keep vegas

boston brothers: a second chance series

book two

Kelly Kay

KEEP VEGAS
Boston Brothers: A second chance series
Copyright © 2023 by DECORATED CAST LLC by Kelly Kay/Kelly
Kreglow
All rights reserved

Visit my website www.kellykayromance.com

Cover Design: Lori Jackson LJ Designs
Editor: Aimee Walker https://aimeewalkerproofreader.com/

Copy Edit & Proofreader: Leah Francic

Chicago. Shakespeare, William. 1992. Macbeth. Wordsworth Classics. Ware, England: Wordsworth Editions.

Published by Decorated Cast Publishing, LLC

To the matriarchs who taught me resilience and how to find the laugh in almost any situation. And taught me how to teach it to my son. Thanks, Mom.
And thank you; Grandol, Grandma, Lynn, Norah & Sue (AKA Mrs. Adams)

There's a piece of each of you in the heroines I create. Thanks.

also by kelly kay

All Books can be found in Kindle Unlimited*

Standalone

SIDE PIECE

A workaholics standalone romance. A hot, hilarious, angsty Instant Connection- A story about cheating on their jobs not each other.

A podcaster and a romance writer walk into a bar...

BOSTON BROTHERS: A second chance series

Standalone stories featuring six friends and the women were lucky enough to find. And then find again.

Keep Paris

Keep Philly - a newsletter exclusive novella

FREE

https://dl.bookfunnel.com/xfkvirgsh1

Keep Vegas

Keep Tuscany-

Keep Rugged (novella)

Sometimes you have to get lost in the woods to find love.

Keep Boston

Somethings are worth losing a bet over.

SONOMA SERIES

Interconnected standalone small town, found family series exploring the lives and loves of five winery families with all kinds of tropes and troubles.

Box Set Volumes with bonus material

Volume One: Books 1-3

Volume Two: Books 4 & 5

Volume Three: Books 6, 6.5 & 7

Volume Four: Books 8, 9 & 10

Or available individually

LaChappelle/Whittier Vineyard Trilogy

Crushing, Rootstock & Uncorked

Stafýlia Cellars Duet

Over A Barrel & Under The Bus

Gelbert Family Winery

Meritage: An Unexpected Blend

Residual Sugar

Pietro Family

Bottled Up

Langerford Cellars

Complex Finish

Prohibition Winery

Grand Cru

CHITOWN LOVE STORIES

Intertwined standalone loves stories set in the Windy City

Rockstar duet

Shock Mount & Crossfade

Present Tense

Carriage House Chronicles

Hilarious spin-off novellas

Follow Me

Rockstar, Second Chance, Forced Proximity

Sound Off

Grumpy Sunshine, Enemies to Lovers

For the Rest of Us

Holiday M/M , Marriage in Crisis

Something Good

Nanny, Single Rockstar Dad

————

EVIE & KELLY'S HOLIDAY DISASTERS vol 1*

With Evie Alexander

VOLUME ONE

Cupid Calamity

Cookout Carnage

Christmas Chaos

(*Not available in Kindle Unlimited but at all retail outlets)

————

Reading orders available www.kellykayromance.com

a note from kelly

Welcome!

This is book two of the Boston Brother's series but it was intended to be a **standalone.** If you've read Keep Paris or my free novella, Keep Philly, it's another story with all the guys and the women they were lucky enough to meet and then meet again. But if you've never read them, you'll be more than fine with Tony & Makenzie's story.

Here's an odd thing- I don't think this book has any traditional triggers. If anyone feels that there is one - please reach out and I'll definitely add it to the book. But other than sex and language, I think we're good.

part one
vive la france
12 YEARS AGO

tony

Paris–Twelve Years Ago

"*F or a charm of powerful trouble, Like a hell-broth boil and bubble.*" I dodge the shoe thrown at me.

"Shut up, Tony. We all know you got an A on your *Macbeth* paper," Colt chides from across the room.

"Yes, but I'm bored." I walk from one end of the room to the other and finish my witches' quote, then turn to my friends, who are not drunk enough, and say, "Good Knights, a wager?"

"Odds?" Danny looks up from the poker game he's currently crushing and grins. My roommate and one of my best friends is always up for a bet.

I survey the room. It's small but workable for the next few months as we revel in a semester in Paris. I drain my beer, then pop another one.

This guy from Texas who just appeared at our poker table speaks up, "What in the hell y'all betting on?" I've dubbed him Tex.

I crouch on the bed like a gargoyle. "Let's wager"—we always have a bet going in some way or another — "how long it takes Colton to find a hook-up." Danny and I fuck around

3

all the time but our best friend, Colt, he always has a steady girl.

Colt pipes up, "End-of-term history paper."

"Are you saying you won't get a steady girl the entire time we're in France?"

Colt nods. "Yes. And I'll do your end-of-term history papers if I do." He puts his hand out to shake at the same time Danny texts his older brother and I text mine.

"Do we have to involve everyone?" Colt groans.

I shrug. "You know we don't bet without the big brothers, you silly rabbit." I glance at my text from my brother. "Dax is in."

"I'm not writing college papers, you assholes." Colt winces. He forgot it's always a five-way bet. The text chain pops off.

DAX: Tell him it will be for Earth Sciences instead of History.

COLT: No fucking way. I'm not writing a fucking college paper on rocks.

ROBBIE: I'll take cash—50 bucks.

COLT: 50 bucks to the assholes who aren't in Paris, and I write papers for the idiots standing next to me if I fail.

Colt looks at Danny and me, and we all shake on it.

TONY: Candy. Baby.

"Now, let's find something to tempt you with, good and just knight. Sir Cockitup!"

Colton groans, "Dude. I'm so sick of being a knight. Come on. Can we drop the round table shit?"

He's a surly one tonight. We started fucking around with being knights and jousting in the fall at prep school. It makes me laugh, so I keep doing it. And it's so fucking sweet when I rile Colton up. His voice gets this annoying comedic pitch. Everyone's sitting around looking at me, so I amp it up.

"Sir Colton, there's only a fortnight till the good harvest and a celebration will be had to honor the equinox."

"Oh, my God. Knock it off, Tony. This is bugging the crap out of me. And who cares about the freaking autumnal equinox?"

Danny doesn't miss a beat. "Vernal."

"Venereal, vernal, who gives a rat's ass? Let's play cards."

I smile at him and change tactics. "What died up your ass?"

Danny grins. "Colt's ex-girlfriend won't stop texting."

Sucks for him. I'm not above knowing that my friend is a fucking catch. He's got this all-American sandy-haired, greenish-hazel eye thing going on. I'm a tall, skinny, funny fucker with a shock of blond on my head. It draws in a very different set of girls. Danny's the brooding brunette with an artistic heart and quarterback's body. But Colt's newly single and the succubus won't let go. I want to make sure he has a good time here.

I pop another round of beers and sit on the bed. We've moved the beds to the sides of the wall and combined the desks into a table. I'm having an actual round table delivered to the dorm tomorrow. Dorm? Strange old hotel in the middle of Paris? Same thing. But we'll have a proper table tomorrow.

We're here for three months and graduate in four. Before we head off to different colleges around the US, I intend to have a good time. For the next three months, I'm going to party, mess around, and do only what's necessary to graduate.

I pick up the old-school hotel phone in the room and dial random numbers. "Have you unpacked yet, young man? If not, you had better get going. Inspection is in ten minutes." I hang up, and the room explodes.

"Shit, what are you doing?" Danny asks.

"I'm bored. Surely, there's trouble for us to find?"

Colton answers, "No, Tony. No. Stop it with that look. We're playing cards and we're cool until the welcome dinner tonight."

Using my hand, I make a fart noise and then give a thumbs-down. I pick up the phone, and they all go back to ignoring me.

Danny tosses a pillow at me. I grew up calling him a different name back in Boston. But when we got to prep school, there was another kid with it on the football team, so I started calling him Dan, short for his last name, Danson, and it stuck. I don't care what the fuck he's called; he's like a brother to me.

"Y'all play football together?" Tex pipes up.

Colt goes into a long explanation about how he and Danny Boy have played football together in city and state tournaments growing up and are now the wide receiver and quarterback studs at our prep school. I tune them out and make another prank call.

Boredom's not a good look on me. It gives me time to remember all the shit I should do instead of having fun. It gives space to all the fucking rules set out for a Ladd man to follow. My obedient older brother seemingly follows most commands. But I know he secretly has zero intention of settling into the Ladd Enterprise conglomerate tight-ass family corporation bullshit. I jump up and down around the room like a pogo stick to change the narrative in my head.

We need wenches.

I push the number 666 and hope it's an actual room. It's ringing, and I'm getting giddy. Perhaps we need witches, not wenches. I cover the receiver and make enough noise to draw all the attention to myself.

"Gentlemen, are you ready?"

Tex asks, "For what?"

"For adventure!" It's what I say instead of 'Hey, want to

stir up some trouble?' It's like a code word for my friends that I'm about to fuck shit up. And anyone around us doesn't get worried. My friends are used to me; strangers take a minute.

A sweet but sexy voice coos "hello" into the phone, and I ask, "Are you possessed?"

makenzie

The music is super loud, and the girls are popping. This is a good time, and that's all I want out of the next three months. Scam of my lifetime. I convinced my high school back in Reno to let me come here, even though we both know I'm not gonna graduate. I also weaseled a scholarship from a local church. The harder I dance, the further away all the crap from home gets.

I worked my ass off to get here, but not how most people expect. The church assumed I was multitasking my studies and activities. But the hustle was my full-time focus. I fed the homeless, attended every service, volunteered with the old people, and dusted the pews like a good girl.

Sure, I was also fucking the boys from the youth group. Sundays were my days to seek forgiveness and plead my case for Paris. I talked about spreading the word of God through fellowship in Paris. I would have said anything. I just wanted to go to France.

Given the circumstances of my double-wide trailer life, I never saw that in the cards for me. I'll pay them back someday, but for now I get to have the adventure of a lifetime, as my mom calls it. We went to Chicago once, and it was beautiful, but it's nothing like this. The ride from the airport and this dance party have been the best two hours of my life. For now, we dance. I'll get a life when I get back.

I'm good at pretending, and I independently learned French. I can leave my small life behind and be larger. This is my one shot at seeing something besides the wrong side of Reno. The flight rocked, and the moment we hit international airspace, my best friend, Maggie, and I ordered a drink. Then we met two other girls from California on the plane. One's a little goodie goodie for my liking, but who the hell knows? Maggie's a bit like that, too, but she can hang. The California girls, Lizzie and Kris, join us in my room to keep the party going before we have to go downstairs to the welcome dinner bullshit. This dorm/hotel is filled with students from all over the US.

The phone is ringing. I leap over the bed to grab it, turning down the music. I hope we're not busted this fucking early. It's day one, 3:00 p.m. Who cares if we're a little loud or tipsy? Maggie flashes me a look. I hope they only kick me out. It would suck for the others if they got punished for my delinquent vortex.

"Hello, are you going to be interesting?" It just comes out, and I hope to God it's not a teacher.

"Are you possessed?" Is this a man or a boy? His voice is deep, and I hope he's not like a teacher or a chaperone. Actually, who cares? He sounds cool as he purrs at me, waiting for a response. It's a good joke because we're in room 666.

"Not today." I roll my eyes, and Maggie covers her mouth to cover her laugh. They're all standing staring at me, wondering what is happening. Maggie knows me, so she might be worried about what I'll say to this stranger. She's been my best friend since nursery school when this kid we called Booger Boy took her pudding, and I made him give it back.

"Then surely, good woman, you have a magical power to

withstand the evil forces of your current abode. You are of hardy stock. And it seems you're putting me under some sort of spell."

Good woman? I gotta see this guy. I hear something like a party in the background. Hopefully it's not a pervy teacher.

"Why don't you come down and meet my coven? Or I could hex you."

"How large is your coven? Tell the truth, so that I may gather enough merry men in my band and call upon you."

I crack up. "There are five of us, Robin Hood."

"You can call me Tony. And we're much nobler than a mere robber."

"I'm imagining a round table where you all circle jerk each other. Am I close?"

He laughs, big and bold. There's a flicker of something in me that's proud I made this guy laugh. I can't explain it, but I will ride this high for a second or two.

"Then anon, milady, or whatever your village calls you."

"Makenzie, but you can call me Mak."

"Makenzie, but you can call me Mak- I believe I'll use Mak and we shall be together henceforth. I'll bring supplies and my men. Good knights all, but some be surly. Be warned."

"Not scared. We're protected by forces beyond your comprehension. Better bring your runes to gird your loins and as much mead as you can carry." My lips curl into a smile, and everyone stares at me.

"Looking forward to it. I do enjoy a good verbal joust."

I hang up and look around at the stunned women. "What?" I sit on the edge of the bed and pull my hair back. I pick up my favorite red lipstick and apply it. Then toss it to my new and seemingly nervous friend, Lizzie. I pull on a pair of leggings.

"Tony and his friends are on their way down."

Maggie asks with a leading side eye, "Who's Tony?"
I shrug. "We'll find out."

tony

This girl is toe to toe. She's right there with me. After Danny and Lizzie peeled off from the group moments after laying eyes on each other, Mak found us all a club. Colton is already slow dancing with some chick named Maggie as the beat bangs.

Like taking candy from a baby, Colt's going to lose the bet already.

I toss a picture in the Boston Brother's text chain so they have proof of the girl Colt will go all in on.

Kris and Tex are dancing just as hard as Mak and me. We're sweating and jumping in the crowd to some French techno crap. Every time the beat drops, I love the high of release and the fucking surge of adrenaline. I can't stop thinking about touching Mak and dancing. I've stripped down to a white t-shirt that's now soaked through, having tossed my emerald colored sweater somewhere. Her dark, sleek bob is swinging around her face. Her deep brown eyes never leave my body. Mak removed her hoodie about an hour ago and she's dancing around in a black ribbed tank top and leggings. She's slender up and down, but her tits fit on her body perfectly. I want them in my mouth, or just in front of my face.

We've done shots of every color, and I'm pretty sure Colt will have technicolor puke in about an hour. He can't handle the off-color liquors, the green, blue, or hot pink. I don't know what the hell we've had, but I do know if I don't take her soon, I'm going to pop a nut right on the fucking dance floor. We can't stop pawing at each other. She's got a permanent sly little grin. Her red lipstick has worn off and stained her lips a dark pink. It's everything I could dream of wanting wrapped around my cock.

Our hands are all over each other while we grind. She keeps biting her bottom lip. When the music slows, she slides her arms around my neck. She's ready and I'm ready. I stare into her eyes, about to move us to the next phase of fucking. Brown eyes aren't usually this fucking gorgeous. Maybe it's just her. She's breathing heavily, and I lean in as Maggie crashes into us.

Cockblocker.

"Mak! Help me. Stop me. I want to climb on this guy, and I don't do that." She tosses her arms in the air. I hope she's ready to pick out curtains and start saving for their future. Danny and I have always been the one and done type, but not Colt.

Mak walks away with Maggie, and I'm left on the dance floor alone. I look around, and a big-tittied blonde puts her hands on my biceps, pulling my focus from Makenzie. She's DTF, I can tell, and I know I could. But my dick shrinks back as she touches me. There's something about that raven-haired hottie that's already locked up my sex drive. I lean into the bubbly blonde to tell her I'm not interested as she grinds on my thigh. Next thing I know, her shirt is yanked backward, and she with it. Mak stands in a power pose and points to the edge of the dance floor. The blonde looks totally surprised, and I bite my inside lip to keep from laughing. Mak points to me then wags her finger at the blonde. Then she turns to me. Her straight hair swings and there's a wild look in her eyes. Like recognizes like. I know just what this one needs, and it's reassurance that a catfight was indeed warranted.

She skips the four steps to me, and I see her launch. I put my arms out like we're in fucking *Dirty Dancing*. She leaps into them, wrapping her legs around me, and before she's even in position, I take her mouth. I kiss the fuck out of her. I don't wait to seduce the kiss into something deeper.

I plunge my tongue into her mouth. She pushes right back, and our lips collide in the most fantastic kiss I've ever been part of. With our teeth gnashing and tongues thrusting, we try to get into each other's space even further. My cock springs to life. Fuck, I think my life just sprang to life with Mak in my arms. But my cock needs more attention than my life right now, so I return to the idea of fucking her.

mak

I can't get enough of him. We fooled around and both got off, but we didn't have sex. I like him and I don't like a lot of people. Usually, I'm the chick who strips first and asks questions later, but the other night, I wanted to wait. I want to see him again, and maybe, I don't know, a date or something. It's stupid to think that, but I do.

I like France. I can be anyone I want to be as long as it's not my regular life. Dancing with Tony was so much fun, but I haven't seen him since. I blew off class this morning to walk along the Seine. I'm starting to know the city after walking around for several days. It's still cold and blustery, so I pull my oversized hand-me-down coat a little tighter. The smell of my mom comforts me as well. I do love my parents, I'm just terrified to become them. My mom has some dumbass health issues, but hopefully is listening to the doctor and cutting back on butter and crappy food.

Speaking of butter and fat, I shake off my home life that's 6000 miles away as I see my favorite little creperie. They have a huge savory crepe for only a couple of euros, and I can snack on it all morning.

The winter sun is crisper than in Reno. I always feel like

there's a film over everything there. Watching the sun playing on the water, it's as if I can see each ripple as clearly as a ridge in my fingerprint. I watch the shadows sharpen, then fade in the river.

My parents are moving to Henderson while I'm here. They said when I return, they'll figure out a place for me to stay to finish the school year in Reno. Ha! They do not know that's unnecessary, but I'll tell them later. I've signed my excuses and papers for so long as my parents that the school wouldn't recognize their handwriting. Getting my report cards and terrible tests signed by my parents has been rather easy. It's also why they have no clue I'm about to drop out.

I bite into my crepe wandering up and down Rue de Monge, looking in the shops. I love imagining a different life, and someone told me there's a French version of the Goodwill called Emmaus Shop. I need a new clubbing outfit. I didn't bring a lot with me, since I didn't want to check a bag for the extra money. And I don't like my clothes very much. But again, the idea of reinvention, even if it's just a French shirt from the Gap, would be exciting.

My phone dings, and I know I only have so much data left, so I glance and see it's Maggie. She's done with class and wondering if I'm out yet. I won't tell her I skipped. Attendance is always taken by a sign-in sheet. They don't care, or so I've been told, who is in the dark little lecture halls. So, I paid a guy. It's all the extra money I had. He's signing me in and turning in the odd assignment now and then for me.

Lizzie's holding her own hand in front of her. "Can we definitely get in?"

Kris rolls her eyes and says, "Of course. Duh. Look, the guy I met last week said, 'if you're hot and young, which we are'." She shoves her shoulder into Lizzie. "We are! Saying 'bizarre' gets us into the club."

I'm so freaking excited to let go. This week has been Tony-less. I explored the city while they studied and went to class. I don't know if he thought I was busy or he's not that into me. If that was our only time together, I should have slept with him. I don't know. He felt different, but I guess he's not.

I've seen a lot of Colton since he and Mags rarely leave each other's sides. And Danny's all gooey-eyed over Lizzie. Kris and I have been hanging out and drinking a lot. We go to a bar around the corner and pretend we're college students. She hooks up, but I don't. But tonight is going to be different. I need to put him out of my brain to find someone who makes me laugh as much and is that fucking hot. That's my goal. To find a Tony that's not Tony. I wish I didn't think about him all the time.

tony

"Yes, ma'am. I know. I'm aware and I'm not doing anything you'd be ashamed of or would bring dishonor to the family. I'm absolutely staying away from temptation of any sort."

I pretend to take a cock into my mouth and roll my eyes as I finish up this call with my mom. Ever since my brother got serious about a girl, and published a small story in *The Atlantic*, our parents decided to ruin my life. They believe his switch from economics to journalism is his girlfriend's fault. Now, I'm not allowed to date until my junior year of college, so I don't get any ideas that will derail me from my corporate path.

My father and mother have been married forever; they're affectionate and perfect for each other. Yet my brother and I are supposed to mate like prized endangered pandas, all in the name of legacy and tradition.

I hang up and scream. Danny Boy puts his hands up, and I punch them. He knows.

I turn to the crew and say in my mother's voice, "You can date when it is an appropriate partner."

They all bust up laughing. It's not that funny. My father's

words have been pounding in my head while I've avoided Makenzie. Shit. I don't think I can be with her and not want to be inside her all the time. So, I've stayed away.

Tex is guiding us to God knows fucking where down a twisty street. Colt's moping because Maggie went out with the other girls. Easiest bet we've ever won.

"Why the fuck do my parents drive me so fucking crazy?"

Danny smirks at me. "Yeah, poor baby has too much parental love and money."

I shrug. He doesn't usually play the shitty homelife card with me. He doesn't want the sympathy or to rub it in our faces, but I'll allow it right now. Mostly because I'm being a dick, and it's his way of calling me out.

"Ok, fine. I'm losing it." I don't tell them how much I want Makenzie. And not just because she can suck a proper dick, but because I want to hear her opinions on things. I want to be with her and talk and laugh and cut up.

"You should fuck it out," says our Texas evening Sherpa.

"What?"

"Just find some hole and fuck it out. All the frustration."

"It's a worthy suggestion. I'll take it under advisement."

I walk ahead, and Danny joins me. "Just go for it, man. See where things go by being with her. If she doesn't want to hang out, you'll know, but avoiding Makenzie is a drag for everyone involved."

"I'm that obvious?"

"Dude, I've never fucking seen you like this. It's like you're itchy. Or your shirt's uncomfortable. You keep pulling it to try and make it fit. And I know you're doing it so you don't think about her. Just talk to the girl."

"I'll think about it."

He's right. And if she hooks up with anyone else, I'll freak the fuck out. Maybe we could do this thing for like a minute, while we're in France and far from our everyday lives. I'll keep it casual, and we'll have fun while we're here. Get it and her out of my system.

Texas yells up at us and reinforces his earlier plan. "You're not getting married just fucking around in France."

I ask Danny, "Is that what you and Lizzie are doing?"

"No, not at all. I'm not fucking around. I'm going to marry that girl." He smiles, and it's bright as anything.

I shove him. "You're fucking serious."

"As a heart attack. But you should definitely stop avoiding Makenzie. She's insane, so just up your alley."

We walk a little further, and I hear a thumping beat, and I love it. I want to fuck it out. But I want to do it with Makenzie. I do something I haven't done yet. She doesn't even know I snagged her number. I text her.

Tony: Hey.

So stupid, but I don't know what else to say. There's no answer. Fuck me.

I look up at the lights flickering on and off in the giant old building down a skinny street. There are way too many college-aged kids in faux fur and feather boas for this to be anything but what I need. I watch them disappear through a door about halfway down the block. This is the place for me to forget I'm a dopey ass waiting for her to answer my text.

"Gentlemen, hard left."

Colton remarks with a groan, "What? Where are we going?"

Danny smirks and says, "You've known him this long and you still need to ask?"

I lift my arm in the air, and even Tex joins in.

In a chorus heard by the gods, "To adventure!"

mak

Kris and I are doing shots and dancing around near the bar. Mags and Lizzie keep their dance circle tight, so no one gets between them. We have a dick parade rubbing up and between us every time we turn around. It's a good time, but I'm kind of pissed the fuck off that this dude keeps popping into my mind. Tony's like an annoying little mosquito bite that I can't scratch. I shake my hair out and do another shot. I'm wearing the little white top I found at Emmaus. It's sheer and tight, and I have a tank underneath, but it's really cool.

We push up against the men trying to keep their place between us, then Kris gestures to the bar. I follow her.

"We need to toss those two back. I need a bigger fish." I laugh. She's six feet tall, and they were both more my height than hers. She surveys the room and points. "There we go."

A giant man is standing by himself against the wall, bopping his head. She shoots whatever the bartender just put in front of us and waggles her fingers at me. She left me with the tab and the bartender scowls as I fake a laugh. I don't have the money to cover these drinks. Fuck. I sit on the stool, so they don't get pissed, and order another drink. I'll sip it and eye fuck someone until they come over, and I can ditch them with the bill. It's my only choice.

I swivel towards the dance floor, and a very swarthy-looking man cocks his head at me. I play with the stir in my drink, then look back up to see if he's still there. He is, and now he's staring at my legs. They are good legs. I cross them, then smile at him ever so slightly. Please let this bait work. I can't make any sudden movements, but I glance over my shoulder just as he steps toward me. Thank God. I'll flirt a little, disappear, and hope we never cross paths again. It's a shitty thing to do, but it's kind of my only option. I don't want the girls to know about my tight budget. I did have an idea today, but I'll see if it pans out tomorrow.

As he leans over me, I quickly finish my drink and signal the bartender to pay.

"You're not leaving, are you? We have yet to share a drink."

Thank you, short skirt.

The bartender puts the check down and my target swipes it before I can even pretend to reach for it.

"Awfully confident I'm staying, aren't you?"

His hand moves to my knee. I don't love that. But I do love that he grabbed the check.

"I was thinking of dancing." I literally bat my eyelashes at him. There has got to be a better way of figuring out my bar tab. He gestures for another round. I smile at him.

"Fine, I'll have a sip, but then we dance." I pout a little. He seems like the kind of asshole that wants a girl to be pouty and stupid.

He puts a finger under my chin and lifts it to his face. I try not to wince at what I can only guess is hummus breath. It could be escargot, but it definitely involves garlic.

I clutch my drink and head to the dance floor, and he's instantly too close. I look around but don't see my girls. I need an assist ditching this guy, but I can't quite yet since he just paid for our entire bar tab. I turn around, and he's on my back, and his hands are on me. I keep turning around like I'm a spinning fool. If I shimmy enough, it will overwhelm him, and he'll give up. His eyes don't seem to leave my chest, and mine can't stop watching his hands. He's not bad looking at all, and I can handle a handsy guy. I just wish he were someone else.

tony

W ell, that's not fucking happening. I storm across this insane secret club, and Danny points toward Lizzie and Maggie. Colt takes off to go join them. Dan shouts in my ear over the loud music, "I guess you decided."

I shake him off, laser-focused on some asshole's hand on what belongs to me. It happened in an instant, and I'm all in now. All the hell in. I'm unclear if it's just for a night or the entire time we're here. I'll have to run it by her, but what is currently happening needs to stop.

I'm vibrating with rage as he feels her arms up and down. I see her not quite responsive, but he doesn't stop. So, he's a pig, and he's touching my things. I stomp onto the dance floor and stand right behind them. She's spinning around like she's in some overhead shot in a movie. His hands are poised to catch her, and then he grabs her hips and pulls her towards him. And that's fucking enough of that.

Things happen quickly. She sees me, drops her cup of whatever she was drinking, and wriggles out of his grip. Her eyes widen as I touch the man's shoulder; she shakes her head no. Before he can touch her again, I pull on his arm, and he rounds on me. I open my mouth, and he cocks his arm. My face must have been telegraphing my insane anger and jealousy.

Next thing I know I'm on the ground with a solid thud to my face. My eye is fucking exploding, and my cheek is throbbing. The music and lights aren't helping. I gather myself, ready to get a couple of shots in, but it's already been taken care of. Colt, Dan, and Big Tex are all up on this man.

All I see are a tangle of legs and arms from my angle, and I have to get out of here. I'll grab everyone and lead the charge out of here. But first I need to get up. My vision is foggy for a moment, but then I see her quite clearly. Crawling towards me on the dirty speakeasy club floor, through the sticky mess of spilled drinks and who the hell knows what, is my little witch.

She's grinning, and when she gets to me, she pushes me back down, lies on top of me and shoves her tongue in my mouth. The kiss is heated and downright filthy. In more ways than on given that we're on the floor. Someone kicks me in the ribs, breaking the spell for a moment.

I kiss her nose. I shout, "MINE."

She wiggles off me and pops up, lending a hand. I glance around, and Kris is at the back door with a giant wall of a man, and she's waving to us. The fight is no longer about Makenzie. It's evolved into some kind of riot. I grab her hand and weave through the crowd. I push, she shoves, and we make it to the door. We exit, and everyone is already in the alley. As the door closes, a man yells in an official tone in French. I'm catching every other word, but none of them are good.

Colt screams, "RUN." And we all do. I slow down momentarily to check if she can run in her heels, and she keeps up with me. All the girls are screaming, and Danny scoops up Lizzie because she's lagging behind. He's running, faster than all of us, with her in his arms.

I, not being quite as athletic, turn to Mak as we continue to run. "I'm not doing that shit, so if that's what you want, bail now."

She laughs, bright and breathy. "No. I only want you."

My heart soars. We're on the same page. Fuck my parents and their rules. And fuck my brother for screwing it up for me. I can have a girlfriend for three months and be totally fine. They'll see.

We land around the corner from our dorm at a small place with cheap shitty beer. We sit on squeaky old vinyl stools all lined up at the bar. Mak alternatively kisses me and holds a towel full of ice on my bruised cheek. Even though we've only known each other for a week, and I avoided seeing her for days, we're reuniting like I've been off at war. I can't stop touching her, and we haven't even gotten to the dirty stuff yet.

We make our own club, dancing to whatever's on the jukebox. The old guys at the end of the bar join in, and a couple of women on a mom's night out grind it out too. I look around at the old dusty bar with Christmas twinkle lights draped over the ceiling that resemble a mouth missing teeth with their random burned-out bulbs and try to burn this night into my brain. Because it's absolutely perfect.

"Fuck, you feel so good. Mak, don't dance with anyone else for a while. Because I'm not sure I can find someone of your caliber."

I moan as she puts my dick in her mouth. She sucks and swallows me down until I can't believe how deep I am. I'm not a small fellow, and she's an expert at this.

Mak pops off but keeps her hands moving up and down my saliva-slicked cock.

"Caliber of what?"

"Dick handler." She stops and I sit up and shake my head. "No stopping. There's no stopping when my head is this hot and angry."

She laughs and climbs on me. I grab her hips and settle her on top of me. She leans down and her nipples brush my chest as she kisses me. I swear I'm trying to climb into her fucking mouth. I can't get close enough to her. She's moaning from the friction, and I gasp; it's so good.

"Mak. Put me inside of you." Finally!

"With... wait." She leaps off me and her stunning naked body is at the foot of the bed instead of riding my dick.

She searches in her little bag, and I realize what's happening.

"Condom?" I say. And she shakes her head. I have a stocked mini fridge, regulation-sized poker table, and the best sheets money can buy, but I don't have a fucking condom.

I flop down with a groan.

We could probably find one, but all our friends are hooking up and coitus interruptus is a hard boundary I won't cross.

We both crack up. She slaps her hands together and backs up like she's chalking up for an Olympic vault. She runs and then leaps onto the bed as I move out of the way and catch her before her head slams into the wall.

"What the hell was that?" I ask.

She licks her lips and says, "That was the opening cere-mony of the Oral Olympics!"

I toss her down on her back and pull her legs open. I grin and say, "Oh, I'm going to get a gold medal in this."

"You think so?"

"I might medal in all three events."

She laughs and tries to sit up on her elbows. "And those would be?"

"Speed, distance, and pairs competition."

She smiles and raises one eyebrow. "Pairs?"

"The 69."

I kiss her inner thigh as she says, "Let the games begin."

mak

I only bought this one dress, and it's this sparkly silvery thing. I thought it would be cool for clubbing, and my new boss at Emmaus Shop gave me half off. Total score. I'm working part time at the thrift shop while they go to class. Now I can afford to go out and keep paying people to sign the attendance sheet for me and do a couple of papers. I also have enough money left over for tomorrow's jambon crepe, coffee, and to buy a round or two tonight.

The dress is short and moves in the light. I will be like a human disco ball when I'm on the floor. It's simple and hangs just under my nonexistent ass. Maggie helps with my hair. There really is nothing to be done with it, but she puts it up in the back, and then we pull two straight black pieces down the sides of my face to frame it.

I swipe on my *Enchanted* lipstick and step into some high-ass heels. I love heels and shoes. I don't own a whole lot of them, but I'm hoping some cool shoes will come into the shop. There are a lot of busted, stretched-out ones right now. I'm actually excited to work tomorrow.

He knocks on the door, and Mags fixes my hair and swipes

the top of my lip, then whispers, "Perfect." She's in sweats, and I'm sure Colton is coming over so they can make out for hours before meeting us at whatever club Tony's picked out for tonight.

I open the door, and he's in a fucking navy blue suit. His blond hair is styled with a bit too much shit, but he's like a magazine cover. His eyes glaze over and get a bit darker as he looks at me.

I smile at him and do a little shimmy. I feel a bit underdressed when he's so formal.

"Always under your spell. That's what's happening. Fucking stunning. Hey, Mags."

"Hi, Tony."

His eyes never leave mine as they greet each other. He puts out his hand and leads me down the hallway to the elevator. When the doors close, he leans in for a kiss. This one isn't like our usual hello kisses that are like feral squirrels stuck in a bag.

His lips are lush against mine, and his hands slide down my back. The doors open, and he pulls back. I step in front of him, and I swear he growls.

"Is everyone else meeting us there?" I look around, and his crew is missing.

He takes my hand. "Just us tonight. Are you ready to be wined and dined?"

I shake my head. "Where are we going?"

"Dinner."

"What?" I grasp at his biceps. "I thought we were going clubbing. I'm in a clubbing dress. Do you see how short it is?"

His hand drifts down my ass and flirts with the hem as we walk. "It's my favorite thing about it."

"Stop."

"Actually my favorite thing about this dress is you in it. But it's also going to look excellent with you out of it later." I giggle a bit. The boy has turned me into a giggler. I usually bust out with a guffaw or a throaty laugh, but he's turned me a little more feminine. He pulls me to the street.

"Are you sure I look ok?"

He squeezes my hand.

We walk another block or two, and his arm is around me. My dress is riding up because of it, and I keep yanking it back down. It really was to stand around dancing. Not walking or, God forbid, sitting somewhere. But I'm sure we're doing something else after we grab a bite.

"Hey, fancy boy. Why the suit? You look completely yummy, but it's a bit much, don't you think?"

Tony wrings his hands. His voice is a little softer than it was a moment ago and I think I've offended him with the fancy boy comment. He says, "I have to tell you something."

That doesn't sound good.

"You're thirty-five?" I try to joke around it.

He laughs but it's hollow sounding. "No. But I've had to pretend I was thirty-five since I was five."

"Don't understand."

"I don't care about it, but people may recognize me at this restaurant."

I ask, "Are your parents like athletes or actors or something?" I have no idea. His name doesn't ring any bells. He is movie star handsome, so maybe they are.

"Not actors in the traditional sense. But they have a lot of money. Like old money, not Europe old, but Boston old." He walks a little slower, and I try to figure out what he means.

I shrug. "I don't really care. But how rich are we talking? Like you're buying dinner rich or let's grab the Chunnel tonight rich?" He exhales, and somehow, I can tell that he needs to know I honestly don't care. He looks at his shoes, and I duck my head down to capture his eyes.

31

I speak again so he believes me, "Doesn't matter to me, I was just teasing. Let's not talk about it, ok?"

His voice is rough and raspy, "I could buy you an island right now rich."

We continue to walk slowly, and there's a big silence caught between us. It's as if he's separating us by this ridiculous imaginary wall of money. I won't have it.

"Who has time to run an island? The politics, the maintenance, and then there are the tourists. No thank you."

He pulls us to a stop and pushes me up against a wall under a streetlight.

"Hey, watch what you're doing back there, unless you want to share that view with everyone."

He kisses me as if I have all the oxygen he'll ever need in the world. I give as fucking good as I'm getting. I want to wrap myself around him.

"My view. You get that right. I know we just got here, but I don't want to be with anyone else but you. You're funny, sexy, and smart."

Smart? Nobody has ever called me that. I scoff a little. "What? You object to being called sexy?" I smile. "Surely, that's not it since you chose this dress for our dinner."

"Again, I chose it to grind up on you in a crowded club where it would blend in," I remind him.

"Fair." He removes his glove and traces my lips. I open slightly, and he gasps as I slowly lick my lower lip. Then he slams his lips to mine and holds my face in place. It's so fucking hot being controlled by this guy who just called me smart. His hand slides up my thigh, and I shiver.

Then I double down and aggressively chase his tongue with mine. I can't get enough. I've kissed a hell of a lot of frogs, apparently. But this guy, holy shit, he can kiss.

He breaks away, putting his hands up, and I come off the wall.

"Are you still interested in dinner?" I gasp.

"I want to take you somewhere as special as you seem to be."

Not sure how to react.

"Tony."

"Makenzie." He shoots back.

I tell him, "Thank you, I'm having a really good time with you."

"We haven't even done anything yet."

He kisses my hand, and we stop in front of an elegant building. He pulls me to him.

I fight my heart from showing too much expression on my face. I ground myself in his beautiful blue eyes. "You've done more for me in a week than pretty much anyone I know."

"Girl, you crazy. What the fuck are you talking about? I do lick a mean clit, but—"

I put my fingers on his lips. "Let's just say, I don't usually get taken care of. I'm not usually the one who gets heard in the room if I'm not on top of a table screaming for attention. And you see me, and it appears you like me."

He takes my hand and places it to his heart. "I haven't begun to take care of you the way you deserve. Because, girl, your little witchy soul sees me too. I'm under your spell and I'm not looking to break it. Now, let's go in here and run up my parents' Amex." I grin.

He pulls me up the marble staircase, and it's like stepping into a fairy tale with crystal chandeliers and an ornate golden lobby filled with plush green velvet furniture. When people dream up where rich people eat, this is it. Holy shit, I'm out of place.

I don't make eye contact with anyone so I won't know if they're looking at me. I don't know which fork, spoon, or teacup to use. I thought we would get a burger or some street food before clubbing. I understand food you can eat with your hands. This is another level. A man steps to us after Tony gives his name. He takes Tony's coat, and I panic. I'm about to light this joint up. When that soft, stunning, megabucks old-timey chandelier light hits my dress, I will end up blinding someone. Like when your phone catches the sun and momentarily flashes your field of vision. But I'm about to fucking blind the entire waitstaff and patrons.

"Mr. Ladd, follow me, please." Another guy comes out of nowhere. There are like forty people standing around in black-and-white outfits. The women are stunning and look like they know not to wear a short skirt to a fancy place. But I couldn't have imagined this kind of fancy.

The man whisks my coat away, and I'm standing with a tiny piece of aluminum foil wrapped around my middle. I kind of wave to everyone as they take notice. Tony is oblivious and takes my hand. He kisses my cheek.

We're both helped into a chair, and I immediately put my napkin on my lap, all spread out, to hide how far up my skirt is riding. I'm a freaking teenager with this hooker dress on, smiling at our personal waitstaff of forty people. It's like *Downton Abbey* introducing the staff to the guests. Tony's pushed back from the table with his legs crossed while they speak. I'm clutching my purse and scoot underneath the tablecloth as far as I can. They're still introducing themselves. There's one called the bread steward, one in charge of wine, and another is our main waiter. Whatever the hell that means.

A woman steps to me and smiles. "Mademoiselle Preston, c'est pour votre sac."

"Qu'est-ce que ? En anglaise, s'il vous plaît." I doubt if I heard this woman correctly.

"Mademoiselle Preston, this is a shelf for your bag." Nope, I heard her correctly. She's kneeling at my side, taking my small clubbing purse and placing it on the tiny bench.

I lean over to her and say, "And if my earrings get a little heavy later, is there a shelf for them?" She laughs lightly and says, "No, but there's a golden bowl for them." Then she winks.

A mini cart full of all kinds of tiny breads and rolls arrives. Tony smiles and gestures to me. "Pick your bread." I point at one and then realize the man who brought the cart is still speaking about each individual roll. He talks a lot about gluten and spelt. I glance around, and people are noticing I don't belong here. Or it's the vibe I'm throwing off. Panicked, poor teenager in a dish towel. That's the right vibe for this place, right? I don't want Tony to be upset or kicked out of here, so I'll keep it under wraps. A couple of small rolls are placed on my plate. I search for butter, and another man appears with different pots of varying colors of yellow spread. He explains that each roll is paired with a specific regional or compound butter. What the fuck? Tony doesn't even think it's fucking weird that someone is buttering my bread. Tony scoots his chair in, thanks the men, then chomps on his bread.

"What looks good?" I pick up my menu, and I'm baffled. I keep turning it over, then whisper across the table. "What's with the name and date on this? And where are the prices?"

"I told them your name. The menu changes daily, hence the date. And the prices aren't listed."

"Then how can I identify what's good?" I'm so out of my league here.

He laughs and I pretend it was a joke, but seriously, if it's not expensive, how do I know what's supposed to be their best thing? And what the fuck is a langoustine? I'm fucked. I'm going to embarrass the hell out of him. This is terrible. I don't even know what half of these foods are, let alone if I like them. I pull my dress down again and pull the tablecloth a little to try and cover my thigh. I sip my water, and Tony looks at me.

"Ok, what the hell is going on? You're all jumpy."

"Just excited to be here. This is so decadent and lovely." My voice is high-pitched and I'm sure it projects desperately trying not to freak out.

A waiter I haven't seen before appears with two plates of tiny bits of food. Almost looks like someone ate half an appetizer. He explains that it's an oyster something, a bit of roe, and a frog leg. And I'm out. Not doing it. Can't do it. Frog leg. And which one is the fucking frog?

He walks away.

"I didn't order this, did you?"

"No, it's an amuse-bouche."

"Gesundheit," He laughs, but we need to leave now. This isn't us, or it certainly isn't me.

"A chef's bite. It's a tiny constructed pre-appetizer to get your palate ready."

I pick up a fork, and Tony shakes his head. He picks one up and places the entire thing in his mouth. I follow suit. It's creamy and rich and tastes a bit like the sea. It's not bad, and there's a weird crunch that I don't want to ask about. But I survived that one.

We both toast with our tiny next bite, and I pop it into my mouth. It's like popping boba but really bitter. I swallow it down and finish my water. I can't entirely hide my grimace.

"Not a caviar fan?" My eyes get wide. Like I've had that before. I look at his plate, and he's not eaten his. "Me neither."

Which leaves the frog. Oh God. It looks like something is smeared on it.

"Don't think. Just eat."

He pops it into his mouth, chews, and swallows it with a big smile.

"I love foie gras."

"Oh. Not frog leg but foie gras." That's so much better. I pop it into my mouth, and it's like an earthy butter with a pop of citrus. There's a sweet bit to the chew and then a touch of heat on the end. It's sensational. I've never tasted so many things in one bite.

"No, it was both."

I smile and purse my lips. "Of course it was." I straighten my back a bit and decide to brave walking in this dress and go to the bathroom. I retrieve my purse from its pedestal and place my napkin on the table. But before I know it, my chair is being scooted back, Tony is standing, and I'm being guided away.

"The restroom is just here. Do you need any help with anything?"

And what the hell will they do in the bathroom with me? I push open the door, and sure enough, another freaking person is working in there. Shit. I don't have any money. I bolt out, and the bathroom guide is waiting for me. I push past her and get to Tony.

I whisper in his ear, "I don't have a tip for the bathroom lady."

He laughs and pulls out his wallet. He hands me five euros, and I kiss his cheek. It's just about my under-the-table per-hour rate at the thrift store. That's a nice haul for the bathroom lady. Depending on how often these people pee. If I were her, I'd cut the busboys in on the tips and make sure these people were hydrated.

"I'll get you back," I say.

"No need. The bathroom's on me tonight." He smiles and sips a glass of wine that's appeared. I hurry back to the bathroom, give the woman the money, and sit on the toilet for a minute, collecting myself. I'm way over my head here. I bite the bullet and use my data, I shouldn't, but I google him.

"Holy shit." Anthony Ladd has a lot of zeros after his name. My gut reaction is to want to run my double-wide trailer ass out of this restaurant and far away from the man so obviously out of my league. But staring at his face, I have a change of heart. I won't let him always take me to this kind of thing. And I won't let him always pay for me because I don't want him to know just how opposite our bank accounts are, but I feel different around him.

He makes me smile all over, and I don't want to give that up because he's rich. Like billionaire rich. But to me, he's just Tony, and maybe he doesn't have a lot of people around him who think that way. Perhaps I could be the person he trusts not to want something from him other than himself. I have that, and it won't cost me a thing.

I'm guided back, and there's a brand-new napkin for me. Why on earth would I need a new fancy folded napkin when we haven't even really had anything to eat? It's not like I had ribs and got sauce everywhere.

I pull my skirt down as low as I can. I sense people watching me, and I let the guy scoot my chair back in. I cover myself the best I can and pick up my menu only to set it right back down. I whisper shout across the table, "Tony."

"Mak?"

"Order for me."

"Really? How do you feel about offal?"

"I don't feel awful, just hungry."

"Offal. Not awful." I do not know what the fuck he's talking about.

"Whatever is fine." I'm not eating a single thing that I can't freely identify. I pull my dress again and squirm a bit, trying to fit in. I'm pretty fucking sure I never will.

Then I look at him. And he's staring at me adoringly. He's oblivious to everyone's judgment, including mine. I reach out my hand for a second, and he squeezes it. Then another waiter arrives, I assume he's the ordering waiter. I slide my napkins around my thighs like a skirt extension.

My dress crinkles a bit every time I move, and it's starting to make me laugh. I stifle the giggle and look around. Then I look into his face again, and it's solid and sweet. With his ivory skin, he's just so damn sexy. I smile, sip, and bite the inside of my cheek so I don't full-on laugh at how ridiculous this all is. Us playing adults in a place I'm not sure either of us are enjoying.

tony

She keeps pulling on her sparkly dress. I'm a fucking moron for bringing her here. I don't even like this that much. Even I've only been to a couple of places like this. This shit is next level. The amuse was awesome, and so is this girl. I'll gauge whether she wants to stay.

"Little witch, what's brewing?"

She shakes her head. "Nothing. I'm cool." Her voice is strained, and she's smiling a bit too much.

"You are, but that's not what I'm asking." She moves around in her seat again. This skirt must be too short or something. But who cares. She's been super squirmy all night.

"You look gorgeous. Stop messing with the dress. It's perfect. You're fine. Really." She rolls her eyes and tries to pull it back down again. She fidgets with the silverware in front of her.

"They'll bring you the fork and knife you'll need for each course."

"So, this whole setup with the plate and like a full set of cutlery is for what? Show?"

I smile and laugh. "Yes."

"Tremendous waste. I assume they have to toss it in the

dishwasher, even though I didn't use it. What's the purpose of the butter knife when the butter boy is going come over and spread it anyway?" I bust out laughing, and she does too. I'm happy to see her relax. I think we should bail on this. I lean forward to ask if she wants to go and she's squirmy again.

She tries to fix her skirt situation by half standing up. One waiter is there in a flash and pulls out her chair as if she's headed to the bathroom again. She sits back down without knowing, and there is no one on earth that can stop this shit from happening. She lands with a thud, and four more tuxedoed waiters rush over. I'm up in a flash, almost jumping over the table to get to her.

"Makenzie!" I don't make it around the table before the men lift her up. But she weighs next to nothing, and there are two men who don't account for her slight frame and lift her a little too quickly. She's now hoisted over their heads like she's the baby lion in *The Lion King* and glares at me. I can't help but laugh as she's presented to the room like she's mid-ice-skating lift. Wrapping my hands around her waist the men back off. I place her feet on the floor again.

She tosses her arms up and yells so everyone hears her, "Now can we get the fuck out of here?"

I hand a credit card to the closest waiter and tell him I'll be back tomorrow to collect it. But to run the whole bill. I take her hand, and she looks down at her shoes. She adjusts her dress again, and I whisper in her ear, "You look so gorgeous. And good God, you're my favorite thing to watch. You're like my favorite show."

She mutters, "Shit show."

I laugh and say, "All of the shows. Are you ok?"

"Yes."

I curl my arm around her waist. "Look, I'll take the shit and the not shit. Doesn't matter. I got you. I'm so sorry. This was stupid and I'm so sorry about it all." She curls into me as we make our way around our table to the exit. When we're almost out of the dining room, I see a devious glint in her eye. There's my bad girl. She grabs a bottle of wine from someone's table, takes one giant swig, then offers the bottle to me. I glug down some very good red hooch and quickly exit the building.

As we spill onto the street, she roars with laughter. We run down the road, and I hear the maître d' yell about the bottle we stole. I'm sure we'll be charged, but who cares?

Once I know we're in the clear, I lift her chin, kiss her jaw, and reach her lips. She greets me with a sensual and wet kiss. She lightly moans against my lips. I'm so fucking underwater, drowning in all things Makenzie. It's cold, and I don't know where we're headed, but a shop is closing, and I pull her inside. I grab two coats, a couple of dopey beanies, and gloves. I pay with one of the other credit cards in my wallet.

She pulls the pink beanie down over her hair, not caring if her hair's been done for tonight.

I say, "You look derpy in that."

She laughs hard. "Then I'm never taking it off." She puts on a navy coat that swims on her slender body, and I grab a different size.

She shakes her head and explains, "It's fine. I like a big coat. It feels more like a hug, and I can pretend it's a hand-me-down versus something that's too expensive for a date. Next time get me flowers." I kiss her quickly as she shoves the gray beanie on my head.

"Deal."

"Or shoes. I like size seven and a half shoes."

I look down at her feet. "Noted." She kisses me sweetly and lingers a little longer than we should in front of the shop girl. I know she'd never accept shoes from me, which makes me like her all the more. She only took the coat because she was freezing.

"You know you look derpy too."

"Then I'll never take it off either. We can derp it up together." She actually looks scorching.

We walk on, and I give her the space to find what we both know she's curious about. We're strolling and holding hands for about twenty minutes when finally, she talks again.

"What's it like?"

"To have the money?"

"Yes."

"You won't like my answer."

She turns and smirks. "You're going to tell me it's good, right?"

"Nope. I was going to say, I don't know what it's like to have it because I've never been without it."

Her lips part in a small gasp, and she nods as if she gets it. "Just like I don't know what it's like to have it."

"Exactly." She takes my hand and puts my arm around her.

"My turn."

"What?"

"I've never been to Reno," I say.

She shrugs and replies, "It's a nice place to be from. Well, parts of it are great."

"And your part?"

"It's fine." She looks away. She's avoiding the subject, and I'm going to let her for now.

I'm weaving my fingers in and out of hers as we turn another corner. She looks around and smiles widely finally looks comfortable. I have no clue where we are, but she seems to know exactly where we are.

She says, "I hate to tell you, but your date was a fucking disaster."

I swig and pass her the bottle. "And you could do better?"

"I already have." She leads us down a street with a sharp left. Then I see how close we've wandered to the most photographed romantic spot.

She's running and yelling at me, "I've never seen it at night. Holy fuck. Holy fuck, it's so beautiful." And as her coat flips up and I see her sparkly dress and her eyes glisten in the streetlights and the crisp of a February night, I feel the same. Holy fuck, <u>she's</u> so beautiful.

"Fancy an elevator ride?"

I stare up at it. I've seen it a hundred times before; my parents made sure we know what metal was used and all about the architect, we've taken all the boring ass tours and been quizzed on its cultural significance, but with this girl in my arms, I realize I've never really seen the Eiffel Tower. Even though she's avoiding talking about herself, everything else about her is infectious.

She pulls me along and I'm happy to be led, for a moment. We start rushing. "How are you running in those heels?"

She shrugs and says, "I don't know, it just feels right."

I whip her around and pull her into a hug. Her body smacks into mine because of the centrifugal force and she's laughing. I pull her hair out of her face and say, "I know what you mean."

Her lips meet mine in a soft but suggestive way. They're slightly parted as if waiting to be complete and I oblige by gently tickling her inside lip with my tongue.

mak

"Monsieur, nous sommes obligés de monter au restaurant, il y a des gens qui nous attendent et nous sommes donc très en retard."

{Sir, we are required to go up to the restaurant, there are people waiting on us and we are so very late.}

He answers in English, "I'm sorry there are no more reservations this evening."

Tony grins and I know he's thinking of slipping him money, but I can't have that. No, thank you. I can get in here without the money. I like him. He's funny, cute, and sexy.

I turn back to the elevator guard.

"Sir. My boyfriend is about to bribe you and I think that's the wrong approach. I'm not going to lie again, but it is very important we find our way up there. Like vitally important. But if we bribe you what does that say about your character? How much is your soul worth that you would take something as cheap and tawdry as a payout to let two people who are having a terrible date try to turn it around in the most romantic way? So can you let us up, for romance?"

He doesn't hesitate, "My soul costs 200 euros." Tony

shakes his hand, and he steps aside as the elevator doors spring open.

I stare at both of them.

"Cynics." They both laugh.

I lean against the back wall of the elevator and shake out my hair as I remove my hat. Tony stares at me as if I'm precious.

"You're perfectly framed, and the lights and your hair. Jesus, you're everything right now. If you were a spy, the door would slide closed, and you'd shoot me just as they meet."

"And if this were a different kind of movie?"

He enters, his eyes flash darker, more sexual, then the doors slide behind him and he kisses me quickly and completely. I feel his scruff coming in and I like it. It's odd, it's not blond like his hair but darker as if he hides a secret. It's a soft kiss that amps up until we begin to move, and the glass elevator is filled with the lights of the tower and the city. It's beyond anything I'll ever get to see or know. All the cracks of self-doubt and longing to be somewhere else or anyone else are filled with this light and the way he's looking at me. The city of lights makes sense to me now, so bursting with beauty you can forget everything but light for a moment. For three minutes we stand side by side watching the tower in front of us and hold hands.

When the doors open, he kisses me quickly, winks and guides us to the bar.

No one is acting like we shouldn't be here. I think the guard at the elevator does believe in romance, he must have called up.

Tony orders two glasses of pink wine. My aunt always drinks that kind of sweet swill and I'm not sure why they'd serve it here.

I don't want to be rude, so I take the glass and raise it as Tony says, "To the best date ever."

"Maybe not the best but it's up there." We clink and I take a small sip. "This is not sweet."

"No, It's a rosé."

"I like it."

He grins. "What do you like about it?"

"I don't know."

"Just say what you think it tastes like." The bartender is listening.

"It's not sweet but like strawberries and a little like, and this is going to be totally weird, but rocks."

The bartender slaps a towel onto the bar, and it startles me.

"The mademoiselle is right; it has a mineral taste. Enjoy."

"Mineral is a thing in wine?" I say.

Tony puts his glass down. "Apparently. Who knew?"

"I'm guessing you did but thank you for not patronizing me."

He weaves his fingers through mine and says, "Not knowing something doesn't make you anything less than spectacular. It just means you don't know it yet."

We've snacked on cheese, sipped our wine, and people are staring at him. He puts his head down a little. I don't know if they know him or not. Or they just think he's gorgeous like I do. I put my hands up like I'm framing a headline. "Bazillionaire Bad Boy, Blunders Bad Date with Gorgeous Enchanting Stranger."

He laughs loudly, and the waiter takes his card.

"I feel shitty about all the money he's spent. The rosé is great, but this was insane. I sip and say, "I promise this is a one-shot deal. McDonald's on me, next time. It's just down the street."

"How do you know that?" I gesture to the hint of the Golden Arches. It's a shame that's part of the view, but it somehow sets me a little more at ease. That I belong a little more at this incredibly beautiful, expensive, and unique place because McDonald's is here too.

"You seem as if you know everything."

"I don't," he says with authority.

"Name something you don't know." I poke his chest.

"What you taste like tonight."

I gasp and clutch his knee. "That can be arranged."

"When? This is fucking spectacular up here but what I really want to be doing is fucking you," he whispers in my ear with a slight nip, and it makes me excited and nervous.

I feel so much older than we are, and everyone is treating us like we're adults, which is fucking weird. I look out over the city and then back to him.

"Look at the view," I remark.

"I am." I roll my eyes and he turns his barstool so we're both facing the city. We say nothing as he lets me drink this all in. The view, his touch, and this wine which is delicious and foreign to me. I wish I could draw or like paint or something so that this moment could be captured, and I could take it out when I'm back in my real life. I know it will be a story I tell myself in the future that's not only wildly romantic but really fucking cool. I never want to forget even a second of tonight, not even falling flat on my ass at the snooty place. And I want a purse worthy of its own stool, but I want to figure out how to get it myself. Tony makes me want to figure out who the fuck I'm going to become.

After I sip the last drop, I turn towards the bartender and when our stools flip around, his hand goes higher on my thigh. He leans over and starts whispering things he wants.

"I'm aiming to get you off within the next ten minutes."

The idea of it makes me squirm in my seat, although I

don't know how it happens - but I want it. I lean to him and bite his ear hard. He groans and adjusts his dick. I enjoy controlling his dick.

I shake my head wildly. "Yes."

"How fast do you think I can get you off?" he says while kissing just under my ear.

"I'll do my best, but fucking trust me, I'm ready." He scribbles his name on the bill, grabs his card and we race to the elevator. I try to lead him towards the bathrooms. When he pushes the elevator button, I'm a little disappointed. I'll have to wait so long. He must see it on my face.

"Don't misunderstand me, my little witch." The doors open and the moment they slide closed, he pushes my front against the window, pulls my hips back slightly, and his greedy hands find my clit as he hikes up my skirt.

"Oh, God. Here? Now?"

"Three minutes and all of Paris is waiting to watch you come." His dick is hard and digging into my back, and I lean my head on his shoulder as he slips a finger inside me and thrusts slowly while pinching my nipple. "So fucking wet and ready."

All I can do is moan and be turned on by the glass elevator and the fear that someone will catch us. It's intoxicating and fucking hot. Jesus, it's so wrong, and I buck into his hand when he crushes his palm to my clit. I feel it building so quickly.

He's kissing and nipping my neck. I gasp, "Harder. Fuck me harder. I'm so close."

"You fucking ride my hand and come for me."

He slips a second finger and pumps into me, then he pinches my clit and I'm fucking gone. My body floats higher, getting tighter and tighter until the elevator rattles for a second and so do I around his hand. He whispers me through my orgasm, and I realize he's been watching me the whole time in the glass. The lights of the tower dotting my reflection just like he just lit me up. I come down with a gentle easy slump into him. He removes his hands and I turn to look at him. He licks his fingers and raises an eyebrow.

"Mineral."

I bury myself into his chest and laugh hysterically.

tony

W e're trying to fall asleep, and I should be fucking exhausted. I don't want to miss a second with her. I've experienced nothing like her. The only way I can think to explain it is she fills all the spaces, inside and around me. She's everywhere and I like it. But it's spaces I never knew needed filling. Or maybe she's like a great flashlight illuminating parts of myself that were hidden. Or maybe she's just fantastic at fucking and my cock has taken over my brain. There's been a dick takeover and I only hope he's able to get my math home-work done as well as dream up impossible scenarios to fuck her. I want to take her up to the roof and do her up there. Perhaps I have a thing about almost getting caught.

She rolls over and flops on my chest. "Why can't I sleep?" Her stomach growls and it's like mine is talking to hers. "I'm fucking starving."

I slide my hands into her hair and let it run between my fingers. It's so soft and sleek.

"Everything around us is closed."

She sits up and I get a view of her dark brown nipples and my dick brain begins to figure out a way to get hard again. But then she's out of the bed and throwing on a t-shirt and a pair of my boxer briefs. Not sure I'll ever recover from how fucking hot she looks right now.

She says with a knowing smile, "Not everything's closed. Come on."

I toss on some black sweats and my Xavier Prep sweatshirt and follow her, I have no idea where.

She rubs against me in the elevator and when we get out, she sneaks down the hallway to the kitchens of this hotel/dorm.

I whisper, "They're going to be locked."

She smirks and picks up a paperclip. She unfolds it and twists it. Then she jams it into the door, hip-checks it, and it springs open. My eyes are wide as she tugs on my sweatshirt and pulls me in, closing the door behind me.

"The peanut butter is over there. Grab it and I'll get the jelly." She flips on the lights, and I'm stunned she's so familiar with this kitchen.

"How often do you break in here?"

"Enough."

"And can you break in anywhere?"

She turns to me and smiles. "Pretty much. I'm kind of a delinquent."

I hustle over and take her in my arms. "You're a badass not a delinquent."

She shrugs.

"And we're not having peanut butter and jelly." I lift her and place her on the big metal prep table.

"That's all I can make."

He grins. "Then you're in luck that I've had a series of nannies and cooks that taught me well."

I find some chopped onions, celery, and some ground beef. I set about making a simple sauce.

"Can you find canned tomatoes, you little grifter?"

"Thought I was a witch."

"That too."

"And garlic if you can find it. Cream and parm. And noodles."

She beams at me as I pull out pans. "Yes, sir."

I sauté, and she fetches. Then she sits back up on the big table after gathering plates setting up a little tabletop picnic area.

"You're a fucking catch," she says. "And your ass is fantastic."

I turn from the boiling pasta. "Look who's talking."

"Nah, I'm just Mak."

I abandon the stovetop and take the back of her neck. I pull her towards me and say, "Exactly. I don't know many people who are just themselves. I don't know how to be a boyfriend. I've never been one before."

She's shy and her eyes soften as I stare into their endless depth. "You're doing a pretty good job."

"I think it has more to do with you instead of me," I correct her.

Mak tosses her arms in the air. "I've never really had one before so we're both fucking flying blind on this." She kisses me softly, and I melt into our own definition of what this is.

"Let's figure it out together," I say quietly, then her stomach growls again.

I grin and turn to plate our makeshift Bolognese.

We're seated crisscross applesauce facing each other and I wait to get her verdict. She bites, swallows, and chews but says nothing.

Then Makenzie looks up at me and says, "Remember how hard I came in the elevator?"

I dip some bread in the sauce, which is really fucking good.

"Yes."

"This is better."

I laugh and toss a napkin at her. She dodges it and takes another huge bite.

"Will you cook for me a lot?"

"As much as you'll let me," I say.

She shovels a giant forkful of noodles in my mouth and grins. Then kisses the errant bit of sauce off my lips.

She sighs. "I think I'd let you do anything."

"Good to know."

She kisses me slowly and whispers against my lips, "Best date ever."

I flip open my phone to see what time it is, and I've missed fourteen calls and twice as many texts. I pick through my texts.

DAD: What the hell are you doing?

DAD: Explain yourself, young man.

DAD: We give you a lot of leeway and a wide berth, but we expect you to respect us and study hard.

MOM: Honey, call us. We just don't understand the bills rolling in from last night. You were supposed to be at a lecture. And you're on a strict budget.

I roll my eyes because we all know what a Ladd-style budget is. I privately text my brother.

DAX: Dude. They tried to dispute the charges, but a waiter had a picture of a girl being held in the air and you standing next to her. They're way fucking pissed.

And another one comes in from my parents. Apparently when Mak was lifted up some asshole filmed it.

DAD: Who is she? And could her dress be any shorter?

MOM: Darling. You shouldn't be drinking anything, but certainly not with a girl. You know the stipulation. You may not date until college. This seems to break our rules and our trust in you.

I don't get why they are getting involved. Jesus, leave me alone. Dax texts again.

DAX: The bottle you swiped - $8200.

Fuck, it wasn't that good. Oh shit. What's done is done. It must have been from that dude's private collection. I guess it was good but kind of dusty tasting, so that makes sense. But who cares what my parents are pissed about. Yeah, it was a lot of money but that's not why they're angry. It's the girl. My perfect girl, so I'll take the heat for the money, but as for her, I'm going to stick. How can they stop me?

I love that my room smells like the magnificent Makenzie. All girly and sexy.

We won't spend a night apart from now on. I plan to keep her as close as possible. Because I've never slept as well as I do with her in my arms.

I roll over, and Mak's arm tightens around my chest. Her hair is splayed over the pillowcase, and she has a slight smear of red wine residue on her lips. It's probably about 100 bucks worth. I grin. I'll catch hell, but it's not like they can come to France and stop me. She's worth all the hell I'll catch and every dime I'll have to work off with command performance visits to relatives or shareholders.

I kiss the top of her head, pull her body closer to mine, and throw my phone into the toilet with a perfect swish.

mak

Work at the Emmaus thrift shop plugs along and I'm collecting pieces as they come in. Every second I'm not pretending to be at class is spent with him or here. I did a couple of quizzes, well, the guy from Tampa did them. I pay him weekly to sign me in attendance wise and occasionally he does a quiz for me. I told him my grades don't really matter, but I don't want to get kicked out of the program. I figure a C or a D will get it done.

I'm lying on the floor staring up at the stars Danny painted on the ceiling. They're kind of funky and cool. He said he was bored, and I told him have at it. Maggie basically moved into Colt's room last week and Tony and I go between our two rooms.

He doesn't knock but enters and stands over me. He's got on tight jeans and a wide striped sweater of tan and navy blue. His blue eyes sparkle down at me and it's hard to believe this is my first boyfriend. I've slept with a ton of people and fooled around but no one ever made that status official. And I didn't care about labels until now, but he makes me believe this will last.

"Hi."

He's leaning over still. "What's with the face? That's a happy face."

He leans all the way over and kisses me upside down.

I sit up and we lean against opposite beds in the middle of the floor.

"Come to Boston." We only have a handful of weeks left and my lies weigh heavily on me, but I don't stop them. I think he'll break up with me if he knows, not only am I not going to college, but I have to repeat my senior year at some point. Not sure Mr. Harvard would approve, so I stay quiet.

"I will visit, I told you that."

He scoots over to me. "No. Transfer to Northeastern. You said you got in. Come be with me. They're eleven minutes apart." My body freezes. Pretending to go to class has been exhausting. The lying is painful. I can't keep up this circus and pretend to go to college. Can I? Maybe if I work all summer I could afford to move there. But I'll have to tell him and let him know I'm kind of a fraud.

"That's a big ask."

He leans forward. "Mak, this is something. I don't know what the fuck it is and we're young and shit, but I think this is something."

"I feel it too." I let myself slide into my imaginary life. "Being away from you is unimaginable for me."

He sits up and guides me onto his lap, and I snuggle in. He's kissing my hair and I'm clutching him.

"You didn't answer me though. We'll figure it out. It was just an idea." I swallow down all the happiness I can in his arms and hope it lasts.

"The fashion merchandise program is so good at ASU. I have a scholarship and Northeastern is too expensive, and I will not let you pay." He holds me as close as possible. I knew this moment was coming, it just sucks how much it hurts to turn down what might be perfect for me. But it wouldn't be perfect for him.

I don't know what the hell I'm going to do in life. I have got to get my shit together. I want to be worthy of him. Maybe I could get into a Boston Community College or something if I ever graduate.

It would be cool to work in fashion, but I kind of want to do something to help people. No one should have to feel like shit or be treated like shit when they're feeling shitty.

Mom's been having a lot of health issues lately, and I watch people disregard her because of her weight. Or they'll rush her out of tests or appointments, and she never gets to ask questions. I know her heart has an issue, and they're doing that thing in her neck to clear it out. And when I get back, she promised to start walking with me. Or doing whatever physical things she can. I don't fucking know, and it's not like we have the money to get someone to help us out.

I'm lost in my head when his hands start to roam, and I like the change of subject from my own thoughts.

"It's selfish to want you with me. And I know there are things about your life you hold close, but trust me. I'll be here for you. I can't imagine not being here for you. Like for a long fucking time."

I sit up and look at him. "Not selfish if I want it too."

"Just think about it."

I grin. I can do that. I say quietly, "Ok." His lips brush over mine and chills spread throughout my body. I lick his bottom lip and lazily sweep my tongue into his mouth.

I'll bury all the lies for tonight and dig them back up tomorrow to deal with. I've been calling my mom every morning on my way to work. She wants me to have a good time. I want to have a good time, but my fake life is getting complicated, as well as my feelings for him. We have three weeks left, and it hurts to think of my day-to-day without him.

Maybe I'll tell him and go to Boston and figure my shit out there. No maybe about it. I have to come clean with all of this stuff that's weighing me down.

I exhale, and my heart is lighter, knowing I've decided. I'll tell him and go to Boston. I'll just hang out there until he forgives me for lying. Then we'll be together.

tony

She's knocked out, and her phone is going off. I put it under a pile of clothes, but it's still bugging me. Our finals are almost upon us, and then I want to take a week and go to Italy with her before we separate in the States. I claw at the fucking walls of my mind and heart, thinking about her not being tucked against me every night. I actually looked into Arizona. I'm going to spend a lot of fucking time on a plane if she'll let me visit often. I'm rubbing my fingers up and down her arms.

My family would kill me if they knew how gone I am for this girl or if I drop out of Harvard. I want to look into more marketing and social media growth potential versus straight finance shit. I don't care how the sausage is made. I just want to package it pretty and find new revenue streams as the world shifts to digital.

I inhale the faint scent of sandalwood on her hair. I'll make this work. I haven't said it. She hasn't said it, but it's right there in every move we make, dance we share, fuck session, handholding walk. All of this is about that four-letter word. She brings me exotic French snacks, and I make sure there's always the bubbly orange water she likes in my fridge.

That. That's the part that will kill me, the little shit. She'll get a new favorite soda, and I won't know. She slays me.

I kiss her shoulder and whisper, "I love you so very much, Makenzie. My little witch, you are all I could ever want in this life. Not sure what magic is woven around us, but I know it won't ever be broken. Fuck. I love you."

She says nothing but flinches a little when I rub my finger lightly up her arm again. I flip her over, and her eyes are glassy.

"Sap." She smiles.

"For you, absolutely," I say, then kiss her quickly.

There's a moment where I hover near her lips, then she says, "I'm not sure I've ever loved anyone, other than like my parents or Maggie. But if the feeling means, I don't want to be anywhere else, and you make me feel like I matter, and you don't see my flaws then I love you too."

"That's a lot of conditions." I grin.

"How about this? You're my favorite person," she says so absolutely.

"Yes. That's it. That's perfect. You too."

She puts her hand on my cheek, and I sigh.

Mak's eyes are stunning in this low light as she says, "I didn't know love felt like this. You're all I care about, and I really should care about some other things. I love you. I love you so much and I have to tell you something and then we're going to figure it all out, because I don't want to go home or to Arizona. I want to stay in your arms."

I slide her to me and take her lips. They're firm and yield to my touch. I kiss her once, twice, and on the third gentle peck, I pull her lip down with my own and lightly wedge my tongue in to find hers greeting me. It's a slow and sexy kiss, and just as it starts to get good and gaspy dirty, her phone vibrates again.

"Did your laundry just jiggle?"

I laugh, and say, "Your phone has been going off."

She kisses me, and I lose all rational thought as we make out. We're both naked and ignoring the constant erection digging into her hip bone. I can't stop it. It's all the damn time with this girl. My phone is buzzing now too.

I prop myself up as someone bangs on the door.

"YO! I'm trying to tell my girl I love her and then show her for like twenty minutes or so."

She laughs, and says so only I can hear, "Only twenty?"

I kiss her nose. "How about two twenties? One ten now and then I'll do it again in like an hour. Fuck, I love you." I kiss her.

She smiles against my lips. "Tony Ladd, I love all that you are and will ever be."

"Girl, that's heavy."

"We only have a couple of weeks, gotta dive in." Her perfect bowed mouth widens into a full body smile.

"Took us long enough to get here. I promise not to be afraid of how hard I love you," I tell her.

"And I promise not to hide from how hard I love you. We talk after you fuck me, ok?" There is something weighing on her, but my dick will not be denied. Thank God, she loves it.

The banging is back, and then I hear Maggie's voice. "Mak. Makenzie, come out. Honey, something's happened." I react without thinking tossing on shorts. She's in her leggings and my t-shirt. I whip open the door, and she joins me. I put my arm around her.

Maggie's eyes are wet with tears. Mak leaves my arms and pulls Maggie into hers. "What's wrong? Are you ok?"

"Mak, we have to go. It's your dad. Your dad's in the hospital."

She pulls back and looks at me. I know she wants her phone, and I grab it.

She looks at her texts and bursts into tears.

"Is he ok?" I ask.

The girls just hold each other. Colt looks at me, and as much as we want to be here for the girls, the reality of them leaving immediately, as they should, is killing both of us.

Colt says, "He's in the ICU. He had a massive heart attack." She leaves Maggie, and I take her into my chest as she sobs.

"She's the sick one. He's fine. My daddy is fine, I know he is. Oh, God. We have to go."

Maggie wipes her face, and says, "I'm praying for him." She squeezes Mak's hand. "I'm going to pack."

Kris is in the hallway with Danny—not sure where Lizzie is—and she says, "Take only what you need. We'll pack the rest and ship it to you. Don't worry."

Danny says, "And let's see if we can get your tickets changed."

Colton says, "Magpie, it's ok. We're ok. I'm here."

She's so emotional. But then I realize, as tears tickle my eyes, it's because she's leaving. Shit. This is it for France and my girl. This fucking sucks. This all sucks, but I hope her dad is ok.

I say, "Don't bother changing the tickets. I'll buy them. Kris, could one of you do this while Colt and I put the witches back together?" She nods. Everyone clears out, and Mak sits on the edge of my bed. I squat before her and put my hands on her knees, so she knows I'm here.

She bursts into tears as she looks at me. "I have to go. And I feel like shit because I want you to come with me."

"Oh, my perfect, beautiful girl, you know I can't. But I can get to you quickly when I get home. But if things don't go well, I'll be there. Fuck school. If things are ok, then I'll be there the moment I come home from France. That's three weeks. Then we have six weeks until we both graduate. We'll find all the time to be together this summer. We can spend all the time before we have to move into our freshman dorms. I promise. I love you so much. Go be there for your dad."

She inhales sharply and nods at me. I see her straighten up, and steel takes over her spine. She says as a matter of fact, "I love you. We'll be fine."

Then she dials her mother and I hold her close. When her mother picks up, I see her start to waver, but then she's back to the fearless caretaker I know her to be. That's who she must be at home.

"Hi, Mom."

mak

I fell asleep, and now my eyes are even puffier. Jesus, never cry and then get on a transcontinental plane. I'm going to have to pry them open. I look down, and Maggie is still holding my hand. Thanks to Tony, we're in first class, and it's fancier than I thought. Dad was stable before we got on the plane, and I hope he still is when we land. My mom's heart is the one that's shitty. I was prepared for my mom but not my dad. And now I'm annoyed at both of them that Tony's just gone from my life.

I've cried, and Mags has cried. There's no more place for more tears. I keep trying to fool myself that I'll see him again. That it's all fine and will work out. That it doesn't matter I blew off class to the point where I won't graduate. Or that my father's in the hospital, and my mother won't be able to take care of him. Or that I have no idea if they paid the insurance this month or not. Because that's a bill we can afford. Oh God. I saw my whole life for a moment in his eyes, but I should have known better than that. The bubble was always going to burst.

End of Part One

part two

viva las vegas

PRESENT DAY

tony

Las Vegas-Present Day

"And we're here, why? It's fucking July in the desert."

My mostly silent brother, Dax, has agreed to come out of his on/off love den in Boston and grace us with his presence. But he's not a fan of heat.

I toss a look at him. "Ask Mom. She's the one who gave birthed in the summer. Bitch, drink up." He laughs and slaps me on the back, then gestures to Hayden to see if he needs another drink. We used to call him Dan in prep school, but he goes by his middle name now. It suits him.

The rest of my 'brothers' are either scattered or en route here. I try to see one of them every month. I flew to Paris last month to meet Hayden for a drink. They're the only thing that makes me feel comfortable in my skin these days. My 30th birthday has become a reunion for the six of us who struggle to find time.

Colton's late because he had some dance recital to watch. He's a total girl-dad.

He's the only one without a blood relative in the mix. Colt usually ends up mediator between all the actual brothers. Ironically, he grew up in a neighborhood between the Ladd boys and the Danson boys.

Our house was the brothers' safe haven growing up. My parents never minded if Hayden, his two brothers, or Colt showed up for dinner. The Dansons had a shitty beginning, but they've all made something of their lives. Our parents always supported our relationship with our friends from different neighborhods.

Hayden's younger brother, Law is scooting a lilac-haired hottie off his lap, and joins us at the bar. Hayden explains to her that Law's moved on.

Old-school Hayden would already have had lilac hair upstairs long before his little brother would have had a crack at her. The dude always worked fast, but he's locked up his libido for anyone other than the love of his life, Lizzie. They live in Paris, and sometimes it's hard to talk to Lizzie because it reminds me of the one thing in my life I never got to keep.

Lawrence splashes his drink as he gestures, and the droplets fly about, then slams a shot of something clear and dangerous.

I toast him, "To the greatest pitcher Arizona will ever know."

Law slams his hand on the bar and yells, "Fuck yeah!"

I adjust my turquoise shirt and sip my beer.

Law leans back on the bar, propping himself up on his elbows, and surveys the room. "Why the hell aren't we at some fancy bullshit your wife planned. The kind where I'd have to think twice before I adjust my crotch in public?"

He winks as a group of women walk by. I'm not sure I can stop him from getting every venereal disease there is tonight. We can all pull, but not like him.

Ignoring all the women recognizing him, the oldest of us, Robbie, skulks up. He's recently retired from the NHL but has no need for puck bunnies. He's been locked down since he met Claire in middle school. Robbie's the protector, Hayden's the artistic one, and Law, the cocky one. Scratch that. They're all cocky as fuck.

Hayden slaps me on the back and says, "Feels like you're denying Laura media coverage for her pretty dress. The king of Ladd Media is turning thirty." I wish they'd fucking let this go. I'm not ready to admit shit to them.

Dax, my actual brother, chimes in. "He's getting a divorce, so we're doing this instead." I hang my head. It's fresh, but now I know she's contacted our family attorney. Which means my fucking parents know as well. I was going to tell them, but I went to Vegas instead. I actually asked Laura if she wanted to come here and get a quickie divorce; she smiled wickedly and said no.

Fortunately, there's a prenup, but after two years, she's got a pretty nice payout coming if she doesn't fight for more. My last divorce was messy as hell. The one before that was easy, cut and dry. But the marriage lasted only three months. Basically, when we sobered up, we realized it was a mistake. But she got a lovely half million as a parting gift. She was the bargain bride. I still talk to that one occasionally.

Robbie's voice booms from the barstool three down. "Holy hell. Again?"

Hayden puts his hand on my shoulder. "So, you fucked up again?"

I jerk his hand away, and Colton arrives just in time for the story.

"Tony, fuck up, nah. That's impossible," Colt says as he pulls me into a hug, then makes the rounds backslapping the others.

Of course, I'm the screw-up again. I know I'd say the same thing to them, but fuck them if I don't feel every jab like it's a fresh wound after the last couple of days. I lost a deal on a new social media platform which turned out to be a colossal mess and made everyone remember my billion-dollar disaster from a couple of years ago.

I'm going to flip this script so I can have a good time tonight instead of wallowing. I want to be with my friends and that's it. I don't want to be Tony Ladd, Media Mogul, tonight, just Tony.

I stand on a barstool and look down upon these men.

"Gentlemen, despite my lack of maiden, or marriage I can make work, I would choose to be with you assholes every fucking time." I reach down, grab a bottle of Dom, and proceed to spray them down. Dax wipes his face with a cocktail napkin and puts down the family black card.

Hayden grins. "We're not going to remember a thing in the morning, are we?"

Law says, "Not if we do this right. Colt, you in?" He hesitates for a moment then stares straight at me.

"Happy thirtieth, asshole." Colt takes the bottle from me and swigs while we all cheer.

I thrust my hand up in the air as I jump down. "Let's ride, gentlemen. To adventure!" I head off into the night, so I don't think about having another failed marriage.

There's a haze of cigar smoke over our heads like a halo of sin. Law has just returned to us from banging our waitress. His grin says all the things polite company wouldn't want to discuss. He grabs a Scotch from our private bar and lights a cigar as well.

"Can we discuss this divorce of yours?" Colt changes the subject, and they all lean in a bit from their leather-backed chairs this club has provided. We dined on steak and sipped Scotch, doing all the manly things. We'll go clubbing in a moment, but for a second, I wanted it to be us.

Dax nods at me.

"Laura used to be fun, warm, sweet, but she changed. Usually I can pinpoint some dickish behavior on my part, but there wasn't any. I thought our friendship was enough for a marriage. Until we fought so much that one day I bought her a condo, hired a crew to pack her shit then handed her a card and a key to her her new address."

"You kicked her out?" Law asks.

"Ok, maybe I was a little dickish at the end. But she left willingly in a chauffeured Bentley. She's fine. No one told me I shouldn't have married her."

Hayden puts his hand up, and then they all do.

"Fuckers," I hiss.

Dax smiles and says, "Yeah. We did. But you do what you like. Now who has money on tonight?"

We've bet on lots of shit over the years.

Colt leans forward. "What's the over/under?"

I say, "On what?"

Robbie answers while crossing his tree trunk legs in a delicate manner. "Whether you get married again tonight."

"Not fucking happening. Never again. And, dude, I'm still married."

Dax says, "Technicality."

Hayden crosses the room and does a pivot. "Love ya, man, but you can't stay single."

Colt fills in the blanks, "You can't be alone."

"What the hell are you talking about? Law fucks everything and Hayden bedded most of Boston to get over the love of his life. Which didn't work. And Robbie's never been alone. Like ever. Colt, my man, you've been married up since like we met. Dax, you would be alone if you stopped puppy dogging back to your on/off woman. So, fuck off, dudes."

All of them are laughing. Hayden squats down in front of

me, and says, "Six months." Then pops up and walks back to his chair. He's nimble as fuck and always moving.

"Is that your bet when I get married again?"

Hayden offers up, "Interesting idea, but no. That's the longest you've been alone since high school graduation. You're a serial monogamist. You have to have someone."

I guess I started holding on to one person after the only person I ever wanted let me go.

Dax stretches his legs out, and says, "Third divorce before thirty and toss in the two other engagements. It's like you have this desperate need to lock it down before it gets away."

"I'm thirty tomorrow and won't be divorced. Technically only two divorces in my twenties."

"And two failed engagements." Law adds.

"Well..." I don't like how that hits my gut.

Robbie's lips curl up like the Grinch. "A wager, gentlemen?"

Law jumps at the chance. He'd do anything Robbie says. "Stakes?"

Robbie stands and taps his fingers on his lips. And everyone is staring at him. "I've got it. Tony, you stay single for one year and I'll give you a million dollars." We're all wealthy in the room. Some by sports, others by family money, and the other two by hard work. Colton's a genius investor and will never go along with the number, but he has that kind of cash.

Colton yells, "In."

"What the fuck is happening?" I jump up.

Dax laughs and says, "Oh, I'm so in, little brother, you can't go a week without getting serious about a stranger."

Hayden says, "I'll take that bet. I could use a million dollars. We're getting married at some point. And my house in France needs a new kitchen for the second floor."

"What are you assholes proposing? Because it sounds like I'm going to take a million dollars off of each of you."

Robbie says, "Fat fucking chance."

"A fool and his money will soon be parted." I cover my heart while I say this to them. I seriously am done with people in my space and telling me I have to go to dinner with people I don't actually like or attend functions to be seen on her arm.

"Ok, Yoda, how much does Laura get?" Dax says.

I point at him and stand up to walk the room, drawing their attention to me. "Good marks, gentlemen. Good marks, all, but I can stay single as long as I want."

"A year," Law says as he drains another Scotch.

"Yeah, a year. One year, no relationships," Colt emphasizes.

"Surely, you don't expect me not to get my fuck on in the next year." I thrust to make them laugh.

"One night only." Hayden beams.

Robbie seconds him, "I don't care if there's 365 different women, as long as none of them take your name, have your correct phone number, or get a second date." Harsh.

Dax talks with a mouthful of cake, "Mom will be devastated you're not settling down again." Everyone busts out laughing. "But then again, you've been settled enough for all of us."

"Yeah, and I've been married for a decade," Colt pipes up.

Robbie clinks glasses with Colton. "Amen to that."

"What is the purpose of this?" I ask.

"Fun. Adventure. Surely, you're familiar with that, right?" Colton moves around the room, and everyone busts out laughing. "It's fun to tell you what to do. Honor system, though. You can't secretly find a loophole and get married." We all laugh even harder.

I stand in the center of our leather-clad chair circle and raise my glass. "I stay single, like asshole Law, for one year and you owe me a million dollars each."

They nod, and my brother stands up. "And if you sleep

with a woman more than once or get engaged, married, or otherwise legally entangled with a woman, within the next calendar year, you owe each of us a million."

"Child's play," I say.

Robbie puts his meaty ring finger in the air and says, "Candy/Baby." I flip him off as we all stand and raise our glasses, looking each other in the eye while we clink. I wouldn't want to be on the receiving end of seven years of bad sex when I'm headed into a debauched year of only that. These idiots are basically giving me a license to fuck around for the next year, and then I pocket five million.

Sucker's bet.

We all clink, yell, "Hot Bods," and laugh. One time we were all hanging out during spring break in Boston, playing touch football on the common. There was this clique of girls who always trying to date one of us, and they called us the 'Hot Bod Squad'. So stupid, but we always toast to that.

We've got bottle service and a revolving door of women. Robbie bagged off to go call Claire. Colton keeps checking his phone, grimacing and texting. It's the wifey checking up on him. I don't like that woman, but I say nothing.

My lap is full of a sweet ass I'm going to tap in like twentyish minutes. Hayden's happily dancing with everyone and anyone. Law's already got some woman off while on the dance floor, and now he's back out there.

A swaying Colton stands up from our perch of a table and points. He's white as a sheet.

He yells, "Maggie!"

Ok, cool, we're going with ghosts of relationships past. He's so damn drunk. I kiss the woman's neck, and she pours herself another drink.

He's bouncing on the balls of his feet, yelling, "You need to see this. Magpie. Maggie. Tony, it's Maggie. I swear to fucking God, Hayden's talking with Maggie."

"It can't be, sit your silly, drunk ass down."

"OH SHIT. Dude. She's not alone."

Hayden, Law and several women approach. But it's like a rack focus in my brain. Everything else goes fuzzy but that face. I turn away, and I leave my body. It's as if I have a bird's-eye view of the situation. I stand, moving the woman from my lap.

"I'm so sorry to lead you on, but my plans have suddenly changed." I hand her an unopened bottle of vodka the size of a Prius. "Here, take this."

"What the fuck?" The woman squeaks, and I do feel a tiny bit guilty, but she'll hook someone else in a second.

I shrug and say, "I'm seriously sorry, but destiny won't be denied."

"Who the hell is Destiny?"

"I'm trying to be kind. But you need to go."

"Fuck off then." She shoves bruschetta in her mouth, grabs an open bottle of champagne and some gin. Good on her. I salute her as she storms away, desperately trying to hold on to the clinking giant bottles. Colt laughs. I turn, locking eyes with her dark chocolate ones.

She's here in front of me. She puts up her delicate hand in a greeting, and I return the lame gesture. I don't know how to behave right now, so I finish my drink in one sip and tuck my shirt in.

And then she's standing right in front of me.

She bows deeply at the waist and says, "And good and well greetings, my liege."

Fuck me, Mak's still gorgeous.

mak

I'm freaking out while I'm bowing. Seriously, I never go out. My schedule makes it impossible even though I'm twenty-nine and should go out. I don't even have cool shoes. I thought I'd be up to my fine flat ass in heels once I grew up. Nope. I have two pairs. One is on my feet, and the other is for some fancy occasion, if there is one. I had second hand Manolo Blahniks for a moment but left them at his house when I ran away from Tony. I should see if the maid still has them.

Everyone's chatting loudly about how insane this is, and I'm trying not to stare at him. I have no money, and Maggie's never in town, so I don't go out. I don't like my friends. It's like we ended up together because of past work experiences or because a friend of a friend used to hang out, so now we do. I didn't choose those people. Life chose them for me. But Tony? He's the one thing I let myself have for way too long. And the one thing I never wanted to give up, but it got too hard.

I cried for months and still do if I push the edges of my memory. But right now, the most perfect man is bowing right back and joking.

"Goodie, Makenzie, a lovely treat." Then he kisses my

hand, and as his lips brush my skin, I realize I've only ever lived a colorful life for six months. All the rest of my moments pale compared to him. And I didn't even notice I was in the gray until he touched me.

Colton and Maggie stare at each other much like they did when they first met. But as they awkwardly hug, both of their wedding rings gleam in the glint of the club lights.

I lean in and yell, "Dan."

He puts his finger up and gets in my ear. "I go by my middle name now, Hayden." I give him the thumbs-up, and he shows us that Lizzie has texted six times already.

I lean up to his ear and yell, "Is she still Lizzie?"

He shakes his head no. What the fuck is with them? He leans down and says, "But she'll answer to it. Most people in France call her Elizabeth."

"Whatever it is, it's good to fucking see you, Hayden."

He pulls me in for a selfie. I love that they found each other again. We all lost touch stateside when everyone went to college except me. I'm still working my way through, and I'm almost done with my pre-med undergrad requirements, then it's off to medical school for me. My degrees are my ticket out of a life I never thought I'd see the other side of.

I can feel his stare and his damn heat. I turn back to him. "Happy birthday."

Tony pulls me into a hug, then says in my ear, "You're the birthday present I didn't dare wish for." We hold each other too long, and I can't breathe. My blood pulses in time with the EDM like it's getting too much oxygen. It's like my bloodstream is hyperventilating. Tonight, exactly twelve years ago, I walked away from him. He doesn't seem angry or destroyed. And I wish he'd teach me how to be like that because I'm still destroyed and angry at myself. He just seems like Tony.

I pull out of the hug, and he gestures for me to sit down. Mags is sitting between Colton and Hayden while sipping a cocktail. Tony gestures to vodka, and I nod. He fixes me a vodka soda, and I point to lemons.

He's so much more than I remembered. Christ. I wring my hands in front of me, so I don't reach out and touch him. This is so bizarre. In all the times I've cried over him, fantasized, or dreamed of him, it was always young Tony. I forgot to age him in my fantasy, and it turns out he looks even better all grown up. He's still sporting the blonde hair and dark facial scruff. It's such an odd but sexy unexplained combo. He seems as sure of himself as ever, and I hope my mask of bravado holds.

His body has filled out, and the skinny but fit boy he once was, is long gone. It's been replaced by this cut, trim, ripped man with a fuller face but the same mischievous blue eyes. His blond hair is cut short, almost cropped, and it seems odd to see him put together. It was long to his ears when we met. I remember pretending to study and running my hands through its corn silk texture. I look around the room, and it's all sweaty bodies rubbing against each other in search of connection. The desperate thumping of music bonds them through rhythm and beat. The touch of his fingers on my wrist has my insides squirm like the bodies in front of me. I like it too much and not enough to come clean with him or see where tonight would lead. The idea of slitting open that wound seems unbearable.

Sitting down, I pull down my little black dress. My dark, bobbed straight hair falls forward, and the strand gets caught in my gloss. He's quicker than I am to pull it free and tuck it behind my ear. His knuckle grazes my cheek. We were wild together, but this was always underneath all the shit we pulled. He's always been sensitive and tender, a side of myself I've only ever shown him and Maggie. Lizzie, and Kris saw a snippet here or there, but I can't afford to let any of that shit slip out.

He turns toward me, pulling my shoulder so I have to face him. His drunken eyes are lit with fire. The way he's looking at sweaty me is the way I look at cheesecake or Lake Meade on a hot day. He wants to dive in. We stare, and I'd like to say that time has dulled the heat between us, but I can faithfully report it has not. I remain silent and glance around.

He leans in so I can hear him. "You were the girl who never held back. What's stopping you? I crave your boldness." Me too. I don't do that anymore, but it's fun to remember that girl.

He sips water and studies me further. I hate he can sense my hesitation like he knows me best. I haven't seen him since his eighteenth birthday. It's easy to follow this man's life through paparazzi and social media. I try not to imagine what it would be like if I hadn't run away. I don't want the glitz, I just wonder what we'd be to each other if I'd stayed.

"Nothing's stopping me. Let's dance." I hop up, and he follows immediately. Hayden's little brother nods at me, and he flips Tony off with his ring finger, which makes no kind of sense. I met him on my one trip to Boston, but he was much younger.

Tony yells, "Fuck off." Then I glance at Colt, Hayden, and Dax, Tony's brother, and they all have their ring fingers up as well.

On our way to the dance floor, I lean in to him, "What does the one finger mean?"

He laughs and growls. "It's a promise I intend to keep, but you just made it a whole lot harder."

Even though I don't know what that means, I'm getting swept away. One night of lowering my guard can't hurt, that much.

I put my hands on his biceps. His face lights up as I squeeze them, although I was not expecting them to be unyielding. I love a good arm. I bite my lip and say to him, "To adventure!" And then I throw my arm straight up in the air and lead him to the dance floor.

We're grinding immediately and falling into old habits. He's behind me, and I can feel him. He pulls my arm up behind his head, and I try to clutch his hair like I used to. There's nothing there, really, but he gets the point. And then his face is buried in my neck, nipping and kissing. We got here super fast, but it's always been fast with Tony. I used to be impulsive and a touch hedonistic, and Tony was the height of it for me. I wanted him all the time in all the ways. Sweet and tender, rough and sexy, and it never mattered where we were or who was around. We were almost always in constant contact. He used to study with me on his lap, or sometimes we just linked pinkies under a table. I've never connected like that again.

"I can't help it." That is all I can hear in my ear. My body is light, but my skin is on fire. We keep dancing, and I don't dare turn around, or he'll stop. And if he stops, he might remember I hurt him.

His erection is digging into my back, and I want to climb up on it. He's bulkier and muscled and so fucking gorgeous. He flips me around and pulls me to him. I bite my lip and he brushes his thumb over it. Then he pulls my hair back, and as the club thumps to a Cardi B remix, we sway as if we're hearing a different sound.

"Fuck it." His eyes light up, and he leans in and brushes his lips across my cheek, then holds me as close as possible. The tension is broken by my confusion. I thought I'd wrap my legs around him, and then he'd carry me out of here to the closest semi-private flat surface. I could use that. He kisses the top of my head, and we continue to sway in a slow circle in our own spotlight. I don't mean to, but I melt into him. I'm protected and connected. That shit doesn't happen in my everyday life. It's the escape I need, not the one I thought I wanted. I cling to his shirt and let go of everything weighing me down.

Then he's in my ear and whispers my name. "Makenzie. My Makenzie. Why? Where did you go the moment you left my side? How are you here with me now? You're a dream and I don't deserve this moment, but I'm going to take it anyway."

His breath creates a series of chills down my back and arms. The rumble of his deep voice touches all parts of me. I have to get away from this because it's too much of what I'll never have.

He'll jet off tomorrow, and I'll still be alone in the desert.

tony

I want to fuck this woman into tomorrow and for the next month. No one has ever felt totally right since her. It's only now, as we dance, I realize everyone else was just playing house. All the wives and girlfriends were merely square pegs in round holes. I don't know if we can pick up where we were. I'm a different person now, but would it be a mistake to try?

Besides my heart, which gives itself up pretty regularly, it could be a five million dollar slip-up. I hold her closer, slowly dancing amid chaos and electronica to stop me from taking her right here. I only get one shot at being with her this year. If I fail four hours into the bet, these assholes will never let me live it down. Technically, I wouldn't fail until I begged to see Mak tomorrow, the next day, and the one after that.

Her smile is wistful, and full of melancholy, and I feel all of that with her. As well as the intense pain of the hole in my heart I've tried filling with wives and fiancées is because this one left me.

We stroll to the table, but she sits in the vacant seat near Maggie. Colt's still staring at Maggie, and she's oblivious to the power she still holds over him. I guess Mak has it, too.

I'm flanked by Hayden and Dax. My brother slaps my

knee, and I turn my head to his. "Easiest money. She's right there, the girl that got away. I know you."

"Fuck you. It's just nice to see her."

Hayden leans over. "Man, look at you. She looks fantastic and can't stop staring at you. It's the same hungry look and feel from Paris. You walked in that door twelve years ago and you both jumped to life."

"That was a pretty powerful door." I nudge Hayden, and he grins and closes his eyes. I'm sure he's thinking of his girl in Paris.

"It was. But, dude, you're screwed. Now, if you don't want to wait to run after her, you can slide me the mil right now." I punch him in the arm.

Dax leans forward, puts his drink down, and walks away, nodding to the others, then jerks his head a little, indicating I should follow him.

"Be right back." I say it to everyone, but mostly so she knows I'm coming back. When I squeeze her knee, and she covers my hand with hers. And zing right to the crotch. My dick and balls just woke up to be part of the conversation. They're saying, "*Her. We want her.*" Settle down, junk. We'll get to it.

Dax stops abruptly near a way too trendy restaurant. "She fucking flattened you." I might have taken the breakup badly, but that was over a decade ago.

"It was a dance and a nibble. Be joyous. Wish me a happy birthday." I try to tease my brother out of whatever he thinks he needs to say here.

"Happy birthday, she fucking flattened you."

"I danced with her. I can totally handle seeing her, and I promise you I'm not going to marry her."

His expression softens, and finally, I see my brother staring back at me. "We can call the bet off—"

"No, I can do this—"

Dax continues, "But you shouldn't. You need to figure out how to be alone." He puts his hand on my shoulder, and I shrug my brother off.

"Fuck off. I can totally be alone. I've been alone in all my marriages."

He doesn't laugh. He should. That shit is funny. Instead, he says, "Dude, three times in twelve years. And you were engaged twice more. You don't know how to be alone. Not since she left you."

I spit back at my brother, "Says the whipped fucker who's chasing the same scared tail from Chicago to Boston to New York."

"Don't compare my relationship with Sophie to your nameless, faceless marriages."

"What relationship? She dumps you, you chase her, you're happy for a minute, and then you become this morose mutha-fucker all over again."

He slugs me in the arm.

"What the fuck?" I yell at him.

"Figure your shit out, and I'll figure mine. But the bet just got amped up, asshole." He scowls at me and my phone pops off in my pocket. Even if every bone in my body is screaming to get closure or laid tonight with Makenzie Preston, I can win the bet.

Actual Brother (Dax): I'm doubling down on my bet. Makenzie will crack him tonight. He can't marry her, but sure as fuck will date her.

Brother From Another Mother (Hayden): Agreed. Book it.

Brother In Arms (Colton): Is this a frivolous use of our money?

Actual Brother (Dax): I'll give mine to the charity of your choice.

Brother In Arms (Colton): Deal. Double it.

Another Brother (Law): {Thumbs-UP emoji/MoneyBag Emoji/Money Bag Emoji}

MotherFucker (Robbie): You assholes are still up? Jesus. I've been asleep for hours. And Makenzie Makenzie? Like Paris Makenzie? Like dumped your ass in a text after walking out of your 18th birthday party, Makenzie?

Brother From Another Mother (Hayden): Yes. Makenzie Makenzie.

MotherFucker (Robbie): He'll be at a chapel in twenty minutes.

TONY: I'M STILL MARRIED. Dumbasses. Double whatever you want. I can't marry Makenzie.

MotherFucker (Robbie): If anyone can find a way, it's you, my brother.

Actual Brother (Dax): We said date.

I stomp around in a circle, and I want to fucking kill my brother. Jesus, cut me a fucking break. I deserve one night with Mak that's not about pain.

He shakes his head slightly, and I lose it. I'm sure I'll be on some bullshit viral gossip tomorrow, looking like a lunatic.

Flicking my wrists at him, I say, "Seriously, what the fuck is wrong? I'm done with this bet, dear brother. Message received. I marry the wrong women. I like being with someone instead of alone and desperate like you. Laura wasn't it, and it turned out she's a boring lay. How the fuck do we know it's not Makenzie?"

Thank God it's a casino, and people around us can't hear me, and no one's paying attention.

"Get the hell out of my face."

I cross my arms over my chest like he usually does and cock my head. I'm done being messed with.

Dax tosses his arms in the air. "Dad's signing papers on Monday to divest you of Ladd Media."

"What? Why?" My voice is insanely loud and high-pitched. And my entire body has gone icy cold, like I'm in one of those fucked up ice bars.

"Two-fold. He's done having way too many women on your romantic fallout payroll. And Bugle."

"Jesus. Bugle again. That tech nightmare was six years ago. I learned that fucking lesson and the division is in the black again. We're building content, not buying flawed tech."

"The majority share and top management are freaked by how much money you've spent to launch your new venture."

"The Cookery will work." My back is up because this idea and the work we've put in will fucking pay off. It's the gamble of my career, but it's a sure bet in my mind.

Dax continues, "--- after trying to buy that over priced tech last year and let's not forget your billion-dollar fuck-up with Bugle—"

"It wasn't that bad."

He squeezes his eyes closed. "You went all in and pushed it to be the next big social. The platform and code crumbled under the weight of what you were doing."

I scrub my face with my hands and walk around in a circle. It was that bad, but I've already atoned for this shit. What I'm doing now is an enormous investment, and I thought I'd sealed up all the doubt with my father and the board.

"For someone who has stayed far away from the family business and wants nothing to do with the company, you sure have a lot to fucking say about it. Why the sudden turn? Business has nothing to do with the wrong women I break up with."

Dax puts his hands on my shoulders. "Dad sealing your trust and Ladd Media if you don't stay single. Optics. It looks erratic and irresponsible."

"I should knock up some woman and stay in a miserable marriage? That's not the example we have. That's not the brass ring of their fucking perfect relationship."

"Your divorces are undermining the entire company and the shareholders are wigging out. This shit is serious."

My heart bottoms out because my job is the only thing I'm good at. I love it. I'm shit at relationships but I rock at work. And money. I'm fucking lucky, but I don't know a life without it. Making it comes naturally to me, and spending it is my forte. I've been yelled at for giving too much away, but never threatened like this. Other than the threats about getting a girlfriend before I was in college, this is the first time they've put this over on me.

Dax catches my shoulder and pulls me into a hug. More like a headlock, but still our kind of hug.

He says directly into my ear, "It's why I created the bet, to stop you before it all blew up."

"Does everyone know?"

"No. I thought if we teased you enough, you'd cave to a bet and stay strong. I didn't plan on Mak being any part of your next year."

"That's a bet we all would have lost." I slap him on his back and look around. I look at everything in the room but my brother. "When's Dad bringing the hammer down?" Our father is a phenomenal and patient person, and it appears I broke him. Not the first time, and pretty sure it won't be the last. But at least I'm maintaining my black sheep status.

I ask, "How long? You know this is fucking stupid, right?"

He nods.

I continue, "Paying Gavin to draw up these bullshit papers will cost more than Ariel's monthly palimony."

"Your mermaid was the worst one." Dax shakes his head.

I'll play along because the my multimedia gamble, the Cookery launches soon. "I've developed too much to abandon it now. But the mermaid's deal runs out this year. That's one off of the books."

"It's gonna take a sizable chunk to unload Laura."

"Hey, that's my wife." I grin.

Dax smiles slightly, then says, "Give Dad a year to calm the fuck down. Be wary. He knows every dime you spend and every penny your serial monogamy is bleeding your bank account and the trust. Their trust money and their actual trust are hemorrhaging."

I run my hand over my head. "Simple. Nix dating, don't screw Makenzie, successfully launch a super fucking unprecedented stellar concept, gain back Dad's trust and look fucking good doing it. I'll fuck around, have threesomes, make everyone happy." But I do want to screw Makenzie, like desperately. I'm willing to find a loophole that leads to her hole. That was a joke my dick would make. Not a dick joke, but one he would make if I were listening, but I'm not. Because I'm keeping my job.

"Terms of the bet if you still want to honor it." I shove him back and cock an eyebrow. "You can't fuck the same woman twice and you can't date anyone."

I scream into the casino in frustration, and no one even bats an eye. It's loud and crazy and no one is noticing.

Makenzie appears at the club door, looking around for me. Her dark hair falling on her bare shoulders is breathtaking. Her slender frame sways to the music, and as I watch her hips, my mind is no longer in control.

But I *can* fuck her once.

Just once.

mak

He's been gone for like a half an hour—the perfect timing for me to sober up a bit and realize all the things I'm thinking are a terrible idea. I've acted on enough of them to know. There's an ease to my head and soul when I'm around him, and I can't believe I feel the fucking same way I did twelve years ago. But I have to go before it's too hard to walk away again.

This time I'll say goodbye. I owe him that after the way I broke up with him. We had an amazing time the day before his eighteenth birthday. All the weirdness of being apart ceased to exist once we were in the same space. I'm scared that it feels the same as that. But when I bolted, I was young, and family, friends, and money surrounded him. He was unaffected. I was very affected and aware I didn't belong there so I literally ran out of their Martha's Vineyard mansion, and down the road to a ferry. I eventually texted him. But that day, I left a giant piece of myself behind. I don't know if he's aware he's been holding it for me all this time.

His nature, his heart, and his humor were things I felt came so easily for him. And for once in my life, I wanted to be a part of something easy, so he let me. He didn't know I gobbled up our happiness and swallowed it down, devouring every moment with him, hoping it would rub off on my life beyond Paris. When I flew back to my house, I was reminded I didn't belong to him or in that world. His parents dismissed me in a way that was both cliché and painful.

My parents are good people and love me, probably shouldn't have had a kid, but here I am.

His sexy mouth tugs upward as he taps away on his phone. I'm experiencing a rush of memories and feelings that were once neatly tucked away as I walk toward him.

I didn't want him to see any of my real ugly because his world was so sparkling. I didn't want him to know I flunked out of high school. That I partied and fucked around because I didn't want to go home. I certainly didn't want him to see my parents in their ancient striped faded barker loungers, eating on TV trays binging old *Columbo*s and new *Law & Order: SVU*'s. And having heart issues because they both really love the KFC bowls. And their issues were never about the quality of food, just the reasons they kept on eating.

I want to help families to find their balance in life, so I'm going into family medicine. It took me twenty-two years to find it myself, and I dragged my parents along for the ride. I'm proud of turning my life around. But I can't fucking tell him because he doesn't know anything about my family or my real life. He was only ever privy to my heart and soul. I can't hang around to find out if that's enough.

But that fucking dark-ass day when I flew home and saw our house filled with junk and neglect was the moment I wanted to make my lies true. Looking at a long stretch of sad loneliness, I began to empty our house and fill our lives. I made room in my life to be something more than everyone assumed. I gave myself permission and space to step into my own light instead of mocking it, lying, or running from it. It was the day we all began to dream.

I never reached out because by the time I was proud of myself, he was married. And married. And I believe he is currently—married.

His blue eyes and rich honey hair. His nose is a little crooked, and I'm sure he broke it in a fight at some point. He was always good at starting them and terrible at finishing them. It adds character to his face. The outline in his jeans is undeniable and he's casual, sexy, and, well, not mine. He skips to me grinning like a madman taking my hand.

"Where did you go?" I ask.

He shakes his head. "Nope. That's a question for you to answer. Come on."

"You're married."

He laughs. "Not for long."

"I'm sorry."

"Also, nope. No sympathy. It's not my first time." He wiggles three fingers of his bare left hand at me.

"Three divorces. So, I've heard." He's not exactly out of the spotlight.

He nods and laughs, then says, "Never would have happened if you hadn't broken up with me. Totally your fault." I laugh, but I hope that's not true. Ok, I hope it's a little true.

He drags me with him, and we're flying through the casino and laughing. I should pull back, but I want a piece of the old fearless and sometimes reckless Makenzie back. Maybe that's the piece he's been holding for me all along.

We look like a couple that people would envy. Or at least I think we do. It could be the vodka talking. I avoid looking in a mirror because I think I look smoking hot. The reality is I probably have eyeliner smeared under my eyes and the faded edges of a once perfectly lined lip. I let myself get lost in the way he makes me feel beautiful for a second. Maybe we can have that moment and avoid digging up all the pain we seem to be ignoring. And getting laid by someone I know is packing and is fantastic at fucking, wouldn't be the worst idea I've ever had.

That one is reserved for the Reno church I scammed into sponsoring me to go to France for three months. I've paid them back but I'm still working off that moral debt with odd jobs for the church.

He yanks me into the present by taking me in his arms. I'm out of breath in this confined space with this mythical man. Like my favorite childhood toys, the Sand Dollar Café and Poolside Paradise Beach Lego sets, I've both built him up and torn him down a thousand times. By combining them, I made a kind of resort. I'd rebuild them at least once a week, always altering and trying to perfect the beach scene. I'd place and replace the figures or move the chairs around and reposition the pool, change up the color patterns of the plastic bricks. Then finally, I'd imagine living there and being carefree with an umbrella drink. Snapping the cup into my Lego figure's hand when it felt like paradise. It was always the final piece. Then I'd tear it apart again, knowing I'd have nothing like that. Perfect doesn't exist.

I imagine a life if I'd stayed in Boston sometimes. I build it up tall, just like the beach Lego. I move the pieces around in my mind, conjuring perfection. But I know I would have wrecked it somehow. Even when I think about it, I tear it down quickly in my mind, so I don't have to see all the imperfections in either the dream or surrounding me. The scattered colored bricks return to their box, so I can build and try another day.

"Take me to bed," I blurt out.

He raises an eyebrow. "In a minute, little witch. There are things to do and things that need to be said first." My heart almost explodes as he uses my former nickname. I adjust my black dress and wring my hands. His look is so reverent I don't know how to respond.

I whisper under my breath, "Adventure."

He whips me around, and I end up facing him. He kisses me quickly and mumbling against my lips, "Adventure." I gasp a bit, and he spins me back out of his arms and leads me through the maze of the casino.

"Where?" I say as he madly types on his phone.

"So nosy. You used to be a lot easier to be around." I guffaw loudly.

He talks to the bell captain guy as a sleek black car pulls up. The driver gets out and hands him the keys.

"Get in."

"Are you kidnaping me?"

"Yes." Then he looks around at the bell captain, doorman, the valet, and the driver and says, "You guys cool with that? They may question you later and I really want to come off well when you describe her assailant."

The valet says, "Yes, Mr. Ladd." I swivel my head to him, completely confused.

He grins and peels off several bills and distributes them around.

"I forgot. You're rich."

"That's the nicest thing anyone has ever said to me. Get in, my good witch."

I slide into the passenger's seat and see a picnic basket in the back. I ask, "I thought this was spontaneous? When did you have time to set up a picnic and a car?"

"When you rent out the presidential suite and connect it to the chairman's suite so your buddies can each have their own bedroom, and Law can do his laps in our private pool in the morning, they get you anything you want very quickly."

He spent a year's tuition on his thirtieth birthday party.

I'm quiet. He looks over at me, and I inquire, "Tell me you do something good with all of it."

He nods. "I donate as much as the trust will allow. And I bid on the things, go to the parties, walk the dogs, and ladle the soup once or twice a month."

I smile, but I don't think his head has touched reality in a very long time. "Do more."

He nods, turning onto the street, lacing his fingers through mine. It's comfortable, sweet, and all wrong. But I clutch it nonetheless, and the grin on his face grows impossibly larger. How does he still like me? He doesn't even know me.

tony

I'm hoping the concierge who set all this up, came through with this last piece. I had to get out of the hotel and away from my room. My suite has an epic shower with benches and different sprayers. It would allow me to fuck her in so many filthy ways. I plan to fuck her at some point because I can't stand not being inside of her. But if I want to keep my company, I only get one shot at it, and it's not going to be a quick hook-up like she asked for. It's not going to be in a sloppy, drunk, rushed way. I stopped drinking long before she showed up at the club. Although there was lots of alcohol around, I wasn't feeling it. And then, when Dax told me what my parents were up to, any semblance of buzz wore off.

Now, I'm riding the high of holding my wicked little witch's hand. She's squirming. I know her. She's the type that both wants me to hold her hand and give her space. She wasn't affectionate at first, but eventually, she'd curl up into me on the Metro. I needed her touch like I needed to breathe. Still do, apparently. Didn't know that until right now when I realize I've been holding my breath for a decade.

I'm not sure I could take letting her go again. We pull through the gates, and she smiles.

"I love the Valley of Fire."

"Do you come to Vegas a lot?" I knew she left Reno for Arizona. I think she's still there—she's tagged on social media once in a while, but she never posts.

She doesn't say anything as I ease the car over to the side of the road. We're an hour or so from sunrise. And they instructed me in my texts to watch our step because of snakes and critters. They wrote the word critters, like things that could kill you could still sound cute. I grab the blankets in the back and the picnic basket. I set it all up on the hood of the car, and we ease back against the windshield.

We stare at the stars, and I swear to God I've never seen this many in my life.

She interrupts our silence by inching her hand closer and saying, "I don't go to the Strip often. And I sure as heck don't see this that often either."

I weave my fingers into hers and clasp. "Me neither."

My words die on the stilted air all around us, and I let them. She sighs, and it's this lovely little moment of resignation. She's decided to let me in.

"I know things feel messed up. But aside from not talking to you in a decade, the wrenching pain when you left, and let's shelve my intense carnal desire to claim you, I missed you. I missed your laugh, your storytelling, the dancing, the closeness. I missed you trying to figure something out and then doing it your own way. That's it. I missed you." I missed having her know me best.

A tear streams down her cheek as I glance at her. She lets it slide onto her shoulder, then shudders a bit. I let her take the moment.

Then she says, "This all got weird fucking fast. Dude. You can't say things like that. Give a girl a chance to catch up. You're like a million steps ahead of me. I'm seriously just trying to recover from the shock of seeing Colt, Hayden or

Danny or whatever he's called now. I certainly wasn't prepared to see you. So back it down, boy. Start small. It's all I have to give."

"I'm not good at small," I remind her.

"Says the man who apparently marries on the first date."

"I'm an all-in kind of guy." She's giving me shit, and I love it.

"I remember," she teases.

With a few snaps of my fingers, I try to come up with something to start with. "Ok. Small. I can do small. Do you have a pet?"

She laughs long and hard. "No."

"Where's your favorite place?" I hit her rapid fire.

"How is that catching up?"

"I'm starting small. Jeez. Give a guy a break." I squeeze her hand, and she tightens our grip. I inch a little closer to her, and we're both still staring up.

She asks, "What's your favorite place?"

I say, "You're not ready to hear that." She turns her head to mine, and I stare at her beautiful and sweet face.

"Paris?"

"No. I'm not all Francophile, like our friends, but it has a special place in my heart. But no. What's yours?" She's not ready to hear that it's here. Right now. This is my favorite place. Wherever she is. I don't wait for an answer before I speak again. Fuck small, I have to dig in.

I say, "Huh. Cool. Interesting. Ok, I'm dying. Where do you live? What do you do? Do you have someone? Do you like eggs now? What's your favorite sushi roll? Are you married? Are you engaged? Are you happy? What's the meaning of life?"

She can't stop laughing at me as she sits up a bit. I shift and grab her and pull her to me.

I kiss her lightly. Her lips are firm, and I wait until she

yields. I don't push it. As soon as they're soft and lovely against mine, I pull back. "Is that small enough?" My whole body flutters.

She gasps, and her eyes look dreamily at me. "Perfect."

"Great. Now start answering me, woman."

She smiles. "Kind of all over, but I have a small apartment in Los Angeles. I style commercial shoots for mid-range fashion brands, dragon roll, no, almost, sometimes, and look up."

I grin and look up as the sky yields to the day. There's a glow forming, like the world is on a dimmer switch, and it's slowly turning on. We scoot back, my arm around her, and her head leans on my shoulder. It's like it's made for her.

mak

Holy shit! What the fuck am I doing? The lies keep slipping out. It's like I have a sickness, and there's no cure. I want to be with him, but I don't want him to know about my life. What is that about? The pit of my stomach churns as I curl into him. The same feeling I harbored in Paris the whole time we were dating. That horrible, *what if he finds out I'm not fabulous*, feeling. The one that comes with lies that could unravel everything. Shut up, Makenzie. We've talked about everything in life except the reality of mine. He doesn't know what my home life really was like. And hid the whole dropout thing who thought it was more fun to have sex and skip out on everything than make dioramas for World History. Someone should have sat me down and told me dioramas are more fun than a GED and community college.

"Mak?" He breaks the silence, and I relish the distraction from my own thoughts.

"Yes?"

"If you could do one thing from your past differently, what would it be?"

"Wear a longer dress to eat foie gras and frog legs." He laughs, and my head almost bucks off his chest. What I'd actually do is tell him my whole truth when he told me he loved me and trust him. And I'd trust me. But now I'm so whipped up in this mess that I'm not sure it's worth telling him everything. He'll be gone in a minute.

I lean on his chest, facing him, his arm slung behind his head and the other wrapped tightly around me.

Ironically, I ask, "Tell me something true."

"My father is threatening to take away my piece of the company."

"Yikes." I wince, and he laughs.

"And I'm great at what I do. I've grown the media, digital publishing, and communication division to be the pillar that holds up the rest of Ladd Enterprises."

"Did you kill his dog or something? Eat the last of the Cheerios?" He is laughing and tickling me to stop me. I keep going. "Put the milk carton back empty? Did you lose all the office furniture in one of your dumb bets?" He flinches, and I know I'm getting closer.

"I'm getting divorced again. Let's just say my relationships have cost a bit more than our Eiffel Tower night."

I shake my hands out. "Damn."

He grins and pulls me back. "Tell me something true," he says, and it stings slightly, given how truthful I've been tonight.

"My parents are doing great. It's been a long struggle with health for them, but we're getting there."

He holds me close. I let my head rest on his chest, and he kisses the top of my head. "I'm sorry. That must have been hard."

"It's fine." He drops it, and we sit for another minute wrapped up in each other.

"What is this?" I ask.

"Indefinable."

"I like that."

"Tell me about your twenty-fifth birthday."

Truth: My mom was in hospital suffering from complications of a heart procedure. A fun time brought on by her lack of activity and consuming too much over the years with no regard for how it would affect her, my father, or me. But I lie so I don't get his sympathy kiss again.

The lie: "Mags and I went to New York. It was kind of low key. And then we went out to the Hamptons for a shoot I was on and got to stay on the property." I'm like an improv savant.

His eyes light up. "Where?"

"East Hampton." Is that a place? Shit. Abort. "What about your twenty-fifth?"

"I was on a honeymoon."

"Which wife?" I wonder if he had fun.

"Number two. She was a peach. The nastiest, most expensive divorce to date, but the new one may outdo her. Granted, I was only married for about ten months to number two. Laura has three and a half years under her belt between dating and marriage."

I move to face him. He sits up, too, and pulls out chocolate. His face is chiseled, and the angles welcome the light as dawn breaks. I want him to know me. It's not what I should say, but it's what I can say right now.

"Tony."

"Makenzie. I don't like the tone you're taking."

I move out of his touch. "Someday, will you tell me about what happened when you, well, got my text?"

"Probably not, since I don't like to revisit it. But do you need to tell me something?" That chiseled, vulnerable face somehow tightens and closes up a bit.

"I'm so sorry. I'm so sorry." He puts his hand on my knee. I keep blurting out my apology. "My life was messier than you know and there wasn't a place for me or you. And we were... I don't know. It was the hardest thing I've ever done in my life, and I don't regret doing it, only the way I did it. I should have faced you, and I'm so sorry I hurt us both so badly."

He says nothing for a minute. "That won't help."

"What?"

He smirks. "It won't help that I'm paying off a bevy of women who I connected my life to in order to get over you. The way I see it, you owe me a ton of cash." I push out a small laugh. He squeezes my hand. "Not tonight, ok?"

Leaning over, I kiss him softly. We're still not opening our mouths, but the connection is there, if not the lust. I snuggle into him again. It's not absolution, but it's a start. Even if we never go past this moment, there's a bit of closure for eighteen-year-old Makenzie, and I hope for him, too. I didn't apologize for being selfish, or maybe I did. It doesn't matter tonight. Just the feel, smell, and comfort of him matters.

"Do the words prenup mean anything to you?" He laughs and sits up, cracking open a bottle of sparkling water. I take it from him and sip.

"This one has one, but she's crafty. Should be even more money to fight it than to pay her off." He seems resigned and I hope I didn't do that too. Dampen his spirit. That's not Tony. I stand up on the car carefully, and he holds my legs. I hoist my water, and it splashes a bit.

"I'd like to make a toast in front of every star in this hemisphere." He laughs, and I continue, "I'd like to toast Tony Ladd and the bride he should have had."

I don't know if that's me, but I know it's not any of the ones he's already tried. There's an eerie but beautiful glow breaking across the edges of the world. I sit back down between his legs to bask in it and he pulls a blanket over the two of us. And we watch.

The intense fuchsia gives way to a fiery orange that fades into a rainbow of sherbet peach and pink. The sun appears after its fanfare, and it looks like we could touch it. That it's low enough and close enough to believe this is our personal sun. He kisses my head and the back of my neck. His arm comes out of the blanket, and he takes a picture with the glow of a new promise all around us. Wrapping my mind around his, I exhale deeply. I take a couple of pictures of the sun at our feet and our hands on the blanket. I know they'll torture me later, but I want them, anyway. He holds me impossibly close.

With the sun in full view now, I say, "You have to fight her and your dad. Don't let them take what belongs to you. You're still Tony, but you're less."

He holds me and whispers, "So are you." He's absolutely right. "But what if we could both be more?" he says. I turn around and press my lips to his, and he takes them greedily. "I can't sleep with you, and I can't tell you why."

"That's ok. Just kiss me. And you are married, right?"

His tongue slides into my mouth, and I accept it like the gift it's supposed to be.

"Separated," he says breathlessly, and his hands roam up and down my thighs.

I have a lot of things to unravel, but maybe he won't walk away if he knows all my truth. If he understands the lies I've told are stupid things, and he knows the real me.

He kisses my neck, muttering sweet things, and I hold him tight to me. The smell of him is helping me remember that bold, bad girl Makenzie wasn't totally terrible. I miss being fearless. Finally, a clear decision with no second-guessing. I don't edit or think, and impulsive Mak feels good.

"Can I know you again?" I say.

He grins and slams his lips to mine. We chase our past with our tongues and hands.

"Are you casting again, little witch?"

"Maybe." He kisses me again. This time, his soft lips take their time. Our moment evolves into what we need it to be without getting messy with memory.

"Then consider me under your spell." He slides his hand into my hair, and I moan into his mouth. He flirts with the edge of my skirt.

"Jesus, I want to make you come. I want to see it and feel it."

I gasp. "Same."

He lifts his head and furrows his brow. "I have to clarify something, and I'll get back to you. Rain check?"

"Confused, but yes."

"More of this right now, please." It's sheer blissful torture as he moves me underneath him on the hood of the car. The sun is higher in the sky and spills its light all over us. Perhaps it really is a new day.

tony

I crawl out of bed at quarter to noon. I've been asleep for four hours, and I woke up smiling, despite my abbreviated slumber and lack of orgasm. We fly home today, and I don't want to miss the "recall brunch." Dax named it that in college when we'd all get together and get blackout drunk.

I glance at my phone, and there's nothing. I start way too many days like this—with nothing. Even my bed is empty. Laura has filled my bed for the last three and half years, and she was my successful marriage. Well, we had separate bedrooms for the last six months; she said I snored. We still occasionally had very unsatisfying sex, and then it was all bold graffiti writing on the wall.

I toss on a robe and walk out into our villa. It's like the marble gods threw up in here. As if the height of money and decadence is hard, shiny stone. It's Vegas-perfect. Any less, and it might look tacky, any more, and it would tip the scales to gaudy.

I appear in the archway with my spicy Bloody and raise my glass to the men, who all turn toward me. "Gentlemen! And yoga, yogurt-parfait-eating pussy."

Hayden stretches and says, "The question is, dear friend, whose pussy did you eat?" He licks the yogurt spoon clean and places it on the table.

I shovel mac and cheese onto my plate from the massive buffet with all our favorite foods I ordered in advance. Robbie's favorite breakfast is two. Two complete breakfasts. Even though he's coaching now, he skates every day and trains like he used to. He's still an enormous man.

Colt's breakfast is stunning. He always repurposes and combines food into little works of art.

Law prefers all the protein he can get, being taller and much more lean muscle. Currently, he's working on a full porterhouse and at least a dozen eggs. He probably already did fifty laps in the pool to keep his arm loose for his debut game, pitching for Arizona tomorrow. Glad we caught him in this pocket between minors and majors to hang out.

I empty my pockets and wallet. I surrender my phone and place it all in the center bowl that Colton is currently picking through.

He's piecing our night together collectively. He'll get a working timeline of our evening together. Hence the name 'recall brunch.' Colton's like our anarchy archivist. He's currently scrolling Robbie's phone.

"You seriously text Claire that much?"

"What? We're codependent." He scoops a mountain of brisket hash into his mouth.

"Did you marry Makenzie?" my brother asks.

I grin. "Thought maybe I'd get divorced first. But the genuine answer is, not yet." I waggle my eyebrows.

Robbie smirks, "Do it. Claire wants to put in a pool and buy a beach house. We need the cash."

Robbie can afford anything he wants. Turns out his wonderful wife is an investment genius and has their money in all the right places. I tossed Claire some cash, and apparently, it's doing well. She's actually studying for her broker's license so she can be more than a day trader. She says she wants to manage hedge funds. I love her dearly, but I never saw her becoming a Wolf of Wall Street.

"What did I miss?"

Colt says, "Nothing much. Law took off with a redhead."

Law grins. "Yeah, I did. Wild shit. I mean, wild shit. At one point I was upside down and there was like a ghost in the corner."

"Someone in a ghost costume watched?" Robbie asks.

"Maybe. Or maybe she has like a sex ghost. My dick might never recover."

Hayden asks, "You had sex with three different women yesterday and that one was wild?"

Law looks up curiously. "Two. The chick at the club and the redhead. And technically, the redhead was after midnight."

Dax tosses a matchbook to Law. "Steakhouse waitress." We all nod in agreement, and Law exhales loudly and concedes.

"Yeah, but the redhead and the ghost will live in infamy."

I ask, "You had a celestial three way?"

"Who the fuck knows what happened."

Hayden grins and says, "And her name?" He's ribbing his little brother, who never remembers women.

Law grins smugly at us after looking up at the ceiling momentarily. "Celeste."

Dax slams his hands on the table as all our eyes bug out of our heads.

Robbie cocks his head. "WHAA? Baby bro. What the hell? You made that up."

Colt holds up a receipt. "Can confirm." He passes it around, and it's a casino bar receipt for $124.16 with a lipstick number and the name Celeste.

Law screams, "Burn." Then he shovels half a steak into his

mouth. "Shocks the hell out of me, too. Let's call it maturity." We all laugh, then chatter insults at him, tossing our napkins at his head.

"Quick clarification," I interrupt the assault on Law.

Colt looks up. "On what?"

"What constitutes sex?" I ask.

Robbie says, "Ejaculation."

"Let's go with that," Hayden confirms.

"Fine. Cool. So I can only masturbate once? Cuz, I've already lost the bet."

Dax puts his finger up and says, "Ejaculation with another person in the room."

"Now, what if they come?" I tent my fingers in front of my face.

Law points at me. "You made her come? That counts."

"Nope," I say, holding both hands up. "And I don't think it should count if I don't come."

Hayden grabs his phone and stands, bouncing around the room. I'm sure he's headed to a yoga class of some sort. Not sure where his energy comes from.

"The idea is you can't date. If she comes and you see her again, that's a second date."

They all grunt in agreement. Colt returns Dax's phone to him as mine dings from the silver bowl, and everyone looks.

It's a picture of the sunrise with our feet on the edge of the image. Fuck yeah. I've got her number now. I gave her mine and let her decide if she wants to stay in touch. Everyone stares at me.

"You can't see her again," Hayden says.

I stand on my chair, raise my glass, and put my hand on my heart. "Good brothers, all. I, Anthony Ladd, did not, on my honor, her honor, and let's say, Colt's,"—they all laugh because he's the most honorable of all of us—"I did not sleep with that bewitching woman. We both walked away unsatisfied, unsated, and unencumbered."

They all yell, "Hear! Hear!"

"The rules state I can see her as long as we're not dating or sleeping together."

Robbie says, "But you can fuck her once if you like."

"I will take that under advisement."

Dax smirks. I step down from the chair and point to him. "What?"

"Good luck."

Another picture comes in, and it's of Maggie, Makenzie, and Colt. He's in the middle, but glancing at Maggie instead of the camera. That's loaded. We all yell, staring at the picture.

Then we settle our gaze on Colt. Shit, he's the most upstanding of all of us.

Law throws a napkin at him. "Wait. Dude! We need to discuss your unholy behavior. You closed your eyes."

"I didn't." He shakes his head, but I see it too.

I pop in, "Um, you did. Just now and last night. You wanted to shake her hand. She hugged you instead, and you closed your eyes while she hugged you."

Hayden raises a bottle of water and hitches his mat under his arm. "And you smelled her. I saw you."

Robbie says, "You're a mess if you think she doesn't still own a piece of you."

Colt puts his hands up. "Ok. Fine. I closed my eyes and smelled the girl of my former dreams. But it was nostalgia, nothing more. I'm a settled family man."

I say, gesturing with a considerable piece of pancake, "Looked pretty current."

"She's married and I'm married with kids. I'm not that man. She's happy and I'm happy for her." He's not. But he wouldn't jeopardize his girls. Considering what he did and still does for them, I believe him.

There's a long pause, and Colt seems relieved we've let the subject go.

Then Robbie barrels in and adds, "But you didn't say you are happy."

We all howl, and Colt flips us off.

Best birthday ever.

mak

He didn't respond, but I know he got it. I wonder if he's still in town or if I was slipped a hallucinogen.

I roll over in my hotel bed and see Mags is awake, and her face is a little too dreamy.

"Hey. What was that with Colt last night?"

She rolls over, and we're both snuggled in our beds facing each other.

"Who knows? Maybe it was simply catching up. It hurt to see him, and I didn't want it to, so I guess I acted like I was more than fine."

"He did you shitty." He did to her what I did to Tony. That's how I know it was shitty.

"If it matters, there were apologies and lots of laughs about how stupid it is to turn thirty." Her lips curl into a smile and her long highlighted brown hair falls in her face over her hazel eyes. It's nice to see my friend's face, it's been a while.

"It is dumb. Let's stay twenty-nine for a while."

"Agreed," she says. "My highlights from last night are insignificant. What the hell was with you? Did you make love to Tony?"

"Uck. No. I would have, but he took me out to Valley of Fire, and we watched the sunrise instead. Our conversation was both everything and nothing at all. We did some super-hot kissing and cuddling under a blanket. Then he gave me his number."

"What did you do?" She sits up. "This is huge! You never cuddle. You're a *wham bam thank you ma'am* kind of gal."

I laugh and turn onto my back, stretching while looking at the reality kaleidoscope that is the Vegas Strip. So different from the dusty brown view at home, which is twenty-five minutes and a world away from here.

I sit up and shrug, pulling a pillow onto my lap. "I didn't give him my number until like a minute ago."

"Why?"

"I lied," I confess.

I walk to the bathroom, but Mags is up and following me. "What? Why? Wait, when? About the old lies? Stop it, Mak. You have a problem."

"I know!"

"You're like the most forthright person I know. And you lie to him? I thought you were done with all of that. I do not approve. No, ma'am. Tell me all of these details now. If we're going to process the love of your life popping back up—"

I stop brushing my teeth, spit, and turn to her. "Hold up. No one said love of my life. He's a guy I used to be with. And—"

She pokes me. "Bullshit." Then Mags does a silly dance and twirls around. "Love. You looooovvve him. Lurve him. He's your lurver!"

"Stop."

"He's the love of.... Wait. You lied? When?" She sees my face.

"Yeah, I lied. I mean, from before." I can't tell her I did it again.

"Before what?" She knits her brow. Sometimes she's a little

lost in her own world. She's sweet and funny, but every once in a while, she loses the thread of a conversation.

"In Paris. I told him I was choosing between going to Northeastern and Arizona State."

"That's not even a choice," she says matter-of-factly.

"What are you talking about?" I shake my head.

She counts on her fingers. "You go to Arizona State. It's warmer, there's a better football team, and you're closer to home. How is this even a question?"

I push past her and grab a bottle of water. "Oh my God. Maggie. I didn't graduate from high school, remember?"

With a long groan of recognition, she says, "Ohhh. I see. That's right. Are you choosing between those colleges now?"

"Mags! No. That was one of the old lies I told Tony. Remember?"

"Oh yeah. But you're in school now. What did he think of that?"

I shake my head like I'm the crazy one. "What does that have to do with the lie from twelve years ago?"

"You're correcting it all."

I throw my hands up. "Yes, but he thinks I already went to college. And that I live in LA."

She jumps on the bed and kneels. "That would be fun. You should move to LA."

I snap at her face. I know it's rude, but I need her to pay attention. "Maggie, focus up. He thinks I graduated college from ASU with a fashion merchandising degree and live in Los Angeles. And that I travel all over the world working as a stylist on commercial and advertising campaigns for mid-level fast fashion brands."

She looks at me and takes the bottle of water from my hand. "Why does he think that? You're a rec director in an elder care community living in your parents' back room, that really should be a study or something. There's too many windows for it to be a decent bedroom."

"I know! He thinks this because I told him those things. I don't know how to untell him things."

"I get it. You layered lies on top of old lies as if they were still alive and moving on with their lives."

"Stop talking. I lied. That's the point, but I may not be able to tell him the truth."

She wags a finger in my face. "You have to or it's going to end up like a frustrating plot of a Netflix show I can't watch. It will bring me such anxiety thinking about you perpetuating the lie."

I sit in the desk chair and stare at my daffy friend who speaks the truth. She always does. Maggie's incapable of guile, deceit, or cruelty. She's my yin. I'm just a big ole dumbass yang.

"I know. I fucked up."

"It's ok. Everyone makes mistakes. But if you still want to be around him, you are going to have to untell."

"Why are you still friends with me? I'm not sure how someone as good as you started hanging around with me."

"You didn't care."

"Care about what?"

"Looking cool or judging me for worrying about everything. You're still my only friend who has always made me feel as if everything I have to say, whether it makes sense or not, is valid."

I smile at my best friend. "Same. You never cared that I screwed up."

"Oh, yes, I did. Lots of worrying about you, but you're figuring it out. If he matters, tell Tony. It's not like you're a couple. If he wants to be your friend, he should know what a great friend you are. And the freaking truth."

I laugh. "We'll see. I wish you lived closer."

She reaches out her hand. "Me too." Portland is way too far.

We hug. Then she goes to reach for another bottle of water.

"Stop! We can only afford one minibar bottle."

She picks it up and grins. "This one is on me. I'll send you the cash for it."

"In that case, crack open the M&M's, I'm starving."

My phone dings, and Maggie picks it up. She squeals, "It's TONY!"

"We're friends. Nothing more. I've screwed up so many things in my life. I don't want to screw up my pre-med thing."

"You need to tell him you're going to be a doctor."

"At this part-time rate I'll be a doctor when I'm forty. That's eleven years from now."

"Exactly!" she says with way too much excitement. "And you get to be a doctor for sixty years! That's a good deal."

Always the optimist. I exhale and look at my texts.

T: Gotcha now.

MAK: I guess you do.

T: Nice feet.

MAK: Thanks. I only bring them out on special occasions.

T: Thank you.

MAK: For my feet?

T: For letting me in.

Oh shit. I did not do that. I will not do that. I have to do that. Should I do that?

I have to tell him.

tony

I neglected to tell her the full extent of my father's threats and conditions. It's killing me but I can't be with someone else while in the middle of a custody battle over my couch. And my parents will disown me, the company stock will freaking bottom out, and the lovely third Mrs. Ladd will get a boon of a payout.

Laura should walk away with $248,900.26 worth of jewelry and clothing as well as 3.4 million. I'm an idiot, but I'm not stupid. Not a dime more, and I'm on the straight and fucking narrow until this is all settled.

Alerts from multiple trash paparazzi sites pop up with pictures from Vegas. The pictures have been circling for two weeks now as I've avoided my father. It's all typical thirty-year-old birthday stuff with the dudes. I'm usually only in them if I'm with a woman, making deals, or fall-down drunk. But Law and Robbie cut a big shadow, and when we're all together, the paps can't resist. Not even my own media company can stop them. I posted a picture one of us from dinner then I leveraged the coverage. It's clickbait to get them to the Ladd Media site so we can remind them I'm basically launching an online, multi-platform cooking network in the coming months. I'm not too proud to whore out my own birthday party.

The steakhouse where we ate is hosting our launch podcasts. I'm swallowed up right now in all the moving parts of this thing and apparently my entire career hinges on its success. If it works, then the bullshit can fade away and I can see if Mak is something.

We weren't publicly photographed, thank fucking God. I can't stop thinking of how she smelled, fit in my arms, and made me feel. I'm a whipped, spell-bound pussy boy. And I'm all about her pussy, so this divorce needs to be fast-tracked. I glance at my reflection and restyle my hair. It's pulled back with product but not stiff. It's got the wave in it I like, and I'd give it an eight out of ten today, and sometimes, that's the best you can hope for. We've texted with some frequency lately and I like it.

TONY: I'm going in. And I'm wearing the yellow tie he hates.

MAK: Who is this?

TONY: Your knight in shining armor.

MAK: Thought you were a king?

TONY: Can't I be both?

MAK: I've learned in life—you don't get both. Choose and live with the consequences.

TONY: That's a little loaded for 9:00 a.m. EST and 6:00 a.m. your fucked-up time, but I'll take it.

MAK: YELLOW 4 EVA!

MAK: I LOVE YELLOW.

TONY: He hates it.

MAK: All my underwear is yellow.

I laugh.

TONY: Prove it.

MAK: It's all in the wash. Another rain check.

TONY: You owe me a panty pic. Text me later.

I silence my phone so I can believe she'll text me later then wave to my father's assistant, who giggles.

I say, "How is it possible you smell that good all the time?"

"Oh, Tony. How are things at your building?"

"You know I don't own it."

I moved the Ladd Media Group across town about a year ago to get distance. I needed them to look to me not my father for leadership.

"Well, things are going really good over there but I miss seeing you here." I'm more disconnected from him these days. I wink at her.

I fling open the door, and my mother is in his lap. "Ah, the parents. And I'm not scarred at all." Their marriage is enviable, but I don't need the details.

My mother laughs, kisses my father, and stands up, opening her arms. I pick her up and give her a big hug. Her ashy dyed-blonde, perfect hair bounces right back to the exact place she's had it for decades. I've avoided this meeting, but he cornered me at Butter the other night. He knew I'd be there for steak on a Tuesday.

Mom puts her hand on my scruffy cheek, pinching a bit too hard.

My father stands and puts his hand out. "Really, Pop? A handshake?" He smiles and we do that hug with a manly back-slap thing.

"Sit."

A series of legal-looking bound folders are on the coffee table, and I sit on the brown leather couch behind them. His assistant arrives and places a perfect latte in front of me.

My mother sits in the pony chair opposite me, and my father takes the matching one off to the side. His office is decorated in a collection of vintage, reproduced, and knocked-off pieces that span decades. His black, glass desk is a holdover from the era that brought us *Friends*, mismatched dining sets, and birch cabinetry.

"This shit stops," he says, as if I'm twelve and stealing extra cookies after dinner.

I cross my legs and sit back, draping my arm on the back of the couch. My mother winces as my father swears.

"So, I've heard." I stare back at them.

"Honey, what happened with Laura? She was lovely, not like Nicola or—"

My father interrupts her, "If you want to remember their names, darling, perhaps just look at the corporate checkbook that pays these women every month out of Tony's salary. It's a miracle you have some left. No more." They're so melodramatic.

"Ever?" I raise an eyebrow. "Don't you want grandkids? Legacies to take over your empire. Maybe one of my kids will have a head for figures like you. Or dimples like your lovely bride." My mother puts her hand on her heart. She doesn't have the stomach to punish us.

My father is pissed, and I'm baiting him. I want him to get to the point.

"Why don't you let Dax take care of grandkids. You need to stop fucking getting married. It's costing us a fortune and we're losing face in the public. You're making a mockery of the company and our business by looking like the cavalier idiot who marries and pays out on a whim. Who's going to trust you with multibillion dollar investments if you can't seem to stay in a relationship? Laura's suing for more."

I stand up quickly and point at him. "I may be a wicked serial monogamist, but I've always been fair in the breakup. If she wants to money grab let her try. There are no skeletons, nothing to negate the prenup. But quick disclosure, I kissed a woman in Vegas, but we were completely alone and I'm legally separated. I didn't cheat or violate anything. And when does it matter who is in my bed when it comes to the bottom line of this company?"

I circle around the power desk because I need to move around. Their heads swivel to watch me. I don't say anything else.

My father circles the room. He puts a hand on my shoulder. "Kissing a woman while you're separated, not admirable, but you're right, not a violation or cheating. Just don't marry or date this one. Tell me it was a drunken hookup."

"Dad? Really?"

"Sweetie, we just think you need to be unattached."

I nod and my father says, "I'm so frazzled by a third divorce and the fifth member of your fan club to go on our post-Tony-relationship payroll."

My mom blurts out, "Wait until you figure out what you do want instead of trying on all the wrong ones."

"Not to be weird, but I want you. I want a partner. Someone who still excites me after years together." My mom reaches over and takes my father's hand.

I smile. "See. How the hell am I supposed to find the perfect relationship when I'm living up to this shit?"

My mother gives me the stink eye.

"Sorry. I want someone who wants me. Just me. And I'm so afraid that they'll slip through my fingers that the moment I like someone—"

"You marry them." My father finishes my sentence.

"I see now that's not a good plan." I cross my arms. I know what's coming, thanks to Dax.

"Tony, I hate doing this. But I need for you to stay single."

"Seems everyone wants that."

Mom pipes in, "Not your friends. They'd lose the bet."

I scoff as I lean back on the bookshelves. "Does Dax tell you everything?"

My mom answers, "Yes."

"Give us some time, like a year to clean up this divorce, survive the media cycle, which I'm hoping you'll control as much as possible, and get past this. We need to shore up some voting blocks of shareholders and I can't have you giving them ammo. Two of your past paramours' palimonies will be off our books in eleven months and then we'll revisit this. I don't want to remove you from the company, but I will. You need to sign these documents that state you'll step down if I say so."

"Can't you just ground me?"

My mom laughs. "I think you need to be alone for a while. You need to get a hobby. Take up yoga like Hayden or gardening like Colt."

I roll my eyes. "Work and getting married are my hobbies."

My father puts his hands on his knees as he sits down.

"Fine. I'll endure this shitty deal for the good of the work I love and the beloved fucking money. But here's my counter: I stay single. I forgo, even if I find the one, any relationship and I get Ladd Media, free and clear. I walk away with all my assets, resources, staff, support staff, and I buy you out of the stock. I want to take it private. I'll change the name if you want, but I'm done bolstering the appliances and insurance divisions while getting hung out to fucking dry because I suck at being married."

"Son."

I interrupt him, "Seems like a dream deal to unload your black sheep."

He reaches out his hand. "Deal. But I'll give it to you, you don't have to buy me out." Then he pulls me into a hug and says only to me. "You can fuck around, son, but you need to reexamine your screening process. Laura has a real dick of a lawyer, and it's going to get very, very ugly."

My mother speaks up, "Her power-hungry, social-climbing parents won't have it any other way. Her father is a shark, and he smells blood in the water, I'm afraid."

"She's a pawn and he's coming for me through you."

"Understood, let him try." Our holdings have been shaky, and we might be in a tight spot, but I'm sure we're fine.

My dad slaps my back and says, "I'm doing this for your protection. For the company your great-grandfather built and to ensure that it's around for a long while. We need to finally put Bugle in the rearview." Always the legacy and God forbid we have one business conversation where we don't bring up my billion-dollar Bugle blunder.

"I'm sorry I'm such a fuck-up."

"I've never seen you as that. Now, take the year to figure that out for yourself and nail this new project. It's vital you keep your head down and get this done, son. No fodder for the shareholders or the divorce attorneys. Keep it tight, son."

My mom pinches my cheek again. "And don't get married, or engaged again until you've dated for at least a year. And don't date at all this year. Do you hear me? No more infatuation ceremonies or rings. Ugh, the wasted jewelry you've handed out."

"You knew, didn't you?" I ask her.

My mom takes my hand and leads me out of my father's office. She puts me just on the other side of the door.

"I did." She nods.

"You knew none of them would survive the test of time."

"Yes. But I thought I was being a good actress. How did you figure it out?"

I lift her hands. On her left is her wedding set, but on her right is my beloved grandmother's wedding set. "Because you never offered me this." I run my thumb over my grandmother's ring. She grins and nods.

"When you know, for real, that's when it comes off my

hand." She kisses me on the cheek, and I see my father wave to me over her shoulder. Then she backs up and closes the door in my face.

I hear my father's laugh booming as my mother's muffled voice says, "Now, where were we?"

That. I'm going to get that.

mak

"No. I promise. First thing in the morning it will be on your desk. Work got in the way. Won't happen again, ma'am."

"See, that it doesn't, Ms. Preston."

I rush to my car, so I don't explode at my lab partners for fucking this up for me or cry. Most of my classes have been online, but as I move into the practical labs of my science degree, they're in person. Online was great for me because I fit the work in between double shifts or the middle of the night. But now I have to take a split shift, bolt out to UNLV, then hightail it back to work the second half of my shift.

School's kicking my ass, work sucks, my parents suck, my house sucks, and it's 120 degrees outside. It's like the surface of the sun. I'm hoping Alaska needs a forty-year-old doctor.

I have a shift in twenty minutes, and it will suck since I have to pull bingo tonight and do a tuck-in at building B after med distribution.

I assume I'll have to go international for my medical degree. I'll be in Mexico or India or some shit. Although for the first time in my life, I am proud of my grades. I'll be headed to med school where it's the cheapest. I've only had one B, but I'm not sure anyone is looking to hand out scholarship money to an almost thirty-year-old for medical school. Some semesters I could only afford one class or two if work permitted, but I saved and took a full course load about a year ago so I could at least finish up undergrad. I'm not sure I remember what sleep actually is.

I'm so close to being done and thrilled with my MCAT score. The residents have helped with proofing papers and quizzing me. A couple of retired doctors and nurses help out with tutoring. I've got a great advisor at UNLV who is pulling all the strings to help wrangle me a spot at an in-state med school, let alone anywhere domestic. I want to do this on my own, and that's why I haven't told Tony about the med school yet. I'm afraid he'll take pity on me or see me differently and try to pay. I'm not cut out to be a kept woman.

BZZZ. "That's not a word!"

The rec center is hopping today. It's too hot for these people to go to the pool, and they don't like to stay cooped up, so they're here with me in the air-conditioning. Ironically most of them keep complaining it's too cold. Three of them have blankets wrapped around them. I'm still sweating.

I scold, "Scott, it is a word. Stop it now."

BZZZ

BZZZ

BZZZ

Some asshole gave these people the game Taboo. That horrible buzzer is driving me to drink. I stretch my arms over my head and say, "It's ok, go ahead. Say your words."

"I damn said them all and this old fool keeps buzzing me," the usually reserved woman says.

The fight continues between them. The whole rec room is

debating whether or not 'sulk' is too close to the word 'Hulk.' And none of it even matters since the word they're trying to guess is 'chair.'

I move towards Scott, and he engages his scooter. He knows I'm taking the buzzer away. I walk slowly like I'm trying to catch a rabbit. He grins and then buzzes Ellery again. The crowd gets as animated as they can. In my experience, senior living isn't as peaceful and calm as they make it out to be in the brochures. Sure, they nap, but they also drink, fight, cuss, and fuck. They live like the cast of *Yellowstone*. Cowboys not giving a fuck and taking what they want when they want. They have more sex in a week than I've had in a couple of years. We regularly have to test them for STIs, and every time one of them yells at me that they, "Don't have the damn clap." Or "If I had VD I'd know it." I roll my eyes and hand them another cup to pee into.

And then we silently give them chlamydia meds with their regulars once we clear it through their families or doctors. And those are my favorite calls to make. I swear to God, telling someone their mother has genital warts from screwing strangers at eighty-four is the best. Makes my day every time. It's a lesson in seizing the damn day. These people do not give a shit anymore.

A crowd has gathered, and I'm almost to Scott, who is distracted by new holiday decorations in the rec room, and I lunge for the buzzer. He jumps his scooter forward, and the chase is on.

He's cheered on by his latest paramour, Dottie, and I sneer at her.

"Go, ya big hunk of burning love. Let her rip. Open her up." He's doing a doughnut in the rec room, and I can't approach him without the Slippery Seniors taking me down. I call them that because ever since they discovered body oil, they're all covered in it. I've learned I must wipe down the chairs at the end of the night. These four women are shiny enough to look like they were part of the *Thunder Down Under* cast or a bodybuilding competition.

Someone thought they were doing the old folks a solid and dropped off a supply of this body oil and lotion that apparently never ends. It's faux floral and stinky as hell. Four women claimed it, and now permanently smell like acrid, sweet two-week-old roses mixed with what I believe might be menthol. It's totally messed up the plumbing systems in their apartments and houses. The pool has a rainbow film on it after aqua aerobics class. If you happen to touch them, your hand slides right off. Poor Dottie had to give up wearing bangles because she couldn't keep them on her wrist. When these dear women die, I swear if they're cremated, they'll go up in a fiery burst of glory, and if they're buried, that silk will be grease-stained forever. Chelle, Julia, and Lana pat Dottie on the back in solidarity, but I glare at them not to interfere. They like to stir shit up.

Scott eyes me, and the women all swoon. Three of the Slipperies are real trouble. Dottie just wants to be in the cool crowd, and I can control her.

"Give me that buzzer, Scott, and no one gets hurt."

"You'll never get me, copper!"

He's in the hallway careening around a corner, *BZZZZZZZZZZZZZZZZZZZZZZZZZZZ*. People are jumping out of the way, and I step it up.

I catch him rather easily once I run in earnest. Still, I'm afraid he'll accidentally drive over my foot if I get too close.

"Scott, stop it or I'll make sure no one serves you down at the pub. I swear to God, you'll go to bed sober and alone with nothing to comfort you but that buzzer."

The scooter stops immediately. He swings around abruptly, taking out a portion of the hedge.

"You know how to get a man in the nads, don't you?"

"If you're saying I'm good at my job, then yes."

He offers up the buzzer, and I approach cautiously. I snatch it from him before he can back the scooter away. I knew he wasn't ready to surrender it. He charges at me, and I have one shot at this. I skid the buzzer like a shuffleboard puck, and it slides under his wheels, and with one last gasp of a BZZzzghark, he runs over it.

"There! Nothing's taboo now." I yell.

He glides past me and smacks my ass. "You got that right." And cackles the entire distance back into the rec complex.

I collect the pieces and throw them away. Game day is always lively and often ends in violence. I'm not sure why it's still on the agenda. I want to share this with Tony. Maybe if I start small. Tell him I work at an old folks' home. Well, a retirement community for the elder set of people in the world. That's how they describe it.

Shit, if I unravel one thing, it all comes down.

tony

Work is madness right now, but she's all I think about. The texting is nice. But I don't like how I have to keep checking for a response. I rub my eyes and try to clear the long day away.

My assistant, Lill, plunks down a sandwich on my desk.

"That's a sad looking grey-meated sandwich."

"It's all they had."

I wink at her. "Then salmonella it is. It's late, you should go. I need to see if the coding works and check on the edits for the first pod."

"They want you to come by the booth when you've finished dinner."

I sip a Negroni and wink again. "This is dinner."

"You're gonna need some more fruit in your drink to make it a balanced meal." She sits.

"What?"

"Not leaving until you eat."

"Eh. That's the weirdest fetish ever." She laughs, and it's throaty like she dug it up from the bottom.

MAK: Hi.

I look down and smile.

"Keep it in ya pants, Romeo. No more weddings. I like this job."

"I'm still married."

"You're such a good husband." She stands up and puts her hands on her hips. I take a big bite of the squishy white bread, pre-packaged turkeyish sandwich.

I'm chewing the limp lettuce and talking with food in my mouth. "We live in one of the major culinary cities in the world. Find me a fucking dinner that's not this." I pick up my garbage can and spit it out.

She lets loose with another giant throaty laugh. "Bacco's is in the hallway, lobsta ravioli and a green salad. I just won a bet though."

"Shit. Is Dax here?"

He walks into the room, laughing his ass off, and texts the group chat in front of me. He puts a large to-go bag of food on my desk.

HAYDEN: Did he eat it?

DAX: He chewed and spit it out. Does that count?

ROBBIE: Yeah. If he tasted it.

TONY: What's with this fucking sandwich?

LAW: Dax saw it in a machine, and we bet him he couldn't get you to eat it.

COLT: Then he told us Lill could get you to do it. I lost $100 bucks. Was sure you wouldn't do it.

TONY: Thank you, man. Now you all owe Lill some cash.

My brother unpacks our last-minute dinner, and I only want to text Makenzie back.

TONY: Hi. I'm with people and need to get back to you later, but I'm so happy you texted.

MAK: Didn't mean to bother you.

TONY: You did. You bothered me so much. I'm going to think about you all night. Gotta go.

MAK: Ok.

Dax hands me a plate, and we dig into the best fucking mac in the world. I love this place.

"Thanks, man. What's up?"

"You ok? Laura's bullshit charity piece in the *Globe*." She strategically placed an article about her benevolence.

I ask, "Sophie out of town? Is that why you're here?"

He doesn't say anything. I stare at him while I tuck into my salad. He avoids the subject, so I know it's off again.

"Sorry," I say.

He shrugs. "She has her reasons."

"Which are bullshit, I'm sure."

"Same damn shit, actually. And perhaps if she keeps pushing, maybe I should listen. That's what Monica says."

"Monica?"

"Hayden's old assistant from Eva and Rinaldi Agency. You remember her?"

"Oh, yeah. She was cool. Where is she? You did her, right?"

"Yeah, never tell Hayden. She's working for the Boston Science Museum now. Still in admin but working with the educators' programs."

"Promise I won't tell him."

My phone dings, and Dax's does not. He nods, knowing it's not our Boston Brother's text chain. I look down and stifle a smile.

MAK: Have a good night.

"Work stuff."

I text back as Dax says, "You're at work. Go fix it. No need to text."

TONY: Night, little witch.

I slept on my office couch because we're running through the beta testing of the site again in twenty. All components of the Cookery tests went horribly shitty all night. The coding is flawed and the fucking components don't work. But I'll smile and pretend it's all as it should be. Rotten dress rehearsal and all that. I'm in the foulest of moods as I change into my clean emergency suit I keep stashed here.

It's early where she is, but she's always up.

TONY: Morning.

MAK: Hi. Sorry. I have to run to work.

An idea sparks to pull me from my crap ass mood. We keep missing each other because of work. After we do a bunch of testing this morning. I can take the day off. If I leave in an hour...

TONY: Are you at home?

MAK: Yes.

TONY: Are you going to work in your town?

MAK: Yes, you freak. Gotta go.

I yell loud enough to be heard on the entire floor. "LILL! Spark up the jet."

mak

S hit, I'm tired from teaching scrapbooking this morning and my quiz. I have a rare day off. It's still early, since these people get up at the crack of dawn, my scrapbooking workshop was at fucking 5:30 am. My plans for today, nothing but lay in my way too sunny room. Maybe a movie.

I turn my phone on to a series of texts. I keep him as "T" in my phone because I don't want my parents to know I'm back in touch with him. They remember vividly how hard I took the breakup. I could never explain satisfactorily that it was my fault. They just knew I was a different person after I left him. But it's been months of texting and it feels normal to have him in my life. Texting helps me to keep lies to a minimum. Our schedules don't allow for more right now.

T: Address, please.

What the fuck is he talking about?

T: I'm here. Where are you? I want to see you. Our texts are boring. Let's have a conversation.

MAK: You're where?

I CAN NOT deal with this. Oh no. He can't be.

T: LA

Fuck. Fuck. Fuck.

T: Have a late lunch with me.

MAK: You were in Boston.

T: Yes, and now I'm here because you said you were home and not traveling. So, pony up an address, please. Where are you?

Spark up the lie machine.

MAK: I'll come to you. I had an early shoot in Palm Springs. Not sure if I have to stay the night or what. Can you wait or do you have to go home?

I'm uh. Well, that just popped out. It would be so much simpler if he went home. Please go home. Please.

T: I'll be at the Hotel Bel Air's pool. Come find me if you come home today. Bring a suit if you want to swim, and we can hang out. I'll fly home in the morning, but only if you have breakfast with me.

MAK: Wow. I mean, wow.

Fuck. I speed home and throw shit into a bag. The chicest stuff I have since I'm supposed to be a stylist. Shit. Shit. My car won't make it, so I'll rent one. I can't afford to fly, so driving it is. Am I really doing this? Spending money, I don't have to keep this fucking ruse going. But in the middle of my packing insanity, I settle at the thought of him. I'm not spending the money to cover my lies. I'm spending it to see him.

"What's all the fuss about, Leech?"

"That nickname never gets old, Dad." He appears at the door, sipping a green smoothie. I'm secretly jumping for joy. They don't always make the best food choices, despite their heart issues. But over the last couple of years, I've had to monitor and nag a lot less. I hope it's not a mint chocolate chip shake.

"Well, Papa Slug, there's someone who wants to see me." My voice is lighter and brighter than it's been in a long while.

"Do you want to see this person?"

I flop on my pull-out couch bed that's rarely folded up, grinning madly.

"That's a good smile, pumpkin. That's a hall of famer, the kind your mom brings to my face."

"What would you do to see her, if you couldn't?"

He grins and looks to the hallway. "What wouldn't I do?" He winks. "Will you be here for dinner? I'm giving shrimp fajitas a shot." I grin. "With yogurt instead of sour cream."

"Dad, you can have sour cream, just not the—"

"My darling daughter, you worry about you right now. We're good. You can do something for yourself for a change. You're welcome to dinner, but it seems you were packing."

I lie back on my bed and wonder how far I can push this before I have to give him up again.

T: I don't know what's between us, Makenzie, or what will come of it, but I can tell you I need it and you right now. I need to be with the one person who lets me sit most comfortably in my skin.

"Dad!" I shout into the empty hallway. Regrettably, I won't be present for dinner.

He yells back, "Atta girl." My mouth won't stop smiling. Tony makes me bold.

MAK: I'll be in your lap in a couple of hours.

T: I'll put a reserve sign on it. Property of Makenzie Preston.

MAK: Hope the other women won't be disappointed.

T: What other women?

Swoon.

I toss my hair into a low ponytail and clean myself up in the hotel lobby after my land speed record-breaking trip. This bathroom might be the nicest place I've ever been. I'd like to move into this bathroom. There's a couch bigger than my bed.

I valeted my rental car and told them to put it on his room. I'll pay him back if he says anything, but the hold on my credit card for the car and the gas and snacks wiped out all my money.

My paycheck goes in tonight, so I'll be able to get home. I had, like, two of those fountain drink vats of soda. I'm a little wired, but I think I can maintain it.

My eyes feel really dry. I keep blinking, but it's not helping. What do you wear to work if you're a stylist? I told him I'd come right from work. My stomach is a massive ball of butterflies and sparks. I'm so excited to see him and I can't believe he came to find me. I toss on a floaty dress that could be a coverup. I told him I'd been in the desert, and this is desert cute.

I'm exiting the bathroom when a baby-voiced woman approaches me. "Are you by any chance Makenzie Preston?"

"Why? What is happening here? How do I know you? Did I do something wrong? I'm so sorry, I took some of the tampons in the bathroom." I dig into my bag to return them. She places her hand on mine.

She laughs. I don't want to be laughed at right now.

"No. I work here, and you can keep them. That's why they're there. Mr. Ladd asked for us to watch out for you and escort you to his cabana. Is there anything you need?"

I had to choose between a Kind bar and a Slim Jim for lunch, and he's sitting here in a cabana. I'm not angry about it; it's just surreal. I want to shrink away. This was stupid of me. I should have told him I was out of town. Hell, I should have told him I flunked out of high school twelve years ago, but here we are. I exhale, look at the woman, and nod.

"Do you need a swimsuit or anything?"

"Nope, just the tampons." I shake my head. I could go into that shop and get a million things, but that's not what's exciting about this man crossing the country to go swimming with me. She hands me a basket with a towel, a full spray can of sunscreen, another smaller face sunscreen cream, a visor, and what appears to be a pair of fancy flip-flops. Score.

The elevator opens, and she points to one of the six elaborate cabanas. There's no one else at this stunning pool oasis. She places her hand on my elbow. "You have complete privacy. He booked out all the cabanas." As one does on a Tuesday. I often book all the cubicles at the library, so I have complete privacy. I roll my eyes, but then I see him.

My breath catches, and I get a moment to ogle him. His chest is toned and tanned and so much broader and cut than when we were in high school. That's a man's chest. A very hot man. His leg muscles are ropey and thick, and his arm is casually draped over the top of his head as he lounges in front of one of the cabanas near the stunning pool. His blond hair is a little wild, and the ends are curling in directions of their choosing. He has let it grow out since Vegas. I can't help but lick my lips.

I shed my dress and bag and tiptoe over. I get right behind him, and that view, damn. Even baggy swim trunks can't hide what I know that notched V leads to under that royal blue patch of cloth. I take off running and leap into the pool in front of him. He sits up just in time to get a face full of my cannonball splash. As I go under the water, I hear him yell, "Fuck!"

When I come up, he's dripping on the edge of the pool.

"I swear, I thought you were some obnoxious kid." He jumps over me, landing a few feet away, and pulls me under the water. Then we both come up laughing.

"Hi." He smiles, wrapping his arms around me and kissing me. I'm shocked and back away to tread water a bit.

"What was that about?"

"It's all I've thought about for weeks. Those lips. You

always look like you've eaten summer berries. And you're that delicious."

"I'm so fucking confused about why and how you're here. And then you toss in a kiss. I have no clue what to do with that."

I dive under and take off swimming to the other end of the pool. He chases me, and I smoke him. When he finally gets to me in the shallow end, he cages me to the wall, and when I try to escape by dipping down, he puts his feet on either side of my waist under the water. He's bracing himself on the wall.

"Where are you going? Don't you want me to answer those questions?"

I hold his biceps and try not to lick his chest. It's just so pretty. I eventually look into his forever-deep blue eyes. Not only does he look turned on, but he also almost looks relieved.

"What's wrong?" I ask, knowing he's hiding something. It's easy for me to spot because I'm the queen of that. There's something off.

His lips curl slightly at the corners, and he pushes off the wall and into a backstroke. I chase him, catching him easily. I push down on his stomach, and he goes under. He pops back up laughing, and I swim to the sun ledge. I look up at him, and he's wet and stunning as he walks through the shallow area over to me. He sits and we both lean back as he wraps his fingers around mine.

I turn to him and smile. "Why are you here? And it's not just to see me. Out with it."

"I wanted to have lunch with you, and I couldn't wait for your ass to visit Boston. Because we all know how much you love Boston. Perhaps we could have gone out to the Vineyard." I laugh, but I'm also wincing a bit.

He squeezes my hand, and the water whooshes between our fingers. "Seriously, it's ok. Someday we'll talk it through, but today I'm pointedly teasing you."

"Deflecting, but I'll let it go. Tell me later."

He sighs and says, "I needed some laughs and lunch."

A waiter finishes up in our cabana.

"Hungry?"

"Not *that* hungry." I gesture to the full table.

"I ordered everything because I don't know what you like anymore."

He leaps out of the pool, and the water spills off the ripples of his back. I can barely contain myself, so I hold my own hand, so I don't run over and rip into him. He grabs something and plunks down on the edge. I slip back into the pool and swim over. He wraps his legs around me, and pulls me toward him. I'm staring at a very lovely view.

"You're looking at my dick, aren't you?"

"It is eye level. I thought you were flexing?"

"My cock is swole right now, but I'll let you look anywhere you want." He smirks.

He hands me the menu and I look it over. "Didn't you order everything?" I ask.

"Yes, but what would you order. I guessed based on a previous lifetime."

"Chicken sandwich."

He pumps his fists in the air, and says, "With fries, Swiss not cheddar, lettuce, no tomato. Ranch dressing on the side instead of mustard or mayo?" My stomach flips.

"Are you fucking kidding me? You remember what I'd order?"

He slides into the pool and holds me closer. "I remember everything."

He kisses me lightly, and I gasp, smiling into his pliable and perfect lips. Then I dunk under the water and swim to the ladder. As I climb out, he groans.

"ACK. Your body in that suit, damn. Wear nothing other than that white bikini, ever." My skin pebbles in the sun and at his words. I turn towards him. "Even better. Chef's kiss, really. That body, that suit, that face…" His voice drifts off as I float away on his compliments.

"And what?" I pop my hip.

"That heart."

I turn away from that kind of sweetness. I'm playing a dicey game with a man who ordered me a simple sandwich that probably costs fifty bucks at this place. It's all a study of opposites. I towel off my head. I sit at a massive table and pluck my chicken sandwich from the mix.

He joins me, toweling off his abs, and again, I'm mesmerized by those ripples. I want to lick those water droplets off one by one.

I blurt out, "You really are out of this world, hot. You're the hottest of the hot."

He smiles. "I know you are, but what am I?" I laugh. "Pick out my lunch."

I know exactly which is his order, but I'm not sure if I want him to know how much I remember. I wait.

"Go ahead, scaredy cat. You can admit, even though you broke our hearts and disappeared, you can admit you know my favorite lunch."

I shrug and grab mac and cheese with a side of bacon bits and sliced tomatoes. Then I grab what I think is a vanilla milkshake and a hot dog.

He jumps in the air, shouting, "You still know me!"

I sit back in my chair and pluck a glass of wine from the table. This is the moment I could tell him my truth. But I want him to confide in me, and if I tell him I'm a big fat liar, then I break whatever this is.

"Sit over there." I place his meal at the other end of the table.

"You're afraid of this rocking bod and the damn percolating heat between us."

I sit down and stare at him.

"Absofuckinglutely, I am terrified."

"It's burning up everything around us like we're reentering the atmosphere. Everyone is talking about it." I laugh. "They're all afraid for us. If we let anything happen, it's possible it could be so scorching, it will cause another big bang." I grin at him.

I take a bite, swallow, and say, "What you're saying is, if we had sex, an alternative universe would be formed."

"Among other things, but yes. We would create a billion new stars and planets. Just from the heat of our fucking."

I shake my head.

"Nah, I'm on the pill."

He laughs big and loud, and so do I.

tony

We're sitting on the chaise lounges by the pool and her body is on full display, the bikini clinging to the areas I'm dying to uncover. I'm sipping something clear and fresh, and she's opted for a dangerous fruit punch full of whimsy and vodka. We flirted and kissed a little, and she let me hold her hand like I'm doing now. The feel of her fingers in mine is something I miss. Laura was never a big hand holder, and now she's gone off the rails. Of all my relationships, other than Mak, I thought Laura and I might end civilly. She and I were friends and laughed a lot. We used to joke and talk for hours. We had something, even if it was just an amped up friendship, there was something. Then she turned cold and cruel out of nowhere. It wasn't like we were on solid ground, but she's the one who moved to the guest room. Even though she was obsessed with making appearances and being in the right place at the right time, she was so cool the rest of the time. Now, I wonder if I ever knew her at all. I miss my friend but can't wait to get rid of my wife.

My favorite voice brings me back. She's lying on her side, looking at me. She says, "Now why are you here?" I roll over to face her.

"Work was fucked up."

"You're hiding?"

"No, I needed to feel good, and your face always makes me happy."

She screws up her face into what she thinks is an ugly version. I laugh and she squeezes my bicep.

"The test launch of my current project was an utter failure. One of our podcast hosts screamed at my producer and a celeb chef while we were doing a taping. Then the coding failed with the recipe finder and the platform for the local ingredient swap did nothing. The SEC rejected two of our channels for streaming rights. The contracts for SAG talent are all fucked up. My dad's disappointed and furious. I don't know how to fix any of it. I can't seem to get divorced, and I was feeling out of sorts. You always brought me clarity. Even when you were nothing but a memory. I wanted to see you, hope that's ok. How was your day at work?"

We pause as I take a breath.

"That's a lot." She leans over and kisses me like it's something we do now. A casual, reassuring kiss that lights up every fucking part of me with its familiarity.

She settles back into her chair and, as much as I want to put her on my lap, I don't. I grip the sides of the chair instead.

She says, "Start talking. That's your avoiding face." I reach over and stoke her sun warmed cheek, and she leans into my palm.

"Ladd Media—"

"I'm familiar with it." While on my feet, I hurl a towel at her.

"My focus has always been on tweaking and improving. But this project I'm trying to do is pure creation. It's a multi-platform simultaneous launch. My concept, my build out, my people, this is all me."

She sits up and sips her cocktail. "Explain to those of us

who don't work in, say, um, tech or media. Give me your stairwell pitch."

"Elevator."

"What elevator?"

"It's an elevator pitch." I correct her.

"Then give me that." She shakes her head and waves her arms around.

I laugh at her and toss a towel over her torso. "Stop distracting me. I'm buying you a caftan so I can have a conversation without losing all sense of reason and blood in my brain. The Cookery is a large-scale multi-tiered beast."

"Go big or go home." I grab my dick and she laughs.

"I'm creating a living cookbook through podcasts, mini reality shows, websites, blogs, all socials. All modeled after my favorite cookbooks."

"You still read cookbooks?"

I nod. "I like the ones where it's kind of bio, a bit of skill, technique, and part recipe. But it's the story they tell through their food that matters."

"I agree."

"You read cookbooks? This is a strange coincidence."

"I saw your shelves in Boston long ago and I was intrigued. It became a habit."

I rush back over to her and hold her face in my hand and brush my lips over hers. Then pull back quickly so we don't get caught up in orgasms.

She sits up and her smile is impossibly beautiful. She sighs and then says, "This is astounding. What's a mini reality show?"

"Five-minute original content pieces scattered throughout the day from a monthly highlighted restaurant."

"And it will all be viewed through what?"

"No clue, and it's all fucked. The big guys want too much

money and YouTube isn't the right fit. The Cookery is too much all at once the way everyone warned me it would be."

"Hmm."

I let her derision sit over me.

"Hmm, what?" I cross my arms and circle back around the lounge chairs.

"Can't imagine anything being more of an adventure than to create five or six things that never existed all at once. I expected better from you."

She's right. I fix this and I do this. I tower over her chair. She shields her eyes to look up at me. I scoop her up and pop us into the pool, holding her close. She's laughing as we hit the water. When we surface, she circles her arms around my neck.

"Mak." My hands slide down the sides of her body and my cock has never been harder. My dick is super pissed off that my brain is going to win this battle.

"Yes." She kisses my neck lightly and wraps her legs around me.

"As much as I'd like to big bang you right the hell now. As you can surely feel. Universe creation is going to have to wait until I'm divorced."

She pouts. "This will put the schedule for the new solar system behind, but I can wait." It's everything I need to hear.

Now it's time to trade a bitch for my witch.

tony

Rolling over, I answer her call. I love that she's calling me now. It's not just me chasing her. It's a nebulous, awkward and often confusing thing we're growing together. We say good morning and sometimes talk at midday as well. Three days ago, we spoke for three hours while watching TV. It's excellent but painful not to be with her. I had to keep getting off the phone to masturbate yesterday. I'm unsure if I can forgive her for all of it. It was so painful, and the thought of her fucking blindsiding me again and disappearing is utterly terrifying.

I found a charm bracelet in a funky antique shop near my house in Boston. I pass by it twice a day. It always caught my eye, but it wasn't until a couple of weeks ago that I saw it had Arc de Triomphe and Eiffel Tower charms. I bought it for an inflated price because the shop is on Newbury, but I had to have it. And really, is a couple of hundred that bad? I want her to know I am thinking of her.

I'm a moron who's going all in on a girl who broke my heart in two. I'm currently married, in a bet to not date, and contractually bound to my father to not get into another relationship for a year. So this is all a super great idea: keep flying

148

across the country to cuddle because that smacks of a one-night stand, casual relationship. I roll my eyes at myself. Four months into this thing and she's all I think about.

"Shouldn't you be at work?" she answers, and my heart soars.

"It's my company." I'm still in bed. I've ignored Laura for a minute while I dove into fixing work. She's probably angry, but she's been angry lately. It's like a switch flipped, and she's the anti-Laura now. The lawyers can take care of it.

"Still, it sets a bad example," she says, teasing me.

I sit up. "We were up until like 2:00 a.m. working. I gave everyone the day off but I'm sure they'll all work from home. Because they're beasts."

"Wow. Some boss you are."

"Sometimes it's good to be the king. I'll send them all chocolate or something."

"No, you won't. Lill will send them chocolate."

"You should get a Lill. She's the best."

"Getting a Lill is on the list after getting my muffler put back into my car." I hate that. I want to buy her all the mufflers, but I know she won't let me.

I get out of bed and scratch my twitching dick. Her voice does it to me all the time. Hey. That's not cheating. She's not even in the room. It's a miracle I didn't sleep with her in LA, but there's too much riding on it. I'll happily pay Laura money if kissing while legally separated counts as cheating. She slept over at the hotel instead of going home and we tried to sleep in separate beds. That lasted twenty minutes before I had to hold her. I smooth the sheets on the other side of the bed and imagine Mak is there.

I snap back and ask, "You're up early. Whatcha thinking about? Are you in LA?"

"Home. Yup, I'm home."

"I can't handle it when you sound gravelly and sexy in the

morning." I suck on my lip, hoping to take this up a notch. I'm desperate to come when she's all cozy and perfect as she wakes up.

"I remember," she says, and her voice is seductive. Oh, I am going to have to get off very soon.

I push. "What else do you remember?"

There's a pause.

"Tony, what are you up to?" Her voice lilts.

I trudge forward, advancing on my goals. "UP is the operative word." I ease onto my couch and flirt with my waistband. I wait for the green light from her to grab myself. But I'm aching to come. My dick has been hard since she answered the phone.

There's another round of silence, but she's breathing rapidly. My toes curl at those breathy mewls and gasps. They haunt every sexual encounter I've ever had. She's turned on.

I whisper low and filthy into the phone while reaching for my cock. "Tell me exactly what you're doing."

She says in her dark turned on voice, "Licking my fingers and circling my nipples."

I groan. "That's fucking perfect. Pinch them once they get good and stiff."

"Stiff?"

"Like my dick, hell yeah. Hard as steel and I'm about to fist my cock pretty good unless you say otherwise."

"Dry?" Her voice is deep and strained. Christ, I need her.

"Tell me how wet you are. I'll see if I can find something around here to feel the same."

"This is a good morning."

My voice almost comes out as a growl. "Listen up, that's not what I asked. Come on, little witch, how wet are you?"

"Fucking soaked. Dripping."

I head across the room to my bed while listening to her

talk about her dripping pussy. I ease down on my pillows and grab the lube from the drawer.

She says, "Tell me how hard I can fuck you?" She's panting.

I scold her, "Don't you dare come without me. Get your hands off of your swollen and perfect clit."

"Yes. How hard? What have you got, Ladd? My ass is in the air. Can you handle it? Can you take me that way right now?" I groan as I increase the pace of pulling my cock, imagining her bent over a railing. "Grab your balls for me." I do it. I need to come right the fuck now.

I sputter out, "How many fingers?"

"Two." She moans.

"In and out at my command. And I'll stroke the same pace. I want you out of your gorgeous head."

"Fuck. Tony."

"In, out. In, out. In, out. Fuck. We come now. Let go, fuck me, Mak." I jack faster, and my orgasm rages down my spine and shoots out onto my stomach as I scream her name.

"Come now, my filthy perfect witch. Come now. Fucking explode all over those fingers. Come."

She pants, "Tony." Over and over, and I keep stroking through. I speak quickly and low into the phone.

"I blew my load all over myself. Mess yourself now. Mak, let go. Fuck yourself good, the way I want to. I'm grabbing your hips and slamming into you while I drag some of your dripping mess up to your clit. Now. Now swirl and pinch so you come. Come. Come. Come now, my sexy-as-fuck witch. Fuck. Do it. Jesus, it's driving me crazy that I can't see you come."

"TONY."

"There's my good girl."

"Oh, Tony. I like being your good girl more than a bad girl

with anyone else." She purrs, and my dick threatens to throb again.

"Jesus, how you talk."

"So hot. Oh my GOD!" She screams.

I turn on the shower but stay on the phone. "You ok, sweet witch?"

"Fuck, yeah I am."

"You're not weirded out?" I wipe my stomach and dick off.

"Hell no. That was awesome, you're better on the phone than the last few guys I was with in person. This is a hot new era for us."

Thank God. I lick my lips and wish I was there to hold her. "That it is. But there's one thing missing," I say.

"Toys?"

I laugh.

"You in my arms."

She quietly sighs. "I don't know what to say."

"Well, think about it and call me later." I go to hang up, and I hear her again.

"Tony."

"What?"

"Never mind. It's just I have to tell you about some things at some point."

"Vague much? Whatever it is, I'll listen. And I should probably tell you some shit too. I have to get to a meeting with my lawyer."

"I wish you were divorced."

"Me too."

"What the fuck is up with you?" My lawyer motions to his

assistant to grab me more coffee. My goofy grin hasn't left my face.

I glance out over his offices through the glass walls of the conference room. Fucking my hand has never been that satisfying. Everyone should get themselves a Makenzie on the other end of the phone.

"Hey, why are all law offices beige and brown? Who decided that wood makes you appear trustworthy and like an expert?"

"No one smiles this much at a divorce proceeding. And if you tell me you got laid, I will fucking kill you."

"Chill it out. No. Did not get laid. I'm playing by all the rules of the many people who laid them out for me. Didn't break the fidelity clause, didn't lose the bet, and didn't disobey the fucking legal document you and my father cooked up for me to be a good boy." I'm the king of the loophole. I came, she came, and later we'll eat dinner, watch TV or something together with 3000 miles between us. I'm dating but not dating.

Just saying good boy sends a spark to my dick as I remember what she said about being my good girl. I will most assuredly lose this bet at some point, but the rules of my father's document and the bet says I can sleep with her one night. We won't sleep for twenty-four hours, just fucking and more fucking. It will have to sustain me through the rest of my indentured sexual servitude. Seven months is a long-ass time to jack off to her voice. I'll have to time our one night exactly right.

Laura breezes in, and her hair matches her curated Chanel suit, which is probably new and sitting on some credit account I pay for.

I greet her and she bristles and puts her cheek out. I air kiss it, and she pastes on a strained grin. Her lawyer follows behind her, as does her friend Teddy. I like her. They've always been close, and I got to know her well on her visits. She's funny, driven, and in the PR department for NBC out of New York. Not sure why she's here now.

"Teddy! What the hell are you doing here? Gathering material so you can win the divorce for her in the court of public opinion?"

"Tony. You were always a good time. Now pay her."

I laugh, and we hug. I say, "Every penny she's worth."

Laura asks. "Stop. Let's be civil."

"Cool. That will be new," Teddy bites back, and it's not directed at me.

Laura crosses her arms and sits back in her chair like she's above rolling in the mud.

"I apologize for my client." I rest my hand on my lawyer's arm.

"Hold on, I have one more." She rolls her eyes. "What are you going to do now? You know, that your M.R.S. degree is getting revoked."

Laura half smiles and says, "First order of business, getting me out from under your black sheep cloud."

I lean over the table and hold up my hand. "Good one. Up top." She lightly slaps my hand and smiles. Everyone laughs, and so far, this is my favorite divorce. Of course, she's about to find out I'm not budging on the offer.

Her attorney slides us a thick-ass folder. "Artwork. There's a blue circle by the pieces that Laura will be taking."

I sputter out a huge laugh. She's not taking anything.

Gavin flips through the pages. He's aware I'm immovable on this point. He closes the proposal, and everyone waits. "You've put a lot of thought into this document."

"Thank you," her lawyer says.

"Nope." Is all I have to say here.

"No to what?" Laura leans forward and stares at me. And I answer her instead of my lawyer.

"There's no more, Laura. The prenup clearly states our individual assets before marriage with the exception of the outlaid jewelry, presents, and the Catskills house, remain. Basically, dance with the one who brung ya. And really? You fucking think you get to take four Hayden Corelli pieces? He's my best friend. That's insanity. The art was all purchased before you said 'I do,' which means, you don't. Get it, that is."

Laura slams the table. "You bought the Mistral and the Brancusi while we were dating."

"And I had a standing bid at Christie's for those two pieces for the last six years, waiting for them to come to auction. That means they superseded you, baby."

Teddy speaks, "Don't call her baby." Her lawyer pats Laura's hand. So, I pat Gavin's as he attempts not to laugh.

"I'm not trying to be cruel, but your greed knows no bounds. Raid your parents' art collection. It's vast, impressive, and enviable, but mine is off limits. This is insane, right? You loved me for what? Six months?" She winces like she's all of a sudden found her humanity. She's a stranger now. "What makes you think because we shared a bed for almost three years that you're entitled to the equivalent of a Powerball lottery ticket?"

"Stop," Gavin chides.

Laura states, "I'm looking for a fair and equitable settlement and over the past three years things have changed and I require more than is in the agreement."

Her lawyer slides super-legal-looking paper over to us. I sit back in my chair and rock it on its hind legs.

Gavin questions, "You're petitioning the court to get the prenup overturned?"

Then her pinhead clarifies, "We'll be seeking all the requested artwork, furniture, Ladd Enterprise stock, a staked partnership in Ladd Media, the smaller Martha's Vineyard house, and an additional sum of $125 million dollars."

The only thing I zero in on is that she wants in on the business. Hello, that's totally her father. Her parents are making a power grab through her divorce, and I'm starting to feel like a mark.

I laugh at what a fool she is. She just woke every bad instinct I've been tamping down. She may succeed in getting the prenup dissolved, but she'll never get any of those things. In fact, I'll make sure she gets less than the original payout.

"I'll rip up the prenup on one fucking condition." Everyone talks over each other.

Her lawyer yells over the din, "Laura is in no position to—"

She stands up. "What condition?" Laura blurts out and silences the room. I want out. I want Mak, and that can't happen if I'm tied to her. I stand up and face her across the table and put my hand on Gavin's shoulder to keep him in his seat.

"You sign a piece of paper right now that says we're no longer married. We save the financial shit for an open battle. But we file jointly today. And then in three months we're free of each other. Except for your hand in my pocket, but again, let's fight that out another day. Today, let's cut the ties that bind."

Her lawyer ramps up his objection, but Teddy squeezes his arm to stop him. Good friend, that one.

Gavin's eyes are wide. He knows my father will go fucking nuts. But she was going to cost us a fortune in legal fees to contest the prenup before we even got to the settlement. And we probably only had a fifty-fifty chance of keeping it in place anyway, so fuck it. Let's blow the fucking prenup up.

I grin at Gavin, and he slides me the simple agreement that was first proposed. He and the asshole across from us X out all items related to assets and property. And then show us where to sign. I pick up a pen, and Laura hesitates.

I lean over the table, and big and bold, I start singing. "Set me free, why don't you babe..."

Teddy laughs loud and long, then joins me in the chorus.

I stand up and shake my lawyer's hand. I don't need her to ruin my really great day.

"Anthony. You can't leave, we have more to discuss." Laura's voice slices the room.

Teddy stands in my way, and I walk around her. I don't even say goodbye. This morning with Makenzie is enough to float out of here in a good mood. Although saying 'no' to Laura is pretty great too. And I'm free. My wallet and bank account aren't free yet, but I am.

mak

"Why are you never home?" We're getting closer, and he's prying. Every moment that's not working, studying, in class, or with practical labs is his. Not sure how I let all of this happen, but it's coming to a point where I won't be able to keep it all to myself.

"Because I work. I think you do too sometimes," I say while I hide my books. As close as we've gotten, I don't want him to know about the pre-med thing yet.

"Switching. I want to see that sassy smirk not just hear it."

I panic.

"I've just got out of the shower."

That was fucking smooth. I usually have a whole set up for FaceTime when my parents are asleep or I call from my rec center office. But I panic because I'm in my weird sunroom/bedroom. He can't see this.

"Then I'm absolutely FaceTiming you."

"Just wait. I'll call you back." I formulate a plan.

"Are you dripping and wet?"

"Only for you."

I hang up. I don't know what we're doing, but it's fun. It's been eight months of television and late-night calls, and

158

mutual orgasms. We always schedule the video calls. But I want to see him so badly. He thinks I'm in LA. I should get a backdrop of a sunny window with a view of palm trees to carry around with me. I keep thinking he's going to get bored of talking to me or remember how I hurt him. So, I keep pushing off telling him the truth.

I shove my books around and hold up my phone. I realize if I sit at the tiny table in the corner of my room it could look LA sunny. There's a patio out back that connects back to the main rec building, but right here in this corner, it doesn't look too Nevada or elderly community.

I jog to the front of the house. My parents are parked, literally parked in their all-terrain scooters, in front of that America game show hosted by the guy who has been in everything, but no one knows his name.

"Yo. Slugs. How about you hit the chairs? Why are you still on your hogs?"

My dad laughs. "We're going to Bess and Jack's tonight. Seemed easier to park than transfer. What's up, Leech?" They can both transfer without assistance, but old habits die hard.

"I'm jumping on a call with school and wanted to make sure you didn't need anything."

My mom holds up a bucket of chicken and a bottle of water.

I freak out, "Mom. You can't eat that."

She howls, "Gotcha!" She tips the bucket towards me, and it's filled with salad. My father shows me his bucket of salad as well. They're actually not incapacitated, just lazy.

My mom is working on losing weight for mobility, but she's in pretty great health these days. My dad is a long string bean like me, but I often wish I had a little of my mom's curves. I love that my dad is eating salad in solidarity. He does have a heart issue, but he's never found as much comfort in food as my mom did. We go to therapy together on Tuesdays, and then we get pedicures. I kind of love Tuesdays.

"Are you pregaming dinner with salad?"

My mom holds up her fork and smiles. "They always serve ribs and mac and cheese, so yes, dear Leech, I'm filling up on this vat of lettuce before I go over."

The day they brought the scooters home was the day I began calling them slugs, but they love them. So, they still use them instead of getting a golf cart, like most of the residents here at Twisty Acres. The scooters are less about needing them and more about transportation and wanting the wind in their hair at a very low speed.

"We're all good and leaving in about ten minutes. Do you have class tonight?"

"Late shift at the rec hall. There's that knitting circle thing. They're planning on yarn bombing the local Walgreens to protest that they no longer carry Vanilla Coke Zero."

"Those women need a hobby," my father says off-handedly.

"Har Har, Dad."

"Will those slippery ones be there?" my dad asks, and I roll my eyes.

"You know, because you decided to live here at the ripe age of fifty-five, these are now your peers."

"The old people?" My father scoffs.

"You. You are the old people. Even though fifty is far from old."

"We scrimped and saved," my mom says, and I raise an eyebrow.

She corrects herself, "Ok, you sold off our hoarded collections to secure this palace without wheels or blocks, so we could spend our golden years doing just this."

"Sitting?"

My father reaches out for my mother's hand. They both smile at each other. "Yes." They really do love their life now.

"Fine. Also, your golden years aren't for like another twenty to thirty years."

I leave the room. My father calls after me, "Then what are these?"

"Copper. These are your copper years. I'll get you some Moscow Mule mugs to commemorate them."

I close the door, and my phone is buzzing with his gorgeous face; I toss off my scrub top and put on a t-shirt, wrapping my dry hair in a towel. I move to the perfect corner I've set up and answer.

"Hi."

His face lights up, and his eyes sparkle at me. I must care since I've decided to go through this elaborate ruse.

He grins. "Hi. Nice turban. Take it off."

"Mr. Ladd. That's a bit forward."

He laughs.

"How was your day?" I need to change the subject, so I don't make up more shit. My memory isn't big enough to sustain this charade for much longer. I remember every bone, muscle, and gland in the human body, but details of my fake history are slipping. I'm staring at my large model, where I practice naming things. There are Post-its all over it with pneumonic devices like 'Pineal, not Penial the no-fun gland of sleepy time not sexy time.'

I'm soaking up that deep voice and that playful man as much as I can until I have to tell him, and he'll be done with me.

"Fine. How was the divorce meeting?" I ask.

"Mediation for financial shit is tomorrow."

My head is too full of endocrine facts for the exam this week. "Potato/Pahtaaato." I draw out the last word until he laughs. I toss my head back, and my towel slips off my head.

"Well, that's better. You have the shiniest hair."

"Not my best feature." I purse my lips at him. He makes me speak before I think. I used to be like that all the time, ask for forgiveness instead of permission. But, after Paris and my early twenties, that faded because I forced myself to be responsible. I miss that girl and Tony brings her back a bit. Perhaps this time I can use that drive for good and not evil.

"I know. I remember. But since your hair is exposed and your—"

"Nope. Do not name your favorite body part." I pull my hair up into a top knot.

"Come on. It will be fun. I'll name the feature and you uncover it." He waggles his eyebrows.

God, this man gets me wet, and I love seeing his face. "And you'll do the same?"

"Yeah, we can call it StripTime. It's a fun FaceTime game all the kids are playing." I laugh and end up snorting a little. "Adore that little snort." I shift in my seat, and he leans back on what appears to be a headboard.

"Are you in bed?"

"Yes."

"It's like 4:00 p.m. Are you napping?"

He grins, and I realize why he wanted to call me while in bed. What the hell are we doing?

"I don't think I'm ready for FaceTime orgasms. Get out of bed. Right now."

He pulls his phone back a little, and he's shirtless. How the hell does he look better now than he did? Jesus. I'm getting thirst trapped. Help! This not something I can handle. Being in bed with him in LA was the ultimate, but we didn't do anything but be with each other. I cannot combine the phone sex with that face. I won't survive, I'll spontaneously combust.

"Mak. I'm comfortable. I don't have to work today and I'm relaxing."

"Do it in the kitchen."

"You want to do it in the kitchen? I'm game. I can certainly clear my schedule to bend you over a countertop."

My eyes bug out of my head. We've masturbated, but I need to not do this with the salad duo like fifteen feet away. And it's not like I can tell him I live with my parents in a retirement village in Henderson, Nevada without it all splitting open. He deserves to hear all of this in person.

Unfortunately, every part of me is aflame, thinking of bending me to his will or over any surface. Not only has it been ages since someone bent me over something, but I also almost always think of Tony when I orgasm. No matter who's in the room.

I'd slept with six people before him and three times as many since, but he's the gold cock standard.

"Go to the kitchen, grab a shirt. I want to watch you cook. Something not sexy."

"You think this is sexy?"

He runs his hands up those abs. All of them. I glare at him.

"We are not doing this. And on second thought, don't cook because that's sexy too."

He sits up, and I'm left staring at the ceiling. Then his face reappears, looking down at the phone. He's grinning and has a t-shirt on, thank God.

"Maybe not today, but we are doing this. Mak. My Makenzie, don't be silly, this has to happen."

His head suddenly jerks to the left, as if someone called his name. Oh God. He's not alone. Ugh. What am I doing? I have to get ready for my shift. I don't have time to flirt with billionaires full of empty promises and a chest I could literally curl up on and live.

"Mak. I have to go."

Wait, what? No explanation and he went from cute to dismissive.

"Ok. But—"

He hangs up. I'm a bit hollow and confused. I stand and pace around my room. I call him back. He sends me to voice-mail. I text.

MAK: Hey. Did you lose service or did I just get stood up?

MAK: Tony? WTH?

MAK: Ok. I get it.

I hold my stomach with one hand and try not to cry. As if holding my stomach will stop all the ugly thoughts flooding my damn head. I wiggle around and try to shake it off. One second, I was his Makenzie, and the next, he hung up on me. It's like what happened on the Vineyard. The switch between my Tony and theirs.

I jump up and down trying to push it all back behind the Lego wall I've constructed where I tuck away painful memories. I won't wallow, like I did then. But I can't stop this shit from weighing me down right now.

I sit on the edge of the pullout, and I can see it so clearly. The memory of him only introducing me to certain calculated people at his Vineyard birthday soiree. I wasn't at his side or any part of his life at this party. It was just like this, two different Tonys. Then it was as if he put me up on a shelf. As if I should wait for him to come and play with me when no one was looking. I was sectioned off in the corner once people arrived at the party.

His parents threw this large, catered, and insanely over-the-top eighteenth birthday party. And he floated between groups of friends, family friends, and people older than himself. There was family all about, or so I'm told. There's no way I'd know, because other than his brother and some quick and dismissive words from his parents, I was introduced to no one. Colt, Hayden, Law, and Robbie all smiled and waved but at that point Hayden was devastated about Lizzie and I was viewed as the enemy. So, I left. I never want to feel dismissed. And other than right now, I haven't. I'm not sure how long it took for him to notice I left, but it seemed like hours before he texted asking where I was. And then we were done.

This feels the same for some reason. Different worlds and all that shit. But dammit, if I didn't get swept up again. My heart's breaking, like it did then, but I know it's the right thing, despite how I feel about him. The lies I've told, and this shitty feeling make it impossible to have him.

That was our last call.

tony

I hate hanging up on the only good thing in my life these days. But Laura's here stealing my things. It's my chance to catch her. I've noticed things missing: The caviar set, a couple bottles of expensive wine, the crystal cut goblets. I'm like her personal wedding section at Bergdorf's, but instead of registering, she's shoplifting.

The lawyers banned her, but the day doorman is charmed by my almost ex-wife. She doesn't know I'm here. I took the day off, something I never do. But Mak said I looked tired and should have a nothing day. So that's what I did, and talking to her was going to be the icing on my cupcake of the day. Screeching to a halt when I heard the lilting fake laugh as she thanked the doorman.

I'm in the hallway, and she's in the library with my artwork. I have two Kandinsky's and a couple of small Matisse drawings, and she once told me it was the reason she believed I was more than meets the eye. Fuck that. I'm so tired of proving I'm more than my money or my fuck-ups. She hammers home every terrible thing I've said about myself.

I listen.

"Bring the crates in here. Chop, chop, everyone." I pull my

phone back out and call 911. I fucking hate it when Laura says that phrase. Her mother uses it all the time.

"What's your emergency?"

"It's a domestic situation in which my ex-wife, who legally can't be here, is currently in my house stealing from me."

"Not quite an emergency, but I'll send some officers over."

"Please hurry, she'll be out of here in ten minutes."

"Sure. Sure. 1 Franklin Street?"

"Yes. Penthouse."

"That Penthouse?"

"Yes. That one. Tell Randall to let you up."

I toss my phone back into the pocket of my sweats and pad down the hallway. I round the corner, still waiting for someone to see me.

Shit, she is taking the Noguchi coffee table and the fucking Eames loungers. Didn't see that coming. She must have seen the insurance appraisal report of my belongings. I thought I was the only one who had it.

I've offered her quite a lot of money and the house in the Catskills that she insisted we buy. She was guaranteed the stupid Palm Beach condo she and her mother picked out. And then there's the shit-ton of cash. But this is beyond. If she wants these things, she can pay for them. They're padding and wrapping up my furniture, and there are wooden crates and white gloves, so she brought art preparatory here too. I document the entire thing, and as she comes bopping around the corner in her perfectly tailored cream suit, her mouth falls open. I capture the exact moment she sees me.

"Tony." She gasps.

I won't be aggressive and hostile like I want to be because there are witnesses, and the police will be here any moment. But who knows what will go down because the one thing I've learned in this divorce: I never knew her.

I lean in and kiss her cheek. "Laura. What a lovely surprise."

"I'm collecting a few things. Don't you have the team meeting today?"

I grab an apple off my kitchen counter and take a bite. "Canceled. Took the day off."

Her head whips so fucking fast I wish I had it on a boomerang. "You did what? You never take time off."

"Not with you," I say. It is monotone and not hostile. I should win a fucking Oscar for my performance.

She steps away from me, realizing we have an audience. She pulls her jacket down and tucks her hair behind her ear.

"How long do you think stealing from me will take? I have a full agenda of watching trash TV tonight."

She stammers. "Um. No. I. These are mine." She addresses the people in the room.

There's a knock at my door. I usher in two police officers and my traitor doorman. Who, I must say, looks rather pale. Whoops, there goes his holiday tip. And probably his job.

"What is this? What did you do? Tony. Anthony, answer me!"

I step forward, crossing my arms over my chest.

"Ma'am, there's a report of a break-in in progress."

"What?!" And then, like a fucking gift from the gods, the Judas doorman tries to save his skin by shoving my ex under the bus. Hell to the yeah.

"She's not authorized to be in this apartment. In fact, there's an injunction in place as well as a sort of restraining order."

"These are my things," she says authoritatively. The movers all freeze and look at the officers.

"Ma'am, we don't want any part of this." The head mover guy nods to me. I smile widely because this is now the best part of our marriage.

"They're my belongings." She doubles down. She always did have moxie.

I grin and say, "Show me the sales slips. Whoops, you can't. Because I bought them. Hey, fellas, I'll pay for your time if you can rehang my artwork and reassemble my furniture. And if anyone needs them, my accountant has all the receipts."

"This is atrocious behavior. How dare you?" God bless her; she's still huffy as if she's in the right. Her parents fucked her up.

The officer catches wise and rolls his eyes, "Sir, do you want to press charges for breaking and entering with the intent on burglary and what looks to be grand larceny?"

"You know I do. And toss in the doorman too as an accomplice. Sorry, dude, I was home the whole time. I was here when you let her inside the apartment. You used your key, which I did not authorize."

The officers are madly writing. "Sir, you know this is an actual B&E."

I nod. Then I pull a folder from the drawer in my open kitchen and hand it to them. It's the paperwork that backs me up. She's legally not allowed to be in this apartment.

One officer looks at the other. "You're going to have to come with us. You too, sir, to officially press charges."

"TONY. This is ridiculous. What will people say?"

"I don't know. But let's find out." I rub my hands together and talk into my phone. "Marjie, Tony Ladd."

Laura gasps because I've called the Boston Globe. Why the hell not? I'm in media. I have to get ahead of this and make it my story.

"Can you send someone to meet me down at the..." I gesture to the officers.

"Fourteenth."

"...Fourteenth precinct. I'm about to have Laura arrested for breaking and entering... I know... It's a fucking gas. Could not love this more, right? And it's all yours. I won't have anyone cover it. You're welcome. I mean, I do owe you for that thing from the guy from that place..." We both laugh. We often reference Clooney's *Ocean's Eleven* to each other from a failed date like eight years ago. Our friendship is the best thing that came out of it. "Awe, thanks... you too... Drinks soon... You should pay because I've just been burgled."

I slip on some sneakers and grab a coat. "Let's go."

The doorman looks like he shit his pants and won't move. The movers are finishing up. I tip them generously. Laura doesn't move.

"Darling wife of mine, it's time to go get fingerprinted. Chop-chop."

The officers laugh.

"I'm not going anywhere."

"Even better," I say as I exit. "Cuff her. She never let me do it, but I'm sure you'll have better luck."

"AHHHH. Fine. I hate you, Tony Ladd." She storms into the elevator.

"Cool. Save it for the press."

Five hours later, she's out on bail. She put up her wedding ring for it. Teddy bailed her out, and I think I saw her smirk at me when we passed in the station. I'll drop the charges, but I want the doorman fired. Enjoyed every second. Ten out of ten, would recommend. I enter my penthouse, and I'm starving and can't wait to tell Mak this story.

I pull out last night's takeout and eat it from the carton. I love cold noodles. I pop a beer and dial her up.

It's late for my time, but LA time, it's still decent. I don't know if she's on a job or not. I think she's in LA.

She denies FaceTime.

I prop my feet up on the coffee table.

I text while looking over her confused texts from earlier.

TONY: Yo. Why did you deny me?

MAK: I'm busy. And it's all fine. I get it.

I'm insanely confused.

TONY: You get what? You're speaking in tongues. Say it. We're friends.

MAK: Friends? You were shirtless earlier.

TONY: Yes, we're shirtless friends. Your turn. Call me up shirtless. I promise not to complain.

MAK: Jesus, be serious. You have more important things than me. You always did. I'm a moron to pretend any of this was different. It's fine. Take care.

TONY: NO. This is not how this goes. I say, let me call you and tell you the story of what went down tonight. Or you can read it tomorrow in the Globe. But here's the part where you say, "Sure. And you're the dreamiest, Tony Ladd."

MAK: I have to go.

TONY: Mak!

TONY: Makenzie.

TONY: Not funny. Are you seriously upset about something? I hated ending our call, but it's such a good story. Makenzie, trust me. I know this isn't quite how you wanted to hear it, but there's something here, and I don't want to let you go again. Please don't fucking walk away again. This is shitty. You have to start telling me why you keep leaving.

MAK: I'd rather you didn't call. It's easier this way. I have way too many things to deal with, and trying to figure out what the fuck this is, or if you're still embarrassed by me is too much of a head trip. Was good to see you. We should have let the past be despite how we feel about each other.

TONY: Nope. Not even a little bit of this makes fucking sense. Calling you right now. We sort this. I'm tired of living a life in the unspoken.

I call her, and she doesn't answer. And doesn't answer. And doesn't answer. I say the same thing in each of the first five messages, "Call me, little witch, you're not getting off this easy this time."

And then I lay it down. "We're not done. Even the universe thinks so, or why would you have been in that club the same night I was thinking about you. I think about you every birthday. You owe me not to disappear."

I don't even understand what she means about being embarrassed by her. She might be the least embarrassing thing I've ever done in my life. Definitely the only time I didn't feel like I had to prove myself or joke around to make someone like me. Or trust me. This is fucked up, and I need it to become something else. It's time we stopped playing.

Fuck the bet.

mak

I like the night shifts because the rec hall is usually empty after the evening activity.

I won't cry over something that isn't. This is all my fault, but it will be a hell of a lot worse if I don't stop it. I'll get attached and heartbroken, and it will take away from my studies.

"Ms. Makenzie. Why aren't you out with someone young and hot?" The Slippery Seniors are home from the pub. It's just the trouble trio, Dottie's probably with Scott.

"Julia, she looks terrible," Chelle says. Chelle's vibrant red hair is bouncing around her ample breasts as she jiggles on over to me. I know it's a wig, but I love that she's always 'show ready' in her mind. She's in a caftan covered in faux jewels. Julia's cream blouse offsets a flowy aqua skirt covered with bright red hibiscus flowers, as if she's headed to the beach. Lana is in a sparkly coral jumpsuit that flows from her slight body. I'm not sure how her slight body holds that many jewels at once, but she's covered.

They sit down next to me and put their arms around me. I'll never get the grease out of this uniform, but it does feel nice to have them here.

"Michelle, Julia, Lana, thank you. I'm fine." Julia has short, cropped hair and her brown eyes dance against the silver strands.

Lana smiles and yells, "Bullshit, Babycakes!" And Lana with her long, thick, flowing white curls always has her lips done in a perfect hot-pink shade. She's tall, thin, and floats in and out of places like she's liquid filling all the forgotten spaces.

Julia says, "We know that face, don't we?"

Chelle interjects, "Tell us. We see you studying so freaking hard and working your tail off. Even your mom is starting to come around to getting out there. You're the reason any of us have fun. But you have no life."

Lana slaps my arm while crossing her sequin-clad legs. "Hot thing like you. If I had your body and youth, I'd never stop fucking. Why aren't you fucking everything that moves?"

"Seriously, get your freak on," Chelle exclaims.

I laugh and stand up. Michelle takes four paper cups from the cupboard and a flask from her very deep and low-set cleavage. She pours four shots.

She raises her cup and says, "To Makenzie's vagina, may it not grow old like ours before she gets laid again." They all cackle, and I'm touched by them.

My phone pops off for the billionth time, but I refuse to read any of his texts. I glance and then back to the women. I'd turn it off, but ever since France, I always keep it on in case my parents need me.

Julia says, "What was that? That was a something." She gestures between my face and the phone.

I concede to tell them something, so they'll move along. "Maybe at some point in an alternate universe on someone else's timeline it might have been something. But here and now, it has to be nothing." It's better it ends now.

Lana swipes my phone and quickly holds it up to my face.

Before I can register what's happening, Chelle pours more shots, and Lana reads aloud.

T: I get it. You're not talking to me about this. And they call me immature. Mak. Even if you and I don't end up being what I want. I know. I'll always know. But my heart and my dick want what they want. We still need to talk about whatever shit you think went down tonight. And fuck it, I need closure from twelve years ago, and you, young lady, are going to have to face me. If there's a shot we come through this together, we're taking it whether you run away or not. I'll be at your door in six hours.

T: You can try to dodge me, but you know I'll just sit at your door if I can find it until you talk to me.

What the hell? I stand up and jump around. No. This is terrible.

Julia claps. "That's not nothing! I'm going to need to see the whole chain. Who is this?"

"I used to be kind of his, but it's nothing. And now I'm so screwed."

Lana says, "Not by a long shot. But you will be when he gets here!" They all giggle.

"Oh God, you're misunderstanding." I plead, and their faces drop.

"Why? When he gets here, we'll get to the bottom of this. And how's his bottom?" Chelle says, and elbows Julia, leaving an oily circle on her blouse. They must spend a fortune on dry cleaning. But seriously, who greases their elbows.

"You don't get it. And yes, he has a fabulous bottom. A fabulous everything. We were together a while ago. But that's not the point."

"That is the damn point. He's crossing the country to clear up whatever went down today. Why won't you hear him out?" Julia looks up from my phone. I'm freaking out. What do I do? How do I unravel this?

"This can never work. He's rich. Like major rich and I—"

"I don't think he cares if you're poor," Chelle offers up.

"No. He won't, but that's not the real issue. I care. But shit. Fuck. I don't... shit."

"Stop speaking in expletives," Julia chides.

"I lied, ok?"

They all gasp. Chelle slaps my shoulder. "You? What did you lie about?"

Tears stream down my face. "I'm sorry, but so many things. I told him I went to college. I told him I'm a stylist for commercial shoots. I told him I graduated high school on time. I didn't tell him I was a mess or how much he really means to me."

"Settle down. You can explain all of that when he gets here. He's flying here to see you."

Julia covers her heart. "That's so romantic. He'll listen."

"You're not getting it! He thinks I live in LA. Not here with you."

They gasp again.

Chelle slaps my hand. "How do you feel about him?"

"For real. Dig deep, Mak," Julia says, holding my hand.

Lana says while she scrolls for something on her phone, "How important is this? You can blow him off and never see him again. He has no way to really find you, right? We can get you a new number. You're out if you want to be, Doll."

I inhale and exhale, and my whole body is cramped. I'm dizzy, and tears lick at the back of my eyes again. The idea of never seeing this man again is too much. It's nothing and everything. Oh God.

Julia squeezes my hand. "How do you feel?"

"Lost. Sad. Panicked."

"Why?"

It all comes out in a rush of a sob and catharsis. "I love him. He's the only man I've ever loved. Or will ever love like this. I can't get over him and I can't forget him for making me feel less and he didn't even know it. I never told him all of this shit and now I'm even more of a mess—"

Chelle smiles. "You know you're phenomenal, right? Everything you do for everyone around you. You deserve to be happy."

Lana says, "And a man doesn't just fly in from—"

"Boston."

Chelle slaps my arm again. I'm going to be covered in her greasy handprints. "A man doesn't fly across the country just to get a story straight. He loves you too."

"I can't. He'll always need someone more than me."

I let the tears fall. Then the women all crowd around me in a slippery hug.

Julia, who never swears, gets up in my face, "You know that's a bunch of horse pucky right there. Anyone would be lucky to have you. And not only are you enough for anyone, but you're also more than most." She nods violently as if emphasizing her point to a crowd.

Chelle says, "What's it going to take for you to know you're enough? Stop wasting time. Take it from us, there's not enough of it." I let them hug me, and a small knot deep in my soul eases as I decide to tell him.

Lana backs up and shows me her phone. "Go. Find him."

I stare at a plane ticket to Los Angeles that leaves soon.

"I don't have kids. So let me do this." Lana touches my arm.

"This is too much. What do I do?"

"Well, I'd hustle and wash your face because your plane leaves in two hours. I'll book you a hotel." A text comes in with the details and a link to the ticket.

Chelle looks at me. "Let us help you. You don't have to do everything on your own. Even though we know you can. But you should know, we know you can't." They look at each other. "Wisdom, bitch. The sooner you kick the chip on your shoulder to the curb the better—did I use that correctly?"

I nod. "If it's the 1990s, sure."

Lana puts her hand on my back. "Well, the point is, don't let your pride rob you of your present."

My voice is a whisper, "Thank you. But I have to work. And I have class. I can't miss it, or he'll take me down a letter grade. He's an asshole like that."

Chelle offers up, "We can cover for you. If anyone asks where you are we'll say you're running an errand for me. Give me your key card. I'll log you in and out and open random doors through your shift."

Julia says, "Is your homework done?"

"Most of it. I have reading to do. But I can get it done. And do this I think."

"I know you can." Lana puts her hand on mine.

"You broads are ok." They all laugh and then smack me on the butt. And now my ass is covered in greasy handprints too. Normally I'd be annoyed, today, I'm grateful.

"Go. I'll have you back here before class on Tuesday."

"Go. Tell him."

I nod. Of all the dumb shit I've done in my life, this might be the dumbest.

tony

She has to talk to me. Maggie told Colton she lives in West Hollywood. I'll pound on every door. I didn't tell Maggie I was coming here, or rather Colton didn't. They apparently talk all the time. I've got to sort this out. There's something wrong with my life if I let her slide back into the past. Before, I was young and dealing with my parents and Harvard and all that shit, so I let her go.

However, she's never been in my past. It's time to find out why she left on my birthday, why she thought breaking up with me was a good idea, and why she won't continue to give me this second chance. I won't sleep with her, unless she begs me to. Who am I kidding, if I have a shot at fucking her, I'm taking it. But first we figure shit out. Just about nine months of talking and getting to know her has been more than perfect, but now we get to the answers.

When she came to Boston twelve years ago, it was like a dream. We were perfect until we weren't. And now she's put our future in tatters, and I'm not a cocky eighteen-year-old with an 'I can do better' attitude to console him so he could move on. Not only can I not do better, I never fucking moved on from the one thing I now know to be the only pure and perfect thing I'm supposed to do with my life. Love her.

I saw who I wanted to be and tried to live up to that every day since. I was a fucking puddle of a mess for a year or so, but I wanted to be this man for her. Whether she ever fucking knew it or not. She stole that version of our future when she ran. Probably a good idea since I was a hot mess of a human at that time. The only thing I was sure of was her. And that wasn't enough. We both figured out how to be people without each other, and it was fucking hard. So now I want my reward. I greedily want it all.

I'll be past all my dad bullshit and Laura's all done. But if she needs reassurance that I don't want her anywhere but with me, then I'll pay off the bet. Even though any major financial transaction right now will look like I'm hiding money from my dad. Shit. I can't lose the bet. And for the first time in my life, I want to.

As the plane lands, I formulate a plan to head to her work headquarters tomorrow and see if I can swindle an address. She must be subletting or something because the only Makenzie Preston registered on the West Coast with the USPS is a PO Box in Henderson, Nevada.

I spark up my phone, and the one text that might define my life is waiting for me. Oh yeah. I'm so losing the bet.

MAK: Four Seasons Bev Hills. Suite 1804. Key at the desk.

The elevator won't move fast enough. There's not enough oxygen in here, and my breath is quick and fast. The adrenaline is surging, and unfortunately, so is my cock. It's sporting a semi in hopes this all means what I think it means. I'd tell him to calm down, but I'm way too fucking excited to see her.

We should talk first, instead I'm going to make her come. Naked. I need us both naked.

I run, literally run, down the hall and I'm shocked my dick doesn't bang on the door himself. I know I have a key, but I'm too amped up, so knocking is helping burn off the shaky feeling I have.

She opens the door, and I swear it's like twelve years and nine months haven't passed. She looks exactly the same as when Maggie opened the door to reveal my destiny in room 666.

I stare at her as she bites the inside of her cheek. I only have a shoulder bag, and I toss it behind her. She's holding open the door, and I step to her. Both of our breaths catch. And then I snatch her up into my arms and take her lips. She moans the exact way my cock and brain remember. I feel her full lips push against mine as I nip her bottom lip encouraging her to open for me. I pick up this wisp of a girl and move into the room. I don't see anything but her. And if I'm honest, I never have.

I push my tongue into her mouth, and she moans again. Her tongue volleys for dominance. Our heads twisting and turning in a passion I've not known since Paris. Or maybe ever. We were teenagers, and now we can fuck like adults. This is an adult porn, powerful kiss. My hands are everywhere, and her noises are sublime.

"Christ, you fucking gorgeous woman, are you ready to be filthy with me? I'm not holding back."

"You say the sweetest things," she says, grabbing my rock-hard cock through my jeans.

"Trust me, that's the last of the sweet." I rip her shirt off and dive into her neck, my tongue snaking down towards her perky breasts. My hands reach around and undo her bra. The moment the bra is loose, my head dives underneath it to find the perfect nipples—I've compared every other tit to these for a decade. I pull one into my mouth and she throws her head back.

"Fuck yes!" Her voice is throaty, and I have to have more.

I kneel down and unzip her pants, pulling them off her legs as I kiss my way down her stomach.

"Just a touch of foreplay because I'm going to fuck you hard and fast. Let's do this quickly so we can clear our heads and really concentrate on worshiping each other's bodies."

"So, what you're babbling about is that you're not going to eat me out right now, but if I bend over, you'll fuck me?"

I stare for a moment at her black thong and cup her sweet pussy. Then I stand up to see her face.

"If you're as wet as I dream you are, then we're not making it past this spot. But if you need me to help you along, I'm more than willing. But if I was a betting man, and I am, I'm going to bet on wet." I inch my hand into her thong and she's ready for me. "Fucking heaven." I play around with her clit for a second letting my finger rim the silkiest part of my little witch. I press my finger inside of her, shallow at first.

She grins and says, "Always bet on Mak."

I slide my tongue against hers while I push in deeper. I pull back and rip her thong off her as she desperately reaches for my zipper. My pants are barely open when her hand is around my cock.

She licks her lips. "I forgot how perfect and wide your dick is."

I move her off my cock, which is about to go off like a fucking rocket.

"That's it. Hands to yourself! Hands off the cock. Everyone take a step back." She's laughing and standing in front of me totally naked. I lean towards her and without touching anything but her lips, I kiss her slowly.

"You're the only thing I see. When I close my eyes at night or when I wake up. You're it, Mak. How do you do that? How do you permeate every part of my mind?"

"Witchcraft."

mak

I give him a little side eye as he smiles like a predator at me.
"You should lose those clothes."

Then I run into the bedroom and sit down, crossing my legs as if I'm a lady at a tea party and not a dripping-wet, happy slutty slut who can't wait to get fucked by the hottest man on the planet.

He yells from the living room area, "You do know that watching your ass bounce like that isn't helping the situation. If you breathe near me, I'm going to come all over you."

"Then I guess you're going to have to come in here so I can huff and puff and blow your dick down."

He appears in the doorframe. His body on full display. His cut chest and that trail of muscle and man that leads to the large cock he's stroking. He holds onto the doorway and his blue eyes are darker and a bit smoldering. He is so freaking stunning and hot.

"Did you just make *The Three Little Pigs* into porn?"

I nod.

But I don't even get a chance to volley a comeback. He pushes me down on the bed and spreads my legs wide. He notches himself up and thrusts inside of me as we both cry out from the contact.

"Christ. Fuck. You're so big." He kisses me aggressively but doesn't move. I wince just a little, my body not knowing what to do with all of this. He kisses my neck and nips up to my jaw.

"Your body will remember me. Come on. Breathe. Relax, let me in, you fucking gorgeous woman. Command your cunt to remember me."

And my pussy does slowly relax as he rubs my clit. The pleasure is too great, and I open up to him. He slides in deeper with a groan.

"There it is," he says as he pushes in slightly deeper.

"There what is?"

"Home."

I grin up at him, and it's almost too much to bear. He's so vulnerable and earnest. His face is expressing all the things I'm feeling but can't quite communicate. I'll forever remember this moment and the way he fills me so completely. My heart and soul as well as my body.

He waggles his eyebrows as he breaks the moment by pulling out and slamming back into me. And we're off to another destination, this one less sappy and more about the sound of our bodies slapping together. He's so deep as he thrusts into me.

"Wrap this leg around me but give me this one." He tugs me to the end of the bed impaling me further on his cock. Now he's got me trapped and he's watching where we're joined. He's pumping in and out and my hips are rising to meet each stroke. He places my leg on his shoulder and grabs my hips.

"I can't. Oh."

"You are. You're taking all of me. And I'm giving you

everything. Fuck. You're so tight. Fuck. Fuck. This. Is. Everything." He punctuates each word with another thrust.

My head is reeling, and he reaches up and grabs my tit. He holds on and I don't think any longer. My body's in charge and we're coming. I move my hand towards my clit so I can come hard and fast on his dick. He stops me but never stops pumping into me as he repositions my legs around his back. Now his body is giving me friction as I jerk him as close as possible, and he leans down to kiss me. The motion is intense, then his hand is between us and pressing down on my hooded and swollen clit.

Then he almost gutturally chants my name, commanding me to come.

"Mak. Mak. Mak. Come for me. Make me come."

"Yes. Yes. Yes." Is all I can utter as the sensations ripple through my body and get more intense as it climbs and builds to this maddening crescendo in which I tip over the top with a scream of his name. "Tony. Christ. Tony."

And with that I feel a jerk and tug buried deep inside of me and his face contorts in the sexiest way. We're in sync as if we're on the dance floor and finishing each other's movements. I gasp, panting, as he slumps down on top of me. His cock twitching and my pussy pulling him in close and holding him. Until I finally am able to relax into the release.

He picks his head up slightly and kisses my cheek.

"That was epic."

I grin and try to roll away.

"Nope. Let me just stay in here a second longer and then we'll get you all cleaned up. And it's a bit awkward at this point, but..."

I suddenly get what he's saying. We didn't even think about using a condom. I don't think I've ever trusted anyone more in my life.

"I'm on birth control and it's been a while since, I... um."

He kisses my nose and groans as he leaves my body hollow and hopeful. Hopeful he'll fill me again as soon as possible, but hollow for the loss of connection. I didn't realize how much I'd shut this part of me down until he chipped away at that Lego wall I'd built around myself, brick by colorful brick.

"And you?" I ask as I sit up.

"I've been waiting for you. Laura was the last woman I was with and that was a painfully long time ago. Shocked I lasted this long. Your pussy is perfect." My lips tug upward as he sits up placing one sensuous kiss on my small triangle of hair. I'm sure I'm a mess down there, but he doesn't seem to care. He's savoring each part of me.

"Your pussy is looking lovely tonight. I wanted to reintroduce myself before I take her to dinner later."

"Just so you know, she's more of a McDonald's kind of gal." He laughs and pulls me into the bathroom. He grabs a washcloth and turns on the shower.

"Come my beautiful Mak so we can clean the cum and start all over again."

I grasp his dick and when I give it a little pull, it jumps in my hand. He raises an eyebrow.

"Hmm. Seems someone is angling to be tossed up on that tiled wall and fucked again?"

"I could find room in my schedule for that. But let me consult with all interested parties."

He laughs as I bend down and pull his cock into my mouth. He hardens almost immediately. I stand up and stare at him.

"I'm as surprised as you are, but he's waited a long time to be reacquainted with his favorite toy. He's got a mind of his own."

"Well, I wouldn't want to disappoint your cock."

"What about me?"

"No. Not you either." He wraps me in his arms and guides me under the warm water. His tongue slides into my mouth and it's less sexual and more of a forever kind of kiss.

I hope I'm up to the task.

tony

She's lying on top of me. Her nails lightly grazing my body. And there's so much left unsaid. All the dirty stuff has been covered. And if I thought she was the best I'd ever had, well, shit, she's learned a thing or two. She out benchmarked herself.

"Mak, I have to—"

She interrupts me. She doesn't look at me but says it so the universe can interpret it first.

"I love you."

I've never been more complete. I'm so overwhelmed and forget to answer her.

She whispers, "Did you hear me? Because I don't think I can say it again. I hurt you too much the last time I said that, and if you don't, I understand."

I whisper back while I stroke her hair. "I've always loved you and happily still do, my perfect Wiccan."

mak

There will never be a more satisfying sleep than this. We said the thing we've been fighting and holding back. I got to be adored and in love for one night. And now I have to tell him. I have to wake him up, and even when he leaves me, last night was worth it. I'll always know what it feels like to be enough, loved, and completely myself.

I'll hold that feeling because after I give all my truths, I'm pretty sure the feeling is all I'll be left with. I kiss his back gently, and he tugs my arm tighter. I'm sore, sated, and currently the big spoon.

'We had a perfect night." I whisper, knowing he's still mostly asleep, "I love you, Tony Ladd. No matter what happens, please remember that as the absolute truth. That's the thing that's true."

I roll over and glance at the clock. 10:46. I sigh and kiss his back sweetly again, but before he can wake up, the time registers. It surges with absolute sheer panic at my stupidity. I didn't set an alarm. I didn't think it was this late. I thought I'd get us coffee and tell him. Or if I chickened out again, I could just leave. Shit. This is terrible.

I jump out of bed. I only have time to put my clothes on

my body. I'm desperately searching for my bag and laptop. I didn't do the reading. I'm going to flunk out. He'll fucking fail me if I don't show up. Letter grade if you miss. Shit. Shit. I can't. I have to make my flight. The class is at two. I can do this.

"What is happening? You're like a hopped-up cat right now. Stop darting."

"Go back to sleep." I bark at him. I'm loud and aggressive. I don't mean to be, but I can't find my phone.

"Because yelling always puts me in a sleepy mood. Babe, what's going on?"

"Shit! Shit! Shit! Where's my phone? I'm out of time. Everything is wrong. I have to get out of here, now!"

"Cinderella. It's way past midnight. You're cool, we're ok. Not a pumpkin in sight, come back to bed."

"That's fucking funny. Because all of this was provided by a fairy godmother. And I just woke up in tatters. I have to fucking go."

"No. You don't. You stay here with me, and we talk about your crazy-ass behavior, my love."

That stabs me in the heart.

"No. I have to go. You don't understand. I have to go." I'm babbling as I throw everything around the suite in search of my phone and wallet. My ID is in the back of my phone. If it wasn't, I would fucking leave it.

The bold Makenzie I've reclaimed over the past almost nine months weighs me down. With the brash and bold comes the irresponsible. My reckless past is creeping in, and I'm doomed. I don't think I can dust myself off again if I flunk out before I even get to med school. I don't want to be the girl who fucked up again. The one who didn't care enough about herself to want something.

Tony made me want something better and now I'm fucking it up again and ironically because of him.

"You're a mess. Hey, seriously, what is going on?"

He's concerned and sweet. That's a bit too much to take. He leaps up and pulls on his black boxer briefs. He tries to hold me, but I shake him loose. My world is crumbling. My lies are burying me, and I'm about to crush him with my truth. It's all so heavy to carry right now.

"You're fine. Stop this. Let me take you home and we'll spend the day in your bed. I want to see where you live, and we can grab food on the way."

And that's it. I turn, and I don't know who I am at this moment, but it's like I leave my body, and I can't stop my mouth from spewing stuff.

"You don't! You really, really don't want to see where I live. Trust me. And you don't want to see who I really am or what my real life looks like. You're not ready for the entire Makenzie experience. You never were and you never did see it even when I tried to show it to you. You pretended I belong in your world, but I don't. And that's why I left, because it was all an illusion, a spell, or possibly your delusion that made me believe it could be different. But each time my reality crept in I knew I had to keep up the glamour spell. I don't belong anywhere near you."

"Yes, you do. You belong to me not with me. And I don't care about whatever you think you're talking about."

"You will, and this is terrible timing, but I have to go. Holy shit. I've fucked up my whole life for the chance to be yours a little while longer and now I have to go. I can't screw this up, but I've messed up everything. That's who I am, even though I tried to be different, and I was. But then there you were again, and now I have to get the hell out of here. I'm going to be late for class. And if I'm late then it's all for nothing. My grades will go to shit and all that I've worked for will be fucking gone. Everything I've tried to fix. All the damage and bad I've done won't be corrected."

"Class?"

I'm ranting around the room, and he's standing there with his arms crossed. It's like I'm an erratic planet off my axis, and he's the sun trying to ground me with gravity and pull me back into proper rotation. I have to go.

"YES. School. Class! Here it is. I didn't graduate from high school when you did. I was either drunk, stoned, or angry in my youth. I blew it all off. And I don't have a college degree yet. I don't have anything you thought of me. I never should have been in Paris. I scammed my way there. Hell, I didn't even go to class when we were in France. I had a day job so I could at least pick up a beer tab every once in a while. I'm not classy or sophisticated. I don't have a huge family or home. I hustled shit my whole life and now I'm paying the price. The true price of blowing off everything. I never should have tried to be something I'm not. I fucking lied. I'm still lying. I don't even live in LA. You deserve better than a fucking bad girl who lied about everything. Now please help me find my phone so I can get out of here and try to salvage the pathetic life I'm trying to build."

He looks dumbstruck. His beautiful, chiseled face is shattered and hurt. This is all as it should be. It's the only ending I deserve. And I finally get to see the destroyed face I ran from years ago. I hid from the pain I caused, but I'm in it, and I see it. And it's so much worse than I thought it could be.

His voice is steady but low, "I thought we were going to have a life together."

Oh God, how that sounds so simple and perfect. His face will be etched on my soul. The pain is deeper this time. Tears stream down my face, and I see Tony shut his eyes and then pinch away tears of his own.

"You don't want my life." I see my phone under the couch. I dive for it. And he tries to stop me.

I yell again to try to get out of here without him. "Don't.

Don't. I'm a fucking fraud. Nothing about me is what you think."

"What if I think you're smart and funny and kind and challenging, adventurous, and loving. Are those things a lie?"

"Don't be nice to me. Oh, Jesus. YES. All of it is a lie," I blurt out.

"Ok, *now* you're lying. You can't tell me those things aren't you."

Then he looks around at the suite and back to me as I tuck my hair up into a top knot. I gather my things and try to maintain some semblance of grace as I destroy everything I ever wanted.

"Mak, before you go, I need to know. Did you lie to me for my money like the rest of them?" And there it is. He'll never believe me about anything since I built our relationship on a foundation of cracked Lego.

I reach out to his forearm, and he doesn't recoil. There's one truth in my soul. "No. That's one of the two things I didn't lie about."

"And the other?"

I suck in a huge breath and hold my stomach. "The way I feel about you."

He steps back. "Says the liar." His voice is steely, and I let the cold wash over me because I deserve it. I've finally pushed him far enough away that he sees reality.

I nod. There's no way to fix this.

"I have to go."

"So you've said."

I walk out. Neither of us says a word. I hold it together until I jump in a cab. And then I implode. The choice to tell him the truth was always mine, and I played a stupid, selfish game. But even if I had told him I was broke, wild, uneducated, living with my parents, barely employed, and scammed my way to France, I wonder what he would have done. And that wonder will always live as a fucking flesh-eating bacterium on my soul.

I text him one more time as I'm racing for my plane, hoping to God I make it on time.

MAK: Deleting and blocking your number. Don't worry. I won't bother you again after this. But I'm sorry, and I do love you.

I want him to be able to think and say anything he wants. But I know anything I say to myself will be worse, so I'll leave it at this.

MAK: And you should know you and I were never the lie. Just the rest of my life was.

End of Part Two

part three

vive le carrousel à bagages

tony

"**F**UCK." I slam another shot. She fucking walked out on me. "A lot." I'm muttering. She lied a lot and then left.

Law gestures for another one, and I take it directly from the bartender. I shoot it while Law slaps my back.

"Now, are we in a 'get laid to forget situation' or are we regrouping? Also, maybe share what the fuck is happening. And why you're at a bar in Phoenix in the afternoon on a Wednesday. Just curious, man. Good to see you and all, but what the fuck?"

"I'm in love with her."

"Please fuck tell me it's not Laura." He turns away from the bar and leans backward, surveying the land. He nods at a bevy of women as they walk by and wave at him.

"I should have flown to France. You're useless." Law was the closest 'Brother,' so I diverted the jet here.

"Sorry, man, I'm here. Tell me what's going down. Are you ok?"

"First off, if you tell anyone, I'm cutting your dick off."

"That's cool. I can still pitch dickless." I shove him, and run my hands through my hair.

"I owe you two million dollars." He grins slowly and nods.

"Figured. And whom did you sleep with twice?"

"Technically, only once, but I have been kind of dating her for like nine-ish months. However, I'm in love with her." Law crooks an eyebrow at me. "Makenzie."

"That's the least surprising thing you've ever said. Now what the fuck happened? Why have you darkened my desert doorstep? I have three days off and I intend to fuck quite a bit and you're bringing down my average and my rizz with your sad boy vibe."

A woman comes up and hands him a piece of paper. "Do you mind, Outlaw?" Her tits are out, and I see him start to move in. I haven't ruined shit with my sad boy vibe. The man could get laid in a convent.

"Outlaw? What the fuck's with that shit?" I ask while pushing the empty shot glass across the over varnished bar.

She flicks her strawberry-red nail in her mouth and says, "It's what we call him, now. Because his...pitching is so hot it should be illegal."

I toss my hands up and turn around. Law gives her the autograph, and she leans into him.

"What's your name?" I ask her.

Law answers, "Marnie." She grins. He never remembers names so it's surprising.

I look at him. "Who is she?"

"She's the manager's daughter, who is collecting signatures for some charity event." He licks his lips.

I get between them. "Ok. Ok. Everybody take a cold shower." I turn to Marnie. "Forbidden fruit, I'm going to need you to table this seduction for another day. No worries, he's a sure thing. But I have very pressing matters and need his whole focus. So please tuck your very large and extremely attractive breasts back into your shirt. How about you let me buy you and your friends a round and we leave Outlaw's cock in the holster for today?"

"And who are you?"

Law shrugs and points at me with his thumb. "The marrying kind." Marnie pouts a bit.

"But I'm still fun. I'm a ton of fun. You would enjoy fucking me, but the problem is I'm in love with someone who has apparently been making up stories about her life for like a decade. I'm Tony, it's a pleasure to meet you." I reach out my hand to this woman who really should be walking away from us.

Marnie shifts, and her shirt pops open a touch. Law pulls his hoodie off and hands it to her.

Law explains, "If you're going to listen to his bullshit, then I'm going to need you to cover up before I pop a nut."

I toss my hands up and shake my head. I stand up and sit back down. "Why am I here? None of this is helping." Marnie puts on his sweatshirt then tugs at my wrist.

"Come with me. You too, Mr. Off Limits." She winks at him. I'm sure he'll have her before the sun gets around the planet again.

I follow her, and Law grabs a couple of beers, and we sit down at a table with three other women.

Marnie says, "Ladies. You know Outlaw, of course. But this here is Tony. He says he has a woman problem."

I push Law to sit in a chair, then I sit on the other side of him, cockblocking Marnie. I don't trust her not to jerk him off under the table.

She continues, "And my problem is I don't get to have Outlaw until we solve this one's problem."

The girls giggle. They're all extraordinarily tan and have that blonde hair only a second-rate stylist can achieve, but they all reach out to me. They're sweet and kind, and I realize I'm letting my snob show. I tuck back my upbringing and smile at these women who want to help or harem up my friend.

"Tell us. Leave none of the ugly out."

Marnie says, "Start with a picture, a visual to see what we're working with."

Law slurps his beer and crosses his legs, and all the women watch. I'm not unattractive. Should I tell them I'm a billionaire? Maybe that will bring focus back to the problem at hand.

Law says, "He doesn't have one."

I pull up my phone. "You can scroll."

His eyes pop out of his head. "You really do owe me two mil." I nod. "Oh, shit. Let me see. Damn. She is hotter than I remember. How drunk was I in Vegas? I do not remember this little raven-haired snack."

I rip the phone from him and point at him. Then shake my head no.

I look to the ladies and ask, "How much of this story do you want?"

A one of the bottle blondes with lips the color and texture of cherry pie filling bends deeply over the table, so I can be eye to eye with her impressively popped nipples instead of her eyes. I scoot my chair back an inch trying not to be rude at this gift but really not wanting it.

All the women cackle as she sits back down and Marnie says, "You're in deep. Nobody looks away from Wendy's hypnotic twins." She purses her lips and does a reverse wave to indicate she wants it all.

Law signals the bartender for more drinks and puts his palm out to me. I slap my black card in it while he yells across the bar, "And a fuck-ton of chicken wings." Then he turns to me. "Start at the beginning. I don't think I even know the full shiz."

"This bar tab is coming out of your end of the two mil." I raise my eyebrows at my brother from another mother.

Law smiles and puts his hand on my shoulder. The women swoon. Good lord the man could probably do them all right here and now.

He was twelve when all the Paris shit went down. All the Lizzie and Hayden stuff as well as my own story. Law also had many things on his plate then, including club baseball all the fucking time. There's no way he knows most of my story from that time.

"The beginning, well, it's going to sound corny, but it all began in Paris. Senior year of high school…"

One girl keeps wiping tears from her eyes, even though we're way past the saddest part of my story. Marnie gestures to me, and I laugh because her arms are doing a floppy thing. "You look like the blow up figure in front of the gas station where that flops and flies."

"Oh, shit. She can totally dance like that. Do it, bish. Do it," one of the blondes yells and points to her friend.

They all have very similar names with Ws, so I can't keep them straight. Windy, Wendy, one of them might be Wendell. I look over, and the one I call Wendell has stood up and is blowing in the nonexistent breeze. We all bust out laughing, and Law moves Marnie deeper into his lap.

Marnie clears her throat and points at me. "Now. You know what you have to do, right? Even if she's a backstabbing bitch, you have to hear her out. You gots to know when and what." She's smacking her hand with her fist.

She leans towards me and says, "You need to get the deets. The closure. If there's a good reason she ghosted twice then so be it. It is what it is. And you can bail if you like. But if she's like other level, then you need to pound her into the mattress. Either way, you gots to know."

I point at Marnie and yell, "I gots to. You are a wise and very horny woman. I gots to know. I release you, my brother. Go make this woman come." She's a prophet in a plastic body, but the heart is pure. I answer these women earnestly. I'm not sure I've been this drunk in a couple of years. But I gots to know.

They all laugh as Law stands up and places Marnie at his side. He whispers in her ear, then uses his phone.

The girls all hug me as I gather my things and sign the bill. Wendell thanks me for the multiple colorful drinks called ZuZus. "Thank you. Good luck. And if it turns out she's not it, we hang out here kind of all the time. Come on back, cutie." Another one appears over Wendell's shoulder.

"We'll take real good care of you."

I nod to my potential three or foursome and punch Law in the arm. I don't know where I'm going, but I need to get out of here. I'm almost to the door when Law slings an arm around me.

"Come on, sad sack."

I grin, and we climb into a waiting car.

We're perched on his insanely bright white leather couch with our feet up, headsets on, fake shooting the shit out of things on Law's obscenely large TV.

"That's not fucking fair. Asshole. Where did you get that knife?"

"Colt, my dear, I've had it the whole time," I respond.

"Robbie, on your left," Law yells.

"Nice kill," Dax screams too loudly into his microphone. The six of us have been playing CSGo or Counterstrike for four hours. Law knew I needed to kill things, eat pizza, drink heavily, and hear from my brothers.

"Head shot!" Law yells as he explodes someone.

"Did we get the things we're looking for?" Hayden asks.

He sucks at video games. He's perfect at everything else but sucks at fake killing.

I yawn and know I have a long week ahead of me with the *Into the Frying Pan* live launch. This mini talk show will set the stage for the rest of it. After that, I know what I need to do because I 'gots to know'.

The soft launch was a disaster, and now I have to get this all on fucking track. The Cookery can't fail. If I secure this piece then all the weddings and divorces won't matter. I'll be free to create whatever kind of life I choose, work and love.

There's so much pressure wrapped up in this. And I thought I'd run back out to LA, claim my woman, launch my empire, then kick back and celebrate my perfect life. And that went so well. But blowing everything off and leading these assholes into fake battles is the fucking best thing to happen to me today.

"I miss you, jack holes."

"Yeah. Yeah," Dax says.

I need to redeye back to Boston for the launch. "I've got to catch a plane but a good morrow to you all, brave knights." I look at my watch and start to pull myself together.

They all say goodbye and good luck. But just as I'm about to hang up, Law says, "Oh, and he lost the bet," then clicks off. They all yammer, and I hang up.

"Fucker!"

"Code of the bet. You're dating her."

"But I only fucked her once."

"We'll see, but if you're this hung up, you dated her. Look, you know I can't keep it to myself. I'm terrible with secrets and I like fucking with you. Are you really leaving?" Law laughs to himself.

I walk over to him, so he doesn't have to get up. I slam my hand into his. "Thanks. Yeah. The jet's waiting. I could stay if you want me to."

He's texting. "Nope. Please get the fuck out. Marnie will be here in ten."

"Is this a wise call? Fucking the team manager's daughter?"

"She's legal. And I feel like there's a strange voo-doo on my dick lately. I'm hoping her pussy swallows it down."

I roll my eyes. "Love you, brother."

"Love you too. Good luck with the cooking bullshit. And then go get her. You just let her go last time. Get them answers."

I know what I need to do. I shake my head. "I gots to get them."

I try to put myself back together in the car a bit. I turn on my phone, and aside from the many texts from the Boston brothers, work is blowing up.

I only read the private texts from Hayden.

HAYDEN: I know you. I know it's Mak. Don't let her slip into history again.

TONY: Hurts so fucking bad, dude. She lied about a ton of shit.

HAYDEN: You should know Law told us everything.

TONY: Of course, he did.

HAYDEN: He's concerned. Do you really love her?

TONY: The way you love Lizzie. Or the way you describe loving her. Dude, I can't.

HAYDEN: What if you could?

I shoot him a thumbs-up emoji to stop this conversation. I stare out the window and wonder. Marnie's words keep running through my brain. Even if it's all ugliness that gets revealed, I gots to know.

I lift my laptop and begin to unravel what happened over the last thirty-six hours that I disappeared from work.

And then I need to see a man about a post office box.

mak

I made it to the plane—it was delayed—and I lost a letter grade, and I have to be ok with it all. I've talked myself off the ledge. I know I won't flunk out, but if I don't get a scholarship, then this dream might die. Now that I won't be distracted by Tony and all the things that could be, I should be able to pull this off. But instead of getting on a plane back to Vegas, I used the ticket to reroute to Portland.

I'm snuggled on a cozy ecru couch under a soft, fuzzy cream blanket in my best friend's home. I crashed out for the day when I got here. Then I hid in her guest room for the night. But now, I need to talk about it all.

"There are things you need to tell me. Why did Colton ask me where you live?"

"Shit. What did you say?"

Maggie got a sub for her second grade class and sent her husband out to their hunting cabin for the night. Well, his hunting cabin; she doesn't like guns. This house is warm and friendly, except for the den and a bit of the living room. There are heads of dead things, and the colors are all of a sudden jarring green and Seahawks blue. Whereas everything else is rich with warm cream and beige tones.

"I don't lie. And you made me lie so you owe me the details. I said near West Hollywood because I didn't know how much money you made in your fake life, and I figured that was a neighborhood you could afford that I knew the name of. What is going on, sissy?"

She pulls her legs up underneath her. We're both in her "cozies," as she calls them, and they match. The flowy pink pants and floppy V-neck shirts that make us look like we're in a cult.

"Oh, Mags. It's a mess. A fucking mess. I told him just about everything."

"That's great!" She is so sweet, but she doesn't know the full extent of my shit show life. I burrow a little deeper into her soft and cozy couch. My pullout is not this comfortable. I'd like to move into this couch and pull this blanket over my head and disappear for a while.

"After we spent the most perfect night together, and I told him I love him."

"Oh." She sips her tea.

"Yeah." I tuck the throw under my chin.

"How did he take it?" Maggie leans forward as if what I'm saying is the most important thing in the world.

"Mags, I'm here. And not with him. How do you think it went?"

"But you saw him!"

I don't know how she does it, but she seems to make everyone feel that way when they're talking to her.

I inhale and exhale everything. "Well, I flew to LA to pretend I live there and after we spent the night—"

Maggie puts her hand up like a stop sign. "Wait. You flew to LA?" I sit up a bit to face her.

"Yeah. One of the Slippery Seniors bought me a plane ticket because he was headed to West Hollywood to find me."

"Why?" She cocks an eyebrow.

"Because he loved me too."

"Loved?"

"As in before I told him what a horrible person I am. It's past tense now." My voice drops a bit as I try to hold off tears.

"We'll see. Love has a sneaky way of not disappearing." She shrugs and it's adorable.

"How are you the most optimistic person in the world?"

"It's easier than being upset all the time." She glances around the room and winces a little when her eyes pass over the dead animal den.

"How's your life?"

Her face pinches up for a second, then her chipper voice returns, "Great. Kevin and I are painting pottery tomorrow, and this weekend we're going to see the hot-air balloons at dawn."

"Your life is a Hallmark movie." I sip the tea she made for me. Tastes a bit like a candle, but she's sweet so I'll drink it.

Her voice is bubbling and sincere, "Thank you! I love that."

"Thank you," I say, because she's the only steadfast nonjudgmental thing in my life. Always has been. I judge myself enough for the two of us, so I like that her role remains constant.

"For what?" Maggie asks. She honestly doesn't know.

"For putting up with my miserable ass."

"You make life interesting. Go start fixing this. And don't count Tony out just yet, He's incredibly busy with the launch, right?"

"I totally forgot. He's worked so hard on it. I forgot it's this week. See, I'm the most selfish person ever." I moan and toss a pillow over my head.

Maggie says, "Yeah, because all people stop their lives to take care of their parents and then become doctors. You selfish hussy."

209

I laugh. "You know what I mean." I peek out from behind my pillow and Maggie has settled back into her couch opposite my own. I've decided I own this couch now. It's that good.

"Did you know he took a month off from work? Not now but after the big mucky muck cooking launch thing? He's apparently never taken a vacation for real." I cross my legs under her and pause to think about that. Why would he do that?

I say, "I didn't. Colt?"

"Yeah. He told me." She shouldn't still be chatting with him. It's dangerous for her.

"Are you two friends?"

"I, uh." Maggie bites the side of her lip and doesn't fully answer me.

I kind of scold her. "Stop talking to him. He's married with kids. And you know this, you're not the cheating type. And emotional cheating is a thing."

"It's not like that. We don't bitch about our marriages or confide secrets. It's more casual. Other than you, he was the best friend I ever had. We honestly are just friends. But Kevin doesn't like it, so I'll probs stop talking to him."

I stare at her. She never steps out of line, but this doesn't feel right.

"I know what it looks like, but I've never hidden my friendship from my husband. But I'll stop."

I cock my head towards her.

She leaps up and shakes her arms out and says, "I get it. I do. I'm no cheater."

"No, but you are a flirt. Don't dance that line, sweetie."

"I won't and neither will he." I stand up and hug her. She smiles weakly and says, "Do you want to study while I lesson plan? We can go to the craft room which has a giant table."

"Ugh, I need a tutor. Biochem is killing me and after fucking up class today." I pick up my book and then lean against the edge of her couch. I don't want to think about anything except for peptides.

"Hey, sorry. I didn't mean to bring you down with the talk of gathering around my perfect craft table." She grins but then sees my face that I can no longer hide from anyone. My face has fallen, and it can't get up. She scoots over to me and puts her arm around me. And it all flows out instantly. I sob in her arms.

"What if..." I blubber out.

She says brightly, "Exactly, what if!"

I need to focus on getting through each day, knowing he might never be a part of it. I'll return to the half person I was, but at least that person will be living completely in her truth. And hopefully, one day, be a doctor that helps people.

After a while Maggie says, "Is now when we get to dust you off and figure out what we're doing next?"

"Soon."

She holds me tighter, and I relax into her arms. All of this feels unfinished. I just don't know what to do about any of it.

I turn off my phone and push open the rec center doors, and two of the three Slips are waiting on me. Dottie is taking a greasy hiatus because her man was tired of slippery sheets.

"There you are! You owe us some answers. We're so incredibly curious! And Barton said he'll be here to quiz you on some liver functions later," Chelle says, but there's a different rhythm to her voice. She's usually more upbeat than this. I look around the room.

"Where's Lana?"

Julia looks down at her feet.

I panic. "What's wrong?"

Chelle touches my arm. "Her heart was out of rhythm."

"Is she ok?" My stomach bottoms out and I hold it for support. It's the worst part of working here. I know rationally these people are towards the end of their lives, but they're so vibrant and my friends.

"She's over in the med center," Julia answers quietly.

I take her greasy hand. "Then let's go."

I chat with the doctor on call, and he lets me in on some of the med stuff because I'm pre-med. I also have clearance because I'm on her list of medical releases. She has congestive heart failure, and a new heart isn't the answer at ninety-one.

Chelle is rubbing her arms with their prized body oil, and I smile as the women care for her. She doesn't have children or a family. Lana's husband died about fifteen years ago.

I stand behind Julia. Lana smiles weakly at me when I enter the room. She pulls her oxygen down and says in a gravelly voice, "Tell me a story, dear girl."

"I will. Do you want the fairy tale or the Dateline version?"

"Always the fairy tale."

I sit on the edge of her bed and tell the women the fairy tale. I tell them that he's returning to Boston to pack up his life. He's moving us into a beautiful home right here in Las Vegas, so I can keep going to med school and working. That I can stay close to my parents and that I'll be in their lives.

She struggles to breathe, then moves her mask again slowly. "Liar." Her lips curl up. "It's not too late to change everything. I see you. You deserve it all."

I squeeze her hand, and I don't think I can watch. I may not be a doctor yet, but I know. As does everyone in the room. My story doesn't matter anymore. My heartbreak will still be there when we get through what's about to happen. I know it will still be there because it never went away in the first place.

Chelle talks to her, and Julia cries silently as she glances at her friends, and they all exchange a loving look.

I turn back, grin, and say, "Thank you for being my fairy godmother. I'll see what I can do about turning it around." My voice cracks, and Chelle scolds me.

"No. Not yet. And the most important thing we need you to do is figure out whatever you screwed up, and how you're going to fix it and get that man."

Julia says, "Do you love him?"

I squeeze Lana's foot and answer earnestly, "Completely."

She pulls her mask down and rasps out, "Then there's still hope. Adventure awaits you, dear girl."

My breath catches, and my body freezes. Is she a witch? A prophet? What the hell? And then she points at me as best she can as if she's casting. I grin, and I leave her to say goodbye to her soulmates.

It's empty around here. I don't know how else to explain it. I'm baffled at how a 110-pound person could have taken up so much space. The service was delayed due to a water main break. They cremated her and she wants her things shipped far and wide to people she loved and knew around the world. Lana once told me the only reason she was in Henderson was because her husband brought her here. She felt closest to him here. They met later in life, and she'd follow him anywhere he wanted to go. She had twenty-six years with him. She said he was her second act and so she stayed in the area, traveling about, but always coming home. Without any real family to make the arrangements, Twisty Acres said we could have the service as soon as everything was cleaned up. The girls plan to take a trip to Lana's favorite place in Puerto Rico to spread her ashes and then put her house there up for sale.

Chelle and Julia have packed up and are slowly distributing her things. They gave me her favorite scarf and several pieces of jewelry. One I think might be quite valuable is a choker necklace of onyx and diamonds. They also gave me her shoes. There was a small note from Lana on a post it that said, "For Makenzie." They're all so gorgeous. Ten pairs of designers like Michael Kors and Stuart Weitzman and a very well loved pair of red soles. I read that you can send a vintage pair back to them, and they'll resole them. I like the idea of reincarnating a sole. And that my fairy godmother left me my own glass slipper. I once told her about my French second-hand Manolos and how I sacrificed them in the name of fleeing a bad decision.

I'll wear the choker and the Louboutins to her service and then tuck them away. I don't really want to know if it's worth something because then I'd be tempted to pay off some of my student debt with it when I get done with med school.

But even worse than Lana's death is the mourning of Tony. It gets worse every day. I ran away again because I was a coward. I have to face him at some point and tell him all the truths so we can both be set free. The rec room and the little retirement village all feel empty, but I'm a husk of a person. I'm meeting Barton to help me with biochem. It wasn't on the MCAT, so I waited to take it my senior year. I applied to UNLV Med and UNR. It will be nice to be near Maggie in Reno, if I get in. She's moving to Tahoe, but that's close enough to have a shoulder to cry on.

It's funny, when I thought about med school, there was a moment, even before running into Tony, that I thought of applying to some schools in Boston. My advisor pushed for it, but I backed down. I wanted to apply to some of the ones I claimed I had gotten into ages ago. It was like I wanted to make my lies true so they could be erased. As if the wind shuffling sand off the piece of my past could dig me out of the hole I've dug for myself.

I deleted his number in extreme sadness and panic because I'm a moron. I'm a Magna Cum Laude moron, but still a moron. I know Maggie could get it, or I could text Lizzie. I could call his work, but that seems intrusive. And I was never a big enough part of his life that anyone would take my call.

I promised I wouldn't reach out but days like this when the pain of losing him and what could have been are unbearable are days I might crack. I've stayed away from his socials but I am a charter subscriber to the wildly successful, interactive app, podcast hub and recipe builder, The Cookery.

"That's the peptide. It's a chain of fatty acids, do you see how the symbols correspond?"

"Ok. If I move this here, the compound is stable?"

He cracks his hands together, and someone from across the room claps. I look up, and it's Doctor Parry.

I stand up and take a bow.

"Let me see that? I was always better with diagnostics than the chemistry bullshit, but I still remember a thing or two."

I hand him my work, and he grins. These men are the reason I did well on my MCAT. They worked with me day and night when I was finishing my junior year. Then helped me apply to the two med schools 'worth their salt' in Nevada. I found out today I got into both programs. Now, I'm waiting on the money.

I scoop up my work and wave to my tutors and head off to class. Sadly, biochemistry has become my happy place. Who says that?

LIZZIE/BETTE: Did you lie to us too?

Oh, sweet God. I guess I have to atone for it all.

MAKENZIE: Yes.

LIZZIE/BETTE: Why?

MAKENZIE: You can't really be asking that? If he told you about the lie, then he told you about my truth as well.

LIZZIE/BETTE: I just don't see the point in it. That's a lot to keep bottled up. I would have cracked wide open like a nut. I should stop typing. But seriously, that's a lot of shit to hold on to.

LIZZIE/BETTE: Did you think I would judge you? Actually, back in that day, in Paris, I probably would have, but I still would have liked you.

MAKENZIE: Still have that running-at-the-mouth thing, I see.

LIZZIE/BETTE: Mak, you were my friend. You could have talked to me.

MAKENZIE: Thank you. And I'm sorry. I didn't have a lot to be proud of at 17.

LIZZIE/BETTE: Are you really in college?

MAKENZIE: Yes. And I think that's all I can tell you about my life. We may have been friends, but you're Team Tony now. Anything he needs or wants to know, he can ask me. I love you, girl, but you are the enemy.

LIZZIE/BETTE: HA! Hardly, but I get the point. I'll be in the States in a month or so. I don't know if it's possible, but I'd like to see you and hang out. I want to be Team Makenzie as much as I can. You made me a better bitch/witch back then. And I'm happy I knew you, know you. And I want to know you better again. Does that make any kind of sense? Whatever.

I grin. I did always like her, and she always was full of words.

LIZZIE/BETTE: And for the record, and only your eyeballs —Hayden's not totally Team Tony right now. He shouldn't have let you go then or now without at least talking. I promise to find you.

MAKENZIE: That works for me. But only if it's after finals.

I turn off my phone, knowing I'll never meet up with her but feeling more rounded. He did let me go, then jumped right back in without ever really discussing anything. I have to move on, but I don't know what to do with all this love. Once you stop seeing someone, it's not like it goes away, or stuck in a box and shoved in storage. I am filled with it. It's crowding out all other emotions and becoming a problem. What do you do with all of it when there's nowhere to put it?

I'd like to cremate it and shove it into a very pretty box. Will that get rid of it? It will be more compact, but really, what is that going to accomplish? If it's compact, can I tuck it away and pull it out in moments I want to make myself really sad, like a travel-sized heartbreak.

tony

I sling my charger into my bag and hoist my maroon camp chair on my shoulder. Lill procured this chair, and it's kind of genius the way it fits in a bag. It's been about a month since Mak decided what our future should be. Her key problem is she decided something that was a joint decision. I know Lizzie talked to her, but she won't let me in on that action.

I've taken matters into my own hands like the girls in Phoenix told me to. *Gots to get the answers.* She won't return my DMs and blocked my phone. I have no other choice but to go ridiculous, but I'm pretty sure this plan will work. Eventually.

I glance down at my phone and there's a bunch of questions I'll need to contend with for work.

The Cookery is fucking tearing shit up. The three podcasts are solid, and all hit number one in different categories on Apple, Spotify, and Google in the last two weeks. I know shit will even out, but it works. The data is insane all of it is working and the money is rolling in.

The interactive cooking live streams on TikTok, Instagram, and Facebook are pulling in master chefs, money, and numbers. Paramount and Netflix, want to talk about large-scale. We own the platforms and the content. We're not shoving other people's stuff onto Ladd services, we're a complete production house now. And I'm discovering the possibilities, if we can get a hold of it all, are limitless.

My COO, Robin, is in control while I do some important work on myself, but I'm never out of touch totally.

So, yeah, I earned some time off to go a little crazy. Other than getting married or engaged, I worked my ass off and loved every fucking second of it. After the Bugle nightmare and the several bil I blew on that bullshit deal, this one. Big swings buried me, but this big swing might set me free.

And that brings me to my current mission.

I grab the box of doughnuts and the tray of coffees. I push open the door, and the smell of tape and cardboard envelopes me. It's starting to be a comfort. I might miss it when it's gone —when I finally get the thing I came here for. Stubborn, prideful thing. She's an idiot if she thought she could shake me that easily. Unless she's killed someone and has been lying about that, I'm pretty sure we could maybe figure this shit out.

"Morning, fabulous and noble people of my favorite mailbox place. And to you, kind sir."

"Tony! What did you bring me this morning, hun?"

I place my chair and my bag down near the entrance and approach the counter.

"You look busy, is it bubble mailer day again?"

"Yeah, you know us. Tuesdays are for bubbles." Mary Margaret laughs at her own joke. On Tuesday, they do a big bulk mailing for a local candle company that ships their products out of here.

"A chai latte for the lady." I hand it to Mary Margaret's younger coworker.

"Tony, thank you. You don't have to bring us drinks every day."

"I like to. Just say thank you and take a doughnut."

Fred pops his head out. "Is that Tony?"

"Is that Sorter Fred?" He's not always here, but they like to have him here on Tuesdays and on eBay Saturdays. There's a dude who does eBay like a religion, and always does a mass mailing.

"Good morning to you, Mr. Tony!"

I hand him a tall cup of coffee with four Splendas. He likes it fake sweet. He sips it and looks at me, tipping his imaginary hat. "Perfect."

I grab my own coffee and a scone from the box and set up in front of the mailboxes.

Carissa brings me a tall box.

"Thank you." She started doing that last week so I could use it as a desk. Even though I'm officially off work, I check emails for a couple of hours a day. And then, I take suggestions from the crew as to what to watch while I wait. I've binged *The Marvelous Mrs. Maisel* and the not-quite-satisfying reboot of *Sex and the City* this week. It's nice to spend time with the girls again, but I miss Samantha and can't help but be sad that Stanford died in real life.

I open my camp chair and arrange my world in front of PO box 148. It's my third week here. On Saturday, they close at four, and I head to Boston for a couple nights, but I'm always here by ten on Mondays.

She has to check her mail at some point. It's the only connection I have to her. Since she's been lying, I don't even know where to start looking. I could sit on campuses around here, but this seemed like a more targeted approach. Maggie has stonewalled Colt because her husband didn't like them talking, so she's not a resource anymore. Lizzie claims she has zero idea where she is. I'll allow it since Hayden tortured her with his tongue when he asked her.

So, here I sit. The mailbox crew can't legally give me any information on her, and I respect that. I haven't even told which box I'm staking out. I don't even mention her name because I'm afraid of two things. One: I don't want them to get into legal postal trouble. And two: I need an ambush. I don't want her to know ahead of time I'm here. I don't want her to run. So, they let me sit here every day.

The door opens, and Mr. Santee, the eBay guy, enters.

"Must be a busy Tuesday. Any more in the car?" He hooks his thumb towards his car. I head outside, gather the rest of his packages, and deliver them to Mary Margaret to weigh and label.

"Thank you, Tony."

"Help yourself to a doughnut. I didn't know you were coming in today, or I would have grabbed you a tea." I gesture because this week, I've been bringing them the good stuff my concierge gets for me. The first two weeks, I felt I needed to be close to the Henderson mailbox place, so I was at the glamorous local little hotel/motel for $86 a night. I've got the room booked out for a month. I imagine this is what camping is like, but the outdoors probably smell better. The only spoiled rich guy thing I did was overnight Frente sheets, and I hired my own cleaning crew. But I couldn't take it, so I went back to being a spoiled trust fund kid and moved to a suite with three bedrooms on the Strip.

Neither of them feels right. I know who I am in this camp chair sharing pastries, but the rest of it is up for fucking grabs until I figure out my little witch.

My very favorite Mailboxes R US duo arrives. Two daffy women who always smell like a massage room at a second-rate spa. They recently lost a friend and have been mailing her belongings to people all over the world. Apparently, this woman had houses and friends all over, but no blood-related family. As these ladies sift through her stuff, they keep coming across addresses or names written on the back of pictures or trinkets. The stories of Lana are kind of legendary.

I hop up from my camp chair again and meet them in the parking lot. I'm in a t-shirt that says, "It's good to be the king." The assholes gave it to me when I graduated high school. Just as we retired our Knights of the Round Table bullshit. I rub my hands on my dark jeans and pull my sunglasses out of their tucked spot in the neckline of my shirt. I slip on the aviators and wait for the ladies to park.

The driver, Chelle, is all done up. These women always glisten a little too much, but they're adorable.

"Woo, you are a fine man today, Tony! I don't know what I'm going to do without my daily eye candy when we're done with this project."

I laugh. "And I won't know where to put my affection. You're the best part of my day."

"Honey, can you grab the boxes?" Julia hops out and kisses my cheek.

"Any sign of your secret lady friend?" Chelle inquires.

"Nope. Not yet, but still hopeful." I pick up the boxes and glance at Julia, who's wiping a tear. "Why the sadness?" I nudge her shoulder.

"Well, tomorrow's Lana's service and I guess I'm not ready to say goodbye. This is the last of her things. Then it's just the two of us against the world."

Chelle holds open the door for me.

"A formidable twosome if ever there was." I wink at her. I don't know what to say to them.

I place the boxes on the counter, and Julia sets about weighing and paying for them to be scattered around the world.

I sit back in my chair and with my laptop. I sip on my coffee when Chelle comes over.

"Tony, this sad story of yours. The one where you had the girl and then were an idiot and lost the girl, twice."

"I'm familiar with it."

"We have a friend who has a similar story. Would you be in the market to meet someone?" I grin at this well-meaning gal, but I'm not really into an age-gap situation. I don't want to date a friend of theirs.

I put my hand on her arms. "That's so sweet of you. But my girl, my little witch, she's it. She's the only one, and if I can't get it together with her, then it's a life of meaningless sex and loneliness for me." She laughs, but I'm serious. I love Makenzie so fucking much that I've been sitting in front of her PO box for almost three weeks, waiting just to talk to her and see if she's who I think she is. And I don't think she knows that she's worth the fight. She's worth it all, and I intend to show her. If I can find her. I know I lost the bet since we technically dated. My father will kill me if I get engaged before this messy divorce has even been monetarily settled, or the board has signed off on this quarter and the shareholders are stable, but here I am, in Henderson, Nevada, waiting on my little spellcaster and avoiding everything else. Like I should have done when she walked out of my life twelve years ago. I didn't realize in her bold move to save face and a difficult situation that I was the real coward. It's why I'm here instead of hiring someone to find her. I have to do this myself.

Julia approaches us, and her eyes are red again.

"Tony, it was the nicest thing to meet you. This terrible time was lightened a bit by your smiling, sexy face. Your girl is a lucky one, I hope you find her."

"I will." I stand to hug these women. The first day we met, they were in the store for close to two hours. I told them the same abbreviated version I've shared with Mary Margaret and crew.

Chelle hugs me, too, and I squeeze this darling ball of elderly goodness, despite the grease stains that will end up on my clothing.

"Let me know if there's anything I can do for you. Lana sounds like she was quite the pissar." My Boston slips out.

"There's a service for her tomorrow. Would you like to come?"

Julia says, "It's at four and that's almost closing time here. I don't want you to miss your opportunity with your lady, but it would mean a lot to us." I do have a room at the gross hotel for the night. I can do this, and it would be nice to have companionship outside of a quick mail place.

When I lost my grandmother, I thought about all the lives she'd touched. She was a formal and harsh woman but loved my brother and me beyond anything. I feel like she still touches and changes people, much like this woman I never met. I see her effect on these two, and these women are so in my corner, how can I say no.

"Ok. Give me the information."

They leave, and I sit back in my chair and wait for the love of my life to come back to me.

mak

My mother and father look great. They left their hogs at home and walked to the service. Mom's using a cane, but she uses it less and less each day. She and I are starting to see the value in believing in ourselves. I arrive early to talk to the box that used to be Lana.

"I did it. I got an A in biochem. I'm still getting a B in statistics because of the whole missing a class thing." I pause and put my hand on the box.

My mom shuffles over to me. I'm fine if they want to live out their lives here as long as they live. She's been hiding for so long behind her weight or her maladies she forgot she loves to garden or be outdoors. I went to Paris partly because she once told me she'd always wanted to see it but knew she never would. I want to take her there someday and show her my Paris.

I think it was a pivot for me when she told me that. I wanted to make sure I was never that resigned in life. That there wasn't an adventure I couldn't take. Adventure. It hurts just as badly as it did the moment I walked away from him. What I saw as reckless and impossible when I was younger now seems like it might have been the right path.

I'm standing between a woman who tried everything and a woman who's tried nothing. And I'm leaning towards the Lana life philosophy and hope my mom joins me in choosing to be a little reckless but truthful. I don't want to deny who I am anymore.

But if my mom can walk up to me and learn to live without sugar and shame, maybe if she keeps trying, I can remember what it's like to do that too. Med school at almost thirty is ridiculous and could be considered reckless. Still, I've been hiding behind fixing my past for so long that I forgot I have a future.

I put my hand on the box and look at my mom, and tears just flow. I'm sad she's gone, I'm sorry I let myself disappear, and I'm devastated I walked away from Tony.

"My darling, Leech."

I bury my head in my mother's shoulder. The space is filling up, I hear it, and I'm fine that they're seeing me crying. They can think I'm mourning Lana. I am. I wish I could listen to her yell at me to get my life back in gear one more time.

"Mom. I love him so much. I don't know what to do." She holds me closer, and she's not wobbly on her feet or shifting her weight. She's steadfast, and I'm so grateful for her. She smooths my dark hair that I let hang straight for today. I did put on makeup that's now ruined.

"I know, baby. If I could take this pain from you, I would. I've gotten a little too good at pain management. Don't hide from this. Feel it. That's what we've learned, baby, we have to feel the yucky stuff so we can feel the good things too."

I laugh through my blubbering.

I lift my head, and Chelle and Julia come into view. They're dressed in lavish matching pastel gowns and tiaras. They're honoring Lana in the best way possible. And they're escorted by a young, blond, handsome—what the fuck is even happening?

I can't breathe. I can't do anything.

"Mak, you ok? Why are you so white?" Barton yells from the corner. "Get Parry, I think she's going into shock."

Scott yells, "She could use a little shock after the stunts she pulls."

Dottie yells at Scott, "Leave Mak alone. She's a good one. You just cheat at games and Makenzie's good at catching you."

His head snaps from looking at the ground to my direction when Dottie yells my name. We're frozen in a gaze that might define the rest of our life. My heart is heavy, filled with lead and light, as helium leaks from a balloon.

"Honey," my mom whispers. "Honey, what is it?" I point down the makeshift aisle. I keep hesitating. She turns and says, "Is that him? That's your man?" I nod.

Someone behind my mom points out, "Hey, lookie here. Is that Tony from Mailboxes R US?" Mr. Santee says, "What's Tony doing here?"

I shake my head and realize half the people here are saying hello to him. Hell, Mary Margaret is hugging him. What the fuck is going on? My jaw drops, and my knees buckle, and before I know it, he's gently removing me from my mom and taking me in his arms.

"Ma'am, I've got it from here." He smiles at my mother, and she clutches her heart and squeezes his arm. Then she wobbles off to a chair.

Chelle screams, "Hells bells, Tony, why didn't you say it was Mak?"

There's noise, and all the chatter fades into a mess of white noise, things we can discard so we can focus on each other.

The touch, the smell, and the sound of him humming a slow song all work together to awaken my entire being. I return to myself in his arms. And just like that, I fall completely apart, and he's the only one who can help me put myself back together. He's holding me, and everyone around me is staring. And I know Lana had one more trick up her sleeve and one more spell to cast.

He kisses my hair softly and whispers repeatedly, "Shh. I'm here. I'm here." We stay entwined for moments beyond appropriate at a memorial service.

I snuggle harder into him and let all my remorse, grief, and anxiety flow onto Tony's chest. This has to be a mirage in my desert. He can't be here with me.

He eventually guides me to a couple of chairs, and I don't look around us. I focus on sitting and remaining connected to him. I have a hard grip on his hand, and he doesn't say anything about it.

When the local pastor speaks, I dare to look up at him. Tony's gazing back at me. He lets go of my hand and wipes the mascara from under my eyes, smiling.

"You're a mess, Preston." I stifle a laugh. He leans into my ear, his lips close enough to feather over the shell of it and give chills up and down my spine. "But I happen to be an expert at messes. Something dumb fuck-ups have in common."

My body surges with something kind of unfamiliar to me. It's not lust, and it's not the electric pulse I usually feel around him. It's more like a fuzzy blanket. He's the calm and comfort I deny myself.

Our attention snaps to the front when Chelle speaks. His arm stays firmly planted around me, and I rest my head on his shoulder. He weaves his fingers in and out of mine in a languid and slow pattern. The repetition stretches out all the tense parts of my brain and soul, like a good yoga pose.

"There will never be another Lana. And that sucks. She lit up the world and my life when I thought there wouldn't be anything to look forward to after my husband died. She was a kindred soul always wanting to find the fun and good in a situation. And it's goddamned unique to be this age, when you're finally past the bullshit. Past the worry about what sags where or will there be traffic to get to that meeting that I really don't care about. I fucking love being eighty-five, and she made us all remember we're not dead yet. No need to sit around and wait for it, it's coming at some point. Get your ass up and go do something. Today, I'll take a moment to be sad, then Julia and I are getting on a plane and flying to Puerto Rico to sit at one of her houses and have one last cocktail for her. And then we'll go looking for some cock. Some stranger danger that might get us in the best kind of trouble."

Everyone erupts in laughter, and Chelle places her hand on Lana's sparkly box of an urn. The girls in craft hour bedazzled it. She kisses her hand and touches it one more time, squeezing her eyes closed as if telling her tears, this is it, get out. She exhales and heads down the aisle. She squeezes Tony's shoulder, then grins at me. And I don't know what to make of all of this.

The party moves down the street to the wine bar, where I've arranged with the owners for a little reception. Being in Twisty Acres village, the wine bar does exceptionally well and has plenty of scooter parking and wheelchair tables. I should run and check on the arrangements, but I'm afraid if I move, the spell will be broken, and he'll disappear.

Everyone has cleared out, and he removes his arms from me. I knew it would happen at some point. We can't live entwined. We will have to eat, sleep, and bathe, but I'm still not ready to face all of what he has to say.

He turns toward me, and I scoot over, putting a chair's distance between us.

I wipe my eyes and fix my dress. Then I gesture to him to start talking.

"Go ahead. Hit me."

He laughs. "You've got to be kidding. Little witch, you're the one with the tale to tell." I shift my weight, and he stares at me while he crosses his legs. He extends his hand and I shake it, not sure where he's going with this.

"Hi. I'm Tony Ladd. Of the Ladd Media Group. A division of Ladd Industries and Technologies. A company founded by my great-grandfather and built by my grandfather, maintained by my father. I grew up in Boston and Martha's Vineyard. I prepped at Xavier Academy in New Jersey. I have one brother named Dax, who doesn't talk nearly as much as I do, and had the balls to basically reject the life he was groomed to lead. My friends, Hayden, Robbie, Lawrence, and Colton are like blood to me. I've known them since I was little. I had nannies, drivers, and vacations that were photographed for major magazines. I've been engaged twice, married three times, and am currently at the end of a media-heavy, nasty divorce. I love modern art because it speaks to the chaos inside of me and is still beautiful. I own several paintings and sculptures worth millions. I will inherit in the billions. I've never felt like I deserved any of it, that I was always the fuck-up who lucked into a life he didn't deserve. But now I'm learning how to accept my advantages and use them for the greater good. And to get a fucking life of my own."

"Amen to that." I hold up my hand and he high-fives me with a grin.

He recrosses his legs and cocks his head. "I'm a good person, and one who has always been determined to succeed, even if I didn't feel like I was doing it right. I was the one running to catch up with proving myself. I've never felt like I was good enough, smart enough, or completely myself except in one place for a brief time that changed the core of who I am as a person. I need none of the things or trappings or houses or pieces of art. Nothing matters except that one thing I used to have, and I thought I got back. That's who I am on paper, but that's not who I am. Now. Who are you?"

I laugh as I see Julia approaching us. She's all shiny and sparkly. She grins and hands us each a giant glass of wine.

"Thanks," I say.

"Tony, why didn't you tell us you were him?" Julia says, and squeezes his shoulder. He covers her hand with his.

"I didn't realize you knew Mak." He shrugs and she kisses him on the cheek and toddles off.

"I'm so sorry about Lana." He looks at me.

My voice catches in my throat. "Thanks. Did you know her? Is that why you're here?" I'm so freaking confused.

"No. I never had the pleasure. But I met Chelle and Julia three weeks ago at Mailboxes R US when they began shipping Lana's items."

I lean forward with my eyebrows high on my head. "Wait. Like Henderson Mailboxes R US?"

He nods. "You really should pick up your mail more often."

"You've been to my PO box!" I smack his arm.

He laughs and says, "I've been camped in front of it every day for three weeks."

"YOU'RE THE WEIRD DOUGHNUT GUY who brings the good coffee at the mailbox place? Everyone was talking about you at work."

"Start there."

"Start where?"

He asks, "What do you do for a living? We'll get to my postal stalking in a minute."

I hesitate, and he pulls at my hand. "Tell me. It's ok."

I bite my top lip and blow out a large breath. "How far back do you want it?"

"To the first lie."

I need air, so we're walking and talking about nothing and everything. I'm not sure I know how to unravel a lifetime of fuck-ups and lies. I'll try his method.

I breathe in and out, and I let it flow. "Hi. I'm Makenzie Suzanne Preston. I'm an only child, raised in an up-on-blocks double-wide trailer in Reno that used to be kind of nice until it wasn't. I have parents who love me even if I've doubted it from time to time. My fault, not theirs. My parents have some issues, but who doesn't? My mom ate her feelings for a long time. I'm ashamed there was a moment in middle school when I was embarrassed by her, but what goes around comes around. She had her turn to be embarrassed by me. My father held in all the stress of raising me and caring for her. Hence, his heart attack that interrupted our French tryst. I escaped from them as often as possible so their life wouldn't rub off on me. I started going out and getting in trouble when I was thirteen. My first arrest at fourteen was for blowing up mailboxes."

He scoffs and laughs. "SAME! See, we really did grow up exactly the same." I laugh, and his eyes crinkle up in a giant smile that colors my dusty, drab world.

"I lost my virginity at fifteen and kept a steady rotation of people to help me forget my parents were poor, depressed, overwhelmed, and overweight. I didn't notice because I was too busy not graduating and making sure everyone who came close to me got stung with either my attitude or a cruel tone. And I made sure to not go to school. I skated by for years on Ds and an occasional C, bribing people to write papers. In the end, my attendance my senior year caught up to me. I went out more. I partied harder. I studied even less. Because what was the point, I was only going to end up poor, unhappy, and stuck. When the factory closed while I was in France, they decided to move us to Vegas so they could start working in the casinos. Once my father recovered, he got a pretty good job, and they had great health care, but that's when their depression amped up or at least got diagnosed. They're good with each other and me, but they don't love crowds. They coped in their way. My mother ate more, and my father collected things and filled our new, small condo with crap. They'd take memorabilia from anyone who offered it. I didn't graduate from high school and was the town slut, party girl, and fuck-up."

Tony winces. I get it. I'm not ashamed of those words anymore, they're just labels someone else gave me.

He says, "Be kinder to yourself." And the man knocks the wind out of me. I grin through instant tears, but I decide to blink them away. Damn, I'm in love with him.

I hold up a finger and finish. "But once in Vegas I took it to a whole new level. No one ever expected me to see twenty-two without being pregnant, in jail, or a raving lunatic. I worked off the Strip in a bar that would let me work drunk until I looked around one day and decided we all needed a different life. That's who I am on paper. But it's not who I am. Nice to meet you, Tony."

He sits down on the edge of a bench. He says nothing, and it's killing me. I've never laid it all out like that before. This is so painful. It's like everything in the world has stopped breathing while I wait.

"And who are you really?" he asks, keeping his distance.

"I'm a college student."

"What the fuck?"

I grin and continue. "Yeah. One who's about to graduate Magna Cum Laude. I'm a senior recreational facilitator, a girl who wanted to study to help her parents and herself. We all understand, now, that we do not process things well. I'm the girl who sold all their collections that were cluttering our lives and house so they could buy their dream home here in Twisty Acres."

"Seriously? You really are Chelle and Julia's friend. And you live with your parents?"

I nod. "My parents were never the problem. I was. I was stupid and thought I was destined to live their life."

He scoffs. "That's familiar."

"And when I realized I didn't have to, it was almost too late for me. Almost. My parents denied good things except for each other for a long time, a habit I picked up."

We stand and walk side by side but not quite together. We're out of sync, but I guess that happens sometimes in the getting-to-know-you phase.

"I hope someday I have a partnership like theirs, and living their life isn't a terrible idea, but I realized I should probably get one of my own. I stay in their back room and have a mountain of student loans and debt. I give them what I can for food and towards the mortgage. I own a piece-of-shit car. I'm happy except I lost the one thing I can't quite get over giving away. But I'm not a fuck-up or a slut anymore."

"That's a shame." His lip curls up to the right. Oh, thank God for that lip curl. My body zings with love for this man.

I shrug. "Ok, maybe the slut thing is true, but these days only for you."

"Best answer. But the lies. Unwind them now. I get the why, but I need to know they're done."

He puts his hands on my shoulders and his forehead to mine. He keeps talking. "I know this is hard. But I've had too many liars, cheats, and wannabes in my life. You were the only authentic thing, and now, I need to know everything, or I have to walk away. I need to know at least we were true, even if your glamorous home life wasn't. I gots to know the deets."

I laugh at him and nod. Then I walk ahead so I can get this next part out. "I scammed a church congregation into paying for my trip to Paris. I knew a diploma wasn't going to happen. I felt that getting stoned, drunk, fucking around, stealing cars, and hanging out was much more important than pulling up my English lit grade."

He puts a hand on my cheek. "Oh, wild little witch, you do realize that prep school isn't all that different. We just studied., or our fathers bought our grades." I shove him a bit and he smiles.

"Well, I forgot to do that part."

"Study?"

"No, get a wealthy daddy." His eyebrows twitch, then he licks his lips. "Different kind of daddy, but we can revisit." He waggles them again, and I laugh.

We stroll forward and I continue, "The more my grades tanked, the more I didn't think I was smart enough to actually learn."

"Your parents?"

"Horrified at my behavior. I caused them so much stress. I had a lot of microwave meals if I came home at all. I pushed them away as I spiraled. Maggie was my only friend that wasn't a burner. She and I would still get together, and when she decided to go to France, she convinced me to go too. She didn't know I was barely hanging on in school. I told her when we were in France. But I had no money to even get there in the first place, and Maggie said I should try for a scholarship."

"And the church people..."

"I showed up on Sundays in my best dresses and glad-handed, volunteered to bring meals to shut-ins. I was a total lie during the day and a disaster at night. Instead of studying, I worked at the church for the money to go to Paris. The school agreed after I sweet-talked them and turned in some missing assignments, which I convinced a church kid to do. I was passing enough to go. With the caveat I had to repeat my senior year."

I shrug because that's the worst of it.

"Holy shit." Gasps out of his lips. Cool, wasn't sure I could surprise him.

I continue, "Literally. I became a holy shit. But I still haul my ass to Reno once a month to do odd jobs for them. The ones who remember have forgiven me and told me it's ok. But I show up anyway."

We walk around the corner, and I grin at the tiny, fake town that was created at the center of the community. The colors are all bright like it's Disney or what I think a Caribbean island town looks like. It's so out of place here in the desert. I wander forward then glance back with a shy smile.

"Come on, I'll show you around my home."

Tony cocks his head to the side. "And you have nothing to do with Los Angeles?"

I pop a hip and glare at him. "Tony, this will go a lot faster if you accept I lied about all of it."

We float next to each other, and he brushes his hand across mine. I don't think I've earned a handhold yet, but we're closer.

After a while, he says, "This church?"

"Yeah?"

"Do they need new pews or something? Maybe an organ? Can I buy them carpet or a jungle gym?" He removes his jacket and slings it over his arm. His shirt buttons tug a bit as if they want to remind me of his gorgeous chest.

My eyes are wide. "Why would you do that?"

"Because they believed in you enough to bring you to me. Without them, we wouldn't exist. I'll forever be grateful to those saps and suckers that they were taken in by a heathen witch." He grins, and I'm crying, but this time it's happy.

"They need a new roof patch over the chapel."

He pulls me to him, and my breath is gone. He kisses me with perfect soft pressure. It's the dawn of a new day. It's Valley of Fire all over again. It's a chance. "I'll pay you back."

"I'll never be able to repay them for you, so don't worry about it. I'll patch it."

I cock an eyebrow and say, "You're going to buy them a whole new roof, aren't you?"

"Yes." He doesn't hesitate to say, so I don't hesitate either.

"I love you." I stand by those words that seem to only belong to him. I shift my weight back and forth.

"That's good because I'm not sure how I can explain away that expense otherwise." He jokes. "Let's move on. Paris." There's so much, I can't expect him to tell me he loves me. Perhaps church roof buying is his love language. Fingers crossed.

He approaches me, and we walk side by side. "My Paris lies were to cover up my lack of scholastic achievement. I never went to class and never got into college, obviously."

"You never went once?"

I shake my head. "I explored the city a lot. And worked at a secondhand clothing store while you were all studying. Not even Maggie knew that one. I had a sap in each class sign me in and occasional assignments were handed in. Some were done by me. Mostly the science ones. When you kept asking me to come to Boston, I floated Northeastern because you were going to Harvard. And, in reality, I was hoping the church didn't press charges for fraud instead of deciding between colleges."

"All this lying seems exhausting."

"You have no clue. And in hindsight I should have just done the fucking math workbooks and art projects. Would have been a lot less stressful."

He says nothing. Then finds a wall near the bike path and leans up against it. He's in a navy suit, light yellow shirt, and stunning vibrant silk tie that blazes with orange and red. His hair is producted up, and his dark scuff is just coming in. And then there's his blue eyes, deep and full of pain and something else. I hope it's hope.

"So, it's a pattern and not me?" He asks.

"Yes, but a lot of the lies revolve around you. The money's a hard thing to deal with."

"You should have told me that." He shakes his head.

"At eighteen, no. Now, yeah, I should have." I shrug and shuffle my feet a bit.

"And the rest of Paris. All the things we said and did? The things we shared. Lies?"

"I meant what I said. You're the only absolute truth in my entire life. And I'll fight to deserve you."

tony

Her hair is luminous in the hot sun, and her black dress is floating all around her in the very slight breeze. Her dark eyes are so full of pain, but there's a dimension to them I've never seen before. It's like I finally have all of her in front of me. She's waiting for me to respond. She's rocking on her fancy heels, and I have no choice but to love her. But can I live with her and have her? That's the fuck of it all. I love her, and I always will, but I'm not sure if I won't end up devastated. Or if she's fucking lying to me now.

I grab her face and kiss her hard. She clings to me the way I'm clinging to us making it through this.

"My head is so turned around, my love." I run my hands through my hair and look over the manufactured lake and see a rainbow spray of a fountain. For a moment, I'm transported to the Bellagio, when she and I visited them early after the sunrise before we parted.

Her breath hitches. "You still love me."

"That's never been the problem. How do I know you're not going to leave me like you have twice?" I say my biggest fear and I shuffle my feet and look around.

"It's not in my immediate plans," she says, drawing my face back to hers nipping at my bottom lip.

"And those would be..." I grin.

"Anything you want. To get through the rest of this, I need to be with you. If we break up then let this be the end and if we find our way, then let this be the beginning of a new era of Mak and Tony."

"Either way I get laid, right?" I whisper ghosting over her lips.

She kisses me so fucking deeply it's like I can feel her everywhere. We thrash and moan and gasp releasing all our tension.

I say with a lilt in my voice, "I'm trying to trust you but I love you so very much."

She laughs hard, and then she doesn't. Her face straightens out as she adjusts herself away from my rising cock. It's as if she wants this sentence to be taken more seriously than our situation deserves.

"And I'll always love you. As I always have."

My body fills with confidence and warmth I've only ever known in her arms. "You do know we can't be together until the financial circus is settled and things in my life clear up. I hope you'll still be here when I figure it all out."

"I do and I will."

I grin widely. "That has a nice ring to it."

"NO RINGS!" She takes a stance. "And no presents. No money. I don't want any of it. Do you understand? I'm not those other women."

"But I like to give presents," I whine.

"Fine." My eyes light up. "But your limit is a hundred dollars."

"Plane tickets?" I ask, crooking my eyebrow.

"To where?"

"Clandestine getaways with me."

She crosses her arms. "I'll allow it. I don't love you for your money." I slam my lips to hers and our tongues volley in admiration that this is all that matters.

I smile and put out my hand. "Deal." She shakes, then I ask, "Can I please strip you naked and fuck your most perfect body right now and we'll sort through the rest of the shit as we go? Screw now, talk later."

"I live in my parent's sunroom." Thud. My dick just deflated. "On a pullout couch." And now it's crawling inwards.

"Suite?" I suggest not sure how I can drive with this stiff rod.

"I need to show up to the funeral reception." She explains.

That works because I need to fuck her now, and if we end up in a traffic situation, I'll have to pull over and do it in whatever shitty car she has.

"The budget motel it is." I say and she nods.

She continues to joke, but I'm seriously worried she'll get some kind of ick if I fuck her on those sheets. "I hear they have a hell of a breakfast bar."

I respond, "We can toast Lana with warm apple juice and mini yogurts."

"She'd love that." Her eyes get a little wistful, and I pull her closer. What I really want to do is buy her a house right now and a real bed. What I'm going to do is screw her on the first private surface I find.

"You know me. I'm not a snob." She raises an eyebrow. "About most things. Shit. Am I? I don't think I'm full-on, but ok."

"You could explore more of my world, but you're right, you're not a total snob."

I peck her lips. "Here's the issue: sheets. I can't grind your precious and perfect ass into the grossest, scratchiest sheets known to man. I threw away the good ones I ordered. Actually I had Lill burn them." She laughs. "Tell me there's a store where I can get good sheets."

She kisses me quickly. "Follow me."

mak

He raises his eyebrows at my car.

"You wanted the full Makenzie experience." I sweep my hand down my car like a spokesmodel.

"Do they even make Saturns anymore?" He crosses his arms and stares at it.

"It's vintage." I say unlocking the car with a key.

"There's no key fob. That's a metal key."

"Snob." I stick my tongue out at him.

"Even the non snobs in the world would agree with me on this, it's a death trap."

I can't help but giggle. He gets in and looks around. "Do you realize this is the first time other than the room you shared with Maggie I've ever been in your space."

"What do you think?"

"I hate your car. Love you. Hate your car. But at least it's tidy."

"Snob." He grits his teeth as I swing into Target and park. I turn to him, and his face is confused. "You do know what Target is, right?"

"Yes, but do they have sheets?"

"Oh my God, you over privileged man. You've never been

to Target. They have everything. Come on, get out, there's even a Starbucks inside."

We're holding hands as the doors swoosh open, and we're bathed in the chill of really good air-conditioning.

He looks around, and his eyes are wide. Then he closes them and stands under a vent. "Can I at least get the air-conditioning in your car fixed?"

"It works fine."

"Not for Nevada."

"It needs a part that they don't make anymore. It's fine."

He turns to me and puts his hands on my hips. "I'm begging you. Let me buy you a car." It would be nice but probably not today.

"Nope. Unless you can find one for a hundred bucks."

"Yours. Your car is probably blue booked at a hundred dollars. Does this place really have everything?"

"Name something." We pass by the beauty section on our way to the home section.

"Caviar." He smacks my butt.

"Asshat."

I run and jump up onto the cart and it careens down the aisle. Tony runs after me. He cages me and stops the cart.

"Young lady, is that Target behavior?" I turn and get down and kiss him quickly.

"Absolutely."

"Is this whole place divided by categories? Is there like a map or a key so I can figure them out?" he says as I pick up a pack of makeup wipes. I'm here, might as well pick up a few things.

We round the corner, and he keeps scanning the entire area and mumbling the different sections out loud to himself.

"You know most newer couples would be excited to do something domestic together, I'm finding it to be a chore to be your Sherpa through normal life."

"Get used to it, baby. This place is fucking amazing." His eyes won't stop scanning the horizon. He pushes the cart with one hand and stares at me.

I swallow big and exhale. Time to reveal the last bits of my hidden life. "No more secrets, no more lies, right?"

"If you'd like to have an actual relationship, that's the deal." He points at me while continuing to push the cart.

"I'm going to be a doctor with a family medicine practice." I giggle.

Tony's eyes bug out of his head. "What the FUCK are you even telling me? You're wicked pissah smahrt." He hugs me and spins me around in one of the Target crossroads sections. We could go left to shoes or right to housewares. "Tell me more things like this."

"I'm waiting to hear about my scholarship money..." I put my finger up to him. "No, you may not buy me med school. I got it. UNLV or Reno is going to cover me. You steer clear. Remember the rule."

"I hate rules." He shakes his head and removes his suit jacket. He places it in the seat part of the cart, then says, "Stay here."

He runs away looking manic, then grabs a man in a red polo shirt and disappears down an aisle. I slowly walk towards the bedding area.

A couple minutes there's a tinny honking behind me. He pulls into the aisle in a pink Barbie automated convertible. He barely fits on top of it.

"It's only $80.00 which is more than your car is worth." I can't stop laughing as he parks it between dog food displays. He opens the tiny fuchsia trunk and hands me a Doc McStuffins doc box.

I clutch it to my chest as he proudly proclaims, "You'll need this too. I have a boo-boo, you'll need to kiss better later, Doc."

I cover his lips with mine in a long, lingering decadent moment.

"The boo-boo is lower." He waggles his eyebrows and then says, "Nineteen ninety-nine. And apparently if I sign up and get approved for some card, we can knock 5 percent off that, baby. I'm all about the discount."

He keeps talking, and I've never really let myself be proud. I've just kept my head down and moved forward to the next school hurdle. I grin and say, "Thank you."

"Family medicine! You are amazing. You're incredible. You don't want a high-powered surgical job or a lucrative plastics position. You want to help families."

He swings me around like we're dancing, and I laugh.

I explain, "With an emphasis on treating the whole person. Helping families find balance and to understand how the mental can affect the physical. I might double major in psychology. Ultimately, I'd like a wellness practice."

He kisses me long and hard as if he can't wait for us to get to the next part.

"You need to know, I have four more years of school and then six years of another thing and then I'll go anywhere in the country that would take me on as an ancient resident. I have to accomplish something."

He settles behind the cart and pushes slowly. "Can you do these things with me, or do I have to wait another decade for my happily ever after?"

"It's a lot." I don't want to hide anything from him.

"What is?"

I grab him. "You. This. Us. Immediate and the longevity. I don't know how I can do this and I sure as fuck don't know how I don't. I so love you."

"Then we start there. Or can we start with one more thing? I need to know why."

I cock my head, confused. "Why what?"

"Why you left me."

And it's time to face that reckoning as well. Ok. "Oh, that."

"Yeah. Start talking, Doc."

He winks at me and then takes off like a cat chasing a laser dot on the floor. I push the cart over to him and he's putting on some sort of Las Vegas Raiders tie-dye Hawaiian shirt.

He turns around, puffing his chest out, and says, loud enough to scare the children near us and horrify their moms, "Would you still fuck me in this synthetic mess?"

I glance around and see some sort of macramé shirt that I'm not sure how it works, but I put it on as well as a big floppy hat that says, "Mermaid Hair Don't Care," on the brim.

"Will you still fuck me in this?" The families are scattering away from us like we took a shit in their pool.

He leans over and says, "Yes." Then he kisses me deeply.

I moan into his ear, "Prove it."

He says, "Oh, I will. And this doesn't count towards my hundred-dollar cap." We walk on with our outfits still on.

His voice shifts, "Tell me why. It's time."

I look up knowing it all has to be left here on the white-tiled floor of Target.

tony

S he squares her shoulders, takes the cart from me, and pushes on. We round the snack chips and I grab a couple bottles of water. She clearly needs a minute. I guide her to the patio furniture area, and we sit down. With a smile, she sets her floppy hat on the ground. She takes the warm Smart water and expertly opens the top in like a fucking second. I struggle to open the top and she leans over and removes some hidden pieces of bullshit plastic tab.

"You do know this is an overly complicated system to open fucking water." We lean back in our chaise lounges in the shade of a multi-stripe umbrella protecting us from fluorescent lights. I toast her with our water bottles and take a sip.

She doesn't sip, but says, "You never introduced me."

I'm confused. "To whom?"

"Anyone."

What are we even talking about? People walk by and I wave. They ignore me and saunter towards gardening tools.

She begins again, "I was a poor girl from a dusty little town with two parents who only sat on a couch and waited for their next meal or game show to begin. I had no education, no prospects, and the only thing good in my life was you."

We're raw and real in the moment suddenly among the faux backyard setups and red bullseyes everywhere.

I say, "I didn't know how to keep or protect the good in my life. I was a moron, surely you knew you were in love with a moron in Paris. That can't be a surprise." I place my water in the cupholder and unbutton my sleeves.

She inhales sharply and then steadies her hands on her knees. "I always felt as if I was going to be a story you told people about your wild time in Paris. I never felt current, especially after France," she says while cracking my heart a little. She can't think that.

"That's not true."

"It is. In France we were equals. You saw us on equal footing. We were all students without limits or parents. We carved out our own world. We were out drinking and falling into each other's beds, but when we returned to our realities. I was never a part of your life. At your birthday party I felt like an afterthought. You didn't introduce me to anyone there and I was left alone. The first time we were supposed to be a couple outside of France and I realized we weren't. Your parents made me feel intrusive so I left."

My heart plummets.

"But..." She shifts to her side, and then my bold girl looks directly at me, and I see the fire return.

"Until Vegas, and then LA."

"And, now Target." I add.

She says, "Yes, and now Target goes on the places where I felt we were on equal footing."

Thank Christ.

I roll up my sleeves and move to face her. "Who do you want to meet? My judgy Aunt Lisa? Or my parents who forbid me to date anyone seriously until I was a junior in college? And ironically, right now."

There's a silence between us, then things start hitting me

over the head. Things I should have told her but didn't because I was eighteen years old, and mostly, I was thinking about fucking her and getting away from expectations.

Harvard became my exit from the life I was groomed for. I'd put the fire out from inside the house. I studied marketing instead of economics and advertising instead of finance. I carved who I wanted to be in the wake of heartbreak and confusion left behind by my wild girl. I'm not sure I'd be proud of who I am today had she not busted us both up.

I shake my head and refocus on her, pushing my thoughts to the side. "Something's gnawing at you, go ahead. This is the only place and time to do this. Sitting on lounge chairs in a store, hungry, sweaty, raw from a funeral and three weeks spent flying in, sleeping at that nightmare motel, and eating mostly off of their breakfast buffet and doughnuts. So, fucking bring it on, Preston. Let's sweat this out. Let's get to the other side."

"I wasn't important enough to be included in your life. And considering the multiple lies I was juggling, it was easier to leave you that way. But I don't want to be kept in the dark anymore."

"I don't want you to think that you're small anymore."

"I'm not, but you still see me as little. Mostly because I forgot to tell you that I'm larger than life now."

I sit up and take her hand. "You've always been larger than life, you're just aware of your own power now. And as for introductions, Dax, Hayden, Colton, Law and Robbie are the only people in my life worth knowing. My folks are amazing people, but their whole lives are dictated by money. How do we keep it? How do we spend it? What's the legacy the money should speak? There are trusts and codicils and plans for grandchildren who are all a thin whisper of a reality."

I'm on a roll, but she puts her hand on my forearm.

"Should I see if we can crack open some bourbon or something?"

I laugh and shake her off. I'm getting to a point I didn't realize I could make. I'm starting to see my life in a way I haven't been paying attention to until explaining it to her.

"The questions about money never stop lately. How will it all look when it's spent or lost or found? When it's doled out to multiple divorces and engagements? They don't care that I've gotten divorced this many times, they care about the money. What do the shareholders think of my 'antics?' Does the board still care about the billions I lost when I'm about to launch something they don't fucking understand?"

"You lost billions?"

"I never intended to tell you that."

"Wait here." She bolts off her chair and down the aisles. I sip my water and gesture to the family that walks by, taking in my frame in full repose on the patio furniture.

Her hair is trailing behind her while she runs back. She stands at the end of my chair and points a large black gun like thing at me, then turns it on. Fake money comes shooting out of it and all over me.

"Does this help? It's the 'Make It Rain Money Maker' and only fifteen dollars."

I bust out laughing as I roll around on my chair in the fake money. She's laughing, the red-shirted employees are not. There's fake money everywhere as she sprays the cash to the sky.

"Well, you didn't really have to tell me since Forbes pretty much summed up what a colossal mistake Bugle was. But I wanted you to think I cared." She winks at me.

"Cookery is a big fucking deal."

She sits down and hands me the gun. "If it tanks, give this to your dad." I grin again.

"I never meant for my parents to make you feel less than."

"They didn't. You did. And I did."

"Then we suck, because that's so not true."

She grins, stands up and pulls me up too.

I tell her a truth. "I didn't make a big deal to people who didn't matter when you came to Boston because they'd make me break up with you. Not because you're poor but because I'm rich."

She slides her palm against mine. "And now?"

I hand her the money maker gun. "You're rich too."

She laughs fully and pushes the cart down the cereal aisle.

"No more lies or hiding agendas. I'm not allowed to date you. I'm not allowed to fucking do anything right now."

She laughs a little too hard, and when I don't join her, she stops.

"Again?"

mak

He laughs and I feel lighter as if everything is manageable, if that's even possible with a full course load coming and a life I want to lead as well. I maneuver us toward the sheets.

"I don't accept it," I say.

"Not sure it's your choice, with the tabloidist divorce, the expectations of the board, my father and everyone..."

"Never underestimate the bad girl." I grin.

"Or the black sheep." He kisses me quickly.

"Where does that leave us?" I pop a hip, and he smirks, seeing that I've led him to bedding.

He takes my face in his hands. "How do you expect me to navigate this shit storm or anything, including adventure, without my true north?" His lips are quick against mine and I sink into a kiss that's not quite appropriate for where we are.

I grin and grab his ass. "Mine."

"If you say so," he responds. We're a whisper away from each other. "I love you."

"Good. Now get what you need so you can show me." I shoot back.

He claps and yells, "There are so many fucking sheets! How do you pick out sheets?"

"I'm not the one who can't fuck me on motel sheets."

He yanks me to him and puts his lips to my ear. "I can fuck you right here if you'd like. Bend you over the assorted college furniture or perhaps we take a stroll over to electronics and see how well the cameras broadcast on the bargain televisions so everyone can be fucking jealous they don't get to have you the way I do. Don't tell me I can't fuck you anywhere anytime. I just don't want your perfect ass to get sheet burn from the shitty sheets. It deserves the finest silk..." I lick my lips as he picks up a pack of sheets and says aloud, "But these will do."

My eyes are popping out of my head. He grins, picks up several more sets of sheets and sticks his hands inside.

"These are so good. And does everyone know how cheap these are? Do you need some? Do you feel this one?"

I lean back against the pillowcases and watch this dazzling, sexy-as-hell man get excited over sheets.

"Wait until you see the dollar aisle," I say, crossing my arms over my chest, so no one notices that my nipples are peaking from the air-conditioning and the things he just said to me.

He leaps in front of me. "In the words of Tina Fey, 'I want to go to there.'"

"Follow me, it's at the front of the store."

He walks behind me, randomly filling our cart with things that catch his eye.

"I had no clue candles didn't cost like a hundred bucks a pop."

I turn around and step on the cart. He keeps pushing it with me riding on the front like I did when I was little.

"I didn't know candles could cost a hundred bucks. That's insane."

"I'll get you one and we can compare the two. I think

Target might have the edge. Expensive candles always have annoying scents like turmeric, sea foam, oyster, calendula, exclusive nightshade orchid."

I laugh at him. He stops and stares at the mountain display of toilet paper. "What is even happening? Forty-eight rolls for like nothing. Is it good or like sandpaper?"

I step off the cart and hug him. He kisses the top of my head not even paying attention to me as he rips open the top of a stack of Charmin.

"Jesus, this is like a fucking cloud!" he yells in the middle of the paper goods aisle.

I can't breathe for a second. I bend over and finally say, "I'm laughing at you not with you by the way."

"I don't care. I'm buying you some toilet paper. It's so soft, we don't need the sheets. We can fuck on the toilet paper. Get another cart. I'm buying all of this."

"Nothing over a hundred," I warn him.

He looks at the price then picks up four large stacks of toilet paper and dumps them in. "And I'll still have enough money left to get you some Starbucks and a thing or two from the dollar area."

We walk back through the clothes area headed for the checkout, and he stops. He picks things up and examines them like they're a science experiment.

I grin and he examines a pair of pleather loafers near the dollar aisle.

"You know why these shoes are tied together with this stretchy string?"

"No. Why?" I indulge him while trying to take off my macramé shirt.

"Please, they're an affront to man and assault to the senses. They're the most hideous thing I've ever seen, and they have to go to jail. So, they're fake leather handcuffed together so they don't try to escape."

I'm bent over laughing again as he continues. "You think I'm joking. These are without a doubt the ugliest thing I've ever seen. Target, you had me until you tried to do shoes." He glances over and sees a man trying on the exact same pair as he's holding up. He shrugs and says, "Sorry. They look good on you. I'm just an ass. Seriously sorry. Can I buy them for you? So sorry. Do you want this pair too?"

I'm going to die. I take the handcuffed shoes and put them back on their rack, then turn to the man. "I'm sorry, he's from a very rural area of the world and has never been to a Target. Or interacted with many people. He's not good socially."

The gruff man grunts and nods. "Good luck." Tony hands him some cash and says, "Bitte, danke, haben sie keine shoes!" I yank him away as he sputters random German words.

We can't stop laughing and he takes me into his arms. "Can we come here all the time?" I slide my arms around his neck and kiss him. "I fucking love Target!"

"I do too, but don't we have other things to do?"

He pulls me close and kisses me. "Yes, but first I need to buy that big barn wood sign for you that says '*If your doodies be cray, please use the spray.*'"

"I've never felt more loved or seen." My stomach and jaw are both starting to hurt from laughing.

"It's not only good advice, but it's attractive too. Goes with the TP," he says while scurrying over to grab the ridiculous sign. Sitting on top of that one is a sign that says, "Grateful," with a daisy on it. It's hokey and silly, but I am. So very grateful.

He hops back to me and says, "Ok, what's next? Do you need a gross ton of beans? There's some kind of sale on beans in a can."

"Beans? Are you trying to justify your purchases?"

He doubles over laughing and I'm not sure I've ever seen anyone having a better time at Target.

tony

We don't even finish making the bed before I throw her on it. I light a twenty-dollar single-scent candle which smells pretty great. I whip her dress off to finally see her soft and beautiful skin. Her body will always make me weak in the knees and hard in the cock.

"Mak. Someday, I'd like to savor you but —"

She whips off her thong and bra, wraps herself around me, and silences me with her lips. She undoes my zipper to grasp my dick. "Fuck, I love the way you claim my cock."

"And I love how hard you are for me." She squeezes slightly as I shed my pants and boxers. I'm still in my suit jacket and button-down. She doesn't care as she kisses my neck and strokes me. I dip my fingers and find her ready for me. She groans as I gather some of that delicious juice and rub it all over her clit.

We're a series of groans and moans as we finger, stroke, and grope each other. She pulls away and I leap on the bed, shedding my jacket and shirt as I go. She crawls up like a tiger stalking her prey, and there are no words as she deep throats me in one try. My head is spinning and, fuck, it's so good as she swirls her tongue over my slit. I'm dripping into her mouth. She swallows not only my pre-cum but most of me down. Her hand pumping what her lips and throat cannot take. She's humming slightly as she grasps my balls in her other hand. The pressure of that followed by her flat tongue on my shaft is too great. Fuck.

"Mak, I won't. Shit. I can't." She pumps my cock as she bobs up and down while I watch her tits swing. Every time she looks up at me, I see in her eyes how badly she wants me to come for her. I see it and I'm happy to oblige.

I fist her dark hair back so I can watch her suck my cock. I buck my hips to get deeper and control anything about this moment. She moans and I realize she wants me to fuck her mouth.

"Good girl, my dirty little witch. Suck me down. Fuck. Don't move. Let me do what I want to that mouth."

She pops off for a second and says, "Do whatever you want, I just want to swallow all you can give me."

"Jesus. Get those lips back on my dick. Yeah. That's it." I take her head and push to the back of her throat and pull out again. Her tongue trying to get out of my way is even hotter as she drools. She tugs again on my balls when I thrust back in, and I'm fucking gone.

"Makenzie. That fucking mouth is so hot. Suck. Take my cock down your throat. I want to bump the back of it. Come on." She moves her hand to her clit. It's more than I can bear.

"Make yourself come while I come down your pretty throat." I buck hard and she moans louder as her fingers find their way inside of her. "Look at you making us both come. Jesus. So fucking hot. I'm coming."

She moans loudly as her eyes water and it shoots out of me without warning. She groans and swallows it all down. I can't stop. My cock is jerking inside her mouth. Waves of pleasure rippling through me as I lose all sense of reality. I pry my eyes open to see her fucking her own hand as she pulls off my cock.

She pauses, wipes her lips, then snakes her hand back towards her pussy.

"Up here, little witch, bring your mess to me." Her eyes are dark and full of lust. I lick my lips and prepare to be sat on.

She holds onto the headboard. "Down. NOW." I bark at her and her dripping, glorious pussy finds its way to my tongue. I dive in like a starved man and her first words without my cock in her mouth are enough to almost get me hard again.

"Make me come. Please. Please don't stop. Fuck. Spear me. Tony." I find her clit while my tongue fucks her waiting slit. I've eaten a million things worth talking about, but this will always be my favorite meal. Her pussy deserves a feature on the Cookery it's so fucking perfect and delicious.

Thrusting into her as she rocks back and forth fucking my face. Hell yeah. I feel her tense up, and then, in a burst of expletives and my name, she spasms on my tongue. Her body rumbles with passion and pleasure.

"OH, MY FUCKING GOD. Tony. Tony. Ahh. Fuck. Shit. Holy shit. Fuck. Yes. Yes. Yes."

And she shivers violently and flops forward. She leans backward and slumps onto her back like a scarecrow missing some stuffing. I get up and rinse my face off while grabbing a washcloth for her.

She exhales loudly. "That was fun."

"Not as much fun as Target but it will do."

"If I had any command over my body, I'd flip you off, but I don't, because that was a write-home-about orgasm."

"You want to write to your parents to tell them how good I am at eating you out? You're weird," I joke.

She huffs as if it's the only laugh she can get out. I clean her up and wipe the corners of her mouth. Then I toss the scratchy washcloth across the bed and curl up next to her, regretting we didn't buy towels. She drapes a leg over me, and we stay entwined and silent for a while. I've never been more satisfied in my life. Not just because of the blow job but her. I might get to keep her this time.

"Mak, I'm serious."

"About what?" she whispers while twirling my chest hair between her fingers.

"There's love, and then there's this. It's bigger. Like there should be a word for just us that lets the world know everyone else is fooling themselves if they don't feel this."

"Like a universe of love," she offers up.

"An expanding galaxy of love."

"I don't need everyone to know and get up in our business about inventing a bigger love. There will be clinical trials and tests and papers written. It will all get tedious."

My chest moves as I stifle a laugh. "What do you want to do with all this then?"

She holds me tighter and says, "Keep it."

tony

"Anthony Daye Ladd."

"Here, your honor."

"I'm simply a mediator, you don't have to call me your honor."

My lawyer nods to me.

"Sorry. Where is she? I'd like to get this over with."

"She's in a separate room. We'll talk and then I'll bring her offer to you and we'll go from there. A fair negotiation has to be attempted before you can get a court date."

"Then what the hell was all this paperwork before we got married even for? Give her the house in the Catskills and Palm Beach condo. She gets no part of the Vineyard or business. I'm pretty sure someone can make 3.5 work for the rest of their damn lives. We have no children. I think there's a cat at the dreaded mountain house but who the hell knows. Get her off my jock."

The mediator, to her credit, says nothing and slides a piece of paper to me.

Gavin says, "Hell no," before I can see it. "Having handled Mr. Ladd's previous dissolutions, I can say that this is outrageous. He's being very generous. No artwork. None of it was obtained together. She didn't purchase, pick out, or even want any of it until she figured out the worth of the collection. She also has an arrest in association with trying to steal vintage furniture pieces and the artwork listed in this proposal."

"Here's my counter: 2.5 and I'll buy her a paint by numbers kit." I stand up, and my lawyer points back to the chair.

"For this to count, and in order to get to a judge and a court date, you have to counteroffer in good faith."

I look at the rest of the proposal: fifty million dollars, stock, a piece of my trust, a piece of Ladd Media, the Vineyard house, Palm Beach condo, the Catskills house, artwork, furniture, and my Boston penthouse, which I had long before her. There's a long-ass list of more shit, but she wants cars and furs and jewels. Heirlooms are what she's after. She comes from money, not as much as we have, but enough that this greed isn't tracking with the woman I married.

"Keep the ring and the aforementioned houses. I'll buy her out of the Boston Penthouse, which she lived in for two of the twelve years I've owned it. That will be an additional fifteen million, three cars, the cat we may or may not have, and she can have the Noguchi coffee table. I always bang my shins on that thing. And she can have the slippery, pain-in-the-ass ivory sheets she insisted we buy. Final offer. She asks for one fucking cent more and not only do we go to court, but my offer becomes just the fucking cat and horribly expensive slippery sheets. Did you know Target makes a very cozy set of sheets? Toss in a set of those for her too. Final offer."

She straightens the papers in front of her, and Gavin finishes scribbling. "Tell her to sign it and this is over."

The woman leaves.

"I need this done."

My lawyer sits back. "Have another wife on the hook?" He grins.

"Look, my tragic serial monogamy made you a very wealthy man, so shut your piehole. And you're the asshole who drew up the dumb dating contract that ends—"

"July 4th."

"Eloquent timing."

"I thought so. It's a week shy of your thirty-first birthday. But you do know if wifey drags this out you have to remain unattached until you're financially unattached. She's fighting for a piece of the company and we can't give her any ammunition."

"Why does who I fuck have anything to do with it?"

"You can't be serious?"

"Deadly."

"Your reputation directly effects Ladd's bottom line and right now your father is, well, talk to him."

My phone vibrates in my pocket. "I have to take this." I'm not allowed to leave the room, but I turn away from him to read.

MAK: You ok? Are you free? Why does the caged bird sing?

TONY: Waiting to hear. Hey, how did the functions test go?

MAK: Fucking smoked it. Barton tutored me.

TONY: When is your biology thing due?

MAK: Why? Do you want to help with the practical part of the exam?

TONY: Yes. Yes, I do. Saturday. I have a fundraiser Friday, golf Sat morning. But Sat night, I can be in Vegas. Mandalay bungalow or Bellagio? Or do you want to see my baller suite with the pool at Palazzo inside the Venetian hotel?

MAK: Do you just keep suites in Vegas in case I can carve out time to have sex with you?

TONY: Yes. I like to keep Vegas and my cock on notice and reservation.

MAK: A simple hotel room will do since it's just one night. I'll bring the sheets.

The door opens and she slides our piece of paper and a new one across the municipal desk. Mine has a giant X through it.

Hers says, "50 million, stock, a board seat at Ladd, a piece of the media company, and the Vineyard house."

"She wants to go to court, Gavin, find out why?"

He nods. "This job is never dull. Don't fuck anyone."

"See if you can move the pieces to the larger section of the cooklets? And then launch the newsletter using the features we pulled. Impactful and broad scope. If we want to redefine the cooking magazine/book genre into usable pieces, then let's fucking do it. It's the publishing launch of the next phase of Ladd Media. Don't fuck it up. These small digital cookbooks should help the world avoid using annoying recipe sites where you can't find the recipe."

My favorite designer says, "What if we print them like cookbook novellas but the same concept: one chef or cuisine at a time. All information, no fluff?"

"YES. Do that. Go, bunnies, hop to it. Lill, grab lunch orders, nobody leaves until we go live at four today." They all groan. "Stop. How about we go to Chart House for lunch like a freaking field trip?" And then they cheer. "But no booze until 3:45!"

"Then let's go to lunch at 3:45!" my COO yells back at me.

"Done. Everybody buddy up, and, Lill, get everyone matching shirts for the bus."

"Now, I gotta find a fucking bus?"

We all laugh, and Lill huffs off, because that's exactly what I want, and she knows it.

"A trolly will do."

She sticks her middle finger up at me, which happens at least twice a day, and I head back to my office.

I'm fucking giddy about all of this. I wish she were here. The feeling I get when an idea comes together is indescribable. We're on the top of a cliff about to zip-line down, and it's exhilarating. Not like Bugle, when I threw more money at the problems and expected them to solve themselves. This is real-time problem-solving of things we created.

And I want to share it with her, but between school and whatever the hell is going on with the company, I can't.

I'll see her tomorrow night, in secret, in Vegas, but I wish she could go to the fundraiser with me tonight. I want our life together to start instead of this distance.

I duck into my office and ring her.

"Hi, I have to get to class."

"Teaching or learning?" I ask.

"Teaching. I'm a water aerobics instructor today. We walk from one end of the pool to the other to music from the sixties."

"And again, how are you qualified?"

"Oh, not even close. But they're paying me double because I already worked this morning covering the quilting circle."

"Are Chelle and Julia back?"

"No. They're taking another week in Puerto Rico before Lana's attorney puts the house on the market."

"Do their families know where they are?"

"Yeah, but Julia's kids are freaking out because she skipped an eye appointment. They're kind of obsessed with her medical appointments."

"Is she ok?"

"Yes. I think they're freaked out that she's eighty-six and there isn't a single thing wrong with her aside from brittle nails."

I laugh. "I miss you," I say softly as I finger the outside of my phone.

"I lo—"

I hang up on her because my father walks into the office without knocking.

"Son, that's an awful big smile you've got there. Staying clean?"

Like relationships are my drug of choice.

"The Cookery's new slate launches in six hours. I'm freaking giddy."

"I saw your Tweets this morning. And someone showed me the little video you did. How is anyone going to get the gist of it all in fifteen-second clips?"

"Trust me. We already have 600k views on that in the last half hour. I can pull all the metadata if you want, old man, or you can trust me."

He sits down across from me. "I do. At least with this. I was talking to Hammer Andrews on the course about a week ago, always liked that man. He raised a good son. His daughters are a little high maintenance, but Colt's a solid man."

"He is." I do not know where my father is going with all of this, but I don't like it.

"Apparently, you all had a sort of impromptu Paris reunion last summer."

I know exactly where he's going with this. Even though they met Mak briefly, I'd kept her away from them. But years later, I told him that she was the only person I could ever see myself with.

"Your mother is concerned you never told us that you ran into Makenzie. Dax told me to ask you."

"Shocked he didn't spill his guts for you. Yes. We saw Makenzie and her friend Maggie. A good time was had by all, and then Mak and I parted company in the morning." We did. We really did. And then I texted her, waited several months, phone-dated her, got divorced, fucked her, fell back in love with her, told her, got left by her again, chased her, wooed her, and now I'm in a secret but kind of serious relationship with her.

But that night, we did part company.

"Dad, that was like ten months ago. I'm fine."

"She meant a lot. Your mother and I have made mistakes, I'm not too proud to own some of them, I just hope this wasn't one." It was, but I appreciate his kind of apology.

"Pop, we're all good."

"And you're single?" In the sense that I don't currently have an engagement or marriage going on, yes.

"As I'll ever be." Truth, I'm marrying Mak as soon as I can.

"Let's talk next month about what the situation would look like to spin off Ladd Media. It's dicey right now but let's begin talks."

I'm confused, but before I can inquire, he's gone.

mak

I've never been anywhere that looks like this, and I've lived near Vegas for a long time. I've partied in almost every hotel on the Strip since I had a fake ID at sixteen and would sneak over here for a weekend. Suite hopping was basically my occupation from age eighteen to twenty-two, when everyone I knew was in college. I thought I'd seen the opulence, money, and dirty, gritty parts. I've toked, drank, and smoked in the best and worst places in Nevada, but this shit is unreal.

I was escorted to a VIP lounge within a VIP lounge to check in. I know he has money, but I've never experienced it like this. I pull down my black t-shirt, which is my fanciest one, and accept a glass of champagne.

"Ms. Preston, we'll take you to the room now. We've been expecting you."

"Thank you so much." I hitch up my bag, and a man basically wrestles it away from me. It's all I brought because he said to bring a bathing suit and a dress. I thought he'd meet me in the lobby, but he's not here yet. It makes me nervous and itchy to be around the money without him to help navigate.

Out a back door there's a golf cart and a twenty-year-old in pool boy shorts waiting for me. I climb into the front seat and smile.

"You can sit in the back if you prefer."

"Would you prefer that?"

He grins and says, "It would be nice to have some company. It's not a long trip, but I do it all day long and no one ever really talks to me unless they're wasted."

There's a bottle of champagne chilling in the front, and I pour myself another glass. "This is some rich people shit, isn't it?" He laughs and I sip some more.

"You don't even know. Hold on, I'll drive you to your villa. Unless you'd rather go to the high rollers' entrance and gamble a little."

"Let me save you some time. I'm a local. I'm not gambling."

"Fair enough. Are you hungry? Do you want to call for the chef?"

He swings around the back of the building and enters some kind of secret tunnel. "THE chef?"

"Your villa chef."

"Dude, I'm so over my head here."

"So, I'm guessing there's no tip."

I laugh. "Sorry. When the..." I don't know what to call him. Soulmate? Boyfriend? Hot Lay? I don't know. "When the other half of my party arrives, I'll make sure he tips you well." I turn toward him. "But first tell me how much you earn in a day to wear those tight whitey shorts and drive people in a golf cart?"

He grins. "It's not polite to discuss money." I know there's cash to be made in the casinos, but I stayed away. My parents were so miserable, and it fucked them up for a long time. I started out fucked up and really didn't need an excuse to be around all kinds of terrible behavior, so I never went through a cocktail waitress or hotel staff phase. But driving rich people to their rooms and wearing a little skirt, I might be into that if the cash is good.

"Here we are." He pulls up to a door and hops out. We enter the hotel, and he takes me to an elevator and reaches for my key card. When the elevator doors open directly into the villa, he places my bag on the hall table.

"Or would you prefer your bag in one of the bedrooms."

"One?"

"Yes. Mr. Ladd often entertains here. It can be attached to another suite to provide bedrooms for all his guests."

"The Brothers?" He nods, and I'm lightened that it wasn't for orgies.

"I'm good. Thank you so much, Rich. You're the best." I place down the bottle I carried in and try not to stare at the entrance too much. "I promise Tony will tip you."

He nods and says, "You're not out of your league. Most people aren't quite as kind or interesting as you've been. If there's anything you need, don't hesitate to call. Seriously, anything you can think of, we can get."

"Beef and bean burrito supreme, no lettuce, a Meximelt, and a Mexican pizza. And like forty mild sauce packets please."

"Coming right up." He gets on his walkie-talkie and gives someone my Taco Bell order. They answer, "Fifteen minutes. Is there a drink?"

"Hold on." My eyes are wide, and I can't believe no one even questioned it. The Border on demand, now that's some rich people shit I can get behind.

MAK: Have you ever done Taco Bell?

T: Sexual position or fast food?

I laugh.

MAK: Food.

T: If you'd like to call it food, you may. I have had it. I did go to college.

MAK: But you haven't had it in this decade. They've really stepped up their game.

T: No they haven't. Where are you? Are you at a Taco Bell?

MAK: In the room. Hold on.

"Baja Blast. Large. Make it two and add a six pack of crunchy tacos, a bean burrito, two chicken gorditas, Dorito tacos! Get one of each of those, and two soft tacos. And can you please add all the sauces?" I suspect he's lying about trying Taco Bell.

"Done." I hear my order repeated.

Then Rich heads to the door just before it closes, and he peeks back inside. "I once made 17k in a day, but it usually averages around 1000 to 1500."

"Fuck me."

"That's extra." My eyes go wide. "Just kidding. Behave yourself. Your meal will be here soon."

The door shuts, and I check Tony's message as I slowly step into this suite. It's a lot of marble. There really is a private fucking pool with its own bar attached to the hot tub. I'm sure we could get a bartender if we wanted one.

T: I'll be there in like ten minutes. Please do not eat any Taco Bell until I've eaten you.

MAK: Fine, but hurry. Should I warm myself up so you can slip right in when you get here?

T: Christ, I've missed you.

MAK: You know this place is bigger than the rec center at Twisty Acres.

T: I do.

MAK: It's too much.

T: I'm going to fuck you on every surface you're currently looking at. And then we'll explore the three bedrooms.

MAK: So forward, Mr. Ladd.

T: It's our first official date as a couple again.

MAK: That was Target.

T: It's the first time we're not pretending we are friends. We're written on some ancient scroll somewhere about destiny and fated mates.

MAK: Are we wolves or something?

T: I wanted to impress you.

MAK: Do you remember what happened when you tried to impress me on our other first real date?

T: You got fingered at the Eiffel Tower. Are we going to do that again? Yippee!

MAK: I ended up falling on my ass. No flashy stuff I just you.

T: I love you. Look, the suite is on a tentative hold all the time. I never know when all the guys can get together, and we tend to like to hang out and do nothing. It's easier without other people around because of my bullshit and Law and Robbie's sports hoopla.

MAK: But why this huge thing?

T: The best part of the money isn't the size of the room, but the privacy it buys. Get ready to scream. I'm five away.

tony

I slide into my soaking-wet girl after a week apart and we both groan. This new policy of no condom is a fucking dream.

"Such the perfect pussy. So tight and snug, holding my cock so deep. Fuck it's hot. Fuck." I pump into her, and she meets me on every thrust.

She arches her back and comes in a beautiful torrent of screams and gasps, and I follow her down the tunneling path of pleasure.

She rolls over, lying on her back, and reaches for a cold taco.

"Now that was a Baja Blast." She crunches.

We will leave separately. But for the moment, we're side by side on the casino floor to catch our cars. She's stunning, and I glance around, and my heart stops.

"Mak, can you get me some gum?" I have to get her away from me.

"Gum?"

"Yes." I have to confirm something.

"No." I roll my eyes. Of course, she's not going without an explanation. "You're weird."

"There's someone I know, and we can't be seen together. I'll call you later. I love you. Now, go get some damn gum."

She's flustered. I peck her lips and circle back on the other side of the casino. Mak is still standing there bewildered, staring at me. I shoo her away, and she flips me off and heads to her car. I'm rattled, but I inch closer to be certain. I stand behind a nickel slot machine and peer around down the row next to me to witness a true desert mirage. It has to be fake.

"Holy shit." I shake my head and run away quickly.

I'm sitting in her lobby, hiding and frankly, still in a bit of shock. She doesn't know I was in Vegas. But I think in light of her straddling someone else, making out at a nickel slot machine, I can probably trust her with my secret.

She enters, and if I can separate the woman from the marriage, she's stunning and sunny in the afternoon light. She strides across the lobby floor, clicking her heels in a confident cadence. And then her blonde bob flips to me, and her face hardens as I scoot into the elevator while the doors close. I hate that we do that to each other.

I put my hands up. "Lore, we need to talk."

"Alan will be in touch."

"No lawyers. No one knows I'm here. I could have waited in your place. I have a key since I own it."

"And that would be—"

"Sorry. I'm not here to stir up shit, trust me. You once did. One glass of water, that's all I'll stay for."

"You hate water."

I grin. "I do, and it's a problem. But I'll drink it for you right now if you trust me. I need ten minutes and we can release both of us from this purgatory."

She nods sharply. The doors open, and she swipes her key, and we enter her apartment. Which is, of course, beautifully remodeled on my dime.

She points at the couch. "Sit."

She places her baby-puke-green Birkin bag in a manicured ceramic bowl by the door. It fits perfectly; of course, it does. She's been well trained. Everything is supposed to be exactly where it is and stay exactly the way it's supposed to. Her parents, this fucking world, and old money is all a three-headed beast that rules her existence. I don't know if I'm setting her free or complicating her life, but I want out of this fucking narrative.

She walks calmly to the kitchen, and I follow her. She's filling a pitcher with ice water and slices lemons into perfect thin circles.

"Lore, I saw you." She doesn't stop cutting. Then she plunks the lemons into the water and turns to me. "In Vegas."

Her face goes pale as she clutches the sink, and I quickly take the pitcher from her.

"I saw you and Teddy. Why didn't you tell me, Laura?"

I put the water down and hold her because she's shaking pretty violently.

"What do you want? You finally have your out." She pulls out and slides her composure back into place like it's a tablecloth covering deep scratches in a mahogany table.

"No. Not like this."

I walk back to her living room and sit down. She takes her place opposite me, sitting literally on the edge of her seat.

"No one can know." Is all she says.

"Laura, I don't want anything except for us to be done with this. I'm not telling anyone, but you should. I can't imagine living with that kind of pressure, the duality of your life."

Tears form in her eyes. "I did love you. I do love you, but now you understand why I can't love you."

"Why this charade of pain and anger?"

"I'm nothing if I'm not a society girl living up to my parents' expectations."

I slide next to her and put my arm around her. "Then be something else. I can honestly say seeing you kissing Teddy was the least expected, most outrageous thing I've ever seen. And as you know, I'm not one to shy away from outrageous things. Jesus, Laura, isn't Teddy sick of hiding?"

"And you're fine with this?" She blubbers out, "I'm so sorry, Tony. If the divorce was your fault, if I made you the monster who wouldn't give me money, then no one would look closer at me. My parents pushed for all that shit. It was expected, and my father wants to take down yours for that thing that happened in the '70s."

"Holy grudge. When my pops got the promotion in our company over your father?" She nods. "He didn't see that nepo baby shit coming? I work my ass off and am on top of my game, but it's not like he's going to promote someone over me. There's a good chance he'll can my ass soon if I don't succeed, but no one will be promoted over me."

She grins widely. "Nepo baby."

"Loud and proud, as you should be. But your hidden self has royally fucked me over, you do know that. My entire life, including my love life, is on max scrutiny because of this. That's the only thing I'm really pissed off about, is all the shit coming on me because of you." Her face falls and her eyes fill with tears, as they should. She's fucked up both of our lives.

"I know. I know. It got out of control, and I didn't know how to stop it. My parents want blood and I just... I'm just so sorry. You don't deserve any of this."

"No, I don't. But why did we fight? If you're trying to hide, why divorce me? Why not beard it up for a while longer?"

"Teddy wouldn't be with me if I was still with you. The pressure got too great, and I took it out on you. Then my parents got involved and saw company takeovers and expanding art collections. Basically, everything I asked for in the divorce was so my parents could set me up with their exact life. All that shit is what they wanted for me because it's what they have. Art, a company, multiple houses, board seats. You didn't deserve any of it."

"Jesus, Lore. I don't give a fuck who you love, but you've kept both of us from moving on. You live in a major, modern, progressive city in a time and place when gender, spirituality, and possession are fluid. I don't understand the fear. But set that aside, you caused pain to people I love because you couldn't tell me you were gay. We could have come up with a solution together. Your lies screwed us both. And I'm hurt you hid it from me, or anyone. Teddy's a down chick and you're lucky to have her. So, go have her and set me free so I can dig out from under all your shit."

She quickly wipes a tear from her cheek. "I know. I love her, and I always have."

I sit back and wring my hands for a moment to calm myself down. Then I look up at her and her face is open and vulnerable. "I have one of those myself, and I can't believe being an unwitting beard for you kept me from her."

"Let me call her, I can't tell her specifics because—"

And I realize that no matter what pain kept me from being with Mak since last year can only be a billion times worse for Laura keeping herself hidden. She is keeping herself away from the one she loves, who's right in front of her, and she still can't have her.

"Fuck Boston, your reputation, your parents, and the money. I'm guessing you've never come out before?"

"Women in my family are raised to be fundraising, Mayflower legacy, gardening club wives, we don't get to be, you know—"

I whisper, "Say it. I'll be your safe space."

She swallows hard and squeezes my hand. "I'm a lesbian." Her body slumps against mine.

I push her off me and stand up. I face her and open the Ladd Music app and find what I need. I push play and place it on the coffee table. I grab her hand and yank her to standing. She's laughing through her tears. "Sing it with me now."

We dance around the room to Diana Ross screaming, "I'm coming out. I want the world to know…" Her face is wet and red, and she's finally the Laura that I love. The reason I decided to marry her. I never loved her like I do Makenzie, but it was enough. We were great friends who laughed a lot. And she never judged me for being over the top or ridiculous.

We fall down on the couch laughing when the song is over, and she takes my hand.

"You know this is your song too."

I purse my lips at her. "Wouldn't be the first time someone thought that. But Hayden and I really are—"

"No, you misunderstand me. The line, 'it's time to break out the mold and live a new life' or something like that. That's you. We can both choose to leave our gilded cages."

I cock an eyebrow at her. "Can we now?"

"I can't let the world know, right?" Her voice is sadder than it should be.

"When you're ready, you can. Look, I'm the king of disappointing my family, but jump in the water's fine."

"Why do you do that?" she asks.

"What?"

"Undersell yourself. You know they're not constantly

disappointed, they just don't understand you." She puts her head back on the couch.

I lean back as well and face her. We look like little kids in a fort. "Same."

"I can't. And Teddy's furious, and I'm not brave enough yet to face down awful stereotypes and horrific people with their antiquated views." I can't fix this for her, but I do see a way out for both of us.

"Trust me, step outside of our insulated bubble and those stereotypes are fading fast. The only people who will care are people who don't fucking matter."

"Is this advice or confession?"

I grin. "A bit of both, I guess. Neither of us can get away from the money but we can step outside of the class bullshit."

"They'll cut me off."

"Probs, yeah. But you have a very nice divorce settlement coming. And surely, Teddy's cashed up." I inhale and sigh. "Take the money, no art, no Vineyard, no company money. But sell this place, I'll give you half the penthouse and sell the Catskills place. You know we both hated it. And with the settlement money, the original 3.5 million, that gives you approximately 43.5 to 60 million dollars depending on the real estate market. You're never going to do better than that. I'll throw in the cat and a car and pay all the taxes this year."

Her face drops a little in surprise. "You'd still do that? I lied to you."

"It seems to be a trend."

"What?" She cocks her eyebrow and I shake my head.

"Tell everyone. And then tell them to fuck off. Take Teddy and go live somewhere else. Start again as yourselves and use the money anyway you want and send me a postcard from time to time. Go to Europe or the Hudson River Valley. Go someplace that's not Boston because maybe you'll realize that only you cared. Stop living for everyone else. It's a thing I'll try out as well."

She holds me close and doesn't sob. That's not who she is.

"How long with Teddy?"

"Since I was eighteen. She's it for me."

"Why did we have sex?" I ask, truly confused.

"I got married because Teddy and I broke up and I liked you. I thought I might be bisexual, so I didn't exactly hate having sex with you or men. But in the end, bi, straight, gay, I'm not sure I could label myself anything but Teddy's. I'm hers and always have been. I don't know if I can come out officially, but let's at least get this divorce behind us."

I jump up and down, dancing around the room. "Thank Fucking God!"

She laughs. "Hey, why were you in Vegas?"

"I was having a lot of sex with the love of my life, who ironically, I also met when we were eighteen."

Her eyes get wide, and her face cracks in a smile. "NO! Get out! Makenzie?" I smile and nod.

"Yeah and your dumbass has me sneaking around because of the divorce. So, how about we ditch the water and find something a little stronger and you and I tell each other some truths?" Laura winks at me.

"Sounds like a plan."

"That's all I'm looking for anymore. Women who don't lie," I say.

"I'm not sure I even know where to begin." Laura frets.

"Start with the first lie."

mak

I gather all the mail and plunk it in the shallow, chipped porcelain bowl where my parents keep it. I place my keys on the command hooks I installed near the fridge. I look around our dusty little kitchen and smile. For the first time it feels like a home. We always had somewhere to live, and I remember the trailer being home, but it never felt like this. Placemats covered in hydrangeas are set around the oak table we picked up from Goodwill and my father refinished. And the room is neat and relatively uncluttered. He knows collections won't complete him anymore, but he can't help himself sometimes. I've worried about them for so long I missed out on the fact that they're taking care of themselves.

The bell over the door dings and Mary Margaret appears with a giant smile.

"Well, Ms. Mak, how are we today?"

"I'm good. How goes it here?"

"All good. Where's that man of yours? I need to thank him."

I open my mailbox and grab a stack of letters and my heart pangs. "He's in Boston working. What do you need to thank him for?"

She points to the corner and there's an extremely expensive, complicated, and shiny espresso machine. "Holy shit."

She grins. "I know, right? And there's a service contract and coffee shows up once a week. And the doughnuts on bulk mailing Saturdays are a nice touch. You got yourself a sweetie. Can't imagine what he buys you, girl."

My mouth is wide open as if waiting for flies to land in there. What the hell?

"He's a considerate one," I manage to say.

She squeezes my arm. "Wanna latte? I'm getting the hang of foaming things."

Sorter Fred yells from the back, "No you're not."

"Shut your hole."

I laugh. "I'm good. I'll stop by for some coffee another time."

"Please do, we're getting to be as good as Starbucks around here."

Another yell from the back, "No, you're not."

"Hush up."

I head to my car sorting the mail and there's a card from the church in Reno. I panic a little that it's a bill, but I'm pretty sure I've paid my debt to them. I should find time to go there, and if I pick UNR for med school, I'll be able to help out a lot more.

Tears well up instantly when I see it's a thank you note. I dig my phone out of my bag.

"Call me," is all I say to the voicemail I'm getting too familiar with.

I head home and when I enter, I'm greeted by my dad mixing a Greek salad.

"Kabobs tonight, Leech."

"Good on you, Slug." My mom walks in and flips some chicken in a bag in the fridge. She's whistling and my father is dancing to it.

"What's all the happy about?"

My dad looks at me. "We're not supposed to tell you, ever."

"Is everything alright?"

My mother slaps my shoulder playfully. "You have got to stop thinking there's always something wrong. But we are celebrating. Here's what I can tell you. My blood work came back, and they pulled me off the statins."

"What? That's incredible."

My father hands her a giant, icy glass of what I know is Coke Zero. "And she's off her diabetes meds because..."

She turns in a circle and shakes her butt. "I don't have it!"

I throw my arms around my mom, and she kisses my cheek. "Baby girl, stop your worrying. We got this. And after what he did for us, we're going to be fine."

I pull out of her arms. "What?"

Her face freezes.

My dad says, "Well, hell's bells, Leech, you got it out of us." He shrugs.

My mom shows me a Target card and it's a preloaded debit card. "What did he do?"

My father starts sliding chicken onto skewers and my mother slides veggies on another. My dad says, "There's enough on this card to take care of us for now. I think his intention is to set you free, Leech."

My heart is full, but I don't want him to think this is ok. My mother washes her hands. She picks up a letter from the chipped porcelain bowl with the cats on it and slides it across the island counter to me.

"Sweetheart, if he ends up being something else to you, we

will understand it, but to us, he'll always be an angel. We rejected his offer several times, but he's persistent."

My dad pipes in with, "We're supposed to tell you that he loves a loophole and that none of this is for you, so it didn't have to be a hundred dollars."

I'm staring at a bank statement from our mortgage company. He paid off their house.

———

"You rang?"

I'm pacing and spitting mad. I'm outside so I can yell and either no one or everyone can hear me. I don't care.

I come at him with all my venom. "You can't do this."

"Which thing?" he says cheekily. It's sexy and infuriating.

"You bought the church a roof, a shed, and a twelve-passenger van."

"Yes, they were all things on their prayer list, and I answered their prayers."

"You're God now?"

"No, but if you'd like to call me that in certain situations, I'd accept it."

"This is serious."

"Hey, slow down. I talked with the pastor and asked where the greatest need was, that's all. You asked me to patch their roof but apparently it wasn't structurally sound for a patch, so I gave them a roof. I have the means and I told him why I'm indebted to them. You know this isn't a bad thing."

"You can't throw money at things."

"Why not? It's not doing me any good sitting there and they really could use that shed."

"And an espresso machine?"

"Well, that just makes good sense for Mary Margaret."

"My parents?"

"Look, my love. You won't accept anything from me, and I want to give you everything. You specifically told me I wasn't allowed to pay for your tuition, but being the king of the loophole, if I could take the worry and burden from you and your parents about the mortgage, I'll do it every time."

"You can't buy off everything in my life. I said no gifts over a hundred dollars."

"No, what you said was I wasn't allowed to give *you* gifts over a hundred dollars. And I haven't. Well, the bracelet was three hundred. So, I'm sorry about that."

I don't say anything. He didn't do terrible things. I don't know how to back down, and then as if he can tell what I'm thinking, he addresses it.

"My love, let me in. It's ok to need help; it doesn't make you less. I want to buy presents that matter. It's ok to take it. I know you don't want to be indebted to anyone but let me help.

"Yes, but..." I sputter and can't finish my sentence.

"I wanted to spend the money in places that would matter. Kind of a new thing for me. I usually toss it out there into the nonprofit void. I think the shelter dogs are getting what they need, but I've never met the boots on the ground people or the pooches. I care about these people, and I can help. You told me to do better and I'm trying. I felt this is where I could make a difference but not be obnoxious with it. I'm not sorry."

"Money can't be our love language."

"No, your clit is our love language."

"Tony, I'm serious."

"I wanted to ease the tension a bit for places and people that matter to you. You should also know that I offered Chelle and Julia a round trip vacation in one of the Ladd jets to anywhere they want to go."

"Why?"

285

"Because you're my love language. It's all for you."

I wipe a tear, wishing he were standing next to me. My voice is smaller than I like, and my pride is raging. But I push it down trying to see the good being done around me because of him.

My heart bursts open and I let the reality settle over me. "Thank you."

"Was that so hard?"

"Yes. It was extremely hard." He laughs and I exhale loudly. It's like I'm releasing tension in my body and mind that I thought I'd carry forever.

tony

The door slams open, and my father's face is beet red. It can't be the launch, it was cha cha real smooth. We're already amping up to make more money than he could dream of. There's not a media outlet in the world that hasn't mentioned Cookery in the last couple weeks. I hit it out of the park. I'm not the fuck-up, so not sure why he's got the 'Tony screwed something up' face.

"Are you fucking kidding me?" Lill appears as my father bellows at me, and I motion to her to close the door. He slams down a whole shit-ton of papers. I recognize one stack as my final assets agreement that I signed, and the division is in motion. I waited one hundred and twenty days for the actual divorce. But the settlement is in motion and all the assets are in escrow until it's approved by the court. I'm days away from being out from under all of this. It was a sealed deal, so I don't know how my father has it. He wasn't supposed to know yet.

His voice is unnerving. "You gave her an insane amount of money. And you're paying her monthly? Boy, that's quite enough. You're shut the fuck down. I'm not doing this again. I'm not handing over my hard-earned family money again, because you can't keep yourself single."

"Slow up, Pops. She deserves all of that."

"For a three-year fucking marriage?"

I stand behind my desk and stare at him. I'm not his son in this office. "Didn't know we were putting a price tag on monogamy but cool."

"Don't be flippant with me, boy."

"Again, with this boy bullshit." I come around my desk and square off to him. "Thirty hardly qualifies as a boy."

"Well, then act like a man."

"And fuck anything that moves without regard, so we can protect the money? That was your mature plan? Christ, Dad, you inherited, on both sides. As did Mom. We're so steeped in fucking money and decorum that it's become meaningless."

"Is that why you're throwing it away?" I roll my eyes.

"Just because you gave me some of it doesn't mean you get to decide how it's spent."

"Like hell."

He points to the contract I signed about staying single. "This is null and void. Your wallet is on lockdown."

"First of all, I draw a salary. Second, I have my own holdings and my portion of the company far exceeds fiscally the other pieces, so if you want your half of the business upheld, you better treat me with a little more respect."

"All your personal assets and business perks are frozen until you explain this." He pushes the printouts of my bank account and credit cards across the desk.

"You're spying on me?"

"When one takes the corporate jet for a quick overnight to LA or spends more time in Vegas than Boston, it's a bit of a red flag. Antique stores, jewelry stores, whoever she is, she's not a one-night stand. A ten-thousand-dollar espresso machine and some fucking love shack in Henderson. Church repairs? She isn't good enough for all of this."

"Fuck you."

"Your little travel budget to whatever fucking trollop you've picked up in Vegas, who I assume presumes she's going to be the next Mrs. Anthony Ladd, is cut off." He turns to leave, and I do something I've never done before. I've snarked. I've cajoled, teased, ignored but never this.

"DON'T YOU FUCKING SPEAK ABOUT HER THAT WAY. Or to me like that ever again."

He turns back to me and crosses his arms.

"Get the fuck out of my office. Go call up Dax and tell him how difficult I'm being. Go play golf or old man jack each other off in the steam room or whatever the fuck you do to relax at the club, but get out of my affairs and my office. Or you can nut up and tell me what the hell this is all really about? It's not about where I'm putting my cock or how often or with whom. Or how many doughnuts I buy. What is this about?"

He's way too calm. "It's imperative you maintain a straight and narrow path. Do not be the bad boy spending cash on women or frivolous things right now. This divorce agreement reads like you don't care about your money. And these other expenses are not a good look. Your mother and I are in agreement on this after seeing Laura's settlement and the money you've already spent lining up your fourth wife."

I lean back on my desk. I don't want him to know it's Makenzie because she was right. They dismissed her, and I don't want her to leave me because they were snobs.

I nod at him. "Dad."

"Son."

"Believe me, this is different. This is it."

He rolls his eyes. "Son, it is different. We're involved. The work you've been doing is fantastic, but we can't risk another stock dip when you show up with someone else on your arm. Your personal life matters. It's the way it is. You chose to be a part of this company and it's time you took on some of the burden of legacy. We won't weather another woman on the payroll or another bobble in Ladd Media." Love that he called my multi billion dollar mistake a bobble.

He waves my divorce agreement. "Makes no fucking sense. The two of you all of sudden came to decisions without consultation from anyone else. It's childish and the two of you are playing with very real money. The press and our shareholders will eat this up like gossip. You gave her your Catskills house?"

"It was always hers. I've been there once and hated it. You'd hate it too. It's too mountainy fresh. And, Dad, I love you, but this has nothing to do with you."

"You can keep saying that, but it's still family money, reputation, and lives you're playing with. We can't have it for another second. Your wallet, dick, and whatever relationship you thought you were having are all on lockdown."

"In one month and sixteen days you hand over Ladd Media free and clear. You dissolve all ties to the holding company and it's mine."

"We will see. There are other factors at play."

"Then my team and I walk. We own the Cookery and all those assets outright, so you want me to honor your fucking deal, honor mine."

He puts his hand out, and I shake it.

Thank God Makenzie has graduation to occupy her. But I might die without her. It's a short time when put up against forever. But it's hard to wait for forever to start.

My father leaves, and Lill enters.

I tell her, "Get me a phone my father can't tap or trace."

"Go down to a store and get one."

"It's got to be on your account. I'll pay my bill, I promise. I'm good for it."

"Are you? You and your father weren't exactly quiet." I laugh. "Need a loan?"

"Ballbuster. Get me a phone. He's going to monitor mine and I need all data saved then scrubbed. I want all of Makenzie Preston's texts."

"Finally! Ya gonna talk about what's making you so flipping happy these days."

"Good solid fucking, Lill. That's the key to life."

"Ain't it the truth."

Robbie's wife, Claire, has been investing for me, and she's doing quite well. Thank God. It's not jet money, but it will buy a dinner or two.

TONY: Hey. How's my money doing?

CLAIRE: Why? What did you hear? You owe me more time.

TONY: I might need it sooner than later and just want to let you know in case you have to supplement.

CLAIRE: Don't you owe me a couple of million anyway?

TONY: That's not confirmed, and it was your husband I made a bet with, you little minx. And the bet doesn't officially end until my birthday, despite having lost it, I don't have to pay shit until then. We still have like seven weeks. Can you set up a new account in your name and give me access? And I'll need a debit card. Daddy cut me off.

CLAIRE: Classic. I'll send over the statements.

TONY: Can you send them to the old Yahoo address?

CLAIRE: Yahoo? Ok, Boomer.

TONY: Fine. Send them to the AOL one.

CLAIRE: LOLOLOLOLOLOL

TONY: Trying to be on the DL with it all.

CLAIRE: Fine. Whatever. Did you need me to drop by Blockbuster and pick up some DVDs to go with your Yahoo address?

TONY: Tell your wife to fuck off

ROBBIE: Sure, right after we get done listening to Clinton tell us he did not have sexual relations with that woman.

CLAIRE: Dude, come over; we're burning CDs off Napster.

TONY: Fuck you both.

ROBBIE: Just popping a Zima and chillin' in da crib.

My phone pings with a different text chain. It was only a matter of time until my parents brought Dax into this mess.

DAX: What the fuck did you do?

TONY: There are now sides. Choose wisely.

DAX: Always, brother. But Mother's Day is not going to be fun.

TONY: Can you send her to Bora Bora from us? Just sign my name. I'm broke.

DAX: So I heard.

TONY: That man does not sit on a secret. And I'm keeping the girl, my company, and the money. I do like the money, but if there's a choice to be made it was made long ago.

DAX: Mak.

TONY: Yes. I'll choose her over the money, but let's hope it doesn't come to that. Although, I highly recommend shopping at Target.

DAX: I do.

TONY: You do?

DAX: It's why they're not mad at me. I don't spend the money.

TONY: Fuck off.

DAX: Love you too. Got your back.

Well, I guess flying commercial is in my future. There's no way I'm going almost seven weeks without seeing her. I will miss the jet though.

mak

I curl my fingers through his chest hair as he tickles my back lightly. We're in a plain hotel, not on the Strip. There are some machines and a table or two in the lobby, and it's meant to be a desert oasis, not a casino. The sliders are open as the chill starts to take hold of the night. We haven't spoken since we cleaned up and settled into these positions. My heart is bursting. I love him so much, and I finally think I deserve it all. But for the first time since Lana's funeral, I'm worried about him.

He's distant. Over the past weeks his calls are infrequent and from a new number. Not that I have time, but when I do, my mind wanders to the dark side. It's where I don't come out of this scenario whole. I shouldn't doubt any of it, but is he here for closure or to get laid?

We lie in stilted silence for another minute or so, and I can't take it.

"I don't want this between us."

"What, my love?"

"There's something you're not telling me. About your divorce, or why we're hiding even more than we were. I'm an open book to you now. Please don't be the old me. Even though I know I deserve it."

He grabs my cheek and holds it gently. "Where are you getting silly ideas?"

I shift out of his arms. He's only visited twice in two weeks and it's been really weird. Good sex, but weird emotions. "Sporadic phone calls, flowers from Lill, and you're not here even when you're here. You're freaking me out. Where are you? Am I a side piece you're hiding? I can't do that. I respect myself too much to do that, Tony."

"Oh my God. You thought I was hiding you because of Laura? Jesus, this got beyond me without me noticing."

I pull the sheet around myself, and he pouts. I flash him a tit, and he perks up.

"I'm serious. What is it?"

He holds his head and stands up. I enjoy the flex of his ass and those side dimples. Delicious. He puts on shorts.

"It's serious enough you need shorts? Quick toss me a shirt so I'm not so naked, figuratively and literally."

"My love—"

"Thank fucking God you started like that."

He laughs, but my heart sinks as he places a long jewelry box on the side table. Then he puts his hands on his hips. "I told you about gifts. But I do like the flowers." He kisses me.

I open it and stare at him. "This is under a hundred dollars?"

"Ish."

"Oh, this is the three-hundred-dollar bracelet. I'll allow it."

I want to refuse it, but it's an old charm bracelet that needs to be cleaned. It has only two charms, and I've orgasmed in and around both iconic landmarks. I hold it to my chest.

"Thank you. Will you be adding charms of other iconic places we do it? Like the Henderson Motel 6 or The Four Seasons in LA? He laughs and swipes his tongue over my lips, and I instantly open for him. Our tongues tangle, and eventually, his hands slide to the back of my head, but just as we heat up again, he pulls back.

"Thank you. I love it." I fiddle with the bracelet, and he helps me put it on my wrist.

"Christ, I love you. I love you so much. It's my dad."

"If you're fucking your dad I might have to bail."

He laughs hard and moves to the middle of the room. "No, but he is fucking me. I have to figure out what's going on with the company. There's a lot of pressure on me to be industrious, personable, reasonable, and single. Most of the exes are on the payroll, and the parents put their foot down about this divorce, and I gave in because it was the right thing to do. Remember that last day in Vegas together?"

"When you sent me to fetch gum? Yeah, that was the start of your weirdness."

"I saw Laura."

"Oh, shit. Did she see us?"

"No. She was making out with her friend Teddy. They're in love and she's been hiding it."

"You married a lesbian?"

"Technically, according to her, I married a pansexual, bisexual, fluid sexually human who was never honestly into me all the way. Regardless, she loved me just not like she loves her. I told her I understood." He pulls me to him.

"Oh." That worry line on his forehead isn't fixed. I run my finger and trace the furrow.

"Teddy doesn't want to hide anymore, and Laura's first step was to divorce me. But her family got a hold of that juicy bone and it spiraled."

"You people should really stop talking to your parents."

He grins. "There's more."

"Duh."

tony

This woman. I didn't want to burden her because she had so much on her plate in order to graduate.

"Sweet girl, you're the answer to all the questions but not to all of my problems."

"I like that. Did someone say that?" she asks.

"I did. Just now."

"Oh, it's clever and sweet and makes my heart swell."

"It was meant to." I grin, but it's my turn to come out.

I hold her close and inhale her head. I can't explain it, but it's like a shot of Valium to my soul. I say, "My darling, perfect, insane, girl, here are my secrets. I signed a contract and got sucked into a sizable bet that I wouldn't date for a year."

She pulls away from me and sits. She's in my dress shirt with her knees together and her feet apart. So sexy and perfect doing her best broken doll model pose.

"You made a deal and bet not to date me?"

I kneel in front of her. "No, not you. It was anyone. The only reason I attached myself to them in the first place is your fault."

"Wait, I'm to blame for your father being pissed? Cool."

She stands and puts on her pants. This is getting worse, not better.

"STOP. Woman. Sit. It is so not what you think." She slowly turns.

She puts her hands on her hips, "Promise me I'm not the fool in this story."

"Most assuredly not."

"Do not make me hex you." She squints.

"I'd never cross you, little witch."

"Don't make me spark up the coven, you muthafucker. Start."

"Start where?" I ask.

"The first lie." She points at me, and I nod to her and begin.

She drives me to the airport in her piece-of-shit car. I want to come up with an untraceable way to get her an Audi. Maybe I could rig a contest or a radio giveaway.

"And you really locked all those women down because I left?"

"That's how it feels. And there's the therapy piece of it all that kind of confirms my serial legal monogamy is that I'm trying to trap happiness."

She laughs. "I promise not to trap you."

I turn to her. "Then promise not to leave me."

"You know I can't do that. And neither can you."

"Track record says differently. I only broke up with one of those women. I was willing to stay married to a bitter woman who was so depressed and repressed because her soulmate wasn't me. So, I'm not the leaving type."

I say, "Then don't piss me off. And we don't have to get married."

"We don't?"

"You really want to get married again? Forget your stupid family. Answer for you."

Tony turns to me and takes my hand. "I do. I believe in forever, you taught me that, and I certainly hope you'll join me. I only want to get married one more time."

"Probably a good idea."

I laugh as we pull up to the departures area of McCarran/Harry Reid airport.

"Of course, you're laughing. I'd laugh if you'd been engaged as many times as I have." I glance at the airport goodbyes going on all around us. "I've been through this airport so many times in the last ten and half months, it's starting to feel like home." She grins.

"Kiss me goodbye and let me sit with all of this. I wish I could tell you I'll be fine."

"I know. And there's no telling what I'm walking back into or when I can see you again. Or call you again. My life is fucked for the next forty-one days. But on the other side..."

"On the other side." She's not sure of me or herself, and I hate that.

"If I can, can I come for your graduation?"

"I'll save you a ticket."

"And you're set on Reno?"

"Mags is moving to Tahoe, and I can stay at her mountain house and do the program. I qualified for a great scholarship and financial aid package." Kills me I can't pay for school, but she'd kill me if I did.

"Can I move to Reno?" I blurt out.

She puts her hands up. "One step at a time. Finalize your life. Get the company. Restore your wallet. Fix your father. Can I pay your bet?" She smirks as I kiss her.

"I owe ten million."

"WHAT? Tell me that's ten million jellybeans or pieces of

dust, which is still a fuck of a lot of dust but come ON! Dude."

I lean in and pull her to me. I take her lips. She gasps and moans a bit as our tongues meet in the most perfect dance of twisting and grinding against each other.

"You can't do that. You can't pay people ten million dollars because you love me. Let me talk to them. Who are these morons?" I purse my lips.

"You know who they are." I kiss her quickly and she smirks at me. "Don't think about it. I don't regret a penny, and we always donate the same amount as the bet to the charity of the loser's choice. I don't know when I'll talk to you, but I'm so proud of you."

"So, ten million is getting donated where?"

"How about GLSEN?" Her face softens, and I adore her more. "Massachusetts based organization to help LGBTQIA kids in high school."

"Good. And you should tell Laura that as well. Maybe she can donate some of her new windfall too."

I kiss her quickly. She's adorable.

Then she realizes what I just said, "Wait, you don't think you'll talk to me before graduation."

I lean back in the car as a cop whistles at us. "Baby, I get out from under all of this and I don't know what's in store for me. I'll call every spare second I've got."

I kiss her again through the window and then I hear, "Tony!? Tony Ladd. Wife number four?" There's a phone recording me and a giant camera in the background.

Fuck my life.

mak

MAK: We have lots to work on. Like you not paying people shit tons of money for me. I miss you. Sorry about the press. That wasn't fair. Did your dad freak the fuck out?

T: Hi! I have a fucking guard now. I'm texting from the bathroom on contraband. It's an underground device just to talk to you. Seriously, it's a babysitter because I went to Vegas again.
   MAK: I miss you.
   T: Don't use my other number. Just use my LW phone.
   MAK: Loose Wench? Lilac Waste? Liberty Warrior?
   T: Really? Little Witch.

MAK: Hi. Are you ok?

MAK: Good morning. I hope you're having a better day than I am. Missing you sucks. I don't like not knowing what's going on with you.

MAK: Did the LW phone get confiscated?

T: No. Hi. Swamped. I'm so sorry. They're watching me and there's a heavier thing happening and I'm trying to get to the bottom of it. I love you and I miss you. I don't know when we'll be able to see each other. I'll understand if you want to back off, this is a lot.

MAK: I love you too. I'm not going anywhere.

MAK: T?

MAK: Are you there? Seriously, you don't have time to answer me back? That's ridiculous.

MAK: Ok. I love you and miss you. I hate this.

T: Good morning. I'm thinking about you.

MAK: Hi! Can I call you?

MAK: Tony?

MAK: You there?

MAK: Are you still coming to graduation? It's been almost a month without you. My vagina is drying up and withering.

TONY: Ha! I don't know. Things are in turmoil. And I literally have a bodyguard, Toadie. My father needs me to not step out of any lines and I'm fucking trapped. I fall into bed exhausted at night and rush to the office first thing. Trust me when I tell you my cock misses the hell out of your pussy. But not as much as I miss you. I'm so sorry for all of this. This is all getting too much. I don't know how to get out of it or out from under all of this. I'm trying to get to the other side so we can be together and my life will be my own. I'm so sorry. But it might be a little longer than we expected. Love you.

tony

I'm going out of my fucking mind. Teddy and Laura are at my penthouse for the next couple of nights before they make a life together in upstate New York. Teddy quit her job; they're leaving. Wish I could.

We're six weeks apart, and this sucks. I have a fucking asshole on me 24/7, so unless I'm in my home, I can't use the other phone. Mak's messages go unanswered all the time. I fucking hate my dad. We're theoretically two weeks out from freedom. We've missed so much over the last year. I'm putting a chunk of money with Claire, and I'll invest every paycheck so this can never happen again. I want out of all the Ladd business, the trust included. This shit has to stop.

I lean forward to my regular driver and my new babysitter. "Change of plans, assholes. Take me to Ladd Tower. I need an audience with the almighty one." Today's the day I get shit figured out. He can't duck me.

The babysitter of the day says, "No. He's too busy for anything."

"What did you say to me?" He turns around, and I look at my normal driver's eyes in the rearview. He flicks them to the side. I wink and turn my attention to the BSOTD. (Babysitter

Of The Day) I don't play the asshole rich guy card often, but I do have it in the holster.

"Fuck face. You're not to talk to me like that. Forget your little mission or who you think I am and know me as the president of Ladd Media Group. And for all intents and purposes I'm your boss. But fine, take me to work."

I unbuckle discreetly, quietly gathering my bag and nod to the face in the mirror. I smirk. The light turns green, and he pulls over slightly. I jump out, and he speeds off. I take off the four blocks to my dad's office. He'll have a heads-up, but at least I have the corporate key to the family elevator.

I go around the back of the building and enter my code; miraculously, it opens. I hop in the elevator. It opens to my father with his arms crossed and Dax waving behind him. I don't know if Dax was here or if he was summoned in the last couple of minutes, and he rushed over from his advertising office.

I hug my dad despite his stiffness, which is actually uncharacteristic.

Dax hugs me, and we embrace fully. I love my brother and haven't seen him nearly enough lately.

"Sophie status?" He puts his thumbs down and shrugs.

"Dad. Good to see you. Mrs. Doubtfire tattle on me?"

"I was informed. What's on your mind son?"

I ignore him and walk toward his office. This isn't a hallway conversation. Dax puts his hand on my back. "Don't blow up again. It wreaked havoc on him."

"And you think him blowing up my life and holding a leash like I'm a fucking child or a dog is any better?"

"Point taken, bro. Just talk to him."

"I'll give him the same respect. Stop being our go-between."

"What will Mom and I do if not this?"

I laugh.

I enter the room and toss my bag on a chair. I sit in one across from his '90's desk, and he takes his place behind it.

"Dad. I'm going out of my mind. I'm sneaking around, I'm spending my savings and"—I put my secret phone on the desk—"I call her when I'm not being watched or working, on this phone. This is all ridiculous. She graduates today from her pre-med program, and I can't be there. It is slicing me in two. You come clean now. Why the fucking barbaric behavior?"

Dax sits down. "Dad, I agree. What the fuck is going on? The staff is scared of you. We've been kept off corporate board emails."

"We have?" I ask.

"It's not like you ever read them." Dax glares at me.

"And you did? You're a copywriter."

"And a voting member of Ladd Industries, as are you."

"Yeah, I know. I wait for the email telling me how to vote, unless it involves the media end."

My father exhales. He stands behind his desk, puts his arms out straight, and leans towards us.

"You've been embargoed from the board."

"Why? Spill it, old man, I'm done dancing for your amusement. I need to be with her." I cross my legs and sit back because whatever this crap is, it's not my fault.

"Regardless of what I'm about to tell you, she's a bad idea. Anyone is right now. I'm not going to budge on that."

"And letting me make my own decisions? Romantic, financial, and corporate? When does that happen?"

He sighs and lowers his eyes. "I was reminded recently that you can't hold onto a fistful of sand."

Dax walks around the room, but I stay put. Dax says, "Grandma used to say that."

"That she did. The board is entertaining the idea of a new CEO and there's a move to sell on the horizon. People want to take us."

"Can they do that?"

"They can."

"So, you messed with my life because your shit's fucked up?"

My father crooks an eyebrow. "In a way. But I didn't marry those women and I'll never understand why you let Laura get away with it all."

I purse my lips. I say as gently as I can, "Let her tell you someday. Not my story to tell."

"I'm so confused. And I don't know what to do or where to turn. I'm spinning plates, boys," my dad says.

Dax clears his throat, but I put my hand up, indicating I'll take this one. "Dad, are you kidding? Who cares? Retire. Go fuck Mom in exotic locations. She loves you, and for some messed up reason, she still wants to do your wrinkled ass. Tap hers. Go. Who are you spinning these plates for? Grandpa? Take the money. You earned it. I know what I said about inheriting, but you built this company, now give it up. Take the massive payout and let the legacy go. Let us go."

Dax is quick to back me up. "As crass as he can be, he's right. You know I don't want any part of this company. Clearly, Tony only wants what he's built over the last decade, make it part of your severance package."

"Yeah, you can sit on my board and shuffle papers around. Hell, you can run useless meetings if you want to. I don't care, just get me out. Get us all out."

Dax finishes, "Release him and they can do whatever the hell they want with the antiquated insurance division or the real estate shit. You have always hated that part and the corporate structure. You did it because you were told to, and you raised us to think for ourselves. That we didn't have to do what was expected."

My father and I stare at Dax.

I break our silence. "That's honestly more words I've heard from you in the last year in total."

"I save it up."

My father falls into his chair. And then I follow suit.

"Dad. You ok?"

He cracks his knuckles. Dax and I glance at each other and back to him. "It's not that easy but I'll take it under advisement. I'm proud of both of you despite your disastrous love lives. I'm so sorry you've been held hostage to all of this." He seems remorseful.

I protest, "Hey! Mine isn't. This is the healthiest I've ever been."

My dad grins and puts his head to the side. "Says the man who has no idea what a healthy relationship is."

"Love that you called me a man, but I know exactly what it is, and so does Dax."

He nods and says, "Yours."

Dad always gets a dopey grin on his face when he thinks of our mom.

"Dad, where does that leave me?" I ask.

"My hands are tied. You made your own bed, and I can't get you out of it right now. If you want your division to become its own company, you have to see this through."

"How long?"

"Six months, a year?"

"Christ, no. I'm not waiting that long to start my life because of some old fucks. If I pull my people, does your world implode?"

"Yes."

Dax puts his hand on my arm and pushes me back into a chair. "Dad. Where does this leave you?" he says.

"I need to figure out what's worth fighting for."

I offer up, "Dax would tell you it's love. But he can't even keep his shit locked down. And how come he never gets shit about his fucked-up love life?"

"Sophie hasn't cost us a dime." Dad raises his eyebrows. "A string of call girls would have cost us less than your escapades. And do you know the private jet bill your so-called new perfect love has cost us? It's public record and the *New York Post* and the *Boston Globe* are running your bootie call tally this weekend."

"Point taken. But believe me, she's different this time."

"Time will tell. It's all we have. Your word on this matter does not have a good track record of holding onto our stock or your furniture."

"Leave my wallet alone."

"Son, you can't do anything, I mean anything, to jeopardize our position, or we could lose everything. I really am sorry that you're stuck because of things I've done with this company or my desire to hold on to it. You haven't helped, but it is a really fucked-up situation."

Dax smirks. "Everything? Bit dramatic there, Pops."

My father doesn't smile. "I wish I were. Tony, I'm so proud of what you've done with Cookery and taking that division into a space I couldn't even envision."

I stand up and run around the desk and hug him. He hugs me back hard. Then I dance away from him, singing a made-up song, "I do have Cookery. I have a whole hell of a lot of Cookery. Do you? Do you need some Cookery?" Dax snaps but doesn't dance to my made-up tune. "Hey, Big Poppa, do you need some Cookery? Or do you need Bora Bora with Mom?" Our mom has always dreamed of living in a hut in Bora Bora with Dad. It makes us laugh because they'd last maybe three hours and then check into the Four Seasons.

"You can have it all, Big Poppa." I twerk for him while rapping. "You can crush that ass in the tropics and all you have to do is dump off this fucking albatross of a legacy."

He points to the door. I walk up to him, and he kisses me on the head.

"Pops. Get me the fuck out of this sooner than later. I can't stay chained here. I can't sacrifice the love of my life or the future of a lot of people who worked extraordinarily hard for me and you."

"I know. But it's a long fight."

Dax addresses him, "Father. I'm tired of you being tired and cranky. What are you fighting for? We don't want your life. Time to find your bliss." We both grin as Dax repeats an oft-repeated phrase from our parents.

I collect my Makenzie phone and shake my ass on the way out as I hum the tune for the Cookery song.

She's just waking up. I sent all the things I could. I wish I could go and be there. There's a hole in my soul. That would make a great song. I'd sing it for her, but she's kind of over me at the moment and this distance. I feel it. I know it's not irreparable yet, but we're close.

TONY: I'm sorry. I'm so fucking sick of saying sorry, and I know you're sick of hearing it. But I can't. Fuck. Congrats. I'll be there for everything else you achieve. Or I'll try to be. But for now I have to stay far away from you. The company is in trouble. Everything is in jeopardy. My father won't get out and I'm stuck. I could lose Ladd Media, but I don't want to lose you.

TONY: I don't know what to do to salvage all of this and save you from a life of long-distance dating. But if it means choosing between my family, the company, and you—know that I'm dangerously close to getting a job at the local Reno Target and doing whatever it takes to be near you. I love you so desperately but give me a second to figure all this shit out. But, I swear, you say the word and I'm stocking candles in the home goods section. Congratulations my brilliant, beautiful witch.

TONY: You're everything. I'm going to figure out a way to save you from a life of unanswered calls and broken promises.

mak

"**M**akenzie Suzanne Preston." I take the rolled-up piece of paper that gives me chills. I've often been flippant about it being just a piece of paper. It doesn't give me worth. It doesn't. But it does tell me and everyone on the planet that I worked my ass off for this and what's to come. I hold it up, and I'm clearly one of the oldest graduates, but the whole section stands up and cheers me. I scan the crowd. I haven't spoken to him in two weeks, and I know he can't be here, but I'm pissed, and it stings.

I wave and bow to the crowd and my family. My mom is so great she stands and jumps. My mom with her beautiful curves looks so beautiful. All the weight stuff was always about her health to Dad and me. But now she's a jumping person, and that's gorgeous, mostly because of how she feels about herself. It's infectious. I try to put it out of my mind, but he's not here.

I step off the stage, and someone shoves a bunch of flowers into my arms.

To adventure.
Love you, T

I try not to take it personally but I won't live in the margins any longer. We've reached a critical moment and I have to figure out what's best for me. My stomach lurches and my heart seizes with possibilities and outcomes. I push it down because there's a party planned at the rec center for us all to celebrate. It's as much their accomplishment as mine.

The music is kicking up. I thought, somehow, he'd surprise me. I thought he'd call. I don't know what his fucking cryptic text was about. He hasn't answered me. I should call Lill. But I can't do one more second of missing out on each other's lives. I don't want to build mine one more second without him. This shit sucks.

My mom walks over; she's been up and down and all around. The two of them are now planning to travel. They're going to Branson, Missouri. Not Paris, but it's a start.

I sip my warm punch and smile. I've been hugged and back slapped. I gave a speech thanking Dr. Parry and Barton for all their help. I'm going to keep my job through the summer and look for something else in Reno when I get there. I don't actually know what's happening with Tony. My mind plays that super fun game of, 'Is he over me or is he lost?'

My mom sits and says, "All of my buttons are busted. I'm so proud of you."

"Now that I've accomplished something," I joke, and my father takes my hand.

"None of that now. We've always been proud of the person you are. Not all the behavior at times, but you've always been so confident, strong, kind, and smart. There's nothing more we could want from a daughter. Except maybe for her to get the hell out of our house. You made this happen."

"I did." I grin and laugh.

My father sits down with us. "Leech, you've outdone yourself."

"That's a real compliment from a Slug."

"Daughter, I'm not proud you're going to be a doctor. I'm proud you figured it out. It took your mom and me a while, but you're going to be better off. And you did it all while pushing our slug asses to treat ourselves better too. That's our whole job in a nutshell. That our kids do better than we did. Thank you for pulling your head out of your ass and for helping us with way too much. You're almost perfect, there's just one last thing. A parenting push if you will." My father raises an eyebrow.

He slides me an envelope. "You've always gotten everything you've wanted and truly went after. We knew you took the church's money, and we also watched you not only pay it back but continue on helping out where you could. All so you could see Paris."

I grin. Tears pop into my eyes. Tony.

I take the envelope, and my mom says, "Stop waiting for the rest of this to take care of itself. You've never backed down from a challenge. Go."

I rip open the envelope and pull out a plane ticket to Boston.

"Honey, go set him straight. Go fight whatever's been keeping him away."

"A digital ticket is easier."

"Yes, but it wouldn't have had the same impact." My mom winks at me, and the tears flood down my face.

"I don't even know what to do."

"You won't know if you don't try. We're tired of your mopey ass. We haven't been the most active parents, but I will kick your ass if you don't go get in a car right now. Honey, you're the strongest person I've ever known, a fighter, go fight for the life you deserve."

I bite my cheek to stop myself from crying and shake my head to look at them. "This is a lot of money for you guys. Thank you."

Everyone is staring at us. Chelle pulls me to stand. "Go get our man." I smile.

Then I look at the rest of the envelope, and there's a check for $12,415. I scan the room and realize what's happening.

"You all can't do this." I burst out in tears.

Barton smiles and says, "Each of us gave what we could. We know your scholarship doesn't cover living expenses and we hope this will help. At least get a decent car."

"I can't take this."

Dottie says, "You can. We're so proud of how hard you've worked. If you're hellbent on not spending that cutie patootie's money, then spend ours." I hold it to my chest and wipe my tears and smile wider than I think is possible. Their kids are going to kill me.

My father whispers, "Plane boards in an hour. Get a move on, Leech. Go give 'em hell."

I throw my arms around my parents. "Thank you. You're the best slugs ever."

He texted he didn't know how to save me. Maybe I was always meant to save him.

The car can't get there fast enough. It's late, but not too late, and he once told me he works into the night often. I'm here to fix this. But my fight doesn't start where I thought it would. It's the future I want, not the semi-present. No more distance because other people say so. If I have to find a med school in

Boston, I will. I can talk anyone into anything, but I'm finally ready to fucking claim all I deserve. There's nothing and no one who can stop me from getting to him. I'll go to his house if he's not at the office. This all needs to start with him.

I storm into the building. "Hello, I know that it's late, but I need to see Mr. Ladd. It's a matter of life and death, and I will be family someday."

"Ma'am, I can't let you up. And you're not the first to claim to be the next Mrs. Ladd."

I grin at him and chuff at his joke. I square my shoulders and look him straight in the eye. "If I sneak up there, what kind of time am I looking at? Is it a fine or an arrest? I used to be able to pick a lock in under twenty seconds."

The beefy guy stands and leans over the counter. "You'll get thrown out of here." He pauses, then arches an eyebrow. "What kind of lock? I used to be pretty good at that too."

"Well, criminals make the best cops. I'm going to be a doctor, but you get it." He stands up straight, and I lean over the counter.

"Ok—"

I put my hand out to shake his. "Makenzie Preston."

"Ok, Makenzie Preston, I'll make you a deal. Give me your ID. You pick a lock in under thirty seconds, and I'll let you up with the promise that you're not here to kill anyone."

I open my jacket wide, then hand him my wallet. "Call whoever you want on me. Not gonna kill a soul."

"Choose your lock picking equipment?"

I open my hand and show him the unmarked key card and paperclip. I palmed them when I leaned over the counter.

"Nice work. Come here." I follow him down the hallway to the stairwell door. It's a one-way lock, and I only have to pull a couple of pins. Fucking child's play, but I need an insurance policy.

I get behind him, slap him on the back and lift what I

need. "Thanks so much for the opportunity to hone my skills." He laughs and backs up, giving me room to work.

I unfold the paperclip and double it up. I put it in and bang with my hip while lifting the handle and turning the paperclip. The door pops, and I open it.

"Ten seconds. That was fucking impressive, but this was all for my amusement. I can't let you up without security clearance and it's too late to call up. There's a strict do not disturb going on."

My eyes brim with tears in a virtuoso performance on my part. "Doug, I do understand. If anyone asks and if my opinion matters, I'll give you accolades. I'll come back tomorrow morning."

"I'll put a note in the log, so they help you out first thing."

I put my hand on his arm and squeeze. "Thank you. Is there a bathroom I could use?"

"Sure." Look, I'm not proud of the skills, but I have them, and the end justifies the means. I'll make sure this guy gets a raise if the Ladds ever talk to me again. But he's about to get fucked.

He points to a hallway, settling back behind the desk. I walk slowly, and he watches for a moment. I push the button without looking and duck down the hallway out of his sight-line. I wait against the wall for the ding. I can't quite see it, but I know I'll only have a moment when I hear it. My palms are sweaty, but my brain and blood are buzzing.

I whisper to myself to calm myself down and to hype myself up, "To adventure."

There's a ding, and the door slides open. I dart into the elevator quick as a cat. Doug realizes what's happening. I wave as the door slides closed. I know his office is on the 50th floor, and I use Doug's key card to get the elevator to move.

I look at the security camera and mouth the words, "I'm sorry." Then I do that heart thing with my fingers over my chest. My breathing is erratic, as is my heartbeat. It's kind of a bad girl rush, not gonna lie. I'm doing this, and I feel sorry for him because I'm busting in with no more fucks to give and fight roaring through my veins.

The elevator opens, and there are people scattered around. Before they look at me, I grab a folder off an empty reception desk. I'm in my dress from graduation, and I'm sure I look tired, so I fit right in with this crowd. It's 7:00 p.m., and I walk over to a small group.

I wave the folder and say, "Excuse me, I have to ask Mr. Ladd a quick thing for my boss down on twelve. Could someone point me towards his office?"

Without even acknowledging me, they point down the hall, and someone dismissively says, "In the back corner, his assistant will be able to help you out." I wave to them and make my way down the hall trying to stop my hands from shaking. The assistant is missing, and I'm overjoyed.

I knock, and a deep but tired-sounding voice yells, "Come in." I slowly turn the doorknob and slip in the door. I steady my nerves and knees. He looks up.

"Is that for me?"

"No, sir." I put down the folder. "Do you remember me?"

He sits back and pushes up his sleeves. His eyes reflect Tony's, and his gray hair is perfectly done even after an exhaustive day of running the world.

"I'm sorry. It's been a long day, and I meet so many people. I'd like to be able to say I know all the people who work here, but that's impossible. Is there something I can help you with? Is Helen out there?"

I step closer, and he seems uncomfortable. I get it, a younger woman, after hours in an office with the biggest boss there is. I stay rooted to my spot.

"We met almost thirteen years ago, not that you would remember, but it kind of changed my life. I'm a friend of well... um... I'm Tony's. And I'm here to change my life again. He'll do anything for you and your family, that's part of the reason I've put up with this ridiculous distance, because family matters, but it's time. Mr. Ladd, hand over his company now, not in a month or a year, but now. Release him from whatever hold you have and let him be happy. More specifically, let me make him happy. Sir." His face relaxes, and he stands up.

There's a slight grin as he says, "I'll be damned, this time *is* different. My God. Makenzie?"

"Yes, sir. And we have about five minutes until security busts in here to yank me back to the street."

"He never told me it was you. How did you get up here?"

"I swiped the security guard's card." I step forward and place it on his desk. "Can you give this back to Doug? And you should give him a raise. It wasn't his fault. I'm on a mission and there's not much that's going to stop me."

"What are you here for?"

"Tony."

"Are you aware of his situation?"

"Yes, that you disapprove of him falling in love, because he's the boy who cried monogamy. But I assure you, I'm not temporary. I know every detail of everything, and I do believe you are the reason he hasn't called in almost three weeks. And there's some work bullshit that means the tower of Ladd will come crumbling down if he's seen with me."

"Not you specifically, dear. But that sums it up."

"Why?" I ask.

He shifts his weight and crosses his arms. He's standing and staring at me, and I gather all my grit not to sway or run away. I'm resolute.

"I don't understand." Crooking his eyebrow, he looks just like Tony. And it pangs my whole body that he's not here with me.

I square up to this man and continue my assault. "You're happy with your wife, right?"

He nods.

I continue, "And you have more money than most European countries. Like you're more liquid than Italy, right?"

He laughs and nods again.

I don't stop questioning him. "You're one of the most respected men in business."

"Thank you, but where is this flattery leading?" he asks.

"Why?"

"Why, what?"

"Why do you need more?" I walk towards him as he flumps down in his chair. I lean over the desk. "Tony has figured out what he wants and what will be enough for him, because you gave him those values. But he's still here and missing my life moments and missing out on building his own life because you have him feeding your vision, not his."

He sips his brown liquor drink and stares at me. He gestures to offer me a drink and I shake him off. I'm high enough right now without alcohol.

"Congratulations on your scholastic achievement today, Ms. Preston. You're an impressive and formidable person."

I nod sharply. "Give him the media division, dissolve his agreement with you, set him free. He's incredible and cares more than you can imagine. I won't let you stand in our way because he wants to make sure you're ok. We both stood in our own ways long enough, dancing under the weight of shadows we set for ourselves. But I'll be damned if someone else gets to fuck up our forever. I'm done waiting for my adventure to start. It happens today, right now. But not unless you release him, sir."

"That's a passionate speech."

"I'm passionate about him. You have no idea, so I'm going

to tell you. Stay seated, please." He nods and sips his drink but gives me a little wink. "I've lied, cheated, and screwed up more things than most people have tried. It's how I know he's the only one for me. He's the only thing in my life that's always been true. Be proud of him the way that I am and back the hell off so he can live up to his own expectations instead of trying to reach yours."

He comes around the desk and sits down in a chair, motioning for me to sit in the other one across from him. At that moment, a stunning woman, who I also met thirteen years ago, comes busting into the room with Doug on her heels.

I pop up and point at Doug. "Him. Make sure you give him a raise. It was nice to meet you again, sir. Please heed what I said because other than getting tossed out of the building, I'm not going anywhere."

I put my hands out as if Doug is ready to cuff me. He laughs and Mrs. Ladd covers her heart.

"Sit down, dear," his mother says. Mr. Ladd tosses Doug his key card, and he salutes me and exits the room. "That man told me a woman broke in and was headed up here and I panicked. But he didn't tell me it was you."

I shake her hand. "Nice to see you again, Mrs. Ladd."

"Cheryl."

"Really? Cheryl Ladd? My grandmother loved her."

She sighs. "It's unfortunate, but there are two of us. I'm more concerned with you, Ms. Preston, and what I overheard. Do you truly love Tony, or do you see him as helpful?"

I'm all in, or I'm all out right here.

"I'm aware I'm not the girl you saw for him or dreamed for him. I have a record and a sketchy past, but I worked my ass off to get the life I want and deserve. I graduated second in my class today with honors. I'm headed to medical school on scholarship and financial aid. I'll be the oldest in my freshman class, but I did it on my own."

I plant my feet and stare at both of them. I'm finally standing in my own light, and, for maybe the first time, I see myself clearly. I don't see the shadow of the things I've done. I'm not judging myself for past mistakes but looking forward to making all new ones.

I say, "Do I find him helpful? Hell yeah. He helps me feel more myself than anyone or any place on earth. He helps me remember that life is worth pushing forth and finding adventure. He helps me feel fulfilled and hopeful. He helps me keep motivated to want more from myself and from the world. And he helps me know that I'm loved. But as for your skepticism, I'm going to be in his life if he'll still have me, so why not drop your attitude? I'll sign anything you want. I don't want a dime. Not a penny. If you want to put some of your money in a trust for our kids—" She gasps, and I kind of do internally.

"That's between you and Tony. But I won't spend your money, and I respect your legacy. Look, I made him promise me he'd never buy me anything over a hundred dollars. All that other stuff he did was for my family and a debt I owed, but not one cent was for me. Except the Vegas stuff. That was a little for me and I did sleep in the suite willingly and eat all the Taco Bell, but I'm getting off on a tangent." I put my hands in front of me and breathe in and out.

His mom whispers, "You're doing fine, keep going."

"Every bouquet of flowers he sent over the past eight weeks, I looked up the cost and they were always ninety-nine bucks. He listens to me, and I hear him. Something you two have forgotten to do. Listen when he gives you a good idea and tells you he's in love with me for real, or back then. You banned him from dating me once, I won't let you do it again."

She nods at him, and he squeezes her hand. I'm going to

burst into tears in a moment. I can't believe I said all those things. My body is wrung out but my mind is pinging.

He speaks to me with a grin on his face, and I don't know what the hell that means. "You're wrong about one thing."

I shrug. "Probably a million things, but what are you talking about?"

"You're exactly who we dreamed of for our son."

And I exhale.

tony

No one's here, but I can't drag myself home. I'm in a terrible mood and Laura and Teddy are all happy and at my house.

Mak won't answer my calls. I'm out of my head with guilt over missing her graduation, not talking to her, and what the hell to do about my dad? I distanced myself for what? I'm missing the most important part of myself. I fucking gave it away in order to do what? What the hell? I'm choosing work over love? My father never had to make that choice, or maybe he did. Who the hell knows? I'm pacing my office, and I can't be this inactive. I'm done. I'll take my people and find the capital. I'll live off what Claire's made for me. I'll sign everything away when I get back. Mak and I can find a double-wide without a hole in the floor and shop at Target for everything. Jesus, I love Target.

I dial her phone again, and it goes to voicemail. Fuck it.

TONY: Not coming to say goodbye to you but stay at the penthouse. There's somewhere else I need to be.

LAURA: If it's not by that girl's side, you're not the wildly romantic man I should have been in love with. Sit tight, things have a way of working out.

TEDDY: *Being with the right woman can change everything.*

I dial up the one number I'm not supposed to. If I bring down the company for this, then fuck it.

"Can you ready the jet? The smaller one. I'll be there in an hour."

"Sir, we have to get authorization."

"I AM the authorization, or you're fired. We leave for Vegas in an hour."

She's done with school until the fall. I'll spend the next couple of months proving to her I've been a fool, and the only place I need or want to be is next to her. I'll build a new company wherever she wants. I don't need Boston or the money. Or any of this shit. I only need her.

I sling my bag over my shoulder and rush to the door and stop in my tracks.

"Going somewhere?"

My whole body freezes then vibrates. It's her. The most beautiful thing on the planet right here like I summoned her with my mind. That's eerie.

"How the hell did you get up here?"

She waves her hands around in front of her. "It's a whole thing. Do you want to hear it, or do you want to kiss me?"

I drop my bag near a chair and before it thuds on the ground, Mak's in my arms.

Her lips yield to me instantly, and her hands find their rightful place around my neck. I tug her to me, and my body comes alive. She teases my lips with her tongue, and I deny her and kiss her neck while talking.

"How did you know the exact moment I pulled my head out of my privileged ass?"

"Same moment I remembered my forgotten stubborn wild streak. Finally, we're in sync."

I back up and take her face in my hands, and my eyes tear

up. "I don't know how this happens or what will happen, but I know I can't do another second of this life without you by my side." Tears fill her eyes as well, and she bites her lower lip.

"That sounds an awful lot like a proposal."

"Not yet it is. I have to talk to some people first."

She pulls something from her purse and hands it to me. "Taken care of. What else is standing in our way?"

I take the ripped-up papers and see that it's my agreement with my dad. And unripped papers that dissolve Ladd Media from Ladd Enterprises.

"What did you do?"

"I've slain all the dragons and charmed all the problems."

I cock my head. "Sir Makenzie, what else have you done?" She hands me her phone.

MAKENZIE: You don't know me, but he trusts you. If he comes home before I find him, let me know so I can chase him there.

LAURA: Go rescue our damsel in distress. I'm glad it's you.

MAK: And I'm glad it's not you.

LAURA: And if the press takes him to task, I know the exact story to tell them to get the heat off of the two of you.

MAK: You'd do that?

LAURA: He makes us all braver. When you finish up finding him, come by his penthouse, and we'll all have dinner.

My eyes are bugging out. "How did you get in touch with her?"

"Your mom."

"What? And wait, Laura would come out, so we could be together?"

"Apparently. What else you got? I know you want me, but what the fuck else do you think is in our way? Bring it. All the lies, secrets, obstacles, roadblocks, whining about sheets ends right here." She rolls her hands, and I back up and take in her magnificent soul.

"I love you so hard," I say.

"I'm going to need it hard and quick in a minute, but are we done?"

I smile. "I have some debts to pay, I guess."

She pulls her phone out again. "Dax helped me out with this one and put me on the chain. But I took care of that too."

HAYDEN: Delightful doing business with you.

LAW: Cha-ching!

ROBBIE: Candy from a baby. Let's go double or nothing, he yells, "To adventure" soon.

COLTON: This one had me sweating. Did not want to give up that cash. But, Tony, you never disappoint.

DAX: And somehow, you got Dad to pay.

MAK: No. I did. (Makenzie) And from now on, leave my love life out of your little betting pool.

HAYDEN: Woo-Hoo! Mak! Lizzie says, you de witch!

LAW: We'll see if she can keep her spell cast over him for more than his longest relationship, three years.

MAK: Fine, I'll freaking play. Double or nothing.

HAYDEN: In.

LAW: In.

COLTON: I'm sweating, but no offense, Makenzie, I'll take that action. They're still together in three years.

DAX: In. But if you get married, this bet is null and void.

I type quickly into her phone.

MAK: This is Tony—gentlemen— Candy. Baby.

She pops a hip and closes the door behind her. "There's nothing standing in our way."

"Except your clothes."

"Well, that's easily handled too. Jeez, give me a challenge." She whips her dress off, and I get to see her fantastic body. I pick her up, and she wraps her legs around me. I lower her onto my couch.

"I love you, Tony."

I whip off her cheekies and outline her clit with my finger. "Prove it." Then she licks her lips and moans a bit. "Always wet for me. How do you do that?"

"Practice." She sighs and kisses my neck.

I hitch her up a little higher so she can feel what she's doing to me. "I'll bet I could spend the rest of my life proving it."

"I'll take those odds," she says with a smile.

I lean up, kiss her, and settle into the very best feeling in the world.

"Come with me. Right now, to the Vineyard, where you will enjoy yourself so much this time, you won't leave me."

"Cocky much?"

"Confident."

"Can we fuck on your couch first?"

"Duh."

We gasp and fall down next to each other, panting and waiting for our breath to return. We're staring up at the living room ceiling spread out like deflated balloon animals.

"I can't think of another way to fuck you."

"We could always start at the top of the list again." Her eyes flash at me, and my depraved, perfect girl fills my heart. I haul her to me. I'll never get enough time to hold her. We'll be apart while she works this summer, and I'll fly back and forth creating my company. We're rebranding. Round Table Media sounded better than being saddled with my last name. Dax has agreed to join the company, writing copy, and helping build the print publishing end of it all. Mak's transferring to a school in Boston, for real this time, next year if I promise not to help. But she doesn't know that I'll move my whole fucking operation to Reno in the blink of an eye if she decides to stay there. The text came in this morning that Dad's retiring, and I'm proud of him. He cited my girl for crystalizing what Dax and I have been saying for years. Always bet on Mak.

She kisses my nose and caresses my fatigued dick.

I buck into her hand and speak for my cock. "Yeah, he's got nothing. You can try if you like, but I'm not hopeful."

"He feels cozy and nice."

"You're insane." I kiss her. "In only the best ways. You can hold it 24/7 if you like, but it might get weird at meetings."

"If you only ever do video meetings then I can hold it all the time. But the distance is going to kill me, I think."

"We've done it for a year, we can certainly handle a measly couple of months. And now I'm allowed to fly to you and fuck you whenever I like."

"You think so, do you?"

"Hmm. What should we do with the rest of the week? The beach, but it's got that Vineyard chill tonight. We have this warm cozy fire that we've already done it in front of for days on end, but what should we do? Movie?"

She laughs.

"Quick game of Ringolevio?"

She sits up and leans over to me. Her long dark hair falls straight over her face. The light is perfect, between the fire and the summer sunset outside. I know we only have a couple more days before my parents reclaim their house. But right now, the world belongs to Makenzie Preston. She owns me. And if I'm honest, she has since that witch answered the damn dorm phone.

I tuck her hair off her face.

"Dodgeball, build a sandcastle, paint the fence, open a deli? World's your oyster today. What do you want to do?" I say to this most beautiful girl.

"Get married."

My heart and brain freeze like I chugged a cherry Slurpee.

She straddles me and cups my cheek. I'm a little distracted by the breasts now dangling before me, but I close my eyes hard and refocus. When I open them, she's smirking. "Baby, I don't want your money, and I sure as hell don't want your company or your job. I'll happily sign whatever lawyers say. I can't afford one, so I'll get a terrible deal in the prenup."

I sit up and lean against the couch collecting her onto my lap. Can't help it, I take her breasts in my hands and kiss each nipple. Then I let go and look at her again, trying to not suck her spectacular tits. "I'm putting these in the prenup, so if we break up, I get visitation rights."

"I'm serious, Tony."

"I get it. You want to lock this shit down. Chain it up, lay claim to all of this. My condition is that I keep the boobs in the maybe divorce." I glide my hands down my torso, and she sputter laughs. Like she's surprised she found something suddenly so funny. It's my favorite of the Makenzie laughs.

She takes my hand. "Marry me. I know you won't ask, and if you do it will be long from now, and that doesn't work for me."

Then she leans over and kisses me, and my heart breaks so wide open, letting in all the light and sun in the world. As her lips leave mine, it closes around us, and I'm afraid of nothing in this life except being without her.

I kiss her neck. "Fine. Let's take the week off to celebrate our engagement."

She says, "You know I don't have time off from work, right?"

"You know you don't have to work, right?" She smacks me on my chest, leaving a red mark. "Oooh. New territory! We could always explore that."

"After the wedding. And I'm paying off my loans and contributing to our finances." I kiss her deeply, and she sinks into me.

"That's the sexiest thing about you."

"Stubborn?"

"Driven." I'm kissing her jaw, as I caress her ass when a tear drops on me. I pull back, and her eyes are glassy.

"I love you so much."

"Right back atcha."

She jerks her head up. "No."

"Sorry. Glib is a hard habit to break. I love you so fucking fiercely and deeply, Makenzie Preston, I'll never find my way out of it."

"Better." I laugh. She rocks back and forth and my cock miraculously jumps to life and hardens under her.

She smirks and grinds down. "And after this time, I've got to get home."

I roll her over onto her back. She steals my breath as her breasts fall perfectly so the sunlight hits them and frames them. I'm staring at her, and I lose all train of thought.

"Are you trying to say something poignant?"

"Possibly but hold on." I lean up and draw one nipple into my mouth, and she laughs.

"And here I thought you were being serious."

I speak with her boob still in my mouth, "Silly witch."

She sits up, and my mouth pops off her nipple. She tosses a blanket around herself. I stare at her and spread my arms out wide.

"Your perfect tits aside, I'm saying I have nothing if I don't have you."

"You have 17.6 billion dollars at your immediate disposal."

"I mean, I have that, but nothing else."

"You have everything," she says, and I take her shoulders and stare into her eyes.

"And if I lost all of it, that's fine because I'll still have you, and that's everything."

She quips, "I don't know whether this is charm or smarm.

My head is reeling. You don't know how to be poor. That's super romantic and very gallant of you to offer, but there's no choice for me. Poor, rich, dumb, smart, smarmy, ridiculous, my heart has always chosen you. You really were the fairy tale king and I was the queen plucked from the commoners."

I grin, take her in my arms, and say, "You're my witch not my queen because you bewitched my heart so long ago, and that spell has never been broken despite both of our efforts."

"Thank you," she says reverently.

"For loving you?"

"For seeing me." We hold each other as tightly as possible and stare into each other's eyes. The last of our resistance slides off both of us like rainwater off the slimy seniors.

tony

Watching Makenzie getting dressed was one of the saddest moments of my life. I love her body. I love her naked, and I love that she's mine. I'm taking her home, dropping her off, checking in with Dottie, Chelle, and Julia, and hanging out with her parents, the slugs. I'll sleep in her little back room on a pullout couch. I cannot wait to see what fresh hell that will be. But I promised not to buy a hotel suite because that's what she wants for this week in Vegas. And she wants to hike, whatever that entails. I swear it's just walking, but we shall see. And apparently, so we don't die of heat stroke, we have to do it in the middle of the fucking night with critters all about. But if it means I'm with her and by her side, I'm all in.

I fell asleep before she did last night, and when I woke up a couple of hours later, she was feverishly working on something. I thought she'd finished all her scholarships and grant paperwork, but I guess not.

I wake her as our plane touches down. "Baby, we're here."

I kiss her lightly and scoop her up and set her down so she can walk ahead of me off the plane. We flew commercial because she insisted I not use the jet. But she did let me buy first-class tickets.

At the end of the jetway, I hear the telltale electronic bells and whistles of everyone's last chance at McCarren Airport or Harry Reid as it's now called. The slot machines that occupy the gate cul-de-sacs where people wait to leave this place are noisy at all hours. I never thought about what Vegas meant to me. It's always been a place you go, never a place you stay. But I'll always keep Vegas as a part of me now.

I see the beauty and light beyond the neon and glitter. This airport now means I get to see her. It will never be anything else. In those moments when I couldn't fly private, and rushed on the first airline that would have me to get to her side. And the misty melancholy of leaving her here. Leaving a piece of myself here. But now we're both complete, and I welcome the airport revelers and the good faux vibe smells of Cinnabon mixed with the fetid grease traps in need of cleaning. Bring it on. It's the perfume of my life now.

She takes my hand and drags me towards baggage claim. She's giddy as she checks her phone. I hear a lot of notifications. We're practically running.

For the first time in my life, I'm not frantic to be legally bound to someone because I know I'll always be bound to her. We're an intricately woven spell that will never be broken.

She jumps on the escalator and turns around.

"Kiss me." She commands as the iconic Vegas sign floor mosaic comes into view at the bottom of the escalators. Vegas enjoys reminding you where you are. There are signs everywhere in case you forget, even for a second.

I lean down and kiss her as I was asked. It's sweet and soulful.

"Do you trust me?"

"Loaded question."

"Marry me."

"In due time." I laugh that she's proposed again. I kiss her nose.

"Right now." She kisses me again, but I don't close my eyes as our escalator almost reaches the bottom.

As baggage claim comes into view I spy folding chairs set up and a white archway. There are people standing and cheering, and she's beaming at me from the step below.

My mom stands at the bottom of the escalators and there's a crowd of strangers forming around the spectacle. Mom hauls Makenzie in for a hug. I can't focus on anything as it's all gibberish in my brain. My mom opens my palm. I watch as my mother takes off my grandmother's rings, and I form a tight fist around them and fight some tears. I kiss her cheek, and she nods.

Mak smiles larger and brighter than the sun, as I place the heirloom diamond on her finger and kiss her. She puts her newly ringed hand on my cheek. I smile and pocket the wedding ring.

Then she's whisked away, and a large arm gets flung over my shoulder.

"Bonjour, asshole."

"What the fuck is happening?" I yell as Hayden hugs me hard.

Lizzie rubs her belly. "Your real wedding and get on board with it because I'm dealing with one super bitchy cranky tired boy and our upcoming son as well."

Hayden looks at his wife and says, "Ha. Ha. Come on! You're no freaking picnic right now, Mrs. I think I want some ice cream, can you get up and go get it?" I grin as they bicker. They're pretty cute at it.

Maggie throws her arms around me. "I KNEW it!" I hug her back. She's a ball of sunshine, always.

"What did you know, little Miss Optimist?"

"I knew you were hers. From the moment her face lit up answering that phone. And I knew you'd forgive her."

"We forgave each other. Now, if I'm supposed to be getting married, where the hell did my mom take her?"

I'm handed a drink by my father. Robbie and Claire are at his back. I hug them both tightly, then my father. I look around, and Colt is wrangling his children, who are six and twelve.

Hayden says, "Law's a little busy, but he's here."

He flashes his phone, and it's on FaceTime. He's in the dugout at the All-Star game.

"Sup, assface? Hot Bod Squad reporting for duty. Make this one count. Who's got odds? Mak's original bet is null and void due to the dumbass perfect baggage claim wedding. Let's double down. I take five years max."

My father intercepts, "NO BETTING. This is the one." He puts his hand on my shoulder. "Son, she's an admirable woman and not just because she helped make you a more complete man or took me to task. She did it on her own. Just so you know. I did not interfere, but I reached out to an old college friend. If she stays on course with her GPA for the first year of med school, there's a free ride to Tufts Medical School for next year. She could go Harvard too, but Tufts has a better family med program. And you should know, she earned it. She'll have to keep producing to stay there, but this is the kind of woman you want at your back."

Claire hoots and claps. Maggie shrieks. Even if she's mad we all know how intelligent she is, I'm beaming with pride.

"She was coached by double board certified, handsy seniors and some highly intelligent former nurses. She stands on the shoulders of an entire wrinkled village pulling for her. But we go where she wants. She chooses."

Claire chimes in, "You've got quite the challenge on your hands. She's much smarter than you."

"Nah. If that were the case, she wouldn't have broken up with me in the first place." I dust off my shoulders.

Everyone laughs, and I look around for her.

Lizzie points at me. "Nope. You don't get to see the bride before the ceremony. And if you'll excuse the rest of us ladies. Just hang with the Hot Bod Squad." We all laugh and then I correct Lizzie.

"Ladies?"

Maggie slugs me in the arm. "Elizabeth is a lady."

I correct Maggie. "She's a knight, don't forget that." Hayden goes gooey-eyed, looking at his woman as she bows to me. I bow back to Sir Lizzie, who I knighted on that fateful night in Paris so long ago.

Maggie laughs. "I forgot. Good King, I'll take my leave and fetch your queen."

She disappears, and Dax hauls me into a hug. He whispers in my ear. "Come on, let's push you towards adulting."

I lean back toward him, bite his ear, and lick his cheek. "Never."

Everyone hears me and laughs. The announcements of arrival flights and the billboards high up telling us who is in residence are all dulled when my mom guides over two familiar and fabulous people.

I kiss Mak's mom's cheek and shake her father's hand. "I would have asked for your blessing, but she proposed and apparently got a blessing from my folks."

"I'm glad to have you, son. That's who she is. Not one to wait when she finally figures out what she wants." Her father quips. But her mother puts her hand on my heart. "But hasn't that always been the way with our girl?"

"I promise to love her forever the way she deserves. And let her be as wild and free as she wants to be."

Her father scowls and says, "And you'll let her finish her

school. I have a feeling someone who got in all kinds of creative trouble may be too smart for their own good."

"She is, sir. And I have it on good authority, she's going to be a doctor."

"Of course, she is, she can be anything she damn well pleases."

"Agreed."

Chelle and Julia walk down the aisle first, spreading petals. Then they try to give me a hug. I air kiss them instead to avoid the oil. They're in their Lana dresses and tiaras. I love that they're Makenzie's flower girls.

Everyone looks, and I see her. Dark hair straight and dusting her shoulders, she's stunning in a long, fitted, cream satin slip dress with a cowl neck that dips in all the right places. She's flanked by the women I met her with and my mom. Everyone scurries to their seats. My brothers line up with Dax at the center. Of course, Dax got ordained. Robbie's holding his phone with Law's face filling the screen while in the dugout.

I stand at the end of the aisle with tears in my eyes as I realize all the shit I've done and will ever do was to get me to this moment and to her. Every prank pulled, test blown off, horrible idea, fabulous time, work achievement, drunken lost weekend, failed relationship, and alimony check all led me to this beautiful soul. And now I'm ready for her. I shake my head and jog down the aisle to her.

She scoffs at me. "You're supposed to wait for me at the end of the aisle."

"Nope. Done waiting."

She leans toward me and dusts her lips over the corner of my wet smile. Then turns down the aisle with me beside her, squeezes my hand, breathes in deeply, and says, "To adventure."

I raise my first in the air as we move forward.
"To adventure!"

epilogue

Mak

I have very limited time off so we need to get this shit going. I have boards to study for and hospital follow up to do, but I took off these two weeks, and so did my husband. Because it's too good. I made this one, and I want to rub it in their faces.

I'm standing on a monstrosity of a lawn that belongs to the Red Sox's newest pitching sensation and World Champion.

I'm backed up by a very cool and appreciative fire department. Tony has a fireman's hat on and everything. Law once told me I couldn't find water in a storm. It was my final year of med school, and I was exhausted and fucking pregnant, and nothing I said in that year made sense.

Tony hitches our kid, Salem, up on his hip.

I pull out my bullhorn and yell, "HEY! LAW! I found some water, now find your checkbook! Spark it up, boys. I'm gonna make it rain!"

They aim their hoses at his roof. I make it rain, literally. Law bolts out of his house just as the hoses set off a stream.

"What the fuck is happening? AHHHH. HOLY SHIT! Fuck." He runs out of the way of the water. "Tony? Makenzie, what the fuck are you doing?"

I'm laughing and dancing in the spray that's making a rainbow. I grab Salem, and we spin around as Tony approaches Law. I signal to the fireman to cut it. Law is dripping wet, and I snap a picture of him.

Tony's laughing his head off. I dance up to him with Salem on my hip, who can't stop laughing. She reaches for Law; she always does. He takes her.

"Little princess, what the fuck is wrong with your mommy?" She giggles.

"Pay up!" I gleefully scream.

"What?"

"You once bet me I couldn't find water in a rainstorm. I found water. I've also been happily married for five years and one day, which I believe means you owe me double the original love bet and that comes to—four million dollars." He groans and looks up at the sky.

"She's a shark." Law laughs big and loud.

"Nah, she's a witch with an axe to grind. Pay up," my love says.

"Fine." He taps his phone, and I hear a whoosh. Tony picks up his phone. They all have an account hooked up for instant transfers. It's the first time I'm actually making them pay. Claire's in charge of the account. Before they had a lifetime tally of things. Well, until I made Tony's dad pay up.

Law growls, and I say, "Thanks, man, pleasure doing business with you." I rub my hands together.

"You're not staying?" He tickles Salem.

"We've got a plane to catch." I tell him, and Salem holds him around the neck a little tighter.

"Where you headed?" He nuzzles into my daughter's belly, and her laughter peals through the neighborhood.

"Robbie and Claire."

He guffaws, then says, "Oh, collecting personally this time. Mak, you're too much."

"Mommy too much!" Salem yells at Tony.

"Thanks!"

Tony kisses me and smiles, then says, "We gots to go so we can get to Paris by tomorrow. Colt's meeting us there. And Dax and company are already on the plane. Mak broke in and crawled into their bed this morning. Scared the fuck out of them. She's collecting everyone."

I pump my arms in the air. That one was fun. Colt, being the sensible one, I let that family escape without a prank but did give them a command to meet us in Paris.

Law asks, "H know you're coming?"

"Nope. Wanna tag along?"

"Give me five."

I spark up my bullhorn on this beautiful Parisian Street with the entire band of Boston brothers behind me. All the kids are running up and down the street, and Colt's oldest is holding Salem's hand. I see Hayden in his art studio. It's dawn, and the world is just starting to stir. He once said I was so loud, I could wake the dead. Let's see.

"Hayden Corelli! HAYDEN!!!! GET YOUR ASS AND FAMILY DOWN HERE. Get your checkbook and meet us on the street or I'm going to keep making a commotion like Lizzie did all those years ago." He turns and leans out the window. A paintbrush falls from his top-floor studio.

"What? WHY? What is happening?" He disappears from

view, but we hear him bellow, "Put some clothes on, Elizabeth, apparently, we have company. A lot of company."

Moments later, the azure door flies open, and their children, little Danny and his sister Krissy, spill into the street, followed by Lizzie, who doesn't stop running until she's hugging us.

"This is the best surprise. What are you all doing here? Oh my God." She runs around hugging Claire, Robbie, Dax, Colton, and Law. As well as the other assorted members of our merry band.

Law says while picking up his niece and nephew, "We're here to watch you pay up."

Law, Robbie, and Hayden's mother bounds out of the gorgeous three-story building, squealing, "MY BABIES. All the babies are here. Come to me." Lilliana's a flurry of hugs and kisses and holding her grandkids, both blood and soul grandkids as she calls them. Then she demands her actual baby. Law lifts her up and swings her around in a giant hug. She lives here with Hayden and Lizzie, and her other kids find any excuse they can to visit.

Hayden appears in the doorway. I pull up the bullhorn. "Now can I wake the dead? The deadbeat that is."

Colt points out, "You owe her four million dollars." His eyebrows raise.

Tony hugs Hayden and says, "It's been five years and two days. She'd like her payout."

"You know we don't actually exchange money."

"You do now! Don't ever bet against a scrappy witch with nothing to lose."

Tony looks over at me. "Nothing?"

I take in his face and throw my arms around him. "I guess I have everything to lose, but I'm not going to. I love you."

"Bleck. It's been five years, and you're still like this?" Law says just as Hayden wraps his arms around Lizzie. He groans,

"Ma, get me out of here. Take me inside so you can feed me lots of pasta so I fall into a food coma and can get away from all this bullshit."

He's almost inside when Tony yells, "I can NOT wait until it happens to you."

I've collected twenty million dollars into their joint account, and it's more zeros than I ever thought I'd see. Claire's going to put the money into a scholarship endowment for women seeking STEM-related fields at an older age at their five different colleges. Kind of the ultimate second chance for women seeking a different life. I asked Tony to set one up at UNLV. It's the first time I've asked for something over a hundred dollars.

We're all sitting around Hayden's backyard as our children run around, and our bellies have been filled by Lilliana and Lizzie's mom's cooking. The men are all in a corner, huddled and talking. And I have an idea, and since we're all on the betting text chain together now...

MAK: I've got two million that Law has a secret baby out there somewhere.

COLTON: Candy from a baby. A secret baby.

HAYDEN: I'll take those odds.

ROBBIE: Claire says I have to stop betting, considering I just lost 4, but I'll take that action. And let's put a million on my team making it to Stanley.

CLAIRE: Baby, this is a slam dunk. Take the bet.

LIZZIE: Oh, yeah. No one spreads their seed like Law.

LAW: HEY! I wrap every time.

DAX: Robbie, no one's taking that bet. We all believe you'll get the cup this year. Law, on the other hand.

LAW: Fuck you.

Uncle Dax and crew took Salem for the week in Paris with the help of Hayden and Lizzie. And we're on a vacation that no one should be allowed to afford. A honeymoon we never really had. I was too busy.

The ocean is in front of me, and two hot-pink chairs are side by side next to an infinity pool. There's a pool bar and restaurant directly to our right and a cabana changing area to our left. The warm tropical Saint Lucia breeze tickles my bare stomach and face. I'm awash in gratitude because Tony found this magical resort called Jade Mountain, and he plucked it from my dreams. The architecture is blocky and intricate. My love sits down next to me with a broad smile. He eases back into his chair, and I put my hand out. And as he snaps a fruity umbrella drink in my hand, I let tears flood my eyes as I say, "It's finally perfect."

The End.

Thanks so much for reading Mak & Tony's story.
If you missed Hayden & Lizzie's story
KEEP PARIS
You can catch it at the link above

Claire & Robbie story
KEEP PHILLY
is a newsletter exclusive story. Just click the title and you can grab it for **FREE.** Hockey, soulmates, marriage in crisis, instalust

For **Dax & a total surprise**
KEEP RUGGED.

An exclusive novella coming to my newsletter this summer

Colt & Maggie
get their second chance this summer in
KEEP TUSCANY
pre-order is live
When life gives you lemons, make limoncello - A star crossed
Italian do -over coming in August 2024

Law & Tilly
KEEP BOSTON
Coming early 2025 - pre-order live
He's about to lose the bet of a lifetime but might gain
everything in the process.

All the Boston Brothers' novels are in Kindle Unlimited

And if you'd like to review this book anywhere and everywhere
you can do that. And I'd be most grateful.

hey kel, what else can i read?

All Books Can Be Found In Kindle Unlimited*

Standalone
SIDE PIECE

A workaholics standalone romance. A hot, hilarious, angsty Instant Connection- A story about cheating on their jobs not each other.

A podcaster and a romance writer walk into a bar...

CHITOWN LOVE STORIES

<u>Shock Mount & Crossfade duet</u>
A steamy, funny, rockstar standalone duet.
It's a reverse age gap-rockstar-love triangle-no cheating-second chance- HEA all around guaranteed extravaganza.
Meghan Hannah tripped into their lives, much as she trips into almost any room. But now each man wants to catch her. But Meg's not sure she'll be able to get back up if she falls too far.

<u>Present Tense</u>
How do you have a one-night stand with someone you've known your whole life?
You don't.
You accidentally fall into a relationship knowing everything about the other person only to discover you know absolutely nothing about yourself.
Can Liam and Jillian stop letting the past dictate their lives and find themselves in the present tense?

<u>Carriage House Chronicles</u>
Spinoff hilarious novellas
Follow Me
Rockstar, Second Chance, Forced Proximity
<u>Sound Off</u>
Grumpy Sunshine, Enemies to Lovers
<u>For the Rest of Us</u>
Holiday M/M , Marriage in Crisis
<u>Something Good</u>
Nanny, Single Rockstar Dad

SONOMA SERIES
Five Families Vineyard Romances
Interconnected standalone found family small town series exploring the lives and loves of five winery families.
Box Set Volumes with bonus material
Volume One: Books 1-3
Volume Two: Books 4 & 5
Volume Three: Books 6, 6.5 & 7
Volume Four: Books 8, 9 & 10

Original Full Length novels available as well

LaChappelle/Whittier Vineyard Trilogy
(Josh & Elle) *Enemies to Lovers*
Crushing, Rootstock & Uncorked

Stafýlia Cellars Duet
(Tabi & Bax) *Friends to Lovers*
Over A Barrel & Under The Bus

Gelbert Family Winery
*Meritage: An Unexpected Blend (*Nat & David)
Secret Baby, Reformed Player, Single Dad

Residual Sugar
(Becca & Brick*) Reverse Grumpy Sunshine, Forced Proximity, funny suspense*

Bottled Up
(Poppy & Sal) *Rom Com Mafia, Opposites Attract, Secret Life, My Wife, Touch him and die*

Langerford Cellars
Complex Finish

(Sam & Sammy) The end no one saw coming. An epic second chance

Prohibition Winery
Grand Cru
A series epilogue nine books in the making. You're invited to a wedding that probably should have happened five babies ago.

<u>BOSTON BROTHERS: A second chance series</u>
Standalone stories featuring six friends and the women they were lucky enough to find. And then find again.
<u>Keep Paris</u>
Enemies to lovers, workplace with second chance twist.
Keep Philly
FREE NOVELLA
https://dl.bookfunnel.com/xfkvirgsh1
Hockey, instalust, soulmates
Keep Vegas
Billionaire, soul mates from the opposite sides of everything
Keep Tuscany
When life gives you lemons, make limoncello. Timing is everything. And pasta. Pasta and timing are everything.
friends to lovers, single dad, widow, always been you
Keep Rugged
Sometimes you have to get lost in the woods in order to be found.
friends to lovers, work place forced proximity, one bed, hurt/care
Keep Boston
Some bets are worth losing.

EVIE & KELLY'S HOLIDAY DISASTERS vol 1*

Side by side insane, hysterical, rom-com novellas focusing on one trope and one holiday at a time. With Evie Alexander

They feature Tabi Aganos and Christmas Chaos features all of the 5 Families in the Vineyard Romances.

VOLUME ONE

Cupid Calamity

Cookout Carnage

Christmas Chaos

(*Not available in Kindle Unlimited but at all retail outlets)

Join me at www.kellykayromance.com to stay up to date on all the daffy nonsense that flows out of my brain and onto the page. And all the inside scoop on upcoming books! A workaholics standalone romance.

acknowledgments

SO MUCH joy writing this book.

I have to start with a certain raven haired, sarcastic, bold, incomparable, fiercely loyal and brave friend. I didn't mean to steal your personality for Mak, it just happened. All that happened to her was totally made up in my brain, but her sass and spirit, yeah, that's all you. Thanks Corie Weaver Carlsen for playing along and blame Julia Jarrett.

When Julia read Keep Paris her first question was, "When are you writing Makenzie and Tony's story? And the rest of the guys?" It never occurred to me that there was life beyond Hayden & Lizzie. The Boston Brothers exist because of you. And Maggie and Mak were only ever going to be background, but they wouldn't stop talking in my head. So, thank you for reading this and that, and for opening it all up.

Sandie C, thank you for reading the rawest of words and ideas and seeing the potential. And I promise not to get you lost in the city again. Lower Wacker, isn't your friend, but I'm glad I am.

Lori Jackson- I swear you pluck the cover of my dreams from my head. You truly are a joy to work with and I'm honored to put my words behind your pictures. Thank you.

Aimee Walker, your commitment to my insanity is noble and should be revered. For someone who loves order and schedules to take me on, is well, quite frankly, stunning. Perhaps it's the myriad of animals in your care that prepares you to edit a new book for me. Thank you, my friend, for being my editor.

Leah Franic - You just roll with the -and you coined the phrase- Kelly Kayos. Thank you for your quick wit and grammar skills. And for making sure I know I've used the word 'thing' so many times that it became a thing.

My friends continue to be a source of inspiration and well filling. I'm lucky enough to draw humor and strength from them.

And my fellow HEA authors, who check in, share, and breathe life and light into a solitary pursuit. Adore you, Eve, Tori(s), Avery, and Evie.

I told the story before in the back of Keep Paris. But there really was a room 666, and a set of prep school boys prank calling, and a set of girls who hooked up with them in Paris. Kris was real, Tony's name is actually Tony but the rest of them are pieces of my memories. And for my part, I sometimes wonder where L.M. ended up in life after kissing me under the Eiffel Tower.

But my real life book boyfriend is beyond compare. There's no Kelly Kay without my brilliant and talented everything, Eric Spitznagel. The husband. None of this matters or can be done without you.

Charlie, my beautiful loud and boisterous kid, thank you for learning, "Everlong" and playing it on command.

And **readers.** My goodness, I will never stop thanking you for sharing all of this with me.

What do you say we do it again soon?

about the author

Growing up my best friend and I would write "dreams." We'd each pick a boy we liked, then we'd write a meet-cute that always ended with a happily ever after. Now I dream every day, although now it's a little steamier. I'm a Chicago based writer, married to a writer, mom of a creative dynamo of a fourteen-year-old boy and currently a little sleepy. I'm a klutz and goofball and love lipstick as much as my Chuck Taylors.

Odds are I have a cup of coffee or a glass of wine in my hand right now.

Feel Free to Follow Me in the following places!